Bad
Girlz
4
Life

ALSO BY SHANNON HOLMES

B-More Careful

Bad Girlz

Never Go Home Again

Dirty Game

Bad
Girlz
4
Life

SHANNON HOLMES

St. Martin's Griffin ☙ *New York*

This is a work of fiction. All of the characters, organizations, and events portrayed in this novel are either products of the author's imagination or are used fictitiously.

ISBN-13: 978-0-7394-9624-4

Acknowledgments

I'd like to acknowledge Monique Patterson, Kia DuPree, and all the good people at St. Martin's Press, as well as Angel Mitchell, Eric White, and Da'Neen Hale.

Bad
Girlz
4
Life

1

The Present

Tonya Morris, aka the notorious "Tender," navigated her Mercedes-Benz through the section of Philadelphia called the Badlands and floored the gas pedal, wishing she was already back in New York. In this neighborhood, and in Philadelphia in general, they would steal your car in a heartbeat and she knew it. Still, she couldn't resist the allure of driving the luxury vehicle through its streets. There was a certain pride and prestige that it evoked in her. The car seemed to say she was somebody and that she had made it. Never mind that it was leased.

Tonya had come a long way from her stripping days. She had seriously stepped up her game since then and had been ruthless at times in the pursuit of her goal to become a certified success. Now she was the marketing consultant for Prestige Records and had snagged Quinton "Q" Phelps, the CEO of Prestige Records. Sometimes Tonya was amazed at how funny life was. For instance, she and Q went way back and most of their history wasn't all good. She never would have imagined that they would run into each other again at a party she had been promoting four years ago. And she never would have dreamed that this time he would end up being the love of her life, her best friend, confidant, partner in crime, and lover. Like all roads she seemed to travel with Q, this one had been full of twists, turns, and drama. A couple of times it had seemed like neither she nor Q were going to make it. But she had done what she needed to do to protect herself and, at times, Q. And that was a change for her because no one had ever been the center of Tonya's world but Tonya. Now she would live and die for Q, no questions asked. And she knew he felt the same way about her. She felt so blessed to have him in her life. Maybe she didn't deserve her blessings, but she damn sure was going to hold on to them with everything she had.

Maybe her train of thought was making her paranoid, but when Tonya pulled the car to a smooth stop at a STOP sign, she immediately noticed the young Hispanic male walking in the crosswalk. He walked slowly, too slowly, as if he were purposely trying to hold her up. But her instincts told her something wasn't right about this guy. Or maybe it was his attire. He was dressed in all black from head to toe, big black hoodie, baggy black jeans, and black Timberland boots. Tonya didn't want to stereotype him; after all, this was the hood, her hood. This style of dress was the norm around here. Just because he was dressed like this at night didn't necessarily mean he was up to something. But Tonya's instincts told her that he was.

Tonya had been out of the hood for almost two years now. But one doesn't lose one's instincts, the sense of danger acquired over a span of a lifetime. In this case, Tonya's instincts were like a knife, sharp edged and slicing through her in a painful warning.

Suddenly, in one swift motion, the man stopped directly in front of her car, pulled out a large gun from beneath his hoodie, and pointed the barrel directly at Tonya's face. The man moved from the front of the car to the back passenger side, keeping the weapon trained on her the whole time.

I should pull off on his ass, Tonya thought to herself.

2

Her eyes darted around the area as the surreal event unfolded. Tonya's mind raced with thoughts of escape, yet her driving foot didn't move an inch off the brake pedal.

As if he could read her mind, the man said, "Bitch, pull off and I'll kill you!"

The man put enough emphasis behind his words that Tonya believed him. She had no other choice. She wasn't willing to gamble with her life. The gunman appeared jumpy and volatile. Tonya knew one wrong move could set him off.

Quickly the gunman proceeded to the passenger's door. He pulled the handle, but the car door didn't open. It was locked.

"Bitch, open the fucking door! Now!" he shouted.

Tonya complied, opening the door with a touch of a button.

Fuck it. If the vehicle was all that the gunman wanted, then he could take it. Tonya wasn't about to resist; her life was worth more than a car. She could get another one tomorrow if she wanted to.

"You can have it! Here, take the car!" Tonya said as the man entered the vehicle.

"Bitch, shut the fuck up and drive!" the gunman yelled, poking the gun hard in her ribcage.

While Tonya followed his orders, he scanned the area to see if anyone had seen him. Confident that nobody had, he focused his attention back on Tonya, who at this point was a nervous wreck.

"You can have anything you want. Take my pocketbook and the car. Here, you can even have this chain," she said, starting to feel desperate. "Just let me go."

Momentarily his eyes were diverted to the exquisite piece of jewelry, hanging around her neck. It had been a gift from Q. He had only seen pieces like these on entertainers, in music videos. If he hadn't had something else in mind, then the gunman might have just taken the chain and fled. The jewelry would have put him on easy street, no question. Yet he had bigger fish to fry.

"Bitch, shut up and drive!" the man snapped. "I don't want ya muthafuckin' car, ya chain, or ya fuckin' pocketbook! I want you!"

Tonya felt everything inside her freeze. *Oh my God,* she thought. *This muthafucka is kidnapping me.* Her hands started to shake, and it was all she could do to keep from driving the car into a pole, she was so nervous. She had only read about this type of shit or seen it in the movies. She wished she could spot a cop right now. If she did she would do something to alert him to the situation, like run a red light or beep her horn. But she had no such luck. So in the meantime she complied with the gunman in hopes that she would make it out of this alive.

Tonya's wild ride ended just a few blocks from where it began. From that point on she was led by gunpoint through an alley into a dark house. Once inside, she was subsequently tied up and blindfolded. Two more accomplices later joined her original abductor, bringing the total number of people involved to three. The latter two accomplices were dispatched to dispose of her car in some other part of the city, just in case it was equipped with any antitheft tracking devices. For about an hour Tonya was left alone in a dark room while her abductors performed various activities crucial to the success of their plan.

The situation was surreal to Tonya. In her first few hours of captivity, she spent most her time blinking away tears and fighting a guilty feeling of "it's all my fault." She wondered if this was her past catching up with her. She thought about Q. *I love you, baby,* she wanted to say. She had never wanted to be safe in his arms more than at that moment.

Tonya had no choice but to assume the worst. Of all the thoughts racing through her mind at this point, death was the most prominent.

PART I

How It All Started. . .

2

Four Years Ago

Tonya had just closed and locked the door to her apartment when she heard heavy footsteps coming down the hallway.

"Damn!" Tonya swore. She would know the sound of those footsteps anywhere. She had been trying to avoid that fat, ugly fuck, Anthony Brown, the building's manager, for the past couple of weeks. She was behind on her rent, and that meant he was coming looking for payment in the form of pussy.

The first time Tonya had been solicited by Anthony for sex, she had balked at the notion. First of all, he wasn't her type. He was fat, stupid, and had an odor about him. And second, he wasn't spending any money. She would only be working off a previously established bill. Once before Tonya had successfully been able to fight her notice of conviction in a Philadelphia housing court by coming up with her past-due rent money at the last minute. But by doing so she had only created a new problem, robbing Peter to pay Paul. Unfortunately, she was never able to do it again. As a result, she soon fell right back into the money pit she had just climbed out of. So when Anthony approached her again, she reluctantly accepted his offer.

Tonya despised Anthony, in every sense of the word. She

couldn't help but feel as if each sexual encounter with him was an act of rape. It was unlike any encounter she ever had with a trick, who bought some kind of sexual favor from her. Anthony gave her the creeps, just like her mother's boyfriend, Pete, had.

She hurried toward the stairs, not bothering to wait for the elevator. Tonya breathed a sigh of relief when she finally got outside. Then she felt the sharp bite of the wind and cursed again. Jamming her hands in her pockets, she headed for the bus stop.

Winter in Philadelphia had always been notoriously brutal. A combination of low temperatures and wicked winds had been known to freeze the city. Residents of the City of Brotherly Love were all too familiar with these hazardous weather conditions. Still, life went on for those people who had to venture outdoors to brave the elements. Unfortunately for Tender, she was one of these unfortunate souls.

Routinely, she battled the cold, the wind, and even the snow just to make an honest living. It was days like this that made her yearn to be in her previous occupation as a stripper, where she set her own hours and was paid handsomely.

This morning was one of those days when nothing seemed to go right for her, from the weather on down. Standing at the bus stop, she took a deep breath, completely frustrated as puffs of white escaped her mouth with every breath. Impatiently, she glanced down at her watch for what seemed to be the umpteenth time. She was growing more impatient by the minute.

The bus was now putting her job in jeopardy. Had her car not been stolen a few months ago, she never would have been in this position, late for work, while forced to take public transportation.

If it wasn't for bad luck, I wouldn't have no luck at all, she thought.

Except for the steady line of vehicles that went to and fro, the streets of Philly looked like a ghost town.

Glancing up and down the busy city streets, she saw no signs of her ride. As usual, the SEPTA bus was nowhere in sight. It was just like the police, never around when you needed it. Tender was growing madder by the second. She had to be at work, she had a few clients coming in early today.

Bundled up tightly in her black North Face goose-down parka, blue jeans, and black Timberland boots, it was too cold outside to be concerned with looking cute. She paced the small area of the bus stop in a desperate attempt to keep warm. Underneath her armpit, she clutched the local newspaper, the *Philadelphia Daily News*. It was a daily habit of hers to read the paper while on the bus on her way to work. This thwarted any man's weak attempts to holler at her on the bus. And the other reason was just being plain nosy. She wanted to see who got robbed, shot, or killed last night in Philly while she was fast asleep.

Currently the city of Philadelphia was under siege. The murder rate was at an all-time high, one of the highest in the nation. Neither the mayor nor the chief of police seemed to have a good solution to stop the bloodshed. Operation Safer Streets had only had limited success. Young black males in the hood were still dropping like flies. They were dying every day on the streets of Philly over some frivolous reasons.

I wish this fucking bus would hurry the hell up! she thought. *It's fuckin' freezing out here!*

Looking down the street, Tender thought she spotted something. It was so cold outside she thought her eyes were playing tricks on her. On the horizon she saw a SEPTA bus slowly rambling toward her. It couldn't come at a better time. Her face and toes were frozen. She'd be glad to get on the bus and thaw out.

Finally the SEPTA bus pulled to its designated stop.

"Good morning," the bus driver greeted her.

You late! she said to herself. *Ain't nothin' good 'bout this*

SHANNON HOLMES

mornin'. It'z fuckin' freezin' out here and you talkin' 'bout good mornin'

Her body language and facial expression suggested that she was pissed. So Tender ignored him and paid her fare, then marched down the aisle of the half-empty bus. Taking a seat in the back, she warmed up for a second before beginning her daily ritual of reading the newspaper.

The bold-print headline immediately captured her attention.

TWO MEN FOUND SLAIN

Late last night police were called to the 1100 block of Broad Street. Neighbors reported hearing several gunshots. When police arrived on the scene, they made a grisly discovery. Two unidentified black men in their mid- to late twenties had been bound, gagged, and shot twice, execution style, in the back of the head. Police believe the killing to be drug related. Small amounts of crack cocaine and heroin were recovered from the scene. Neighbors say the house has long been a drug den. People had been seen arriving and departing at all times of the day and night. Police have no suspects in these murders. Anyone with information about this unsolved murder, please contact 1-800-Crime Stoppers.

After she read the article, Tender shook her head in disgust. She wondered just what everyone else did: When would the murders stop? Niggers were killing each other at a record rate, like it wasn't nothing. The young boys were going buck wild on the streets of Philly. And there was nothing anyone could do or say to stop them.

But she didn't need to read the paper to see that times were hard. Or that people were killing each other over crumbs. Tender was from the hood, North Philly to be exact, where that sort of stuff, life-and-death drama, was commonplace.

10

To put the situation in perspective, Tender didn't really care who got shot or killed as long as it wasn't her. She had problems of her own, namely, money. She had legitimate concerns. Her bills were killing her. She was two months back on rent. And her cable was currently disconnected. It seemed like if it wasn't one thing then it was another.

Walking away from stripping hadn't been as easy as she thought it would be. It wasn't like she really missed anyone from her former lifestyle. But she did miss the steady income. It had come so fast and easy. And that's how she spent it. Like many people who lived outside the law, she had trouble making the transition from the street life to real life, meaning that Tender spent money carelessly like she was still in the life.

Tender wanted to become a tax-paying citizen. She figured she was going to need some source of income when she got old. If at all possible, she wanted to collect a Social Security check. She didn't want to be like some of the people in the hood that managed to make it to old age and had nothing to show for it. Or like so many others, who the only time they recognized the law or the government was when they got arrested or received a welfare check.

But retirement plans and 401(k)s were out of her realm of thinking. In Tender's mind they were for rich people. She was struggling, living day to day trying to survive. Any money she earned went immediately to food, clothing, or a bill, sustaining life.

Flipping through the newspaper, Tender went into a daze. At the bus stop she looked up once and cast her eyes on the boarding passengers. One Hispanic girl caught her eye. The girl reminded her exactly of her deceased friend, Goldie. She was a stripper whom Tender had met, and had grown very grew close to, in her not-so-distant past.

Goldie, God bless her soul, she mused. *You deserved better than that.*

Thoughts of Goldie had definitely refreshed her memory about that bitch Kat. She turned bitter at the thought of her. Kat had never been her friend and Tender wished she never had met her.

Fuck Kat! she thought vehemently. *Bitch, you got what was coming to you.*

A long time ago, Tender had heard people say that it was bad to speak ill about the dead. And normally she would have refrained from doing so, but she made an exception in Kat's case. Even death couldn't kill the hatred Tender had for her. The mere thought of her made Tender's blood boil.

Kat was the primary reason that Tender had started stripping. It was she who had introduced her to the game and had helped push her life even further into its downward descent. That girl had been trouble right from the start. If only Tender knew then what she knew now.

When she looked back on her past, she saw a cluster of people, places, and experiences that had shaped her life. Overall she had more than a few ill feelings about the way her life had played out.

Her emotions were understandable. Tonya's years in the stripping game had changed her forever. Gone was the innocent, naïve girl. She had been replaced by a coldhearted and sometimes ruthless bitch. Tender had done so many unscrupulous things in the name of survival, sometimes she didn't even know herself anymore. Her morals and principles had been replaced by a different code of ethics.

Still, there was one redeeming quality about Tender. And that was she was a survivor. No matter what hand life had dealt, she had played it out. And she would always continue to do so. If she couldn't run, she would walk. And if she couldn't walk, she would crawl. But by all means she would keep it moving. She knew if she stopped to question some of the things she was doing she would miss some opportunities to make money. Without a money source, she would eventually die.

12

Tender snapped out of her train of thought. Right on time, too; her stop was only blocks away. Tender stood and prepared for her imminent departure. At first she reached down and picked up her paper before tossing it back down. She decided to leave all that bad news right where it was. That kind of thing was depressing, not something she wanted to be reminded of over the course of the day.

Carefully the bus driver navigated his SEPTA bus into the bus stop. As he did so, Tender glanced at her watch. It read eleven o'clock and she was over an hour late. She knew she was going to hear it from the salon's owner, Paris. Paris always stressed to every stylist, not just Tender, how important being punctual was. A chronically late stylist meant unhappy clients. And an unhappy client was bad for business.

"Back door!" Tender barked. "Would you open the damn back door!"

Exiting the bus, the bitter cold winds smacked Tender in the face. She hurriedly walked toward the salon, seeking refuge from the brutal weather. Taking inventory of her surroundings, Tender suddenly noticed an abnormally high volume of people out and about at this time of morning, in such cold weather. Immediately her suspicions were raised. It didn't take a rocket scientist to figure out what was going on. These people were her people, the local drug dealers and addicts, making their usual transactions. This was a normal everyday occurrence in most sections of Philly, if not most urban inner-city neighborhoods.

Such blatant and unlawful behavior was like a signal that said, *"Welcome back to the hood."*

Hair Image beauty salon was located in West Philadelphia. To be more specific, 52nd Street and Girard Avenue, smack dab in the hood, on a drug strip, in the heart of the thriving illegal drug trade. Still, all the illegal activity outside its doors didn't hurt the business at all. Hair Image salon had a good reputation for being one of the best hair salons because of its highly skilled stylists throughout the city. In fact some of the drug dealers even sent their women there.

Crossing the threshold of the salon, suddenly the person formally known as Tender underwent the drastic transformation to her government identity, Tonya Morris. There was only one person in the entire salon who knew about Tonya's past and her alter ego, and that was a pretty, heavyset girl named Na'eema. She was the only stylist Tonya really fooled with like that. And she was the reason Tonya still had a job there. She always stuck up for her whenever there was talk of firing her. These two had befriended each other over the course of time. They had both checked each other out for a while, from a distance, before deciding that they were cut more or less from the same cloth. And they weren't like the rest of the stylists in the salon, two-faced and talkative. Initially it was Na'eema who struck up the first conversation, about Tonya's hair-braiding techniques. The conversation flowed so easily that Tonya warmed to Na'eema instantly. Na'eema had a warm, infectious personality that made people take a liking to her. Although they may have struck up a friendship at work, it extended well beyond the salon doors.

Without saying a word to anyone, Tonya tiptoed through the salon, seemingly unnoticed, and got settled in, preparing for a long day's work. Almost as if she had smelled her scent, Na'eema came over to her area unannounced.

"Un-uhhh!" she playfully said. "Ya late again. This is not a good look. Not a good look at all, Miss Morris."

"Girl, tell me about it!" Tonya replied. "That damn SEPTA bus iz a muthafucka! And they always hollerin' bout raisin' the fuckin' fares, but they can't neva get a bitch to work on time."

"Anyway, I'm mad at you," Na'eema stated. "You keep shittin' on me."

"Why?" she asked. "How?"

"Why?" Na'eema repeated. "You ain't show up for my party. Again!"

Other than being a hairstylist, Na'eema was an aspiring party promoter. It was her side hustle that a former boyfriend had turned her on to, and a profitable one at that. She threw nice, classy, grown-and-sexy parties for working-class people at various nightclubs in and around Philly. The parties gave her so much needed extra income.

Tonya had totally forgotten about her party. She had other things on her mind besides partying, like surviving. As usual, Na'eema had given her VIP passes, but once again she hadn't used them.

"Girl, I don't know why I even fuck wit you, na'mean?" Na'eema joked. "You never come out and support a sister. Wit friends like you, who needs enemies? That's black people for you, though."

"Tell me about it!" Tonya said. "Seriously, though, ya party slipped my mind. Besides, you know I don't do the club scene. It ain't my twist. Plus you know my transportation situation ain't the best right now. I ain't too far away from walkin', for real."

Na'eema interrupted, "Excuses! Excuses! You know what they say. An excuse is like an asshole. Everybody got one. I coulda came and got you had you let me know in advance."

Na'eema stood in front of Tonya's work area, striking a diva pose, her hands placed firmly on her hips. Despite what her body language may have suggested, she really was sympathetic to her co-worker's plight. She knew Tonya had to commute by bus from the suburbs, Chestnut Hill, to the salon. She also knew that the rent out there was killing her. She would have offered to pick her up for work, but she had issues of her own, like an ill elderly mother to tend to. She was just a single woman doing her best to keep her mother from going into a nursing home, to keep her small family together.

And Tonya understood her plight, so she never even bothered to ask, thus putting her in a position to choose. She didn't want to put Na'eema in an awkward position. Her problems were her problems. Besides that, she was too independent anyway. Tonya didn't need a handout, only a hand up. She was going through some things right now, but hopefully she would pull through.

"Tonya, I told you, my lil' brother steals cars. Why don't you let him get you one?" Na'eema asked. "He can get you some ole fly shit, too. Like a Benz, BMW, or a Lexus. You'll be shittin' on all these hoes."

"Nah, I'm good," Tonya replied. "I'll walk!"

Na'eema might have been poking fun at the situation, but the thought had crossed Tonya's mind on more than one occasion. If there wasn't the threat of jail time attached to the crime, then she might have taken Na'eema up on her offer. If Tonya was to go to jail, then it would be for some major money or somebody threatening her well-being. No exceptions.

Na'eema continued, "Well, you-know-who is you-know-what!"

"Paris knows I'm late?" she questioned.

"Yep!" Na'eema said.

"You hollered at her for me?"

"Yep! You know I did, girl. What kinda question is that?" Na'eema commented. "I'm the only one 'round here who'll speak up for you, who'll hold you down!"

Na'eema may have been a big-boned female, but she wasn't ugly. She stood five foot ten and weighed two hundred pounds. Her hair was cut low in a trendy style, which she seemed to change from week to week. She was light brown-skinned, with chinky eyes and cute pudgy cheeks.

Na'eema was a high-maintenance, fashion-conscious, open-minded chick. But most of all she was good people, fiercely loyal to Tonya, and she knew when to keep her mouth shut and when to speak. She knew when to chastise and when to listen.

Tonya knew she wasn't lying about that. The other stylists at the salon had never liked her from day one, and vice versa. She was cut from a different cloth. Tonya was hood through and through, while they were on some other stuff. The trivial things that they talked about, like customers and guys, wasn't an interesting enough topic of conversation for her. If and when their topic of conversation turned to how to make some money, then she would be all ears. The majority of the stylists seemed to possess an I-am-better-than-you attitude. There seemed to be a touch of arrogance in the air at the salon. She got that kind of vibe from everyone accept Na'eema and Paris, the salon's owner, who if anybody had the right to be arrogant it was her.

Maybe it was a geographical thing, since she was the lone person in the salon from North Philly, and the rest of them were from West Philly. As long as Tonya could remember, there was always some sort of rivalry between those two different sections of town.

"Speak of the devil! Damn, we done talked this bitch up," Tonya said.

Tonya spotted Paris in her peripheral vision as Paris entered the salon. Looking stunning in a full-length white mink with a matching hat, she was accompanied by a dirty crackhead who carried a box of hair supplies.

Paris was a short, dark-skinned woman who also sported a short chic hairdo. That seemed to accent the soft womanly features of her face. Her presence loomed much larger than her height.

Even though she did own the place, Paris walked with an air of confidence, rarely seen. Quietly, Tonya dug her style, though they often clashed. Paris was everything she aspired to be, legal, independent, and successful. To Tonya she was a role model of sorts, someone whose success she wouldn't mind emulating. Paris had it going on.

"Excuse me, Na'eema," Paris said. "Tonya, we need to talk."

"Holla atcha later, girl!" Na'eema responded. "We'll chop it up inna few."

"Listen," Paris began, "I don't know how many times I done told you about bein' late. I understand your situation wit ya car gettin' stolen and all. Na'eema told me. But that's not my fault. You need to find another way here 'cause the way you comin' ain't workin'! Now, another thing! Another one of your customers left before you got here, because you were runnin' late. I'm runnin' a business here. You gotta be here, on time, for your scheduled appointments or not work here at all."

If Tonya was one of the select few stylists who paid rent, instead of working off commission, then her tardiness wouldn't have even mattered. She would have effectively been her own boss, free to come and go as she pleased, just as long as she paid her weekly rent to Paris. But since she didn't, Paris had every right to be up in her business. If Tonya wasn't at the shop on time they both lost money.

"Okay," Tonya replied humbly.

What else could she say in her own defense? Paris had given her the benefit of the doubt on several occasions. And now her patience was wearing thin. She had a long list of better-qualified stylists who would love to work at her salon. Sometimes even she wondered why she kept Tonya around.

"Just so you'll know. The next time you're late I'm goin' to have to ask you to go."

Wow! Tonya thought. *So this is what it has come to?*

With nothing else to say, Paris walked away, thinking she had gotten her point across. This was business, nothing more and nothing less. When conducting her business she didn't care who she offended. Paris was a single mother with kids to feed. And if her children's future or lifestyle were being compromised by any stylist at the salon, then she would fire them. Paris would fire her own mom, and she did, if she wasn't doing her job. She put money over everything. It was end-all, be-all to her.

In the background, Tonya could hear the light sounds of snickering. She looked around and saw the smiling faces of her rival stylists, who had enjoyed watching the confrontation. Her discomfort was amusing to them.

Usually, Tonya would say something to them, but not today. She bit her tongue, knowing she was skating on thin ice. Today was not the day to create a disturbance. So she just made a mental note of everyone who found the situation so funny, promising to get back at them some other time, preferably when Paris wasn't around. She wasn't going to let them clown her and get away with it.

Tonya had too much riding on this job, namely her welfare, to lose it over something like this.

After beginning her day on the wrong foot, Tonya's fortune slowly began to change. One by one her clients began to arrive to get their hair done. Working efficiently, she served them all. Tonya worked her fingers to the bone to give her clients their desired look.

One thing about Tonya when she was in the salon, no one could ever accuse her of slacking off. In the hair salon, Tonya was about a dollar. She always had been and always would be. She chased money as if her life depended on it, because it did. She wasn't one of those lazy hairdressers who were hardly ever at the salon, the kind who came and went as they pleased. Her only problem was getting there on time. Tonya wished the salon was open seven days a week. Surely she would be there every day. The demand for her services was so great that she even did house calls on her days off. Her current occupation was a hustle to her, plain and simple. If the price was right, she was there.

"Yo, Tee, I'm goin' out to get some lunch. You wanna come?" Na'eema suddenly announced.

"Nah, I can't," she replied. "I gotta one-fifteen appointment. But could you bring me back sumthin'?"

"Yeah, I know, I know. A cheesesteak hoagie, no onions, lots of ketchup."

"You got it," she replied. "You need some money?"

"Nah, I'm good. I'll just put it on ya tab," Na'eema remarked.

"Ohhh, Na'eema, could you pick me up somethin', too?" one stylist interrupted.

Na'eema shot her a "you-can't-be serious" look. She had seen them all laughing at her girl. So Na'eema wasn't about to do any stylist in the salon any favors. It was clear whose side she was on.

In a short time Na'eema had grown very fond of Tonya, because she kept it real. There was nothing fake or phony about her. It was what it was with her. She wasn't two-faced, unlike a lot of the stylists working there.

"I won't be back for a while," was the weak excuse she offered her.

Now it was Tonya's turn to laugh. And she laughed long and hard. She drew the ire of every stylist in the salon. She didn't care, though; that was exactly what she wanted to do. She had that me-against-the-world attitude. In a strange sort of way, Tonya loved it when they hated on her. Some days she would use all their negative energy and convert it into positive energy when she was feeling down. It seemed all their hate and envy made her work that much harder to make her hairstyles that much better.

When Na'eema walked out the door the show was officially over. It was back to work for everybody. Tonya's next client sat down in her chair.

This should be quick, she thought.

This was her intial impression because her client was a guy. Tonya knew his hair wouldn't take that long to braid, no matter how complex the designs. Guys were usually easy to please. It was the women who were the pain in the ass.

The young man was there to get his hair braided. From her vantage point, all Tonya saw was a humongous Afro. The guy had as much hair as a woman. It wasn't Tonya's job to pass judgment, to approve or disapprove of his hairstyle. Whoever sat down in her chair, she serviced.

"What's good, Tonya?" he spoke up.

"Ain't nuttin', Mont," she answered. "Evcrythang, everythang, na'mean!"

"I hear that. That's what's up?" he replied.

"Yo, Mont, where was you at last week? You lettin' some other bitch braid ya hair or what?" she asked him. " 'Cause I ain't see you. You been missin' ya appointment."

"Nah, you know it ain't like that. I'm the last person you ever have to worry about switchin' up on you," he responded. "I caughta case fuckin' wit some lame-ass niggers. These niggers was ridin' dirty and ain't even tell me he had drugs in the car. So when police pull us over I'm thinkin' we good. The next thing I know, they searchin' the car and we under arrest. I'm out on bail behind that bullshit now. But that nutass nigga 'bout to take the weight, though."

"Wow, that's messed up. He deserves an ass-kickin' for that. That's foul," she replied. "Good to see you, though. Now lemme get started."

Quickly Tonya began to part and grease his hair. She was doing another intricate design that she had become somewhat famous for. Over the recent years cornrows had become tremendously popular among the hip-hop generation, especially African American males. Guys from all over the city of Philadelphia came to her for exclusive cornrow designs. Her clientele varied, everyone from street hustlers to professional athletes. As a result of her thriving braiding business, she rarely accepted walk-ins. Her chair was constantly occupied.

Around twenty minutes had elapsed, and Tonya was almost finished braiding the young man's hair when she caught a sudden cramp in her hand. A crippling pain shot through the joints of her fingers.

"Ah, shit!" Tonya cursed. "Fuck!"

Grimacing in pain, she desperately tried to rid herself of it by violently shaking her hand in the air. After a few minutes the pain subsided as quickly as it appeared. Tonya was grateful, because the pain was crippling.

With a bewildered look on his face, her client looked at Tonya. He didn't know what to think. Her violent reaction had come out of nowhere.

"You all right?" he asked.

"I'm all right!" she told him. "Caughta cramp in my hands. I'm good, though."

"I ain't know what was goin' on back there," he responded. "I just heard you scream and shit."

When her bout with pain was over, once again Tonya busied herself putting the finishing touches on her client's hair. In under an hour it was done. Carefully she marveled at her work. Then she held up a mirror to her client's head so he could inspect it.

"You still got it, baby!" Mont proclaimed. "That's why I fucks with you, Tonya. You the best that ever did it, far as I'm concerned."

Completely satisfied with his braids, the young man paid Tonya and exited the salon. Now Tonya was really beginning to get hungry. She had heard the rumblings of her stomach, but ignored them while she was working. She was unable to do so now.

Tonya thought about going outside to the store and buying something to snack on. Because it was so cold outside, she began to have second thoughts. She didn't want to battle the elements unless it was absolutely necessary. She decided to sit back in her chair and wait for Na'eema to come back with her food. Just bide her time until her meal arrived.

Sitting in her chair, Tonya couldn't help but overhear the incessant chitter-chatter of the women in the hair salon, stylists and clients alike. Often Tonya managed to ignore it. It annoyed her. The excessive amount of customers increased the level of noise in the salon. Today was Friday and the salon was starting to fill up. Tonya knew she couldn't control how loud people talked or what they talked about. She would just have to deal with it.

This was one of the drawbacks of working in the hair salon, dealing with so many females, so many attitudes. Many times their different temperaments and personalities clashed. Tonya tried to avoid all the politics and gossip at work. She wasn't there for all that. At times she felt the atmosphere inside the salon was catty and cutthroat. Tonya felt it was just as bad or worse than her former occupation, stripping. And that was saying a lot. That said something about the salon. None of which was good.

Some patrons and stylists were more animated than others while they engaged in their backbiting stories. Tonya referred to them as characters because they were liable to be anything at any given time. Their personalities were dictated by who they were currently around. Half the time Tonya thought the person telling the story had no right to even be talking. Usually they weren't all that, appearance-wise, to her. Under these conditions Tonya was forced to listen to this nonsense whether she liked it or not. Their loud yapping was hard to ignore.

". . . . Girl, you shoulda seen her nappy-ass weave. Her tracks was showin' and shit. I couldn't believe that bitch had the nerve comin' out in public like that. No scarf or nuttin'," one patron commented.

"Good! She got what she paid for," a stylist replied. "She went all way 'cross town to that new Dominican spot. Tryin' to save a dollar. Don't she know they only good for wash and sets? Who the hell goes to them for weaves? Un-fuckin'-believable."

"And the funny shit is, she make good money. I heard she's a stripper on the down-low."

Before that statement Tonya had only been half-listening to their trivial conversation. Now she was all ears. She sat nonchalantly in her chair eavesdropping, ear hustling. She was not amused by their brand of humor, to say the least.

What Tonya didn't know was that someone from her past had seen her working in the salon. They told one of her immediate rivals, Imani, the lowdown on her shady past. Imani in turn had spread Tonya's business all over the shop, and it became an inside joke among all the stylists, except Na'eema and Tonya. They didn't have a clue as to what was being said. From time to time all the snickering made her wonder.

Seizing the opportunity, Imani butted into the conversation, adding her two cents. It seemed like she always had to voice her opinion. She loved being the center of attention. Although Imani possessed a slim physical build, the way she ran her mouth, one would have thought she was the biggest chick in the room.

"Girl, fuck them strippers. I can't stand them dirty hoes," she remarked. "Dem strip clubs ain't nuttin' but a cover for prostitution. All dem bitches doin' in there is sellin' pussy. Plain and simple! It don't take a genius to do that."

Tonya had never liked Imani; all she ever did was bad-mouth people and she wasn't feeling that at all. She thought Imani was a coward for talking behind people's backs. Tonya never saw Imani confront anyone. She always seemed to summon up the courage to talk about them when the person in question wasn't around.

Either Tonya was overcome by a guilty feeling or she suspected Imani of indirectly talking about her. Whatever the case may have been, she was dying to say something. Still, she knew to do so might tip her hand. She continued to suffer in silence. At that point a saying her mother was fond of came to mind: "The guilty speak the loudest."

Tonya believed that her background, her former occupation as a stripper included, were circumstances that had indeed influenced her actions. But ultimately she was responsible for what she became. Her destiny was in her and God's hands.

Out the corner of her eye, Imani glanced over at Tonya, to guage her response. Nervously Tonya was rocking back and forth in the chair. That was a sign to her that she was bothered by her comments. A dead serious look now masked her face. Only seconds ago she was expressionless. Imani chose to press on, to get even further under her skin.

She continued, "All strippers are freaks. Most of them just fuckin' just to be fuckin'. It's like they got a white liver or something. They don't even need the money. They doin' it just because or just to get high. They just some nasty, stinkin' bitches who'll fuck any Tom, Dick, and Harry."

The salon exploded with laughter. Laughter that Tonya couldn't help but feel was at her expense. She took offense at these malicious statements, regardless of how true they might be. It wasn't the message that Tonya had a problem with, it was the messenger.

Unable to hold her tongue any longer, Tonya rudely interrupted, "Tell me something, how you know so much about strippers, Imani?" Tonya spat. "Was you ever one? Huh?"

Suddenly the salon went silent, the laughter ceased. It was as if everyone could sense the tension between the two. All eyes seemed to shift to Tonya. She had center stage, their full attention.

"What?" Imani snapped, rolling her eyes. "I could never ever in MY FUCKIN' LIFE play myself like that! I wouldn't even put myself out there like that. Me? A stripper? Get the fuck outta here! My people love me. I could never disrespect my family like that. That shit is triflin'!"

Tonya fired back, "Well, the way you put it out there, it's like you was there. Like you got some inside info or somethin'. I'm sittin' here tryin' to figure it out."

"No, I ain't got no inside information. I know a few strippers, though. I heard how those bitches be gettin' down. How money hungry those hoes really are! I heard a lot of crazy stories," Imani said.

"You heard?" Tonya repeated, puzzled. "So just 'cause you heard somethin' from some other lame bitch, that makes it true? You know what, bitch, stick a dick in ya ear and fuck whatcha heard. Ya heard! You can't judge nobody or their situation from the outside lookin' in. Everybody ain't got family to fall back on!"

Imani smiled. "I musta struck a nerve, huh? Why you speakin' up in defense of dese hoes? Truth hurts, huh? You know what they say, it takes one to know one!"

"Yeah, bitch, I usta strip!" Tonya admitted. "I don't give a fuck who knows, either. What the fuck I did or do, it my damn business. You bitches sittin' here throwin' rocks and most of ya'll live in glass houses. Half you hoes fuckin' for free! Or ya niggers takin' care ya'll. Ya'll settin' out some pussy and a nigger is breakin' ya'll off. And ya'll got the nerve to sit here and talk 'bout another muthafucka, when ya shit stinks. Fuckin' hypocrites!"

Back and forth they went, each side hurling verbal insults at the other, as the onlookers eagerly listened and watched. The clients and stylists became instigators, smiling and laughing at every disrespectful word. The atmosphere in the salon took on that of a schoolyard, where every person was just waiting for a punch to be thrown, a fight to break out. If it wasn't personal before, it was now.

"Well, what's really good?" Tonya finally asked. "I don't like you anyway. I been waitin' for this day. Fuck all this talkin' shit! You tryin' to do sumthin' or what? If not, shut the fuck up!"

Tonya had had enough of this nonsense. She was ready to fight now. And it didn't matter who she fought. She didn't like any of these people anyway. Win, lose, or draw, she was going to make them respect her. It was beyond words right now.

"Come shut me up!" Imani said. "I'ma grown ass woman, I talk when I wanna talk! Ain't nobody scareda you."

Imani had a big mouth, but she wasn't a fighter. Still, she felt like she had to say something to save face. She couldn't let Tonya get the last word. She couldn't let Tonya just disrespect, especially in front of her co-workers. Imani knew she would never hear the end of it. Although she acted as if she wanted to fight, in reality she really didn't. Secretly she prayed that Paris would overhear their argument and come end this war of words before it turned into something.

Immediately Tonya sprung out of her chair, walked directly up to Imani, who stood only a few feet away, and punched her straight in the face. The impact of the blow whipped Imani's head back violently. Momentarily, Tonya just stood there admiring her own strength.

It happened so quickly that neither the stylists nor the clients had time to intervene. The woman who sat in Imani's chair hurried up and moved out of the way. Jaws dropped as the two stylists squared off.

Just like Tonya suspected, Imani was all talk and no action. The first blow she landed succeeded in taking what little fight Imani had in her out of her. From the onset it was clear who was winning. Tonya stunned her with blow after blow. She fought

Imani hard, as if she had something to prove. She was trying to make an example out of her. Tonya was sending a message that she was not the one to be clowned. Don't talk tough if one couldn't back it up.

From the back Paris could hear the loud sounds of a scuffle, beauty supplies being knocked down. Immediately she hung up the phone and came to see what was going on. At the same time Na'eema returned from the store. Both were quite surprised at what they were witnessing. Paris thought all her stylists had too much class to violate her place of business like this.

"Break this shit up!" Paris commanded. "Ya'll fuckin' up my shop!"

Paris's diminutive figure wasn't enough to separate the two combatants. But Imani had managed to grab hold of Tonya and she was holding on for dear life. She didn't want to be on the receiving end of any more of her blows. Na'eema intervened. She used her girth to break them apart.

"Aight, that's enough, Tonya! It's over! Don't hit her no more!" she told her. "Imani, you cool out, too!"

A bewildered look was on Tonya's face, her hairstyle was ruined, and she took long, labored breaths. It was clear to everyone that she still wanted to fight.

A few feet away, Imani wore the beaten look of a loser. Her left eye was slightly swollen and her bottom lip was split and bloodied. Still, she talked a good game. The sight of people interceding on her behalf gave her courage.

"Git off me!" she growled. "Lemme go. I'ma kill that bitch. I can't believe she put her muthafuckin' hands on me!"

"Yeah, let the bitch go!" Tonya ordered. "So I can whip her ass some more."

In Paris's opinion, Tonya was clearly the aggressor. She didn't know that Imani was a troublemaker. She had never had a problem out of her in the past. Tonya, on the other hand, had had a few run-ins, verbal altercations, with other stylists and clients. Her sharp tongue was legendary in the salon. And on top of that, Tonya was chronically late. All of this spelled trouble for her.

"Ain't gone be no more muthafuckin' fightin' up in here! Unless ya'll wanna fight me. Na'eema, git ya girl. Take her ass outside and let her cool off."

Grabbing Tonya's coat, the two women exited the salon. They took a long walk around the block. That gave Tonya time to calm down and give Na'eema the 411.

In the aftermath of the fight, Paris tried to sort out what happened. All she wanted to know was who hit who first. She knew there were three sides to every story: Tonya's side, Imani's side, and the truth. It was too bad for Tonya that Paris got all her biased information from stylists, Imani's friends, and clients.

As soon as Tonya left, the finger-pointing began. They all painted a picture of Tonya being the instigator of the entire incident, downplaying Imani's role in the altercation. It was as if she were completely innocent. As a result, Paris had decided to fire Tonya. Another incident like this wasn't going to be tolerated. Paris would clean house, fire everyone, and bring in all new stylists.

When Tonya reemerged in the salon, she fully expected to be vindicated. She didn't foresee the conspiracy that had taken place while she was gone. She expected to continue her work and go home. To her it was water under the bridge. But to Paris it wasn't.

"Tonya, pack ya shit. You gotta go," Paris told her. "I'm not havin' this shit up in here again. I'm sorry. God only knows what would have happened if I wasn't here!"

Paris's decision was a tough pill for Tonya to swallow. Suddenly she felt that Paris had wronged her. It was as if Paris was in on the conspiracy to get her fired. Since she no longer had a job to lose, Tonya lashed out at Paris verbally, giving her a piece of her mind.

"You know what, Paris? Fuck you and this shop!" she snapped. "You let these bitches get in ya ear witout even hearin' me out. These hoes fed you a pack of lies and you ate it right up. You hoes deserve each other. So fuck all, y'all."

Paris stood there with a dumbfounded look on her face. She was in total disbelief. She couldn't believe Tonya had addressed her so harshly.

"Na'eema, check ya girl," she managed to say. "And please escort her outta her. That was unnecessary."

Tonya shrugged her shoulders in response as if she didn't care. She pretended not to be fazed by the decision, but in all reality she was. Right now, doing hair was her bread and butter. Without the money she made at the salon, Tonya seriously wondered how she was gonna eat.

But that was her problem. Just like everything else that had gone wrong with her life had been. The burden of blame had fallen on her shoulders.

Tonya snatched up her measly beauty supplies and stormed out of the salon. Na'eema followed closely behind, offering her a ride and her unwavering support.

"I knew it!" Na'eema explained. "I knew Paris was gonna do that. That'z that bullshit right there!"

"I can't even be mad at her, na'mean!" Tonya replied. "I gave her the reason she needed to get rid of me. I feed right inta that bitch's bullshit. I shoulda pay them hoes no mind."

Finally Tonya had come to her senses, but it was too late because the damage was done. She was off to her apartment to fret over her dilemma in private. She knew there was no sense in talking about it, hindsight was 20/20. She had gotten herself into this mess and only she could get herself out.

Unlike most people, Tonya didn't have the luxury of a supportive family. All she had in this world was herself. Sink or swim, she was the only person she could count on. Her mother didn't count, since she had abandoned her years ago. Veronica Morris's whereabouts were unknown.

"Girl, don't even worry about it. Everything gonna be all right," Na'eema promised.

Tonya found no comfort in her friend's words. She wanted to believe Na'eema, but something told her not to. She had been misguided by too many people she had placed her faith in. Life had never been so easy for her. And she refused to believe it would be so kind to her now.

Na'eema drove and talked, harping over the situation. Tonya fell silent and she preferred to remain that way. She knew her next move had to be her best move. Unfortunately, success was not an option for her, it was a requirement.

3

A knock came at the front door. Tonya rolled over in bed. At first she thought she was dreaming, her sleep was that good. When she heard the pounding again, she knew she wasn't. Immediately she glanced over at her alarm clock on her nightstand.

"Oh, shit!" she cursed.

The digital alarm clock read 11:15 A.M. Tonya had an 11:00 hair-braiding appointment, so that could only mean one thing. This was her first client knocking at her door. Coming to that realization, Tonya jumped out of her bed. She couldn't afford to miss any money. She had had a full house yesterday and hadn't gotten rid of her last client until almost one in the morning. She had fallen into bed, exhausted after having been on her feet all that time.

"I'm comin'! Gimme a second. I'll be right there," she called out.

Now that Tonya was wide awake, it suddenly dawned on her that she was nude. She frequently slept naked, free from the constraints of panties and a bra.

Quickly, Tonya threw on a Sean John gray sweatsuit with matching top. Even in this oversized outfit, Tonya's shapely figure was apparent. Her round, heart-shaped ass and firm, melon-sized breasts seemed to cling to the fabric, filling out the sweat suit. The chilly air in her apartment made her nipples hard. They could easily be seen pressing against the thick cotton fabric.

Tonya felt like a hot mess as she walked through the apartment to open the door. Her hair was slightly out of place, her breath tasted tart, and on top of that she was still a little bit groggy. It was days like this when Tonya just didn't want to get out of bed. But she had to. She needed to make that money.

"Sorry 'bout that, Rob. My bad," she said, opening the door. "I overslept."

The young man wore a frustrated look on his face. Still, he proceeded into the house as if nothing had happened.

"Damn, Tonya, maybe I shoulda called ya cell before I came over. I been out there for like twenty minutes, na'mean! I bet I won't make that same mistake next time," he told her.

"I'm sorry! My bad!" she admitted. Tonya neglected to tell him that her cell phone had been turned off a few days for failure to pay the bill.

Damn, this broad is so fuckin' fine, he thought as he let his eyes rove over every inch of her body. And he liked what he saw. Tonya's bodacious body was like a ripe fruit whose delicious juice was just ready to be sucked.

"Tonya, I don't know how to tell you this, but you look real good right now!" he began. "When you gone put the young boy on? I'm feelin' you! I been feelin' you. Dig?"

Just like she had in the past, Tonya had once again attracted unwanted attention. Her looks could be both a blessing and a curse at times. Still, Tonya was flattered by the young man's admission, but she didn't have any time for this. Not right now. Her mind was on money.

Besides, she didn't like to mix business with pleasure. It wasn't a good look. Although the young man was cute, other than wetting her vagina, what could he do for her monetarily?

He was a small-time crack dealer who didn't even have a car. So how could he help out with her bills? Outside of the bedroom, how could she even relate or converse with him?

"Rob, please," she said gently. "Ain't nothin' happenin' with me and you. How many times I gotta tell you that? So watch your mouth and save your teeth, young boy."

"C'mon, Tonya, stop frontin' on me. You know you dig me! You been diggin' my style for a minute now!" he said.

"Boy, ga'head in the livin' room!" she replied. "You wastin' time! I got other clients besides you."

With that said, all conversations pertaining to sex ceased. Tonya laughed it off as she locked the apartment door. She had to admire Rob's swagger. Still, that was just his dick talking. From past experience, when dudes let that happen they tended to do and say strange things.

"Rob, have a seat. I'll be right there. First lemme brush my teeth and wash my face," she told him.

"Call me if you need my help," he shot back. "You know your wish is my command. I luv you, girl! I swear I do!"

"Whateva, lil' nigger!" she shouted. "Get ya mind right."

After getting fired from the salon, Tonya had been unable to get hired anywhere, partly because she was an unlicensed hairstylist and Paris had made a few calls to salon owners blackballing her. Another reason was the salons that were interested in her were either clear on the other side of town or the money wasn't right. Either way, it made no sense to her.

In the interim, Tonya had set up shop in the apartment. She was able to maintain an adequate income for a short time following her firing. But her good fortune wouldn't last long. Her bills were mounting daily. No matter how much hair she did, Tonya could never seem to get ahead. It seemed like ever since she had left the stripping game, things hadn't been working out. At least, not the way she planned.

When Tonya was done tending to her hygiene, she exited the bathroom feeling refreshed and invigorated. Walking a short distance through her apartment, she found Rob sitting on a pillow on the floor. Tonya went into the kitchen and grabbed a chair.

Like the living room, her apartment was scarcely furnished. Anything of real value had been sold off a long time ago, in order to help ends meet. She had pawned every piece of jewelry she owned. All that remained was a television, a bedroom set, and some appliances. Tonya's apartment gave off a just-moved-in appearance. It was a far cry from where and how she lived as a stripper. She had gotten used to living in the lap of luxury.

"Is somethin' wrong with your cable box or somethin', Tonya?" he asked. "I couldn't get that shit to cut on."

"Yeah, somethin' is wrong with my cable box, all right," she answered humorously. "It's called 'cut off for not payin' the bill'! Cable is a luxury I can't afford right now. Shit kinda tight."

"Well, why you ain't lemme know? You know I woulda gave you a couple dollars," he told her. "I don't see how you could live without cable. That's worse than not havin' a cell phone."

Tonya couldn't have agreed with him more. But it was what it was, not what she wanted it to be. She adapted to her current situation by listening to lots of CDs and watching DVDs. Any day now she was going to run out of movies to watch. She had seen just about all of them.

"C'mon, boy, ain't got time for all this rap," she said.

Tonya grabbed a comb, some rubber bands, and some hair grease and went to work. Her client sat comfortably between her legs while she braided his hair. Before he even realized it, Tonya had braided more than half his head.

"Tonya, you know a nigger sure could get used to this," he remarked. "Yes, sir!"

Tonya had been concentrating on her job, so his statement caught her completely off guard.

"Huh?" she asked.

Rob countered, "You can say 'huh,' but you heard! I'ma say it again. A nigger sure could get usta this!"

"What? Gettin' your hair braided?"

"Naw! Sittin' between these soft-ass thighs. Smellin' the sweet aroma of your womanhood," he said. "You know I eat pussy, right? I'm good with my lips and hips. I can show you betta than I can tell you, though. Wanna see?"

"Boy," Tonya sighed. "You just don't give up, do you? What parta 'no' don't you understand? The N? Or the O?"

They both chuckled long and hard over her comment. Rob didn't really expect to get some from Tonya, but he felt like it didn't hurt to ask. All she could tell him was no. And he'd heard that before. He felt that his persistence would wear her down one day. When it came to females, he knew that there was no surefire line to get them to drop their drawers. He only knew that if he didn't try, then surely he would never get any.

The rest of the time Tonya took to braid his hair, Rob seized the opportunity to joke and flirt with her. Before either of them knew it, she was done. Rob paid Tonya handsomely for a job well done, then went about his business. Tonya was glad to see him go. She was getting tired of him worrying her about some sex, especially at a time like this. That was the last thing on her mind.

A few minutes after he left, there was another knock on the door, just as Tonya began to get comfortable. Thinking that it was a client that maybe she had forgotten about, she jumped off her bed and headed to the door. She didn't bother to even look through the peephole.

"Yeah . . . ?" Her voice suddenly trailed off.

Standing before her was Anthony, the building owner's son and manager of the building in which she lived. His appearance could only mean one thing: the rent was late, as usual. Seeing his fat black face, Tonya regretted even opening the door.

"Hey, Miss Morris," he greeted her. "How you doin' today?"

Tonya stared blankly at Anthony. He was like the Grim Reaper that came around each and every month, to collect rent money that she didn't have.

"Hi, how you doin', Mr. Brown?" she replied. "I was just about to—"

"I know. You were just about to drop the check off at the management office," he finished her sentence.

As the building's manager, Anthony Brown had heard every excuse in the book about rent, not just from Tonya but from numerous tenants. It never ceased to amaze him how clever and cunning tenants would be when it came to not paying rent. Still, Anthony had managed to turn their inability to pay rent in a timely manner into an advantage for himself. He had a soft spot for female tenants, and he usually was able to work something out with them.

"Well, you know why I'm here. Let's get down to business," he told her.

Predictably, Anthony began to fasten the series of locks on the door. His actions infuriated Tonya. Lately his visits were becoming more and more frequent. But today she didn't feel like dealing with him.

"What you doin'?" Tonya asked, knowing the answer.

"C'mon, Tonya, let's not play games. You know what the deal is," he spat. "It's time to handle your business. Tighten me up."

"Muthafucka, I gotta client on the way," she protested. "We can't do nothin' right now."

"Oh, this won't take long," he promised. "I'll be out of your way in a minute."

Anthony could tell by Tonya's tone of voice and her body language that she was trying to play him. But he wasn't about to take no for an answer. He began to throw up her overdue back rent. And like always, it did the trick. The ever-present threat of being homeless always seemed to motivate Tonya, or anyone else for that matter.

Tonya barked, "C'mon! And you better be quick. I ain't got all day."

Tonya disappeared into her bedroom and reappeared with a condom in hand. Anthony quickly unfastened his pants and let them drop to his ankles. Now he was ready for his favorite sexual act, oral sex.

While dropping to her knees, Tonya looked up at him in disgust. With her teeth she bit into the protective wrapper of the condom. Spitting the small pieces out, she took the prophylactic into her mouth. Before she orally applied the condom, she took one last look at Anthony and his big potbelly.

This nigger probably ain't seen his dick in years, she thought. *Fat bastard!*

Tonya took his penis into her mouth and went to work. Even before she began, the funky scent of body odor began to bother her. His odor was so strong and musky that Tonya attempted to hold her breath while giving him head. Suddenly oral sex became an impossible task.

"Yo, what I tell you 'bout comin' over here like this? All funky and shit! Next time take a fuckin' shower! 'Cause it ain't goin' down like this no more!" she protested. "This is ridiculous."

Still, Tonya went on despite the foul smell. Maybe it was the fact that Anthony held her immediate future in his hands that spurred her on. Often she had wondered how she wasn't evicted already. How was Anthony getting around that? Was he paying her rent to keep her around as his own sexual slave? That was one thing Tonya could never figure out. She didn't know how he did what he did. All she knew was she couldn't keep quenching his ever-growing sexual appetite for oral sex.

Lately, he had begun talking about them having a threesome with a male friend of his. Tonya couldn't bear the thought. But in reality she didn't have very many choices.

Overcome by the funky body odor that Anthony's private parts were giving off, Tonya began to gag. As if Anthony could sense something was wrong, he jumped back. But he wasn't fast enough. Tonya threw up on him. When Anthony looked down, he saw a good amount of vomit on his pants. That was enough for him to end this session of oral sex.

"I don't believe this shit! You just threw up on me!"

It took every bone in Tonya's body to keep a straight face and not laugh at him.

Good! she thought. *I'm fucking glad I did!*

"Don't just sit there!" he cried. "Git me a fuckin' rag, washcloth, or somethin' to wipe it off."

Something inside Tonya made her snap.

"I ain't gettin' you shit, you fat muthafucka! Get out!" she yelled.

"What? You gonna put me out like this?"

"Nigger, you got five seconds to get the fuck out before I holla rape!" she told him.

Anthony looked at her unbelievingly. He couldn't be hearing her right. "You can't be serious!" he said.

"Nigger, I'm serious as a heart attack!" she fired back. "Don't press your luck! I'll have your fat ass locked up."

The stern look on her face told him she was serious. Reluctantly he reached down and grabbed his pants, pulling them up and fastening them. Tonya had succeeded in humiliating him. If looks could kill, Tonya would have been dead. She was lucky that Anthony wasn't a street dude or she very well might have been killed or seriously injured.

Making his way out the door, Anthony turned and spoke. "Bitch, you know I'm gonna get you back for this shit. Your ass is gonna be out on the streets in a few days. Bitch, you better dress warm," he warned.

Tonya slammed the door in his face. From the other side of the door, Anthony could hear loud, hearty laughter. Tonya had turned the tables on him, if only momentarily.

When the laughter subsided, Tonya realized that she had dug herself a ditch. She didn't have a choice now. It was back to the strip club. In a way she was relieved. At least in that world she knew what to expect from a man. There was no pussyfooting around. She had something they wanted, pussy. And they had something she wanted, money.

Tonya had been a little reluctant to return to the shady world of stripping, but now she fully embraced the idea. Tonya was like a prizefighter, a puncher, who was being taught the sweet science of boxing. But as soon as life had landed a haymaker on her, she quickly forgot the art and reverted back to that which she knew.

Money made Tonya's world go round. It was her alpha and omega.

If Tonya ever looked back on her life, she would see that this incident was her point of no return.

4

Goddamn!" a man said. "Yo, look a this broad's ass. This bitch healthy as all outdoors! You'd hit that or what?"

"Muthafuckin' right!" his partner replied. "Inna heartbeat! Shorty the truth! She the baddest thing up in this joint."

The object of their affection and subject of their very loud private conversation was Tender. She was currently up on stage working her set, and currently all eyes were on her. These sex-starved patrons of the strip club made loud, lewd comments, harassed her, and even propositioned her.

"You dick-eatin' bitch, lemme see that pussy!" came a loud voice from the crowd. "You up there fakin'. Lemme see whatcha workin' wit, ho!"

At this point, Tender wasn't the only person the man had offended with his disrespectful remarks. He drew the ire of more than a few customers who stood nearby.

"Dig, let's move away from this nutass nigga, 'fore I slap the shit outta him," one man growled.

His friend added, "I don't know how these jokers even get up in here, but this lame is fuckin' up the game for everybody!"

Not one to throw caution to the wind, the loud guy quickly changed his tune. He decided to be seen, not heard. He knew at the rate he was going, hurling insults, it could get real ugly inside the club for him. And he didn't want any part of a physical altercation. Not over no stripper, anyway.

"*Show me whatcha got, lil' momma,*" Jay-Z rapped as music blared through the club's powerful sound system.

As Tender stared out into the crowd, she zoned out. She had heard all their comments and only acknowledged these savages with a smile. Her beautiful smile was actually a frown turned upside down. Words couldn't begin to explain how degraded she felt inside. She saw the lust in their eyes and the larceny in their hearts, and yet she didn't see them at all. She didn't see faces, all she saw was dollar signs. To her, men and money were one and the same. And both were created to be used by her, in any shape, form, or fashion she saw fit.

Tender had developed this ice-water-in-her-veins approach long ago. She had a willing-to-do-whatever attitude, to go above and beyond the call of duty. It was this relentless money-hungry approach that set her apart from the average stripper. Tender's youthful appearance was quite deceiving. Though she was young in age, twenty-one, Tender was a seasoned veteran of the strip club circuit who made it all look easy. But looks were indeed deceiving. As the days went by it was getting increasingly difficult to pull that off.

"Yo, turn that thing back around!" someone shouted. "Ho, shake that shit! Bounce that azz, bitch! Back that azz up!"

Despite the man's ill-advised choice of words, Tender complied with the request. She was thick-skinned and she knew just what these guys came for and what they had on their minds. Pussy! That's all they wanted, pussy, pussy, and more pussy. To her all men were potential tricks and she would exploit their weakness for her own financial benefit.

Much to everyone's surprise, Tender began to shake her ass so hard and so fast, her butt cheeks began to make a clapping sound. The strip club patrons stared in amazement.

"Git the fuck outta here!" one stunned man said. "This bitch is outta control."

"Bet she can't do that wit a dick in her, though. What you think, man?" another patron said.

"I don't know but I'm tryin' to find out!"

The clever trick she did with her butt cheeks had worked like a charm. The hooting and hollering had gone up to an unprecedented level. There wasn't a soft dick in the club. The rowdy men began showering Tender with dollar bills in appreciation of her show. Few strippers could entertain like Tender and even fewer could perform that trick. It was something she had learned over time and put to good use every so often.

As rapper Jay-Z's new smash hit began to fade, it signaled Tender that her set was now over. Quickly Tender got on her hands and knees to gather up the bills that lay strewn about on the makeshift stage. While doing so she couldn't help but glance into the audience from time to time. Her sexually vulnerable position sparked even more cat calls.

"Damn, Ma, I would luv to knock sparks outta ya ass right now! Hit it from the back just like that!" one man suggested. "How much for a shotta that ass?"

Once again, Tender merely gave the man a suggestive smile. This seemed to only encourage him that much more. If only he knew how she really felt about him and every other male in the club. His voice and the others around him grew louder and raunchier.

"Ma, I got what you need!" he said. "I got that good dick! You need to fuck wit Half-Pint. I'll make you a star for a night!"

Tender stopped in her tracks and shot the man a look that seemed to say, "Nigger, you can't be serious." She knew from past experience that dudes who bragged about having it going on in the sexual department usually didn't. If they boasted about it, nine times out of ten, then they weren't about it. Still, they felt compelled to put it out there like that. It must have been a male ego thing. Usually their big mouths were overcompensation for a small dick.

Strippers bore the brunt of a lot of burdens and this was just one of them. Just because they did what they did, guys felt like they could talk to them any ole kind of way. As if they didn't have feelings just because they took off their clothes, among other things, to earn a living. Tender had heard it all before, but it never ceased to amaze her, what a guy would fix his mouth to say. In general, strippers got no respect.

Nigger, if this was your mother, sister, or somebody from ya fuckin' family up here, would you talk to them like that? she mused.

Still, her facial expression only registered a friendly smile. Her smile didn't betray the wide range of emotions she was currently feeling. But Tender couldn't prevent the sadness, anger, frustration, and annoyance from creeping up on her. As she continued to gather up her money she couldn't help but wonder, *What the fuck am I doing here? Again!*

She was in a precarious position once again, trying to balance herself on the thin tightrope of life, hovering in between what was wrong and what she had to do to survive. Like many misguided souls, with every fiber of her being, Tonya believed she was doing the right thing, if only for the moment.

Ignoring the crowd, Tender exited the stage and made her way toward the dressing room. Once inside she produced some baby wipes from her locker and began the process of cleaning herself. Though the small towels might have succeeded in wiping way the thin layer of perspiration that had accumulated on her body, it couldn't remove that grimy feeling, that physiological dirt that had engulfed her like a cocoon.

Tonight Tender was experiencing some of those same hang-ups she had when she first started, many years ago. And she couldn't believe it. She thought that her return to this world would be easy. And physically it was. Yet mentally there still were some adjustments to be made. Tender knew she would make them, too; she had to. It was just a matter of time, a matter of her reacquainting herself with this strange meat market atmosphere, where the forbidden pleasures of the flesh were bought and sold on a nightly basis.

While those thoughts ran wild in her mind, Tonya continued cleansing herself. She used baby wipe after baby wipe. Tonya was uncompromising when it came to her personal hygiene. To her there was no such thing as being too clean. She knew guys didn't like no stink pussy. And neither did she. Her relentless approach to freshness was all apart of her appeal.

Satisfied that she had cleaned herself the best she could, Tonya briefly inspected herself in the mirror and liked what she saw. Genetically, Tender was blessed and she knew it. All the women in her family were built like brick houses or once were, until Father Time chose otherwise. She stood five foot five, approximately 150 pounds, dark-brown–complexioned, with small firm breasts and a smooth juicy behind. She was well proportioned, to say the least. From various angles in the mirror she turned to inspect her body. She did this every once in a while to make sure she wasn't getting fat. It was a physiological thing with her. Her body was banging, and she planned on keeping it that way.

After passing inspection, Tender quickly pushed aside any lingering doubts out of her mind. Her focus returned to her current reality. There was money to be made out there in the club. And she was in grind mode right now. Tender was hungry right now, in dire financial straits. She hadn't been this pressed for cash since she first entered the strip game. Tender reentered the club wearing a fresh hot pink thong that disappeared up the crack of her ass.

Tender's mind was solely on money. She stepped back out into the club on a mission, a straight paper chase. As she walked around in search of a mark, sexually deprived patrons began to gawk at her body. They stared at her young, firm, succulent body like they had never seen a woman naked before. A few bold men even grabbed ahold of Tender's fat ass cheeks.

"What's good? Who wanna dance?" she called out to no one in particular.

Tender was furious when no one responded to her query, especially with all these so-called players and ballers up in the club. On her way inside the club, she had seen all the trappings of the street life. The club's parking lot looked more like a luxury car dealership. To her this was a classic example of "niggers having short arms and deep pockets." Everyone wanted something for nothing. *That's a real nigger for you,* she mused. Still, Tender was determined to make them come up off some of that dope money.

Now was not the time to lose her composure. She reminded herself to stay focused. Since Tender fancied herself a hustler, she stayed on the prowl. She felt that sooner or later she was going to hit a lick. A come-up might lie within the next guy she propositioned. If she knew anything about men, it was when one won't, one will. She just had to find that trick who didn't mind parting with some cash.

"I'm tryin' to see what that be like, sis. Na'mean?" a hustler announced.

"Put up or shut up!" she fired back. "You know what it is. Money talks!"

"Then you hearin' me loud and clear!" Producing a wad of bills out of his pocket, the man flashed the cash on Tender. Then he put it away. He certainly had her attention now. Though the guy was average in the looks department, suddenly he looked real attractive to Tender. As a matter of fact, with little effort, Tender pretended he was the most handsome man in the club. It was funny how money suddenly changed her physical perception of him.

"VIP?" she asked.

"Yeah, no doubt!" he replied. "Slow ya roll for a minute. Listen, it's my dude's birthday. And, umm, he tryin' to do the damn thang. I mean, we tryin' to do the damn thang."

"What you tryin' to do?" Tender asked.

"We tryin' to get some brain," he admitted. "You know, like a ménage à trois type of thing. Na'mean?"

"I hear that hot shit, Big Willie. You got ménage à trois money? Hope you ain't like the rest of these broke-ass niggers, talk a good game and can't come up with the bread to make it happen," she countered. "As long as you got that cheddar, anything is possible."

"Well, you know what they say, everything's negotiable," he replied. "Me and my man got that dough. So it's a good look, then."

To prove he wasn't all talk, the man flashed a bankroll of money on Tender so big that he seemed to have trouble removing it from his pocket. The sight of all that money seemed to stimulate Tender in ways that sex never could.

"Since you put it that way, let's get it poppin'," she said. "Go get your dude."

The guy motioned for his friend with his hand and he suddenly appeared from a short distance away.

Tender took her customer by the hand and led him through the cramped, dimly lit club while his friend trailed closely behind. They walked past countless scantily clad strippers and the swarm of patrons. Their destination was the VIP lounge. It was there she planned on relieving him and his partner of some of that easy-come-easy-go cash.

Tender gave the big husky bouncer posted up outside the VIP

area a wink of the eye, signaling to him that she was going in to handle some business and that she would take care of him when she was done. In exchange, he would turn a blind eye while she performed some lewd sexual act that was against club policy. It seemed like everyone had a hustle in the club, from the strippers to the bartenders. They all had a price. This was how he made extra money for himself, by allowing the girls to perform nothing short of prostitution. One hand washed the other in life, and the same went on in the club, too.

Once inside the VIP lounge, Tender playfully shoved one man down on a couch, faking aggression. Then she pounced on him. Giving the man a full view of her big ass, she proceeded to grind on him from a reverse cowgirl position. As she sat on one man, she fondled the other man's genitals.

Tender was the kind of chick these guys preferred. She was the kind with whom they could do whatever it was sexually that they pleased, just as long as their money was right. These two guys had tag-teamed plenty of females, twisting them out sexually. It seemed like they were too freaky for the average chick. The things that they wanted to try on them were considered perverted. Still, they had a thing for strippers. They had deemed strippers the most open-minded, or in other words the nastiest. They also fancied themselves to be budding porn stars. It was an inside joke between them.

One man began to softly caress Tender's butt cheeks, gently smacking them, while the other just watched. His penis had risen inside his pants to a rock-hard position. Like most black men, they were ass men. They loved a woman with a nice derrière. So what wasn't there to like about Tender? She had the credentials to back her up in that department. She was young, fine, in shape, with ass for days. Just the sight of it made them want to fuck.

Fantasies of sexual acts dominated the men's thoughts, while visions of dollars danced through Tender's head. A simple lap dance wasn't going to get it. She needed real currency, and fast. She had bills to pay.

Yeah, nigger, grip my fat ass. You like that shit, don't you?

Repositioning herself, Tender turned to face the man before sitting back down in his lap. She began to slowly dry-fuck him, rubbing her crotch back and forth over his erection, working him into a sexual frenzy. He was dying of anticipation.

Tender paused. "Okay, before we go any further, where them dollars at?" she asked.

Without a moment's hesitation, the main guy replied, "Here go mine right here! My dude gone hit you off later when everything is said and done. Half now, the other half when you're done. That way you'll stay motivated."

Tender already had a substantial amount of money in her hand. She didn't have to count it. She saw enough twenty- and ten-dollar bills to make her a believer. She accepted their word that she would receive additional compensation later. They didn't give off the impression that they were going to try anything shady.

Tender took possession of the money, then removed two condoms from her bag, broke the seal, and popped one into her mouth while keeping the other in her hand. In one swift motion she was on her knees, unfastening both men's pants. She took one man's sexual member in her mouth while she gave a hand job to the other.

The man moaned. Tender's mouth was hot, wet, and tight, just like a vagina. Even the hand job that she was giving to the other man was incredible.

"Ummm," he moaned again with pleasure. *She wasn't lyin'. The girl can suck a good dick.*

Tender sucked on the man's dick nonstop, barely getting enough air to breathe. Her fellatio expertise was sending chills up the man's spine. Just as he experienced one wave of pleasure, then came another and another.

He could have sworn that Tender had deep-throated his dick, which was quite a feat since he wasn't small in the dick department. When he felt her tongue tickle his nuts, he was no longer any good. He lost complete control of his body.

At that moment his feeling of pleasure was so extreme that he couldn't take it anymore. The man began to try to pry Tender's head away from his groin, but to no avail. She was locked on him like a pit bull. Feeling this good should be a crime. The man was tempted to hit Tender with a body blow to her ribs, it felt that good. She had taken him to ecstasy and he wanted her to stop.

Suddenly, a jolt of semen raced from his testicles to the head of his penis, swelling it to twice its normal size. There was no sense in prolonging the inevitable, it felt too good. The man unloaded safely inside the contraceptive.

"Damn, baby girl, your head game is vicious!" he proclaimed when she finally pulled back. "I ain't neva got no brain like that before."

Tender shot back, "Don't I know it. I told you I was the bomb."

Now that she had satisfied the first man, Tender repositioned herself between his friend's legs, popped a condom in her mouth, and began to repeat the process. From a few feet away, the first man looked on in amazement as Tender put in work.

Suddenly his cell phone rang. Quickly he looked down at the screen to see the identity of the caller. Seeing it was his baby's momma, he quickly began to straighten up his clothes; he had to go. He didn't want any part of any drama that might lay in wait over him hanging out late.

"My dude, I'm gone," he called out. "Baby mama drama."

His friend merely waved him off. To tell the truth, he was too caught up in the moment to even care.

Within a few minutes the man was feeling the exact same sexual sensations that his friend had experienced. But unlike him, he didn't take flight immediately. Instead he stayed a little longer, in an attempt to get to know Tender a little better. It was as if getting his dick sucked had brought him closer to her. Gladly he paid her for the sexual favor she performed. He definitely had a newfound respect for Tender now. She had his full undivided attention.

The guy was running his game, shooting his best lines at Tender, in hopes of getting her down on his team permanently.

Through casual conversation, Tender learned that the guy's name was Jameer and he was supposed to be some type of big-time drug dealer from the Germantown section of Philadelphia, or at least that's what he said. Tender had her suspicions, though. Dudes that were getting it on the streets usually didn't have to announce themselves. Other people did it for them. The streets were talking, they knew who was who and what was what.

For all of his machoism and bravado, it seemed like the guy wasn't getting the desired effect. He hadn't won Tender over with all his lavish lies about the fast life. From her blank facial expression, she had seen it all and heard it all. At his wits' end, the man had decided it was time to leave. Before the guy knew it, several songs had played. Whether he knew it or not, he owed a debt to Tender. In the strip club, especially in VIP, time was money. And he was being held accountable for all the time they lounged together in VIP.

"Listen, shorty, I'm 'bout to leave. I gotta handle some B.I. But, umm, we definitely need to hook up sometime soon. Feel me? So, dig, why don't you gimme your number and I'll get back at you some other time," he said. "We can hook up outsida the club. Pick up where we let off at."

While talking the man straightened up his attire and walked toward the exit of the VIP, preparing to leave. Tender suddenly flipped the script.

"My number? I don't know about all that," Tender snapped. "But nigger, where you think you goin' without payin' me first? You still owe me."

The man was taken aback by her statement. A dumbfounded look appeared on his face. He didn't understand where Tender was coming from with this. In his mind, he had already paid for the services that she had rendered.

"What? I don't owe you a muthafuckin' thing!" he countered. "You got yours. I already paid you."

"Nigger, like hell we is! Your man paid me for what we did. You still owe me for sittin' here wit' you all this time. It cost to be in up here."

"But we wasn't even doin' nothin' but choppin' it up!" he stated strongly. "You ain't gimme another dance or no head."

"Yo, Riz!" she called out to the bouncer. "You better get this nigger. He tryin' to get slick."

Hearing all the commotion, the bouncer came rushing in. He saw these two standing face to face, almost as if they were about to trade blows at any given moment. Fighting in the strip club was bad for business, so this was something he wanted to avert at all costs, especially while he was on duty.

"Yo, what's goin' on back here?" the bouncer asked, coming between them. "What's good?"

"Main man, lemme tell you the muthafuckin' problem," the man began. "This bitch—!"

"Nigger, I got your bitch! And I'ma good one, too," Tender said.

He continued, "Anyway, this bitch right here tryin' to get over onna nigger! Talkin' 'bout I gotta pay her for sittin' back here with her. Why I gotta do that? Huh? When this bitch is the one who brought me back here in the first place? What kinda shit is that? I wouldn't give that ho all the shit she can eat. Fuck that bitch."

"Yo, family, c'mon now, watch you mouth," the bouncer cautioned. "All this name-callin' stuff ain't gonna get us nowhere."

"You right," the man admitted. "My bad! I'm a lil' tight right now."

Playing the role of peacemaker, the bouncer sought a peaceful resolution to the problem where both parties were satisfied. Beefs and petty disputes were bad for business. In situations like this a little diplomacy went a long way. He knew sometimes it ain't what you say, it's how you say it. In the club one could never be too sure of who they were dealing with. There were a lot of dangerous men who frequented this club on a nightly basis. And he wasn't about to jeopardize his life over some nonsense for some two-bit stripper. He wasn't about to take a bullet for nobody. No pussy was worth dying for.

Gently he placed a humongous arm around the man and walked off with him a few paces. It looked almost as if they were conspiring against Tender. But it was all a part of the game; the guy had walked into a trap.

"Dig right!" the bouncer began. "I know you probably don't know this, but she's right. It's twenty dollars a song. That's the price of a lap dance whether you get a dance or not. Now you been back there for 'bout a half hour, forty-five minutes. DJ done play at least eight records."

"Oh yeah? If you say so," the man countered. "I don't know about all that."

"C'mon now, let's not even go there. You know you was back for a good minute. Listen, just gimme two hundred and we call it even," the bouncer told him.

"Man, I ain't givin that bitch shit! That ho played me!" he barked.

"Look, fam, leave that shit alone, that shit ain't 'bout nuttin', na'mean? Nigger, you know you got it. That shit ain't nuttin' to a baller like yaself. Just pay ya bill and leave that broad alone, feel me? This shit ain't even worth it. You gone beef wit' a broad?"

Just over the bouncer's shoulder the man could see Tender huffing, puffing, and rolling her eyes. The sight of her carrying

on only infuriated him more. If he could get at her now, he
swore he would take Tender's head off. But one look at the
bouncer and he thought better of it. He didn't have any wins up
in the club. If his squad was here with him, then it might have
been a different story. As it stood, they weren't.

After a brief staredown with Tender, the man relented. He
went into his pocket and reluctantly handed over the money.
Quickly he began to walk away. As he left he felt the need to
issue one last threat.

"Bitch, don't lemme catch ya slick ass outsida this club," he
warned. "I know what you look like. I'm do you dirty, ho!"

"Nigger, you gone do what? You gone do whatcha doin' now,
runnin' ya fuckin' mouth!" she cursed. "Nigger, you talk a good
one. But I'm from the Show Me State. You can show me better
than you ever can tell me."

"All right, we'll see," the man threatened. "Bitch, you better
remember this face. I'ma muthafuckin' problem. See me before
I see you!"

"Yeah, nigger, WE WILL SEE!" she repeated. "You know you
ain't built like that! Chump! Git the fuck outta here, you lil'dick
muthafucka."

"You should know, bitch! You sucked it. And I got ya
chump!" he barked. "Bitch, next time you see me you better
run! I swear I'm try my best to knock ya muthafuckin' head off
ya shoulders."

The bouncer waved the man off, as if to kindly ask him to
leave it alone. And the man complied, first exiting the VIP and
then the club. He had more pressing matters to tend to, like his
drug operation. His workers had been ringing him nonstop in
need of more product.

Once he was gone the duo was free to converse, free to divvy
up the loot.

"Yo, Tender, don't do that shit no more. That nigger was real tight about that. What if he jumped on ya ass back here?" the bouncer announced.

"Aww, that nigger wasn't gonna do nuttin'. He was all talk," she replied. "I know a lame when I see one. Besides, that what I got you for."

Even the bouncer had fallen under the sexual spell of Tender. At one time or another they had had their own sexual episodes outside of the club. They chose to keep their affair on the down-low. Tender had sex with him just enough to keep him on her side.

After handing her co-conspirator a fifty-dollar bill, Tender pocketed the rest of the money. She felt it was only right to take the lion's share because it was her hustle. It was she who found the trick in the first place. Besides, she was in need. She wasn't putting herself out there for nothing.

"Do me a favor. Wait right here and lemme make sure the dude left the club," he announced.

Heeding his advice, Tender decided to chill in VIP till the coast was clear. Not that she was scared or anything, but it was better to be safe than sorry. There wasn't no telling what a disgruntled customer would do. Quite frankly, Tender found the whole situation so funny. She had outwitted yet another nigger. And they say women were the so-called weaker sex? Not in her book.

The way Tender saw it, as long as she had a pussy she would always be in power. As long as she looked good, she would always be in demand. Though Tender had been out of the loop for a minute, working a regular job, that was one thing that would never change. Sex sells. Always had and always would. It had been that way since the beginning of time.

Once again, Tender's mind began to drift. Suddenly everything went from so funny to dead serious. Tender took a moment to reflect on her life, how she first came to be in this position. How she began dancing out of sheer desperation, to escape poverty and an uncertain future.

She knew how fleeting success was in this industry. She had had a brief taste of it, some odd years ago, before deciding to quit. Tender shook her head in disgust, feeling sorry for herself, for ending up right back where she started from. Not after all that had happened in the past.

She mused, *I guess history does repeat itself.*

She had been down this road before only to be crushed by disappointment. Her ill-gotten gains had vanished almost as quickly as she had attained them. She knew what lay in wait for her if she continued down this road: heartache, misery, and possibly death.

Tender knew she had to figure something out and quick. She didn't want to do another tour of duty in the strip club. Quite frankly, she didn't know how she survived the first one.

Still, she had to do what she had to do. Tender promised herself that things had to be different this time around. Pussy wouldn't be her bargaining chip, at least not her pussy. She made that mistake once, she'd be damned if she did it again.

Suddenly Tender was struck by a bright idea and she began to formulate the beginnings of a master plan in her mind, a way out. The only drawback was that it would take a little time to execute it properly. Unfortunately for her, time was not on her side.

Tender knew it would take a lot of convincing on her end to get the necessary strippers involved, to put her plan in motion. Still, she felt she had as good a shot as any to persuade them. Tender decided that when she got back to the locker room she would pitch her plan to a select few strippers and see what they thought of it.

5

Later that night, as Tender headed home in a cab, she was feeling very pleased with herself. Her scheme was well under way.

When she had gotten back to the locker room, she had thought over and over about who she could recruit and who she wouldn't. After all, everything wasn't for everybody. Certain individuals wouldn't fit into her plans, for one reason or another. She didn't want any negative energy around her, and from the beginning she was going to make it clear who was calling the shots. She didn't need any headstrong strippers foiling her plan before she got it off the ground. That meant excluding older strippers who were either too set in their ways or couldn't take instruction from someone who was younger than themselves. And no drama queens who would only keep some sort of trouble stirred up. In her mind, less was more. Tender needed people she could control, not people who wanted to be in control.

Cautiously she had approached those she thought would get down with her program. First she had stepped to two lesbian lovers named Starr and Hershee, an odd couple of sorts. Starr was a tall Amazon, big-boned, average in the facial department but blessed with a body that could stop traffic. Hershee was her exact opposite, short, extremely beautiful, yet petite. Hershee looked like an adult-sized African American Barbie doll. Tender understood that they were a package deal, so she propositioned them both.

"Yo, do ya'll want to make some real money?" her sales pitch went. "I ain't talkin' about no chump change, either. I'm talking about some real serious bread! Ya'll wit' this or what?"

After receiving a verbal commitment from Starr and Hershee, Tender moved on to White Chocolate, a white stripper from South Philly who was blessed with the ass of a black girl and the attitude of one, too. She had multiple body piercings from her nose on down to her clitoris. White Chocolate was known for getting down for her crown and being about her dough.

Tender saw the twinkle in her eye as soon as she mentioned money. Money was the bait she used to hook every stripper. She knew that the majority of strippers were money hungry. It was the nature of the business they were in. Men used strippers, but strippers could always use more money. It was a never-ending quest.

Next she got Deja, an ugly, freaky, fat chick armed with a beautiful personality who made more money than most of the strippers in the club, and Unique, a bowlegged, light-skinned girl with chinky eyes who was as cocky as they came. She had a devilish yet innocent appearance about her that attracted men of all ages, including pimps. In many ways, Unique reminded Tender of herself. Or, rather, how she used to be.

Tender had run down her plans to each girl. Yet she refused to give too many specifics when questioned. It was sort of like a wait-and-see thing. When she gave each girl fifty dollars, it sort of sealed the deal. It let them know that she was serious. Tender knew she couldn't properly instruct anyone until she put money in their pockets. But once the strippers heard the plan, they immediately bought into it. Tender's idea was so fresh and original.

The way Tonya saw it, if it was money, power, and excitement that they craved, then she was going to give it to them in large doses.

Just then the taxi pulled up to her building in the wee hours of the morning and Tonya received the shock of her life. She noticed her furniture and clothing scattered about on the sidewalk, as if it had been put out for trash collection or someone had been evicted.

"Stop the cab!" she ordered. "Lemme see something real quick."

Upon closer inspection, Tonya realized that that was her furniture on the sidewalk. She realized that her landlord had finally made good on his promise to evict her. Even if he had done it illegally, he had still done it.

"You fat bastard!" Tonya screamed.

Tonya began to walk swiftly toward her building, unsure of what to expect when she got there. Suddenly her trek was interrupted by the incessant blowing of the taxi's horn. Enraged, Tonya turned around to see what the problem was.

"Hey! Hey! Where you goin'? Pay ya fare!" the cabdriver shouted.

"Muthafucka, I ain't goin' nowhere!" Tonya shouted. "I'll be right back!"

The foreign cabdriver dared not follow her. He knew all too well about the tales of cab drivers being shot and killed by robbers. He didn't know what his passenger was up to, but he decided to wait it out in hopes that the fare would be paid.

Once Tonya reached her floor, she saw that her apartment had been padlocked, so that she couldn't gain entrance. Out of frustration, Tonya gave the door a swift kick. Then she turned and left.

Although she felt completely humiliated, Tonya forced herself to pick through the items she really needed, like her clothing. She gathered up all the footwear and clothes that the taxi trunk could hold and headed for Na'eema's house. She was sure her friend would give her a place to stay, at least for the night, under these dire circumstances.

After explaining what had happened, Na'eema invited Tonya to stay, no further questions asked. As they got ready for bed, Tonya decided to pitch her idea to her friend. If her plan was going to succeed, then she was going to need someone with Na'eema's party promotion know-how.

"I gotta idea that I wanna put you down wit'," Tonya said.

"I'm listenin'," Na'eema said.

"Okay, dig right. I know you throw parties, right?"

"Yeah, and?" Na'eema fired back.

"Well, I got this hot idea tonight while at the club," she stated.

Na'eema interrupted, "What, you wanna start throwin' parties or sumthin'?"

"Can I talk? Damn!" a frustrated Tonya asked.

"Ga'head, my bad girl. Speak ya piece," Na'eema responded.

"Anyway! Like I was sayin'," Tonya said with attitude. "Since you ain't got no patience, I'ma make a long story short. Yeah, I wanna be a promoter. I wanna throw parties, but not like the ones you throw. I wanna throw sex parties, and not the kind where bitches be sellin' fuckin' dildos and shit, either. At my parties bitches gonna be sellin' pussy, pussy, and more pussy."

Tonya paused for a moment to see if her words had any effect on her friend. And she could tell by the smirk on Na'eema's face that she had struck a chord with her. She was obviously interested.

Tonya continued, "And since you already doin' ya thang on the party tip, I figured me and you can combine what we know and do this shit. I got the bitches lined up and ready to do whateva. All I need to know is, you with it or what?"

Scratching her chin as if she were silently weighing her options, Na'eema looked slyly at Tonya. The look said it all. Tonya knew she could count her in even before she verbally agreed.

"Sounds like a plan to me!" Na'eema said enthusiastically. "All right, listen, this is how we gonna do this."

That night in Na'eema's apartment, the two friends laid the foundation for their company, which would later be known as "Dick 'em Down Productions." Na'eema and Tonya became the chief architects of this grand sex-for-sale scheme.

The two friends spent hours in deep conversation. As they ironed out the wrinkles of the plan, going over the positives and negatives, Na'eema gained a newfound respect for Tonya's mind. She learned that her friend had business acumen, and she saw a side of her that she hadn't seen while working at the salon.

There wasn't any class or school that could prepare them for the journey they were about to embark on. Either they had it or they didn't. Either they would succeed or they would fail. There was no in-between. Besides a financial gain, there was a lot more at stake here, namely Tonya's life.

If heartache and hardship had a face, then it would be hers. In many ways, Tonya felt she was destined to succeed. Since her life had been a series of setbacks and failures in one way or another, she desperately needed to believe that this venture was going to be successful. And besides that, she had no backup plan. The way Tonya saw it, if all went well this could just be her ticket out of the strip club forever.

Whether Na'eema knew it or not, an evolution was about to take place. She was about to witness Tonya's transformation from stripper to shrewd businesswoman.

From that night on, Tonya hustled with a renewed passion. She also had the added burden of finding somewhere else to live. She didn't want to wear out her welcome at Na'eema's house.

Every club she danced in, from A Night on Broadway to Top Notch to Delilah's to Moet and Daydreams, Tonya spread the word. She said whatever she had to say to hype her party and pique curiosity.

She even had fliers printed up to help advertise the upcoming anything-goes sexfest. It was billed as "The Ultimate Freak-Off." The graphic artist did a wonderful job on the flier. There were three extremely beautiful minority females, half naked, surrounded by the trappings of success, bottles of Cristal champagne, a fancy European sports sedan, and iced-out platinum jewelry.

Like anything else that was underground and forbidden, word quickly spread.

While Tonya took care of the underworld crowd, Na'eema went after the nine-to-five working-class guys. She cross-promoted their event at her Grown & Sexy affairs. She got tons of verbal commitments from her regular male partygoers to attend the affair. Na'eema promised them that the party would be "off the chain." To her surprise, the upcoming event drew interest from all kinds of men, from every walk of life—corporate types, blue-collar workers, street thugs.

Both Tonya and Na'eema had an equal amount of tickets, which they sold in advance. They made it clear that no one would be admitted at the door without one. Surprisingly, the tickets went so fast that they both regretted not renting an even bigger venue.

A neighborhood recreation center located in North Philly served as the showplace for Na'eema and Tonya's first event. They had secured the spot under false pretenses. The community leaders were told that they would be holding some sort of amateur boxing event for a local boxing team. Since Philly was a big fight town, the lie was believable. A boxing ring was set up, minus the ropes, a day before to further sell the fictitious event.

Tonya assumed a gang of responsibilities that night. She wore many hats, from parent to promoter. She preferred a hands-on type of management. Tonya didn't want to delegate any task to someone else that she hadn't first done herself.

Tonya moved through the recreation center meticulously, going over her mental checklist. She looked for anything that might be out of place, anything that could spoil the event. Tonya wanted everything to run smoothly. She moved from the bar, checking the liquor inventory, to the security guards, making sure everyone was on post, to the fire exits, making sure nothing blocked them. She checked all these places and everywhere else in between.

When Tonya reached the bathroom, which now doubled as a makeshift dressing room, she stuck her head inside. She wanted to see how things were going with her most precious commodity, the strippers.

Tonya was as anxious and nervous as an expectant mother. She was also a pessimist who subscribed to Murphy's Law, which stated that anything that could go wrong, would go wrong. She was determined to take every precaution to make sure nothing happened on her watch.

What she saw was countless naked bodies preparing themselves for the sexual extravaganza. The strippers busied themselves doing drugs like Ecstasy and weed, and chitchatting. They engaged in their usual routines, doing whatever they needed to do to get in the right frame of mind.

"Everybody good?" she asked. "Anybody need anything?"

Either the noise was too loud or they were too high to hear her, because no one bothered to answer. So she assumed that everyone was straight.

Tonya yelled, "Ladies, we gotta bout a half till the doors

open! Ya'll know what to do! Hershee and Starr, ya'll up first. Let's put on a good show. Let's make it do what it do!"

That was as much of a pep talk as Tonya was going to give. If these broads couldn't step their game up and get at all that money that would soon be coming through those doors, then they didn't belong there anyway.

For the majority of these strippers this wasn't their first time performing or selling sex. Tonya was confident that most if not all of them would rise to the occasion with the stakes this high. A lot of them needed money to take care of their children or some lazy good-for-nothing significant other or to feed their ever-growing drug habits. A lot of them weren't young anymore. They were closer to thirty than to twenty. A lot of their bodies weren't as firm or fresh anymore. Slowly they were being used up, so she knew they couldn't let an opportunity like this pass them by.

As she made her way out of the makeshift locker room, Tonya's eyes rested on an innocent-looking brown-skinned girl with large bubble eyes named Cashmere. She was a friend of one of the older strippers. If there was anyone Tonya had doubts about, it was her. The girl had a naiveté and an uneasiness about her that came with one time and one time only. She reminded Tonya of herself her first time in the strip club.

Tonya would be the first to admit there was nothing unique or special about stripping. Still, she knew that this was an individual choice and that every stripper's journey to the strip club was different. She knew that each one danced for various reasons, coming from troubled backgrounds, yet their struggle was the same, to make it in this man's world.

Tonya promised to make it a point to seek Cashmere out and give her the "real" on life as a stripper. It was a shame more people didn't think like that. Then there would be a lot less tragedies in life. Walking away, Tonya had a lot on her mind, and Cashmere didn't help matters any.

Finally Tonya and Na'eema met up at the door. Na'eema showed no signs of being worried. Too bad the same couldn't be said for her friend. To her credit, Na'eema always knew when something was wrong with Tonya. She had good timing and a knack for saying something, cracking a joke, to lighten the mood.

"Tonya, you a mess. Calm down! Be easy!" Na'eema suggested. "After tonight, we gone be the shit."

Tonya replied, "I hope so."

"Don't worry, we will. You'll see," Na'eema promised.

Before either of them knew it, it was showtime. The bouncers began searching and admitting the first group of patrons. What began as a light trickle of men turned into an uncontrollable tidal wave. The partygoers had done their part by merely showing up; now it was time for the strippers to do theirs.

In the center of the ring, Starr and Hershee awaited these sexually charged men. At the sight of the two naked women, the men crowded around and Starr and Hershee proceeded to put on a show.

The smaller of the two women, Hershee, got into the doggy-style position while her lesbian lover, Starr, mounted her and started to pound her out with a large black strap-on dildo. Starr worked Hershee over as well as any man would. They both were really into it, moaning and groaning and making fuck faces. The men pressed even closer, calling out all kinds of comments, they were so turned on by their sexual intensity.

No one had really known just how much of an exhibitionist these two were until now, and how much pleasure and excitement they derived from having sex publicly with each other. It was clear that they were two freaks.

While all eyes were glued to the stage, the other strippers came out of the locker room and began to work the crowd. They began soliciting every man within earshot for any sexual act under the sun. "The Ultimate Freak-Off" turned out to be just that.

Both Na'eema and Tonya kept a low profile, their wide grins signaling their approval. From their perspective, moneywise, it was good to be bad, and the freakier the better. Tonya wanted to put on a good show and give the dudes something to talk about. They both knew that the best form of advertisement was word of mouth.

Starr and Hershee were a tough act to follow, but after them came White Chocolate, who incorporated a guy from the crowd into her act, tying him up and giving him a spanking. She was followed by Deja, who performed one of the strangest acts of the night. She smoked a cigarette with the lips of her vagina, much to the audience's amazement. After that there was a long procession of bodies in the ring shaking their asses.

Tonya and Na'eema carefully scrutinized the performances from the sidelines. It was nothing to Tonya to see these things. Matter of fact, she had seen worse. She had once seen a stripper stick a good portion of a baseball bat inside her vagina.

Although Na'eema was appalled at what she was witnessing, she tried hard not to show it. To do so would mean she was passing judgment on her friend. She didn't want her thoughts to be misconstrued, so she didn't say a word.

It was sad for Na'eema to watch these women demean themselves, sacrificing their bodies, maybe even their lives, driven by the scent of money. Even though she made money off them, after witnessing all of this firsthand, it didn't sit well with her. They did things that no woman in her right mind would do. And all for what?

Na'eema had been raised Muslim, and though she wasn't currently practicing, she felt some sort of moral responsibility. But then she shook it off and tried to think only of the money they were making.

Better them than me, she told herself.

While Na'eema was lost in her thoughts, Tonya noticed the absence of the next performer in the ring. She looked down at her scrap piece of paper, at the half-dozen scratched-off names, and saw one remaining, Cashmere. Silently she cursed to herself. Tonya knew that this girl was going to be a problem.

"C'mon!" Tonya suddenly announced.

"What's up?" Na'eema asked.

"Help me find this bitch Cashmere!" Tonya said, a frustrated expression on her face. "She 'pose to be in the fuckin' ring and she ain't fuckin' there. Where the fuck is she at?"

Na'eema, on the other hand, didn't see what Tonya was so mad about. But she went along with her anyway.

"Look, go that way, I'll go this way. We'll meet up at the bathroom," she ordered. "Call me on my cell if you see her."

Walking through this crowd was something Na'eema had desperately wanted to avoid. She was groped from behind a few times and propositioned more times than she could count.

"You fuckin' niggas betta keep ya hands to yaselves!" Na'eema hollered.

"Hey, Ma, don't act like that!" someone shouted. "Big girls need love, too."

Once one man said something it opened the floodgates for everyone else to make a wisecrack. Normally Na'eema would have turned around and confronted someone. There would have been a price to pay for touching on her body like that, but right now there were just too many hecklers. And knowing herself, she would have said something real disrespectful and caused the man to defend his manhood by striking her. Now wasn't the time or place for it, though. So she kept up the search.

On the other side of the recreation center, Tonya was experiencing more of the same sexual harassment, to an even higher degree. Guys touched her at will. She took the free feels in stride and kept moving. She had other things on her mind, namely Cashmere. Locating her was Tonya's number-one priority. The show must go on.

Simultaneously, Tonya and Na'eema met up in front of the makeshift dressing room. Now they both looked frustrated.

"Did you see her?" Tonya wondered.

"Nah. You?" Na'eema fired back.

"C'mon, let's see if this bitch up in here," Tonya said. "I'll bet my last she is."

Tonya barged into the bathroom like she was the police, with Na'eema close on her heels. They took two steps into the bathroom and saw the stripper in question.

Cashmere had her head bowed with a white towel draped over it. She never heard the door open, due to the loud music. The mere sight of her just sitting there sent Tonya into a rage. She never once took into consideration that maybe something was wrong.

"Cashmere! What the fuck are you still doin' in here? You suppose to be out there puttin' on a show," she barked.

Tonya's tone of voice and colorful choice of words had broken her short period of reflection, giving her a cold hard slap of reality.

"I can't do it. I can't do it!" she repeated.

Tonya was far from faultless, and Cashmere provided a convenient target for her to vent on.

Tonya knew that strippers had game and she didn't know what kind of game Cashmere was playing. All she knew was she didn't have time for it. If Cashmere didn't want to do her job, then she was gone. One monkey wouldn't stop her show. Tonya knew that being the boss came with certain responsibilities. She got paid to make hard decisions, like firing people.

"What?" Tonya snapped. "Fuck you mean, you can't do it? Bitch, have you lost ya fuckin' mind? Matter fact, get the fuck up outta here. I ain't got time for this shit. Bitches gettin' all righteous all of a sudden."

What Tonya didn't know was that Cashmere had tried and

failed to get into the ring and do her thing. She had had a sudden change of heart. Fear and doubt had set in, paralyzing the young girl.

Initially, Na'eema thought that there was a perfectly good reason for the girl to be distraught. Something had to have happened. At least, common sense told her that.

Tonya continued to rip into the young girl, intimidating and humiliating her. She took no pity on Cashmere. That was until Na'eema intervened.

"Tonya, leave that alone," she cautioned. "Lemme holla atcha for a minute outside."

Na'eema placed her big arm around her angry friend and escorted her out of the locker room. Out of earshot, she began to reason with Tonya.

"Tonya, God doesn't like ugly," she said. "Leave that girl be. You can't make her do somethin' she don't wanna do. It ain't in her. Can't you see that?"

Tonya was currently in her "Tender" mode, and her alter ego didn't care about anyone or anything except money. She was hard on Cashmere because life had been hard on her. All she knew was the strong would survive and the weak would die and the only ones that do make it are the ones who put forth the effort, who have willpower.

Once again, Na'eema had a calming effect on Tonya. She had a way of saying things that allowed Tonya to quickly refocus. Her words hit home. Suddenly Tonya realized just how wrong she had been. Life on the street had hardened her to the point where Tonya had little or no compassion for her fellow human being.

Immediately, Tonya thought back to a time in the not-so-distant past when she first entered the stripping profession and someone tried to warn her about the ills and she didn't listen. Maybe if she had heeded the warning, it would have saved her from a world of hurt.

"My bad," she agreed. "You right."

What Tonya did next really endeared her to Na'eema.

Reentering the locker room, Tonya walked over Cashmere, placed her hand on her back, and gently rubbed.

"Yo, you hear me?" she said. "Listen, I apologize for whatever I said earlier. I ain't mean it. Put your clothes on. I gotta job for you. All you have to do is know how to count. You can work the door, be my cashier. You don't ever have to do no shit like this again."

Na'eema wanted to walk over and hug Tonya. She was that proud of her. Tonya was coming of age. It seemed like it took some time, but what she used to say had finally gotten through to her: "Money ain't everything." Tonight Tonya had proved that.

The rest of the night went smoothly and without incident. Everybody got paid, from the strippers to the bouncers to the bartender. This low-budget form of entertainment had exceeded all monetary expectations.

Sure, there were some missteps along the way, but they enjoyed more success than they did failures. Gradually Dick 'em Down Productions grew. Guys bought into their act, literally and figuratively. It generated lots of sexual excitement. After that first night, it took off, growing by leaps and bounds. Tonya and Na'eema had to look for bigger venues to accommodate their ever-growing fan base.

They even started to get some private party requests, which Tonya was more than happy to accommodate. Sometimes it surprised her to see some men at these parties who had good reputations in the community—a few low-level politicians, some cops, community leaders. She thought she even spotted a pastor here or there. But Tonya wasn't about to discriminate. If you had that green, then Dick 'em Down Productions was going to accommodate you.

Things sometimes got wild at these ultraprivate sex-offs, and unbeknownst to the partygoers, Tonya often had a hidden camera going. She never planned on doing anything with the tapes, but she figured it couldn't hurt to have a little insurance, considering who the clientele sometimes was. And a hustler could never have too much insurance.

Tonya didn't know just how far her newfound success would take her. She was like a passenger in a brand-spanking new car. She was enjoying the ride and all the attention she was receiving from her fellow promoters. The money she was making was the icing on the cake; it made everything better. To Tonya there was no need to know where her life was going, because she already knew where it had been or, rather, what it had been: hell.

Tonya hoped and prayed that she had indeed found her way out of the street life, that these parties were only a stepping-stone to bigger and better things. Still, she couldn't be too sure. After all, she had had the same feelings about stripping initially.

After months of making money hand over fist, a crooked cop Tonya had on the payroll, working security for the events, told her that he had heard her parties being talked about by a high-ranking Vice squad detective. The threat of them getting raided or infiltrated loomed large.

Tonya knew that she could have possibly squashed any potential investigation with some of the dirt she had on a few people in important places, including in the Philadelphia Police Department, but she knew it was time to fold. When she told Na'eema about her intentions, she seconded the motion and they began to plot an escape route. Na'eema was growing weary of the large crowds they had been attracting. She just knew that sooner or later they were going to get busted by the cops for prostitution. Things were just too good to be true.

Still, Tonya didn't want to abandon the party game completely. There was too much money at stake to just walk away. Instead, Tonya wanted to shift to more legitimate parties, ones where people actually kept their clothes on. The kind of parties that wouldn't put their freedom in jeopardy.

Tonya could have easily been content with her success, choosing to stay on the street level and be just another ex-stripper. But she had a dream to get out of the game once and for all. And she wouldn't stop until the dream became a reality.

As a small token of their appreciation, Tonya and Na'eema turned over control of the Ultimate Freak-Off to Cashmere, who they discovered had a real head for business and management. She promptly relocated the Dick 'em Down parties to Baltimore to avoid being raided by the police.

In the meantime, Tonya and Na'eema went on to make a name for themselves in event planning, marketing, and promotion. Reinventing themselves as T&N Productions, short for Tonya and Na'eema, they began attracting the attention of some very powerful people.

PART II

Q

6

T&N Productions rose out of obscurity to carve a nice niche for themselves among the partygoing crowd. Backed by a strong street team and cutting-edge promotional ploys, they captured the partygoing crowd's attention. It had been a grueling two years to build their company. She and Na'eema had hustled hard, and slowly the bigger parties and the bigger money had started coming in.

Their coming-out party had been the Philadelpia 76ers star guard Allen Iverson's birthday bash at the Z-bar. The party was such a huge success that it put Na'eema and Tonya's name on the tongues of many very important people. Soon they were getting requests to attend exclusive events and rival promoter parties. When it came to the nightlife, they were on the A-list of celebrities.

Since they were always on the grind, Tonya didn't have much of a personal life. Money was her lover. Na'eema had met her man, Ty, at one of their parties. He was an aspiring music producer and they had been together for two years now. But Tonya didn't have anyone. She had one or two guy "friends" who would scratch her itch or be a handsome escort for some event when she needed it, and that was good enough for now. She didn't have time to be tending to a nigga and putting his needs above her own. However, sometimes, late at night, she wished she had someone to call her own. But then she would remind herself of the bigger picture. The more successful she was, the more secure her present and future would be, and that was all that mattered at the moment.

Club Blue Martini was located on 2nd Avenue and Market Street in downtown Philadelphia. This hot spot was the current location for Na'eema and Tonya's latest extravaganza. Their parties were the talk of the town and were all packed to capacity. A few times the fire department had come and shut them down.

Like any good promoters, Tonya and Na'eema played hostess, meeting and greeting the partygoers. Separately they walked around the club. To Tonya, everything appeared to be in order. Drinks were flowing freely, good music was playing, and people were dancing. Overall, it was a good look. Money was being spent and money was being made.

Suddenly Tonya stopped dead in her tracks. She stared real hard, blinking repeatedly as if she were seeing some sort of mirage.

No, it can't be. That ain't him, she thought. Although she was seeing him with her own two eyes, she couldn't believe it. It had been such a long time.

One thing Tonya was good at was remembering faces. She could spot a familiar one anywhere, and the person she was looking at right now had a face she would never forget. The closer the large entourage came, the clearer his face became and the harder her heart began to pound.

Quinton "Q" Phelps was a music mogul, the CEO of Prestige Records, a Philadelphia native, and the first guy to ever show some genuine concern about Tonya. Their paths had crossed some years ago, under different circumstances, down in Miami, and it had carried over back in Philly. They had shared a brief but torrid sexual affair.

Q was looking damn fine—finer, if such a thing were even possible. Q had boyish good looks, deep brown eyes, a smooth cocoa complexion, and hair braided in small, neat cornrows. He was of average height, but he carried himself with the kind of smooth confidence that made him seem taller than anyone else in the room. He was sexy as hell and Tonya dared anyone to find something wrong with him. Remembering what he had been like in bed—the size, the shape, the feel of him—she more than knew that he had every reason to be a cocky bastard if he wanted to. Plus he had money. So what wasn't there to like about him?

Q was surrounded by a makeshift entourage that consisted of friends from his old neighborhood in North Philly and a few humongous bodyguards. Q had truly arrived. He was somebody. And Tonya was well aware of this fact.

Like everyone else, Tonya had followed his ascension to the upper echelons of the rap industry through the media—MTV, VH1, BET, *Entertainment Weekly, XXL, Vibe,* the Internet.

She watched him now in admiration. Q was like the prodigal son, the pride of North Philly. He was a street cat from the hood who had made it big, a success story of epic proportions.

Tonya couldn't help but think, *That could be me in a couple years. Minus a couple million dollars.*

Q and his entourage totally shut down the VIP area. He bought out the bar, so it was free drinks all night long for everyone in there. He had money and everyone knew that Q was real generous. Wherever he went, he spread the love. It was his way of giving back to the millions of fans, friends, and well-wishers who had supported him by purchasing the music of his recording artists.

Most people predicted that his lavish style of splurging money would soon bankrupt him. Music insiders and critics thought Q was too preoccupied with "keeping it real" with his lifestyle and the hard-core music that came off his label. Despite what anybody thought, Q remained true to the streets and his hard-core audience. It was what put him in this position in the first place.

From the moment Tonya spotted him, it was as if no one else existed. Though she was in a crowded room, suddenly everyone seemed to disappear. She saw nobody but Q. She watched him closely, never letting him get out of her sight.

In a cozy corner, Tonya debated on whether or not to approach him. She still felt the sting of rejection, even after all these years, because Q had chosen her fake friend Kat over her. If it had been up to Tonya, then they might still be together.

At that moment an old saying came to mind: *It's possible for a person to hate that which is good for them and love that which is bad for them.* Q proved that saying true with his choice in sex partners.

It was impossible for Tonya to see Q and not remember the good, the bad, and the ugly. Her mind flashed back to their initial meeting at a private party in Miami, their wet and wild sex romp in the rain, the ménage à trois she participated in with him and Kat, and Kat's tragic murder at the hands of Q's baby's momma, Niecey. All in all, Tonya really had no regrets. Q might have used her to fulfill his own sexual fantasies, but at least Kat had gotten what her hand called for.

After stalking him with her eyes, Tonya decided to let bygones be bygones and walked over to say hello to him. She figured it couldn't hurt to speak, plus she wanted him to see that she was doing well now, no thanks to him.

Tonya crossed the room, passing countless half-naked bodies, sex-starved men, and loud rap music. She was oblivious to it all. She focused solely on the figure in front of her. Tonya's heart began to beat wildly with excitement the closer she got to him.

She mused, *Will he recognize me? Will he even give me the time of day? I hope this nigger don't try and play me.*

But it was too late to turn back now. She had been spotted by

Q. It was unclear if he even recognized her, because he gave no indication as he stood sandwiched between his two bodyguards.

Tonya smiled nervously at him. She didn't know what else to do. Now she was only a few feet away from him.

Just as Tonya was about to reach him, Q was engulfed by a protective wall. She couldn't even see him anymore.

"Can I help you?" a burly bodyguard suddenly asked.

"No, you can't help me. I know Q personally. I was just coming by to say hi," Tonya explained with a bit of attitude.

Q's bodyguard shot Tonya a blank look, as if he had heard that line before. He didn't move a muscle.

Now that Q was a true celebrity, he had been in all kinds of trouble. As of late he had been hit with numerous lawsuits by overzealous fans, men and women alike. Those lawsuits alleged everything from assault to sexual misconduct. So now he rolled with professional bodyguards as an added precaution. Q's attorney had warned him to stay out of the nightclubs altogether. Or hire bodyguards. He chose the latter. No one was going to keep him out of the limelight he so desperately craved.

"I know him," Tonya repeated. "If you move, then maybe he'll be able to recognize me. Better yet, just go tell him Tonya wants to see him."

Q thought he recognized that voice.

"Tender?" he said and his bodyguards stepped aside.

Tonya shot the nearest bodyguard a dirty look that seemed to say, "I told you so."

"Q!" she squealed affectionately when she saw him.

"Tender!" he joyously replied.

Like two long-lost friends, Tonya and Q shared a long, affectionate embrace. They were genuinely happy to see each other. They could see that the years had been kind to both of them.

"Look at you!" she gushed. "Boy, you doin' the damn thing, huh? You got bodyguards and e'rythang. Must be nice."

"You know," he said with a smile, "it is what it is."

"I hear that!" she replied.

"Lookin' good! Lookin' good!" he commented while looking Tonya's body over.

Tender had always been a ten in his book and now she was looking even better than ever. She was rocking a pair of tight Antique jeans, Rock and Republic high heels, and a Salvage top that showed off her sexy flat belly. Her hair was done in a short bob. Her makeup was flawless. She looked like a million bucks. Time had definitely been good to her. Looking at her now, it wasn't hard to remember what it had been like to be between those sweet thighs. Truth be told, he wouldn't mind making another guest appearance in her bed before the night was through.

"Come on over and visit with me for a minute," he said.

Tonya allowed him to take her by the hand and lead her over to one of the plush seats, where a bottle of Cristal was open and chilling. He poured two glasses and then handed one to her.

"To reunions," he said, looking her in the eye and raising his glass. He gave her one of his sexy smiles.

"To reunions," Tonya repeated and could have sworn her panties had just gotten a little wet. *Damn, this nigga has gotten even smoother,* she thought.

After taking a sip, Q said, "So, Tender, what you been up to?" He looked her over from head to toe again. "Because whatever it is, it's treatin' you good."

Tonya took another sip of her drink and carefully crossed her legs. "Well, it's Tonya now," she told him. "I don't go by Tender no more."

"Tonya," he said, as if trying her name out to see how he felt about it. He smiled. "I like it. So, I guess that means you're out of the stripping game?"

"Yeah, it was time to move on. There wasn't any long-term future in that," she said, but didn't eleborate any further. When she had first seen him, one of her initial thoughts had been to

show off her success and the fact that she was making something of herself. She was no longer just a stripper, something
that had kept him from ever thinking about her as more than a
sidepiece. "I'm not good at sharing," he had told her. But she
held back now. She didn't want to feel like she had something to
prove to Q. She didn't want to give him that much power.

"So what have you been up to?" she asked, moving the conversation back to him. Q was only too happy to fill her in on his
latest exploits.

They played catchup for a little while, and their conversation
flowed so smoothly that they could have kept talking for hours
on end. She had never felt so comfortable with a man before. It
was also intoxicating being next to Q after all this time. The way
he looked and smelled and moved and laughed had Tonya open.
And he hadn't even done a damn thing. Every once in a while he
would touch her, real casual-like, and she would feel like ripping
off his clothes and doing him right there in the middle of the
VIP section. She was a mess. Tonya realized if she didn't get
away from him soon, she was going to make a fool of herself.

Tonya looked down at her watch and said, "Wow, Q, it was
great talking to you, but I really gotta run. I have some people to
meet and greet." She leaned in and kissed his cheek. "Come see
about your people sometime, okay?" She smiled and started to
rise.

"Wait, Tonya," he said, reaching out to touch her arm. He
pulled her back down onto the seat. "Listen, I don't want to just
say good-bye just yet." He let his gaze slide over her. "I'm tryin' ta
get at you, girl . . . maybe we can hook up for old times' sake."

Tonya had been dreading and wanting this moment. The problem was that she wanted Q too much, but she couldn't let on. It
wouldn't be in her best interests. To do so would be to show
weakness to the one man who could probably hurt her the most.

A lot of women would have jumped at the opportunity to

sleep with Q. It wouldn't be a stretch of the imagination to believe that he could have any girl in the club he wanted. He could
leave with any of them immediately, if not sooner. Tonya was
flattered that he still wanted her. But it couldn't go down like
that, not again.

Their last sexual encounter had taught her some very valuable lessons. These were lessons that she still recalled now. Q
had played her before, and she would be damned if she let it
happen again.

Decisions, decisions, she thought.

"Q, c'mon, let's not even go there," she said uncomfortably.

He moved in close and touched her face. "Tee, don't do me
like that," he said, letting his voice get low and sexy. "You don't
have to go now. We can slide up outta here later."

Tonya just stared into his eyes and began to get weak. Q
could be real persuasive when he wanted to be. It was hard to
deny him, but Tonya had to. Even though he was responsible for
her very first climax, she had to put that behind her. Tonya
wanted him to see her in a different light. She didn't want to be
just another one of his freaks. If she went down that road again
with Q she wanted to be one of one, not one of many.

Tonya pushed all thoughts of Q's magic dick, his fame,
money, and power out of her head. She told herself this handsome guy in front of her was just another "pussy-hungry" nigger,
that he was no different from any other guy in the club tonight.
That was a lie, of course. Truth be told, Q would always have a
place in her heart. But she needed to downplay the situation
while she fought temptation.

Tonya used the smoothness of a politician to wiggle out of
this uncomfortable situation.

"C'mon, Q, things are different. That was then, this is now. I
gotta man now," she lied. "And I go forward, not backward. Besides, you didn't want me when you had me. Remember?"

Q sure did remember. Quietly he kicked himself for making the wrong choice in women. But that was the story line of his life, from his baby's crazy mother, Niecey, to the late Kat. He always thought with his dick.

"You know what they say, the more things change, the more things stay the same. Love is love. We need to let bygones be bygones."

An awkward silence fell between them and she knew that they were both thinking about the tragedy to which both of them were forever linked. Q's baby's mother, Niecey, had killed Kat. But neither of them broached that subject. It was an ugly chapter in everyone's life that they wanted to remain closed. They both would have preferred to pretend that it had never happened.

Q had to deal with the matter his every waking moment. He had a child by Niecey, so he couldn't just abandon her. He had spent quite a bit of money for high-profile lawyers in defense of someone he had known was guilty as sin. Questionable police work and the sudden disappearance of key witnesses had allowed Niecey to take a plea bargain to a lesser charge. Consequently, she received a light sentence and was due to be released from state prison shortly.

Tonya's reason for forgetting about the situation was simple. There was no statute of limitation for murder and unbeknownst to anyone, she had set the whole thing up. She was an accessory to murder. She had used Kat and Niecey as pawns in a deadly game.

"Listen," she said. "I really do have to run. You take care of yourself, Q."

Once again, Q and Tonya shared a passionate hug. It was as if neither one of them wanted to let go. When they finally broke their warm embrace, Tonya turned and started to walk in the opposite direction, thoughts racing through her mind. She felt like a fool for not getting any contact information from Q. She felt she should have at least asked for his business card.

Before Tonya could get away, she felt a strong grip on her arm once again. She turned around to face Q. Her heart began to pound in her chest as she wondered what he could possibly want.

"Wait," he said. "Tell me something. Do you know the promoters of this party? Do you work for them or somethin'?"

Disappointment registered on her face. Needless to say, this was not what Tonya wanted to hear. But what had she expected him to say? Did she think that he was going to declare his undying love for her? That he wasn't going to let her walk out of his life? Or that he was going to save her from a life of poverty and despair? She shook her head, feeling like an even bigger fool.

"Know the promoter?" she repeated. "I *am* the promoter. Me and my girl Na'eema threw this party. This is what we do."

Q was stunned by the news. He had heard about T&N Promotions. They had built up a huge following throughout Philly. Secretly he had come to this party in hopes of meeting the promoters. Ever on the watch for new talent, Q kept his ear glued to the street. He wanted the most talented and hungry people in his organization. He loved people with a vision and a go-out-and-get-it attitude. Now it was clear to him that Tonya had both. For the first time, Q began looking at her in a different light. She was sexy as hell and she had the fire he was looking for. Q decided right then and there that he wanted Tonya.

And what Q wanted, Q got.

Q left the club at a little after two in the morning. As he walked to his car with his bodyguards, he couldn't help smiling as he recalled his conversation with Tonya.

"Yo, Tonya, you wanna job?"

She had looked at him in shock before she asked, "Doing what, Q? I mean, I already have a job. This is me right here."

Q realized that he was going to have to sell her on the benefits of working for him.

"Tonya, I have to admit, you doin' the damn thing right now," he said. "But realistically, how long do you think your run is goin' to last? Every promoter gets a turn to shine. You got a crowd right now, you the talk of the town right now. But will you be able to say the same thing two, three, or even five years from now? I'm offerin' you financial stability. There'll be a paycheck with ya name on it every week, no matter what. Here you only get paid if the people show up. My company will provide you with full medical and dental coverage. I'll put you up in a furnished crib and let you live rent-free for a year. You can't beat that."

With her arms folded across her chest, Tonya listened intently to everything he had to say.

"Q, you have a point there," she admitted. "I know this shit ain't forever and compared to what you're doing it's nothing major. It's a slow grind, but it's my grind. I'm my own boss. Let's say I did decide to come work for you. What would you have me doing? And what would my job title be?"

"To me it's obvious what your strong suit is," he told her, "and that's marketing. You know how to get the word out to your target market about your product. So I'm thinkin' I'll bring you on board as a marketing consultant. You'd basically be your own boss and you'd only answer to me. You'd have your own expense account, your own budget, and you would be free to put together your own team. Bring whoever you want in with you. I'll make you as comfortable as possible. That'll help ease your transition from your world to mine."

"You got this all figured out, huh?" Tonya asked.

"I wouldn't say that," Q told her. "I just ain't going to accept no for an answer."

Tonya shook her head, not quite able to believe this conversation. "What about salary?" she asked out of curiosity. "I heard you say something about that."

He mentioned a very nice six-figure salary. "How does that sound?" he asked.

He could tell that she thought it sounded good.

"Do I have to give you an answer right now?" she said instead. "This is a major move. I need a day or two to think about it."

Q had expected her to say that. "I'll tell you what," he said. "I'll be in town for a few days. Holla at me. Don't let me leave Philly without hearin' from you."

They had parted ways shortly after that. Q had continued to hang out in the VIP section, and he enjoyed watching her work the crowd. Tonya was a natural. He was determined to bring her to Prestige. He wanted her. And in more ways than one.

Q snapped out of his train of thought when he reached the car. He got in the front passenger side while one of his bodyguards got in the driver's seat. No sooner had they pulled out on the road and gone a couple of blocks when his bodyguard said, "5-0."

Q glanced in the sideview mirror and sure enough they were right behind them. He had spotted the so-called hip-hop police lingering outside the club in their unmarked vehicles when he had entered the club. They were almost part of the landscape for Q now. As soon as Q had been thrust into the public eye, accusations had begun to swirl around him. The media wanted to know exactly where did he get the money to start his music empire? The hip-hop police began to scrutinize his every move. Now Q had to be extra careful, watching what he said and did in public. Fortunately for Q it wasn't what the authorities knew, it was what they could prove.

But to make matters worse, Manhattan's district attorney, Robert Fera, really seemed to want to bring him down. Q was the new wunderkind of the music industry and his face was splashed across every publication in the country, and there was nothing like taking down a high-profile celebrity to make someone's career. Q was sure that Fera was pressuring the police to get something on him. So every once in a while they popped up to harass him on one thing or another.

He also knew that the Manhattan district attorney's power stretched way beyond the New York state lines. He and the mayor of Philadelphia not only belonged to the same political party, but their personal relationship went way back and they had attended the same college, an Ivy League school, the University of Pennsylvania. The same college his son recently graduated from. Q suspected that at Robert Fera's request, the Philadelphia Police department kept round-the-clock surveillance on him, whenever he was in town. Fera had no jurisdiction in Philly, so he was probably just looking for any clues or insight into any illegal activities Q might be engaging in while in town and possibly bring back to New York. And Fera just seemed to like to flex his muscle and remind Q who was the more powerful of the two.

As if on cue, the flashing lights and the wail of the police siren filled the air.

"Pull over," Q said, resigned, and his bodyguard did as he said.

The high beams from the unmarked police car momentarily blinded Q and his bodyguard. From the rear, two plainclothes detectives cautiously approached the Bentley. One of them tapped on the window on the driver's side.

"Roll down the window," the cop said. "License and registration."

"What's the problem, Officer?" Q replied. "Why are you pullin' us over?"

"Your back taillight is out," the cop replied.

Q snapped, "That's a lie. This is a brand-new Bentley."

The cop stated, "I know what kind of car this is. I can read. But like I said, the taillight is malfunctioning. Now, license and registration."

Reluctantly Q's bodyguard handed over the car's registration and his New York driver's license. The cop accepted them and headed back to the car to run his name to see if he had any outstanding warrants. In the meantime his partner stood watch over the occupants of the car. He began to shine his flashlight into the interior of the car, hoping to spot a firearm or drugs in plain view, anything that would give them probable cause to search the vehicle.

"Yo, what you doing, man?" Q barked. "Ain't nothing but people in this car."

"Look, I'm just doing my job," the younger officer stated. "Just following orders."

The cop began to feel a tinge of guilt. He knew who Q was. As a matter of fact, he had some of his albums at his house. He put away his flashlight. After glancing back at his partner, who was still occupied, he leaned down a bit and said in a low voice, "Listen, this is some bullshit, man. You and I both know it. Just sit tight and everything will be over in a second. Here's a little bit of advice, though. If I were you I'd keep my nose clean and a real low profile. Somebody high up must want to bring you down real bad."

Fera, Q thought. *Fuckin' Fera.*

Q shook his head. "Yeah, I know about that, but I ain't doin' nothin' but makin' money off of music, man."

The cop shrugged. "DAs want to be mayors, mayors want to be governors, and governors want to be president. But you didn't hear that from me."

He straightened up when he noticed his partner approaching. "How's everything, Frank?" he asked.

"Everything checked out. They're free to go," the other cop said, handing the bodyguard back his driver's license and registration. "I'm not going to give ya'll a ticket this time. But take the car back to the dealer and have it checked out."

In an obvious show of disrespect, the bodyguard pulled off so hard, the tires screeched as they gripped the asphalt. If Q didn't know before, he knew now that the hip-hop police were watching him. As they put distance between themselves and the cops, Q thought how he had little to no room for error. He wasn't about to let his past fuck up his future.

7

Quinton Phelps was America's worst nightmare, young, black, and rich. But Q hadn't always been rich. He came from humble beginnings. His rags-to-riches story could be traced back to one of society's doormats, the Richard Allen projects in North Philly. Life and living conditions couldn't get much worse than this.

This ghetto bastard was born out of wedlock to a teenage mother, Angela Phelps, and Q would never know his father. He had abandoned both mother and child way before Q was born.

As a teenage mother, Angela quickly discovered that she was unable to adequately provide for her child on her own. She struggled even with help from family and friends. She was soon forced to apply for government assistance. She and her children virtually became "state babies." They depended upon the state welfare agencies to meet their most basic needs, such as food, clothing, and shelter. Ironically, the housing authority had placed her in an apartment in the very same housing project in which she had been raised. She was, in a sense, sentenced to a life term in the ghetto—born in the ghetto and doomed to die there.

Within the next couple of years, in rapid succession, Ms. Phelps gave birth to two more children, two girls, Roshaunna and Karen, by two more different men, bringing the total to three

children by three fathers. Just like the first time, each man abandoned Ms. Phelps, leaving her with another mouth to feed. Feeling hampered by her children, Ms. Phelps knew that no man in
his right mind would seriously want a woman with three kids
fathered by three different men. Knowing this, she accepted her
fate, choosing not to bring another child into this world. She had
her tubes tied and entered into a life of promiscuity. She began
running countless men in and out of her home and her children's
lives. This confused her children. They thought that some of
these men were their father. It was almost as if she bedded different men in an attempt to make herself whole. She needed a
man in her life, in her bed, to define herself.

Her poor decisions in men seemed to catapult Angela and
her children into a lifetime of poverty and despair.

But from day one there seemed to be something special
about her firstborn, Quinton. Although he was born three months
premature, Quinton seemed to do everything quickly, from eating to walking to talking. It was as if God seemed to push him
along in his development a little quicker than other children his
age, knowing one day he would need it. Even as an infant he
seemed to catch on fast to sing-along children's songs. He was
naturally drawn to melodies and music.

The boy was always more advanced than any other children
his age. It was originally predicted by the doctors that he
wouldn't live outside the incubator. But he was a survivor. Proving modern medicine wrong, young Quinton defied the odds.
Quinton Phelps was a fighter, and his will to live was too strong.

During Q's formative years, his mother busied herself with
no-good men, leaving her son free to roam the projects and
streets at his leisure. His role models became the local neighborhood criminals, thugs, hustlers, and killers. These were the
people he gauged himself by. These were the people whose
opinions mattered most to him. These were the people he

aspired to be like, because they seemed to always have a pocket full of money and all the material possessions. They were "hood rich" to him, something he wouldn't mind being.

For a time he accepted his station in life as a have-not. But as he grew older he grew angrier and more frustrated. He began to rebel against society, refusing to believe that his fate was sealed. To him, this couldn't be life; the world had to offer much more. He refused to believe that within this project maze he would meet his doom. No, he wanted more out of life than the projects had to offer. Around this time was when Q's love affair with the game began.

Young Q was a very intelligent kid. But his intelligence couldn't be measured by scholastic tests. What he had was known as common sense. At times Q's common sense exceeded most kids' book smarts, and a few grown folks', for that matter.

"Quinton Phelps," his fifth-grade teacher said, "what do you wish to become when you grow up? A doctor? A lawyer? An athlete? Or maybe an entertainer? What?"

This question kind of caught him off guard. Up until this point in his life Q had never given his future occupation, or his future for that matter, much thought. His problem was that his future was very much dependent on today. He was too busy trying to survive to even fantasize about it. He seriously contemplated the question for what seemed to be an eternity. It appeared that the whole entire class awaited his response. Q was very popular in school, a very likeable kid, so the other students eagerly awaited his answer.

"I wanna be—" Q stuttered, "I wannna be rich! That'z what I wanna be when I grow up."

Well, I'll be damned! Children say the strangest things, the teacher mused.

Not able to fully comprehend her student's answer, coming from a privileged position in society, she shook her in disbelief.

The class erupted into laughter. They thought that Q was trying to be funny. But on the contrary, he was dead serious. Even at a young age he knew that money was the key to end all his life's woes. It was the answer to all his problems, so he thought. Money would make him happy.

The older Q got, the less school seemed to interest him. Yet he still seemed drawn to music. In school it was one of his favorite subjects. Nothing captured his attention like music and the streets. During his childhood in the Richard Allen projects, Q spent most of his free time listening to the oldies, rap and rhythm and blues. The one thing he loved about it was how it brought back both good and bad memories. When he heard certain songs, they took him back to that place and time, to what he was doing then and what was going on in the world. His love of music could be traced back to one thing: his mother.

Angela loved to blast her music as loud as possible, at all times of the day and night, usually when she was depressed or had male company. The reason for the latter was she didn't want her children to hear her holler and moan while she was having sex.

Though Q liked a lot of rappers, especially from Philly, like Cool C and the Hilltop Hustlers, Jazzy Jeff, and Fresh Prince, he grew up listening to hard-core rap. He was still a kid when a group from Compton, California, called NWA, or Niggas With Attitudes, burst onto the scene. This group would usher in the age of gangsta rap. Still, he preferred East Coast rappers, because their reality was his.

"Kool G Rap, one inna million you roll the dice you get sliced the fuck up like a Sicilian!" Q chanted along with his favorite rapper at the time.

At that very moment his mother entered the house. She carried a bag of groceries in each arm. She stared evilly at her son as he listened to the CD in his boom box while doing his homework.

"Nigga, if ya muthafuckin' ass knew ya schoolwork like you knew that fuckin' rap you'd be a goddamn genius!" she snapped. "Now, cut that damn shit off and concentrate on those damn schoolbooks! That rap music ain't gonna do jack shit for you. You just wastin' ya time wit that nonsense. It'z just a fuckin' fad! It'll be gone before you know it. Watch and see!"

Q ignored his mother's negative comments. He didn't care what she said. Long ago he'd learned to block her out completely. Most of the things she said went in one ear and out the other. He was determined not to let her steal his joy. He loved rap music, and that was all that mattered. He lived and breathed hip-hop. It wasn't a fad to him, but a way of life.

To Q, it seemed like his mother never supported him or whatever he liked to do anyway, which explained why he never told her he could rap. He never told her he had literally over four notebooks full of rhymes. He knew she would never encourage him to chase his dreams, let alone become a rapper; it was easier to crush him, since misery loved company. So to avoid all the drama, he would just listen to his music with his headphones on.

In all actuality, becoming a rapper, a recording artist, was never really in his plans. It wasn't even a thought, it was more like a hobby, something he had a passion for. His everyday reality was feeding and clothing himself and his siblings.

From the world outside his window, Q's innocent eyes had witnessed things that no child should: rape, drug dealing, robbery, and murder. His innocence slowly turned to ignorance. Over time these things began to become commonplace, everyday elements of his environment. This very same environment seemed to have set him up to fail. But he refused to lose. Q put the thought in his mind that by hook or by crook, he was going to make it, one way or another. In an effort to escape his bleak surroundings, he decided to take the path most commonly chosen by the desolate and impoverished, the path that led to a life of crime.

As he got older and with no father figure in the house, Quinton stepped into the role of man of the house. The responsibility for taking care of his siblings fell on him. He accepted this great burden and carried out his duty honorably. He never once sought praise from anyone. He looked after his sisters out of love.

Karen was five years younger than him and she loved Q for being there for them while their mother was busy messing with her new man. Q was her hero. There wasn't much she wouldn't do for him, especially when she saw him out there hustling just to make sure that she and Roshaunna had what they needed. She would have been his partner in crime if he had let her. But Q insisted that Roshaunna and Karen stay in school and get their education.

"You let me worry about providing for the family," he told her.

Although they both were good students, Karen was exceptionally bright. She was an honor student. Great things had been predicted for her since elementary school. Karen lived a more sheltered life, thanks to Q. In her mind she just slept in the projects, she didn't live there. It was Karen to whom Q was especially close. He and Roshaunna always seemed to clash, since they were close in age. But Karen blindly followed her brother's instructions. She never questioned him. Karen always felt that whatever he said was for the good of the family. Q had promised her if she went to college and graduated he would have a job for her one day, when his record label was up and running. It was a promise he would keep.

At the ripe old age of sixteen, Q began to secretly sell drugs, along with his best friend, Rasool. Up until then Q had done a little bit of everything to put food on the table, and at that point he was desperate enough to see the endless possibilities that the drug game held and foolish enough to enter it.

Q and his friend Rasool jumped into the crack cocaine trade headfirst. Their operation began right in front of their building but soon spread throughout the projects. In a few years they went from slinging rocks themselves to employing dozens of workers and running numerous crack houses.

As the duo began to flourish in the drug trade, rival dealers began to spring up left and right. In the crack era, gunplay was prevalent. Q proved he was equally as skilled with a pistol as he was with his fists. Q and Rasool were gung ho, reckless with firearms. They began to put in work, protecting their turf from all comers.

On one of his adventures into the streets, his drug-dealing activities drew the attention of a local hood named Big Jihad. Big Jihad was a tall, dark-skinned, stockily built guy who had fallen on hard times. He was a walking contradiction—a killer with compassion. Big Jihad only killed when absolutely necessary. And he only gave it to those shady individuals who had it coming.

Big Jihad's saving grace was that when he was on top, he spread the wealth. He had sponsored basketball tournaments for the kids and threw cookouts in the projects in the summer. His good deeds far outweighed his bad. Truth be told, Big Jihad wasn't the bad guy everyone made him out to be.

But like many of his older contemporaries, Big Jihad had started getting high, beginning a downward spiral into the murky world of drug use. It was just that when he did drugs, he became someone other than himself. When Big Jihad was high and people knew it, they did their best to avoid him. As a result, he lost a lot of respect in the projects. When others looked at Big Jihad, they saw a crack fiend. Yet in Q's eyes he was still Big Jihad, a man still to be respected and feared, a fallen star. Q was a respectful person by nature; he always treated people fairly despite their shortcomings. One day Big Jihad approached Q. It was a day that would resonate in his mind forever.

"What's good, young boy?" Big Jihad said.

Q replied, "What's good with you?"

Inside his coat pocket Q gripped his gun. He placed his finger on the trigger, preparing to shoot first and ask questions later. The game had trained him to expect the unexpected. Q had seen best friends become bitter enemies in a blink of an eye.

It was safe to say Q was more than a little leery of Big Jihad. Word on the street was that he was robbing all the dope boys to feed his ever-growing crack habit. So Q didn't know what was going on. There was no telling what Big Jihad might try when he was on that shit. However, Q knew how he would respond if indeed that was the case: violently. There would be gunplay if Big Jihad ever laid a hand on him or robbed him. That was all it would take for Q to wipe every good deed Big Jihad had ever done in the hood out of his memory banks.

"Lemme holla at you for a minute," Big Jihad said.

Now Q was really on alert. Big Jihad had never said more than two words to him in the past. Where did he get off wanting to "holler" at him now?

With his eyes Big Jihad sized Q up as he contemplated robbing him. Q returned his stare with one more menacing. Something told Big Jihad to leave him alone. Q was not the one.

Big Jihad had seen this look that stayed pasted to his face before. It was desperation and anger that only the ghetto breeds. The hunger that burned inside his soul and shone through his eyes told the story. He was young, black, poverty-stricken, and dangerous. Q's eyes said he had little regard for life or death.

These were soldiers on the project battlefield, on opposing sides in the drug game. Though Big Jihad was twelve years Q's senior, they both were from the same background, and neither one of them was about to back down. Still, there was something

SHANNON HOLMES

about that look Q was giving him that even in his drug-induced state, Big Jihad could see that Q was a force to be reckoned with. So Big Jihad decided to go another route.

"Yo, Q, I'm a lil' fucked up right now. Can a nigga get some help?" Big Jihad said. "They 'bout ta cut a nigga phone off and shit."

Usually Q would have spun him a wicked tale or just said no, but this wasn't an ordinary drug addict before him. Big Jihad had killed many men, and he still possessed the capability to kill again. To him killing was like riding a bike; once you do it, one never forgets. This was a fact Q kept in mind.

"How much you need?" Q replied.

"A nigga need 'bout two hundred," he stated. "But if you ain't got it I'll take a few of them thangs and sling and make the money myself."

Yeah, right, Q thought to himself. *Who you foolin'? Everybody know you gettin' high.*

To the naked eye, looking at Big Jihad one couldn't tell that he was smoking crack. He still had his weight up and his wardrobe hadn't plummeted yet. One had to be in that loop in the street to know, one had to be a dealer or a fiend; either way it was a small world and both parties talked.

Q knew the code of the streets. "Don't kick a man when he's down. Don't deny an addict any drugs when the monkey is on his back." Especially not a man of Big Jihad's stature. With that in mind, Q gave Big Jihad a "pack" of crack that equaled up to roughly three hundred dollars. He looked at it as doing him a favor or as an investment. If Big Jihad ever got off drugs and even if he didn't, surely he would remember this. One day Q would love to have such a ruthless killer like Big Jihad on his team, just in case things got too out of hand for him to handle himself.

"Good lookin' out, young boy. You saved the day. If you ever need anything, just holler. I gotcha."

98

With that, Big Jihad went about his business, to the nearest crack house to get high.

Over the years the two would form a strange bond. Unbeknownst to Big Jihad, it was Q who would come to his rescue, paying off rival drug dealers who Big Jihad had robbed, at one time or another, while on his crack binges. He went so far as to warn Big Jihad of any assassination plots. At times Q even gave Big Jihad money to get away from the hood when things got too hectic.

But Big Jihad's reign of terror was nearing an end. The hood was terrified of him. They either wanted him off this earth or off the streets, whichever came first. Finally the police apprehended Big Jihad before any physical harm could come his way. He was arrested on trumped-up charges of assault and armed robbery. Drug dealers had given a local crackhead some product to testify against Big Jihad. With a prior record that consisted of nothing but robbery charges, he was easily tried and convicted. Big Jihad was sentenced to five to ten in a maximum state prison.

Prison was a blessing in disguise. It literally saved Big Jihad's life. Finally he was able to see the error of his ways and once again devoted his life to the Muslim faith that he had strayed so far from. Once again Q was there for him, sending him clothing packages and money orders regularly. Big Jihad was able to do his time in relative comfort. Acts like these helped forge a bond that would stand the test of time. Big Jihad became ferociously loyal to Q. He vowed one day to repay him, even if that meant taking a bullet and dying for him. So be it.

Soon Q's exploits in the streets attracted many female admirers. Essentially, Q could have almost any girl he wanted, and he loved it. Q discovered that he loved almost everything about the female form—how it looked, how it smelled, how it felt, how it tasted, all the different shapes and sizes. He couldn't get enough.

But then he met one who seemed to stand out from the rest. Her name was Niecey. Maybe Q noticed her over the others because she was wild and aggressive. Niecey did any and everything to get Q's attention. She lived in the Richard Allen projects, too. Their paths had crossed many times during their school years.

Their courtship was brief. Q had impregnated Niecey the very first time they slept together. Since she was carrying his child, Q introduced her to his mother and his sisters. None of them really took to Niecey, though. They thought she was too aggressive. Roshaunna seemed the most upset, telling him that he could do better. But Roshaunna never thought anyone was good enough for her older brother. On the other hand, Karen was less vocal; she supported Q regardless. All she wanted was to be the child's aunt and godmother. Q noted their opinions, but they would have to deal with Niecey, since she was the mother of his only child, and his lover.

But while she was pregnant, Niecey began showing signs of being a problem. She constantly called him, cursed him out, and argued with him over the smallest things. Once she even flushed half a kilo of cocaine down the toilet, for Q's alleged dealings with another woman. Q had been furious; the only reason he didn't beat her down for her actions was because he had sisters and she was pregnant, due any day now. Needless to say, that was the last time he ever left drugs in Niecey's possession. It wasn't that he didn't trust her. He was scared of what he might have to do to her if she ever did that again. He couldn't afford to take another loss like that.

However, Q experienced the thrill of a lifetime when Niecey gave birth to a healthy boy, whom Q proudly named Quinton Phelps Jr. He had always wanted to name a son after himself.

Almost every rich person did. He promised himself that he, too, would be rich and that his name would mean something. The name Quinton Phelps would hold some weight in the world. One day he would be more than just a common drug dealer, he thought. Now the only question was, would he live to see that day?

The child had made everything he and his mother had gone through worthwhile. Lil Q was his pride and joy. But the peace and tranquility that currently surrounded Q wouldn't last long. Trouble was brewing on the horizon and Q was about to find himself in the middle of it.

A notorious gang called JBM, Junior Black Mafia, had just formed. JBM had systematically taken over some of the city's most profitable open-air drug markets and crack houses. They swept through Philadelphia strong-arming and/or murdering drug dealers. This murderous organization was the likes of which the city had never seen. Their motto was, "Get down or lay down." JBM didn't take no for an answer. One either did what they said, or died.

Before long, JBM had set their sights on Q's drug operation. Word was sent that he had to buy his cocaine from them, at an inflated price, or get out of the game. JBM had laid a trail of bodies that stretched across the city, so Q knew this was no joke. He also knew that they wouldn't wait long for an answer, either. No response would be taken as a no. And gunplay was sure to erupt.

The first thing Q did was inform his partner, Rasool, of the extortion attempt. Like him, Rasool bucked at the notion of falling under JBM control. Together they rallied their most loyal followers to let them know the deal. Those who weren't with it were excused, while the remaining soldiers prepared for war.

Q and his team were armed to the teeth. It was business as usual, except they were now strapped on the job. They lay in wait for JBM to make the next move. In an unusual move, JBM sent another messenger to the Richard Allen projects, and Q and his team sent him back in a body bag. The war was now on.

Neither Q nor Rasool knew what they were in for. Every day there was gunplay in and around one of their drug markets. The body count began to rise, with Q's side suffering the most fatalities. Every day Q and Rasool stepped out of their homes, they were well aware that it could be their last.

There was a bull's-eye placed on their backs, a price on their heads as a reward for going against the grain, for standing up to the mighty JBM. Waves and waves of shooters were sent at Q and Rasool, and ultimately they were forced to shut down every one of their moneymaking spots. The war was now hurting their pockets. It was time to regroup.

Q and Rasool decided to leave Philly. They were overmatched. The duo had bitten off more than they could chew. The JBM clique had a legion of loyal followers who did their bidding. Q left the city, taking his clothes, Niecey, his son, and a trunk full of cocaine. Rasool followed him in his car with his clothes and his girl. It turned out to be a blessing in disguise.

They ended up in the state's capital, Harrisburg. Q and Rasool were among the first out-of-towners to hustle there. When they got there the town had been experiencing a drug shortage, which Q and Rasool were more than happy to fill. In Harrisburg they became the major players they could never have been in Philly. They blew up.

Meanwhile, as Q and Rasool were enjoying the fruits of their labor, in Philadelphia, JBM's reign of terror was coming to an abrupt end. A state and federal task force had been formed and secret indictments had been issued. Now raids were being executed on known members' homes.

News of JBM's demise spread far and wide. Q and Rasool heard about it way upstate. They weren't happy about JBM's incarceration, though they could have been. No true hustler wishes that on another. They only wished that they could have toppled the organization themselves.

Rasool took JBM's incarceration as a free pass back to the city of Philadelphia. Although he had enjoyed his run, he missed home like crazy. The only time he ever went back since the beef started was to re-up. He met up with his cocaine connection and then he was gone. At that time it was too dangerous to think about staying.

Upon hearing Rasool's plan to return home, Q tried to talk him out of going back to Philly. His gut instinct told him that the time wasn't right. Unfortunately, his partner didn't want to hear that, and he left anyway, against Q's wishes. Rasool and Q parted ways on bad terms. Q realized that Rasool was his own man, that there was nothing he could do or say to make him stay.

Rasool went home, lulled back by a false sense of security. This notion would cost him his life. Rasool was killed. One of the last few remaining JBM affiliates shot him while coming out of his building, going to see his mother.

Retaliation was quick in coming. Q came out of hiding and rode for his homey, killing the man who had killed his friend, as well as seriously wounding many members of his team.

It would be years before Q returned to Philly for good. He was content with making money in the Harrisburg region. In the back of his mind he knew he couldn't make the same mistakes Rasool had. As long as his family was all right, he was cool. He would just bide his time until things died down and the streets stopped talking.

Around this time he was bitten by the music bug again. It was getting hot in Harrisburg. Out-of-town drug dealers were getting indicted left and right. Now it was time to go. Besides, Q wanted a change. He knew a successful drug run wouldn't last forever. So he sought to do what many other hustlers had tried before him, make that transition from illegal to legal. Q wanted to get out of the game. And music would be the vehicle to transport him to a different world.

Shortly after forming his own music label, Prestige Records, Q stumbled upon a down-on-his-luck would-be rapper named Mikey Raw. They met through a friend of a friend. As it turned out, Mikey Raw would be his meal ticket. In the studio he was a musical genius who had a knack for making hard-core hit records.

Acting as executive producer and A&R for his company, Q personally oversaw every project. He picked beats and criticized some of the content of his artists' raps. Q even supplied some of his artists with stories about the street life, which made their songs more realistic. For his workmanlike effort, Q's first few artists reached platinum status. He was like the goose who had laid the golden egg. He could do no wrong. What was more startling about his achievements was that he did it without the support of a major label. Soon industry bigwigs began to take notice.

A bidding war ensued between several labels. Q wound up inking a forty-million-dollar deal with Universal, where he owned all his own masters. Now Q was set.

Suddenly Q was "that boy." He was labeled an overnight sensation. But what the general public and the media didn't understand was that he was no overnight sensation. His success was a lifetime in the making. He had paid a steep price for it.

Only a select few of his childhood friends had escaped the old neighborhood. Most had succumbed to the harsh realities and traps of the streets of Philly, ending up either in jail or dead.

Though Q's immediate family, his sisters and mother, had weathered the storm with him, unfortunately his best friend Rasool hadn't. That was something Q would regret for the rest of his life.

Q was grateful for his success, although the street life had left him more than a little resentful. Sometimes he even questioned his own existence. His success would have been even that much sweeter had he had someone to share it with. It would have been much more enjoyable had Rasool been alive. He was beginning to feel empty inside. Outside love and support could only do so much for a man of his stature. He wanted more.

8

The Present, Two Weeks Later

P restige Records was located in the heart of New York City, on the fiftieth floor of the Empire State Building. Q felt that since New York was not only the capital of the financial world, but also the entertainment industry, the music industry in particular, he had to base his operations there. And that he did.

Prestige's headquarters were spacious, luxuriously furnished, with all the latest technology, from flat-screen televisions to Apple computers. Most employees who worked there thought of the office as a home away from home. Q had successfully created a good working atmosphere there. When one worked for Prestige Records, it was like working with family.

Down in the lobby, when the elevator doors opened, Tonya and Na'eema were swept up into it along with a crowd of tourists and businesspeople. From opposite sides of the crowded elevator, Tonya and Na'eema stole glances at each other.

Then Na'eema broke out into a wide grin that seemed to say, "Girl, I can't believe we're here. We made it!"

Tonya couldn't help but smile back, signaling her own satisfaction.

But truthfully, in the close quarters of the elevator, Tonya was battling a bad case of the butterflies. At one point she thought she had to pass gas, but she surpressed the urge. She would have had to turn around and go right back to Philly if shedid some mess like that. She was nervous and excited at the same time. She tried her best to disguise her feelings by staring up at the ceiling.

Tonya hadn't felt quite like this since the first time she took to the stage to strip. That experience had changed her life forever. And she was quite sure that this one would, too, but in a good way. Change had been a part of life for Tonya, a constant one. She tended to look at life like this: if she didn't change, then she would die. She kept an open mind about everything.

Now here she was in New York City, with her close friend Na'eema, heading to their first day of work. She still couldn't believe her good fortune. She had a real job. She had to laugh at the thought of her working a nine-to-five. Never in a million years did she envision this. In her mind, she wasn't the type. Still, there she was in an elevator, ascending to the fiftieth floor, dressed for success in a dark blue business suit. If someone would have told her a few months ago that she'd be living and working in New York City, she wouldn't have believed them. But here she was. What she was most proud of was she was able to bring Na'eema along with her. Her accomplishment was that much greater now that she had someone to share it with.

She was still stunned when she thought about how Q had offered her a job, right there at Club Blue Martini, in the middle of her own damn party. She had almost had to ask him to repeat himself. Tonya couldn't believe her ears.

As she had parted ways with Q that night, Tonya had felt as if she was walking on air. She couldn't believe what had transpired. She had a legitimate job offer on the table. Fate was a funny thing. She guessed God had finally decided that she had suffered long enough. And now he had a happy ending in mind for her. If her conversation with her partner, Na'eema, went well, then she was about to turn her back on it all—every negative thing she had ever done thus far in her young life.

She was about to write a new chapter in the book of her life.

Na'eema had been as excited about the offer as she was. From the moment Tonya told her about Q's offer, Na'eema had said it was a good move, even before Tonya told her that she was included as well. But there had been no way Tonya was accepting a position without securing one for her friend, too. She felt Na'eema had a lot to do with her being in this position in the first place. And Q admired the fact that Tonya was bringing her partner and close friend with her. If there was one thing he envied, it was friendship. He hadn't had a real close friend since Rasool.

For hours she and Na'eema had debated the pros and the cons, sometimes speaking about the good times they had had promoting parties. But they both liked the idea of a fresh start and a new challenge.

Na'eema looked at the music industry as one big party after another, and that was the deciding factor for her. She wanted to rub shoulders with the stars on a much bigger level. She never thought about the work her new job would include.

That chance meeting in the club had led to a more formal meeting the next day. It was there that they settled on financial terms and a salary and made verbal agreements and exchanged handshakes and hugs to seal the deal. When she got to New York everything would be finalized. Tonya was confident that Q would keep his word; like most street dudes, he lived or died by it. If all else failed, Tonya had a contract that she and Q had signed to fall back on. At least she'd be compensated even if things didn't work out.

Believing in Q, Tonya and Na'eema jumped on the first plane to New York. But if this didn't work out Tonya didn't know what she was going to do. So this had to work because there was no plan B in place.

Tonya knew that from the moment she got hired as a marketing consultant with her own office and budget, someone in that office wasn't going to like her. As a matter of fact, mentally she prepared herself to face a hostile work environment. Her improbable path into the music industry was bound to rub someone more qualified the wrong way. For instance, Q had informed her that his sister Karen was his marketing director. Apparently he had put her through college and then she had come to work for him.

Q's other sister, Roshaunna, was another story. He couldn't motivate her to do something for herself to save his life. Roshaunna was a lazy, good-for-nothing type, content with living off her brother's riches.

"And how's she gonna feel about you bringin' me and Na'eema on board?" Tonya asked, feeling skeptical.

"Karen cares about the Prestige family," Q told her. "It's number one to me and it's number one for her, too, so she'll be cool."

Yeah, well, we'll see about that, Tonya had thought at the time. Frankly, if it were her and her brother brought two unknowns into her territory, she would be heated. She had a feeling Q's sister was going to feel the same.

But Tonya decided she didn't care. It wasn't her fault she had leapfrogged whomever. In life, they say, timing is everything. This was a prime example of that, and it ain't what you know but who you know.

The position Tonya was placed in, she felt, was no tougher than the struggle she had engaged in with life, or the fatality of the street life that she had overcome. Tonya sensed the urgency of the opportunity presented to her by Q.

With record sales at an all-time low, Q was looking for new and creative ways to jump-start his company's sales. Tonya and

Na'eema were brought on board to provide just that. They had techniques and ideas that couldn't be learned in any school.

The elevator made several stops on designated floors. Waves of people moved in and out. As the elevator became less cramped, Na'eema moved closer to Tonya. A firm nudge in her ribs broke Tonya's trance.

"Girl, I hope this gig works out," Na'eema said. "I could get usta the city. We in the Big Apple!"

Tonya replied, "Who you tellin'? So far so good! Even the hotel was the bomb."

"Girl, I started to clean they ass out last night. Then I remembered we wasn't checkin' out yet," Na'eema whispered. "They had this fly-ass fluffy white robe with the hotel emblem on the breast pocket. I wanted that robe so bad."

"You a mess!" Tonya chuckled. "Take you out the hood but can't take the hood outta you, huh?"

Before either of them knew it, the elevator had arrived at their floor. Tonya took a deep breath and together they stepped onto the fiftieth floor.

Here we go! she thought to herself. *God, please don't fail me now.*

Momentarily, they stopped and scanned the directory, looking for the proper direction to Prestige Records. Once they were assured which direction to go in, they made a right and confidently Tonya and Na'eema strolled up to the door.

Through the thick smoked-glass doors, Tonya and Na'eema could see people moving about. The office appeared to be abuzz with activity, employees going to and fro.

"Oh, great one, you first," Na'eema announced while holding the door open.

"Bitch, I'ma hurt you," Tonya joked, stepping inside the office.

Immediately they were greeted by a receptionist, who asked them to please be seated while she let Q know they were here after they gave their names. Tonya and Na'eema exchanged a look between them and went to sit down in the nearby waiting area.

"Tonya and Na'eema?" they heard someone say and looked up to see a young white woman standing in front of them. "Hi, my name is Annie. I'm Q's administrative assistant. We're so glad you're here."

Tonya and Na'eema were caught off guard by the young woman's perkiness. They wanted to laugh at her unusually sunny disposition, but they thought better of it. Tonya and Na'eema didn't want to start off on the wrong foot and offend anybody.

The slim young white girl had a Plain Jane appearance about her. There wasn't anything noteworthy about her. She was average height, brunette, with brown eyes. She looked like the girl next door in some small town in middle America. Tonya wondered what the hell she was doing here at Prestige Records.

"Hi, Annie," Tonya said, smiling and shaking her hand. "We're glad to be here, too. The pleasure is all ours."

"Unfortunately, Q isn't in yet," Annie told them. "He called and said he was stuck in traffic on the New Jersey Turnpike and that I should give you both a tour of the place and show you your offices. He should be here by then."

A smile spread across both of Tonya and Na'eema's faces, signaling their approval. The last bit of information that Annie provided was a pleasant surprise. They had no idea that they were going to get their own offices. They were so happy to be working for one of the hottest labels in the rap game that it never crossed their minds before. That was icing on the cake.

"Ladies, please follow me," Annie said.

The tour of Prestige Records' offices turned into a meet-and-greet, show-and-tell type of affair. Tonya didn't know how many square feet the office was, but in her mind it sure was big. There was a huge conference room, countless offices, phones, computers, fax machines, and an army of file cabinets that seemed to stretch as far as the eye could see.

As they made their rounds, Tonya and Na'eema were introduced to various employees who held high-ranking jobs within the company. They both had the tedious job of attaching names to all those new faces. Notably missing from the record label's staff were minority employees. One would have thought that since Q was from the hood and a minority that he would have employed more minorities. But such wasn't the case.

Although Q loved his black people, he also knew that sometimes his people could cause unnecessary problems in the workplace. Q wasn't for any additional headaches, problems, or confusion, he was for profits. Q only hired the best and the brightest in the business, regardless of what color they were. It was business to him.

"Excuse me, ladies, I'd like you to meet Tonya Morris and Na'eema Henderson, the new marketing consultants," Annie said. "Tonya, Na'eema, this is Karen Phelps, the marketing director, and Shakira Anderson, the VP of marketing."

Instinctively, Shakira rose from her seat and extended her hand to Tonya and Na'eema, offering them a handshake. It was then that Tonya really got a good look at her. Shakira was average looking in appearance, light-skinned, with dark brown eyes and no curves to speak of. She wore a pair of librarian-style glasses that made her appear superintelligent. There was no doubt in Tonya's mind that she was college educated, and she seemed to be genuinely friendly.

"Nice to meet you both," Shakira said. "Welcome to Prestige Records. You need any help, just let me know. I'm right down the hall."

Tonya knew bullshit when she heard it, but this wasn't one of those times. She could sense her warmth and sincerity and liked her right away. It was in everything from her words to her firm handshake. Right away, she saw Shakira as someone she needed to establish a healthy working relationship with.

Karen, on the other hand, was a different story. Unlike Shakira, Karen was beautiful. She was coffee-complexioned with long hair and a curvaceous figure. She carried herself as if she knew she had it going on. She wasn't as friendly as Shakira, either. Her disdain for Tonya and Na'eema couldn't have been more evident. She never even rose from her seat to greet them.

So this is Q's sister, Tonya thought, not impressed.

Karen gave the new employees a long once-over, as if she could determine their legitimacy just by looking at them.

I wonder where Q found these two bitches? she thought. *I don't see what's so special about them.*

Karen had been furious when Q told her that he wanted to bring in these two. It was like a smack in the face. She felt like he was saying that she wasn't doing a good enough job. Record sales were down for everyone. Bringing in these two nobodies from the streets wasn't going to change anything.

Karen wondered if Q was fucking one of them. Probably not the big one, but the skinny one was definitely his type. And though Q never mixed his sex life with business, she wouldn't put it past him to think with his dick. As much as she loved Lil Q, how else could she explain Niecey?

"Very nice to meet you," Karen said. "It's great that you could join our little family. And that's what we are here, a family. My brother and I work very hard to make it that way for all Prestige employees."

Tonya knew exactly what Karen was doing. She was marking her territory. She was making it clear to Tonya that as Q's sister she was the queen bee around here.

Whatever, bitch, Tonya couldn't help thinking, disliking her more and more by the minute.

"Now, if you don't mind," Karen said, "we have some very important work to do, but don't hesitate to let me know if there's anything you need." Then she turned her back on them and went back to whatever she and Shakira had been working on before they arrived.

After getting the brushoff, the girls continued down the hall on their tour.

"Damn, what's all that about?" Na'eema murmured to Tonya once they were down the hallway. She spoke low enough so that Annie, who was walking ahead of them, couldn't hear her. "Somebody's not feelin' us. Houston, we have a problem."

"We aren't here to win no popularity contest," Tonya said aloud. "We here to do a job. To hell to whomever don't like that. I'm not lettin' anyone stop me from eatin'." She didn't care who heard her.

As they continued their tour, it soon became clear that it wasn't only Karen who was giving them the cold shoulder. The girls were getting their first glimpse of office politics at work.

To the employees who had been with the company for some time, Tonya and Na'eema were a novelty act. Q had bragged all about them long before they ever set foot in the office. He had even gotten some press coverage to announce the hiring, and it had been written up in several entertainment magazines. Q had even taken out an ad in *Don Diva* magazine with an accompanying photo of him, Tonya, and Na'eema. He told everyone about Tonya's background, minus her career as a stripper, and that they were both helluva party promoters back in Philly.

Now it seemed like there was a "too-good-to-be-true" aura surrounding them, and a lot of them were skeptical of their new co-workers. After all, they had gone to college and interned at various record labels before earning their current positions at Prestige Records. Tonya and Na'eema had just been given a position. In their minds, they didn't belong on the same level as them and their presence was not welcome.

"And last but not least," Annie said, "here are your offices."

Their offices were right next door to each other. The girls marveled over them. Each office had a black cherrywood desk with a dark brown, old-fashioned executive chair, a laptop computer, a printer, a wireless phone, and a fax machine. It was pretty much the same layout as every other office had, give or take more square feet and an electronic gadget or two.

Tonya walked through the door and admired the new digs. She sat down in the new chair and slowly spun herself around until she was facing the wall. She envisioned one day placing pictures and plaques on these bare walls.

"I'll leave you ladies to yourselves," Annie said in a friendly manner. "But please let me know if you need anything. My extension is in the directory."

"Thanks, Annie," Tonya said.

As soon as Annie left, Na'eema came into her office and closed the door.

"Yo, I'm so feelin' this!" Tonya declared.

"Must be nice, huh?" Na'eema suggested while grinning from ear to ear. "You came a long way from North Philly and the Badlands. Say so long to the hood and hello to corporate America. This a whole different ball game now, baby. We in the big leagues."

Na'eema sat in the chair opposite Tonya's desk, beaming at her friend. She let her soak up her few precious seconds of fame. She knew it had been a long, eventful trip through life for Tonya to even get to this point.

Tonya couldn't believe her own good fortune. The next few hours felt so magical to her. She just sat in her office enjoying the moment. Meanwhile, Na'eema busied herself on the company phone calling family members and friends. She wanted everyone in the world to know she was now in New York.

About an hour later, Tonya's phone rang. It was Annie telling her that Q was now in and wanted her and Na'eema to come up to his office.

"Sure, we'll be right there," Tonya said. She grabbed Na'eema and they headed two floors up to Q's office.

"This way, ladies," Annie said when they arrived, and with Tonya and Na'eema following closely behind, she led them down a long corridor to Q's private office. Before they entered, Annie politely knocked on the door.

"Come in," a male voice commanded.

Annie held the door open for Tonya and Na'eema, but she didn't enter. She opted to stand in the doorway like some sort of hall monitor.

"Ms. Morris and Ms. Henderson are here, Mr. Phelps," she said politely. "Will that be all, sir? Do you need anything else?"

It was obvious even to the most casual observer just what Annie was doing. Tonya and Na'eema hadn't seen ass-kissing like this in quite some time. They found the whole exchange quite amusing, only they didn't laugh outwardly about it.

On the other hand, Q saw it as a sign of respect. It also tickled him to death every time she called him Mr. Phelps. Previously, the only time he had been referred to by that name was way back in public school, when a teacher was reprimanding him.

He responded, "No, thank you, Annie. I'm okay."

"All right, then I'll be on my way," she explained. "But if you should think of anything, just let me know."

"Will do," he said, before turning to his guests. "Ya'll can have a seat."

After grabbing a seat, Tonya and Na'eema began to look around the office, which was lavishly furnished in Art Deco design. On his walls were about a half-dozen platinum plaques from various rap and R&B artists on his label. They were accompanied by photos of some of the music elite, industry big-wigs from recording artists to executives and music moguls. There were pictures of Q at the Grammys and the American Music Awards with Jay-Z and Dame Dash, P. Diddy, Fat Joe and Remy Martin, Russell Simmons, Kevin Liles, Lyor Cohen, and L.A. Reid, just to name a few. The girls looked at the pictures in awe, particularly Na'eema, since she didn't know Q at all. To her he was just larger than life, even though she was now in his presence.

"So what do y'all think of the place? Did ya boy do it up or what?" Q asked.

Tonya admitted, "This is nice, Q. You did the damn thing. And I really like my office."

"Good, good," he said, nodding. "That's what I like to hear."

Na'eema stayed silent, not wanting to add anything to the conversation. She was still a little starstruck.

"What about you?" he asked her. "Everything good with you?"

"Oh, oh, oh, yeah," Na'eema insisted. "Everything is everything. I can't complain."

"That's what's up!" he added. "For a minute I was a lil' worried about you. You was sittin' over there lookin' all crazy and shit."

"Who, me?" Na'eema exclaimed.

"Yeah, you," he replied. "It's a small thing, don't worry about it. I know y'all wondering why I called you in here, right?"

"I don't know about her, but I sure am," Tonya said.

"Well, the reason I called y'all into my office was to give you a crash course on the music industry. I don't know what y'all know or don't know. But I believe that y'all can do the job as long as you know what your job description is."

Tonya was relieved that Q wouldn't throw them to the wolves without some knowledge of the business. She was grateful that he was personally taking the time out to show them the ins and outs. He was in essence giving them a fighting chance. And that was all Tonya could ask for, a chance.

From what she saw earlier, Tonya knew she wouldn't be able to go to too many people around there for help. She believed that their hiring had caused some rumbling within the company. She was sure that she had a bull's-eye on her back. Initially Tonya thought her hard work would speak for itself. Now she knew that notion was wrong.

"Annie, would you bring those folders I had you make up yesterday?" Q said into the intercom.

Within a few minutes the assistant had arrived with a fully prepared presentation for Tonya, Na'eema, and Q. She passed them out and was gone. Q began, "Record companies come in different sizes. The smallest being your upstart independent labels, run by maybe a handful of people. Then you have your huge corporations, i.e., Island/Def Jam, Sony Urban Music, Interscope, and Universal Records just to name a few. The smaller companies are run by two or more people, while the bigger ones are made up of larger staffs, which have dozens of employees with various different departments. I'd like to think of my label as mid-major, not too big and not too small, very manageable. We got around a half-dozen or so employees on the payroll. Anyway, you got someone called a CEO, which means chief executive officer, who is me, the label head. Then you got ya president, John Wiggins, and vice president, Sandra Jordan, both of whom I believe you've already met. Then there's the A&R, accountants, graphic arts department, publicity, marketing, and promotions, which you two will be working at. And the sales department, just to name a few."

Q went on to explain just what each department did and what they were responsible for. He went to great lengths to explain everything, breaking down the job titles and descriptions, until it was clear who did what.

Both Tonya and Na'eema listened intently, like good students, taking mental notes, absorbing every word Q said to them. Q knew that this information wasn't hard to grasp, since he himself had learned it all on the fly. He was confident that both of them would get it, too. They had to; his reputation was on the line. If these two failed then he would be the laughing-stock of not only his own company but the music industry as well. There were no secrets in this industry. Like everywhere else, bad news tended to travel fast. There were people within his organization and outside of it who would love to see Q fall flat on his face. They were lying in wait for his downfall.

Within the music industry Q was starting to get a reputation. Because of his "keeping it real" style, straightforwardness, and inability to conform to the good-ole-boy system, Q was viewed as a rebel. But because he had a hot product, they had no choice but to deal with him. He currently had a stranglehold on the music charts, with various rappers and R&B artists topping the *Billboard* charts.

"Oh, by the way, ladies, I don't know if anybody has told you, but you'll be moving out of the hotel as of today. We've set you up in corporate housing over in Jersey."

Tonya and Na'eema's new living quarters were in Edgewater, New Jersey, known throughout the music industry as Rappers Row, because it seemed that as soon as a rapper from New York City halfway made it, they would abandon their neighborhoods for a less threatening environment in the New Jersey suburbs.

For rappers, more often than not, in their own neighborhood the same people they grew up with, on the same streets that bred them, the same place that gave birth to their struggle, would target these very same rappers for extortions, robberies, kidnappings, and sometimes even murder. The reason was that they now possessed a few dollars more than the average person

in their neighborhood. It seemed that as soon as a rapper became somewhat successful, jealousy reared its evil head.

Although Q had never lived there himself, over the years he
had placed several of his recording artists there for safekeeping.
He felt that Edgewater would be the perfect place for Tonya and
Na'eema because of its close proximity to New York City as well
as for security reasons. To him, New York City was no place for
two single women.

"Okay, ladies, this meeting is officially adjourned," Q announced.
"I will see y'all later. I got places to go and people to see."

As they made their way toward the door, Q couldn't help
watch as Tonya and her shapely behind left the room. He could
hardly keep his eyes off her the entire meeting. She had told
him that she had a boyfriend, and he wondered if she was happy
with her man. Did he even have a chance? Q didn't make a habit
of rekindling old flames. His ex-girlfriends were his ex-
girlfriends for a reason. But he couldn't recall any specific reason for leaving Tonya alone, other than her former occupation as
a stripper. Right now he was so aroused by the sight of her that
he wouldn't mind sampling her again. But this was not the time
or the place for that. For now he would keep it professional.
Everything else could wait. He'd know the right time to make
his move.

The meeting had lasted about two hours, after which Tonya
and Na'eema returned to their respective offices with a clear
picture of the business side of the inner workings of a record
label and what was expected of them. The talk with Q helped
Tonya get her mind right. Na'eema, on the other hand, was
another story. She was quite smitten by Q. She couldn't stop

talking about him. It had been the same when she first met him in Philly.

"Tonya, Q is so goddamn fine!" Na'eema remarked, following Tonya into her office. "Girl, why you didn't tell me he looked so good in person? I would fuck him in a heartbeat! You think he like big girls? If he do, it's on and poppin'!"

Never in a million years did Tonya think Na'eema would be on Q like this. She hadn't seen her act like this over any guy, for that matter.

"Yo, Na'eema, would you stop talkin' about Q?" she replied. "And you have a man, so you need to be easy."

Na'eema exhaled. "Wow," she said, staring at her. "That don't look good on you. Ain't a good look at all."

"What? What you talkin' bout?" Tonya asked, looking surprised.

"All that hate!" Na'eema joked. "That hate don't look good on you at all. Right now you just hatin' on me. You just mad 'cause Q might want me. Big girlz need love, too. We got more to love."

Inwardly, Tonya laughed to herself. She loved her friend's confidence, but truth be told, Na'eema didn't stand a chance of getting with Q. She wasn't his type. Q liked his women slim in the waist and cute in the face. Tonya knew that for a fact. Still, she was careful not to offend Na'eema. If she thought she had a chance to get with him, then Tonya wouldn't say otherwise. But she did feel it was her duty to inform her friend that she had already slept with him.

"I hear that," Tonya admitted. "But look, I gotta tell you somethin'. You can take it for what it's worth after I say what I say."

Na'eema cracked, "What you gotta tell me?"

"Look, I know I shoulda told you this before, but me and Q . . ."

"Don't tell me that," Na'eema shot back. "You fucked him?"

"Exactly," Tonya said. "We had somethin' goin' on a few years ago. Well, I thought it was somethin', yet it turned out to be nothin'. I was really feelin' him, but you know shit happens. Anyway, that's how I know him. I hope I didn't make it seem like we just met. I apologize for not tellin' you the whole story, but I didn't see the need to until now."

One thing Tonya knew about Na'eema was that she wasn't the type of chick who would fuck behind her. She wasn't the type of person to deal with her friend's ex. Na'eema had some class about her and she didn't rock like that.

"There that go!" Na'eema exclaimed. "I'm glad you told me, though. 'Cause if I would have gave him a shot of this thang here—man or no man." She laughed. "Ain't no tellin' what might of happened after that."

Tonya was glad that they were able to make light of the whole situation. She had only touched on the subject, never really revealing the true depth of her feelings for Q. She preferred it that way. Her feelings were her feelings, they were not open to discussion. And she knew that Na'eema was the type of person who, if one asked for her opinion, then she would give it. If one didn't, then she wouldn't.

Na'eema would never make mention of Q in that manner again. From then on he was off-limits, romantically anyway. She let Tonya off the hook without interrogating her further.

About an hour later, there was a knock at Tonya's door and Shakira poked her head through.

"How's your first day going?"

Tonya smiled when she saw her. "Good so far."

"Well, it's lunchtime and I was wondering if you two were hungry. I could take you out for a bite to eat. My treat!"

"You musta been readin' my mind," Tonya told her. "I was sittin' here hungry as I don't know what."

"Well, what are you waiting on?" Shakira replied. "Let's get up out of here before someone finds something for me to do."

Na'eema interjected, "You payin', we eatin'! Sounds like a plan to me! We right behind you."

The trio hopped into a cab, headed for a small, swanky soul food restaurant called Mekka, located on the Lower East Side. As they dined on the delicious plates of soul food, they got a chance to know each other a little better. During course of casual conversation, Karen's name was brought up.

"Shakira, thanks for bringing us to this spot for lunch," Tonya said. "This food is the bomb. I ain't have greens this good in a long time. From now on this gonna be my spot."

"You know, Karen used to love this place," Shakira commented. "She's the one who first brought me here. We used to have a lot of meetings here."

"What's up with her, anyway?" Na'eema asked. "She acted like she smelled something bad when Annie introduced us this morning."

Shakira looked down while shifting uncomfortably in her seat, clearly not comfortable about talking about her boss. "Karen's great. She's just protective of the company. I'm sure she'll warm up to you guys, especially since Q is so excited about you."

Yeah, right, Tonya thought. The way she saw it, there were new problems on the horizon.

"So tell me who's who in the company," Tonya said, changing the topic. Shakira seemed all too grateful to stop talking about Karen.

For the next half-hour, Shakira schooled them on the lowdown at Prestige Records. Tonya soaked it all up like a sponge. She needed to know who the players were, and she'd need to figure out how to get what she needed from them in order to secure her position at Prestige. Before they knew it, it was time to go back to work. Tonya, Na'eema, and Shakira had enjoyed their meal and one another's conversation and promised to do it again sometime soon.

Tonya vowed to keep the lines of communication open with Shakira for another reason. Should she ever need some information on anyone, she knew exactly who she was going to.

Later that night on the Upper West Side of Manhattan, in her condo, Karen anxiously awaited the arrival of her lover. She was dressed in a sheer black Victoria's Secret teddy, her sexy, petite body on full display. Although it had only been a week since their last sexual encounter, it felt like a month. Karen craved her young lover badly. He was the first man to ever make her orgasm so hard that she almost passed out. He also was forbidden fruit. Not only was he five years younger than her, but a rapper signed to her brother's label. Q would kill her if he found out about their affair. He was overprotective, but he especially frowned down on relationships at the office. In the past he had been known to get rid of one or both people. Not that he would fire Karen, but she wanted to keep the innocent image of herself intact, although she was far from the wide-eyed girl who had left for her all-girls college so many years ago. During her pledge time Karen's soon-to-be sorority sisters had done a good job in turning her out sexually. Karen had discovered the joy of sex and become the campus slut.

Young Fresh ta Def was the name of the rapper in question. He and Karen had started "seeing" each other about two months ago. He had been with the label for about two years now. For reasons beyond his control, his career had stalled. His debut album had been shelved because some label execs felt that the time wasn't right to drop it. His hard-core lyrics would be a tough sell in today's market for a new rapper. Young thought his career was finished, until he began sexing Karen.

Although they had known each other in passing, Karen had never really paid him any mind until a few months ago. Fresh off a breakup with her longtime boyfriend, Karen had only come to the party that night because she was required to by the record label. She had just been about to call it a night when he slipped up beside her in the VIP section.

"Hey, miss lady," Young began. "Did that hurt?"

Karen replied, puzzled, "What are you talking about? Did what hurt?"

"Your fall from heaven. You look so good you must be an angel."

"Wow, that was really orginal." Karen laughed. "How long did it take you to think that one up?"

Young's corny line was just enough to break the ice, and laughter was the only form of encouragement he needed.

"Lemme get you a drink," he said suddenly. "What'll you have?"

"You can get me a cosmopolitan," she replied.

Although there was tons of Cristal champagne flowing freely in VIP, Karen didn't drink any. Champagne tended to give her a headache. She could have bought herself a drink, she could easily afford to on her salary, but since he offered she accepted.

One drink led to another and another, and soon she began to see Young in a new light. They began flirting with each other. There was no denying Karen's sudden attraction to him. She was enticed by the thug element that he embodied, especially after her failed relationship with a corporate type. She ended up taking him home, and after that they hooked up whenever and wherever they could. Karen was open to him because he was so different from the other men she had dated.

For Young, however, it was more than sex; his career was on the line. He saw the immediate advantages of sleeping with the boss's sister. She could act as a go-between and smooth things out. So he decided to string her along, since she was so good to him—buying him gifts, etc. He aired his gripes to Karen early and often. She knew that he had been really frustrated over his career and Prestige's failure to break him out into a major star, which he had talked to her about before. He told Karen that he felt held back by Q.

Young thought that the market was ready for his message. In his mind he was already a star. He thought he could go platinum if only he was given the opportunity. But Q hadn't been trying to hear it. Karen sympathized with him only because the sex was clouding her judgment. There were things she wanted to do for him, but Q wouldn't allow it. He said the time wasn't right to release Young's album yet.

Young had been crushed by the news and had grown increasingly frustrated. With the recent success of independent record labels, Young had the idea to either leave Prestige Records with his masters and go the independent route or form his own label, where he would be the featured artist. He even had a name picked out, Millennium Entertainment. He had run his idea past Karen to see how receptive she would be to it, and she encouraged him to take his career into his own hands. Secretly she had given him the money to hire an expensive entertainment lawyer to get him out of his contract, but Q had rejected any offer they had come up with to release him. He explained that too much money had been spent on production of his album to let him walk away. There was only one way out for Young, to buy himself out. He'd need roughly a half million dollars to do it and he didn't have that kind of money. He was barely getting by now, after blowing much of his advance on a luxury car, platinum and diamond jewelry, and a fancy house. But all was not lost. He knew Karen was the key to getting him out of his current situation. He just needed to be a little more persuasive.

Suddenly there was a knock on the door. Without looking

through the peephole, Karen opened the door. Standing there was Young Fresh ta Def. He was looking handsome as ever, standing in the hallway with a do-rag on. His muscles seemed to bulge under his plain icy white t-shirt. It was this thuggish appeal that first attracted her to him. But it was his extraordinary abilities to please a woman in bed that made her keep him around.

"Nigger, I been thinking about you all day," Karen told him.

"Well, here I am, Ma. Let's do what I came to do," he replied.

Karen reached out and hungrily pulled him inside. She slammed the door shut and began gripping Young Fresh ta Def's dick. He responded by roughly cupping two handfuls of her ass. Soon they began kissing, their tongues tangling until they were almost breathless. Young Fresh ta Def's hands began to roam her body freely. He massaged Karen's breasts before his hands found their way to her vagina. Easily he parted the lips of her vagina and began to gently rub her clitoris. Without warning, she became wet. The juices from her vagina soaked his fingers. By now Karen was in an erotic haze. She was ready for him to fuck her.

Young began to plant soft, grateful kisses on Karen's face and neck. Eventually he worked his way down her body. His touch was so soft and seductive that Karen was getting weak at the knees. His snakelike tongue was finishing up what his fingers had started. Now on his knees, Young Fresh ta Def began to lick Karen's clit, flicking his tongue rapidly back and forth before he then began to suck the sensitive nub. He devoured her and had her moaning for more. Karen gripped his head, trying to get him closer, closer. Her whole body began to shake, and her orgasm crashed over her in a violent wave.

Suddenly Karen pulled him to his feet and she went down to return the favor. Now on her knees, Karen greedily tried to take all of his manhood in her mouth, but she couldn't do it. He was too big. She took as much as she could before she began to gag.

Then she began to furiously bob her head up and down on his dick. Right before he was about to come, Karen pulled back and said, "I want that dick inside me."

Off came Young's t-shirt and jeans, until he was totally naked except for the do-rag that adorned his head. Karen was naked in a blink of an eye. She went down on the floor on all fours, in a doggy-style position. It was her favorite and his, too. Young straddled her from behind and slid his dick into her tight, wet heat. His first violent thrust made it clear that he was going to fuck her, not make love to her. He had no desire to be gentle. Besides, Karen liked it hard and fast. Young began to pound her pussy with thrust after powerful thrust. He knew that after a good fuck Karen was always in a generous mood. He needed a big favor, so he fucked her as if his life depended on it.

Karen was so into it, she moaned and arched her back, digging her nails deep into the carpet. She looked back at Young, giving him a lustful look. Her eyes seemed to be pleading with him to fuck her even harder and faster. He complied by grabbing her by the shoulder blades and forcefully pulling her toward him. Sensing he was about to ejaculate, Young withdrew from Karen's vagina and shot hot semen on her buttocks. Quickly Karen turned toward him and placed her mouth around his dick and swallowed him dry.

After a few more rounds of high-impact sex and numerous orgasms, the couple ended up in Karen's bed, spooning. Young seized the opportunity to have a serious talk with Karen. After all, it was the only reason he had come over.

"Yo," he began. "I'm about to go away for a while."

"Where you going?" Karen asked, immediately getting upset. "Why you leaving me?"

"Look, I gotta handle some business."

"What kind of business?" Karen asked, not liking the sound of it.

"I really don't wanna talk about it. I only told you so if any-thing should happen to me, then . . ."

"Then what, Gary? You talking real crazy right now. What are you about to get yourself into? Talk to me, goddammit!"

This was just the kind of heartfelt response he was hoping to invoke in her. He wanted her to think he was possibly about to get himself into big trouble. And of course she wouldn't sit back and allow that. Not as long as he was giving her that good dick.

"I really don't wanna even do this shit, but I know these Dominican cats. They gonna front me a few kilos of coke. I'ma take that shit down South and get money. I gotta do what I gotta do. That's the only way I'm going to be able to raise the money to pay your brother back his advance. Gotta take back to the streets."

It nearly broke Karen's heart to hear Young's plans. She couldn't bear to think of him returning to a lifestyle he had long left behind in favor of music. In her mind he had too much tal-ent to waste it in the drug game. There was no way in the world she was going to sit idly by and just let him throw his life away like that. There was no way Karen was going to risk losing him. They had a good thing going.

"Listen, you ain't gotta do that," Karen said.

"What? What do you mean, I ain't gotta do that? You know my situation. Where else am I going to get that kind of money to pay the label? Huh?"

"Don't worry, I'll help you," she told him. "You let me worry about that."

Inwardly, Young smiled to himself. He was proud of his per-formance. Hearing that Karen was going to further involve her-self in his plight only excited him. He didn't bother to question how she would make it happen. Young didn't need to know all that. She hadn't lied to him in the past, and he saw no indication that she was lying now.

"Turn over!" he commanded. "I'm going to fuck the shit out of you. Lemme show you just how much I appreciate all your help."

Immediatedly Karen assumed the position. She liked the rough tone in his voice. She knew he meant every word he said. Young Fresh ta Def was a beast in the bed.

9

After their first day, Tonya and Na'eema hardly ever saw Q. He was in and out of town on business most of the time. He didn't participate too much in the day-to-day operations of Prestige Records: He left that to his hand-picked infrastructure of trusted employees.

In the meantime, Tonya and Na'eema were meeting with the record label's artists and getting to know their prospective upcoming projects. They reviewed their marketing plans and budgets. They also placed introductory phone calls to each artist and/or their management teams. They began organizing record release parties, placing calls to various hot nightclubs across the city for any artist who didn't have one planned. Prestige Records had a slew of artists on their roster, but the most important project that Tonya and Na'eema were working on was double-platinum rapper Shizzy Mack's new album, entitled *Real recognize Real*. He was a rapper with a style reminiscent of the late great Notorious B.I.G., who also had the heartfelt lyrics of a Tupac Shakur. He was adored by fans from both coasts and down South. His crossover appeal was unbelievable.

There was less than a month before his album dropped. The girls were all over the city, making sure various street teams had done their jobs, plastering the city with promotional posters for his impending album release. They did a little bit of everything, from demographics to working with local and regional DJs to assure that the record label's artist got numerous spins, in the club and on the radio. They oversaw a street team in each market. They worked on campaigns and helped with the packaging of the product. Tonya found that she had a natural talent for this and loved it. Doing all this grass-roots work excited her. She was meeting the movers and shakers in the music industry. She was also learning that it took more than just a talented artist or a hot beat by some super producer to sell records. It took a devoted team to make an artist a star. And it took a hell of a push to make a record hot.

An electric feeling was in the air, and not just because it was Saturday night in New York City. It was also Shizzy Mack's album release party, and it was as if the crowds that packed the sidewalks outside of the 40/40 club knew this album was going to be a classic. Hundreds of partygoers, gold diggers, groupies, and industry types anxiously awaited admittance into the club, even though it was clear that the club couldn't possibly accommodate that many people. Dozens of party crashers worked their cellular phones, trying desperately to call someone from the label who was already inside to come out and get them. Most of the higher-ups had turned their cell phones off in anticipation of the high volume of calls.

Q sat with his latest flavor of the month in the VIP lounge, surveying the crowd like a king surveying his lands. And he was very pleased by what he saw. Tonya and Na'eema had outdone themselves. This was going to be one of the hottest parties of the year. And speaking of hot, he had just spotted Tonya, chatting it up with some industry cat. Q's eyes narrowed when he saw how the dude was moving in close to her, how he touched her like he knew her like that. He couldn't blame the guy. Tonya looked so fucking good tonight in those tight designer jeans that looked like they had been painted on and complimented every curve that he wanted to put her up against the nearest wall and fuck the shit out of her. And if he was having those thoughts, then he was sure that ole dude was, too. And Q found that he didn't like it, he didn't like it at all.

"I don't care who you are!" the bouncer announced. "If ya name ain't on the VIP list, you ain't gettin' in. It's as simple as that! Fall back!"

When Tonya poked her head outside the door, what she heard and saw made her feel real good. She was in awe of the vast amounts of people lined up outside the club and the standing-room-only crowd inside. Tonya made a quick assessment that the party was a smashing success. This party would be talked about for months after the fact. Realizing this, Tonya felt for the first time that they were now a part of an ultraexclusive fraternity known as the music industry.

Suddenly Tonya caught a flashback looking out on the crowd. This wild scene reminded her of the parties she used to throw as a promoter back in Philly. As a matter of fact, Tonya and Na'eema had arrived at the 40/40 club before the club's doors opened. They were on hand to make sure everything went right.

"Are there still a lot of people out there?" Na'eema asked.

"Girl, it's bananas out there," Tonya responded. "If all those muthafuckas get up in here, the fire marshals gone come shut this bitch down."

Na'eema merely smiled, signaling her approval. She knew that they had had a hand in this. This great party was the fruits of their labor.

Na'eema loved the glamour and prestige that surrounded the event. More than either of them, Na'eema was a party animal. She was the type of person for whom the nightlife pulsed through her veins. She lived to party. Na'eema was definitely not a homebody. She had to be in the mix of action, so this was right up her alley.

"I'm not goin' anywhere near that door again," Tonya said. "Somebody might recognize me and want me to get they ass in. From the looks of that line there's gonna be more than a few made muthafuckas."

"Oh, well," Na'eema countered, "they shoulda got they ass here earlier. I feel for 'em but I can't reach 'em. I'm where I wanna be. Holla!"

Tonya and Na'eema reentered the party, walking around the club with an air of confidence. Everything was going good, and on top of that they were looking good, literally and figuratively. Tonya was dressed to kill in a black corset, a pair of True Religion jeans, and a pair of Jimmy Choo high heels. Not to be outdone, Na'eema was dressed to impress, too. She wore a blue Roberto Cavalli blouse and matching boots. Since she was a big girl, she couldn't get into any of the European designer jeans, so Na'eema wore a pair of Baby Phat jeans. That was the only article of clothing that wasn't high-end fashion. Still, she made it work.

Together Tonya and Na'eema canvassed the party, making sure everyone was having a good time. Cameras were flashing all over the place as the rich, famous, and notorious posed for their media shots. One look at the bar and the sea of people surrounding it and they knew that the club would make a killing on liquor sales tonight. Cristal, Hennessy, Patron, and other expensive liquors were flowing as the partygoers got their drink and swerve on. They knew after this huge turnout that the club's management would rent her the venue next time for next to nothing. They were making a killing.

Continuing her survey of the party, Tonya looked out at the dance floor and saw gangs of people dancing and enjoying the music. On the turntable tonight was a little-known DJ from the Bronx named Stan Strong. Hiring this unheralded DJ had proved to be a stroke of genius for Tonya. He really knew how to rock a party. She had immediately fallen in love with his style while accompanying Na'eema to a few clubs like Speed and Roseland Ballroom. She privately hoped that the headlining DJ didn't show up, since Stan Strong was doing such a good job.

Moving about the party, Tonya chatted it up with everyone who was someone at the record label, from the president of the label to the interns. And of course she crossed paths with Karen. She was holding court with some industry types, some of whom Tonya recognized immediately.

"Hey," Karen said with faked warmth. "Tonya and Na'eema, nice party. You guys really did your thing. Congrats."

They still weren't on speaking terms, but tonight, however, was different. This wasn't the time or place to show any disunity in the ranks. Karen could be cordial tonight all she wanted to, but they knew what was going on. Karen was the enemy, point blank. She was always looking to undermine their projects, finding reasons to slash their budgets.

"Hi, everyone," Tonya said. "Hope everyone's enjoyin' themselves."

Once they were a good distance away and out of earshot, Tonya and Na'eema broke out into heavy laughter.

"You heard that fake bitch?" Na'eema asked.

Tonya replied, "She surprised the shit outta me. You know I wasn't about to speak to that bitch first. It'll be a cold day in hell."

Continuing to make her way through the crowd, Tonya spotted Shakira and frowned.

Shakira was currently surrounded by a few handsome thuggish type of guys, one of whom was showing her a lot of attention. He was shooting some of his best game at Shakira, whispering sweet nothings in her ear. Tonya had made it her business to know who was who at the party tonight, and she immediately knew what was up. This guy was an aspiring manager of an unsigned rap artist and he had latched onto someone at Prestige, figuring that would be a good contact to have. That person happened to be Shakira, and Tonya was pretty sure that he had deliberately picked a female so he could seduce himself into a connection to any possible deal. After all, the music industry wasn't built purely on the talent an artist had. It was about who their manager or liaison knew. Problem was, Tonya doubted that Shakira knew how to handle a guy like this.

"Hey, Shakira! What's goin' on?" Tonya said, coming up to them with a smile. "Everything all right?"

"Hey, Tonya, Na'eema! Oh, everything is fine. I love this release party," Shakira replied. "It's the best I ever been to. Bar none. Oh, let me introduce you to Eric Freeman. He's the manager for an up-and-coming rapper named Sincere."

"Nice to meet ya, Ma," he said. "Your party's off the chain."

"Nice to meet you, too," Tonya said. "Just hope you havin' a good time."

"No doubt!"

"All right, well, I'll see you later, Shakira," Tonya said. "I gotta make my rounds."

"All right, I'll see you later," she replied and took another sip of her drink.

Tonya made a mental note to herself to keep an eye on Shakira. She caught a bad vibe from the guy she was talking to. Besides that, Shakira appeared to be well on her way to becoming intoxicated and Tonya wasn't about let anyone take advantage of her. It wasn't going to go down like that. But right now she didn't have time to babysit.

As Tonya turned to leave, she felt a strong tug on her arm from behind. Thinking it was Shakira, she immediately turned back around to face her. Seeing it wasn't who she thought it was, Tonya reacted violently, snapping her arm out of the man's firm grip.

"You know me?" Tonya spat.

Na'eema added, "Yeah, don't be puttin' ya hands on her."

"Wow!" he countered. "Look, Ma, it ain't like that. I was just sayin' hi. My name is DJ Jus from the *Miss Jones Morning Show* on Hot 97 FM. Ya girl here had told my man who you was and I just wanted to thank you for sending those exclusive songs to the show. Lettin' us break the records before all those other stations. Na'mean?"

Instantly, the man's moniker rang a bell with them. They had indeed sent unreleased material over to him at the tri-state region's number-one-ranked morning radio show. They had even had brief conversations before, but they had never had a face-to-face meeting until now. Both Tonya and Na'eema felt somewhat embarrassed now that they found out who the guy was. Tonya immediately made an attempt to patch up the misunderstanding.

"My bad!" Tonya exclaimed. "I thought you was somebody else. This dude has been harassing me all night long. Talkin' 'bout I look like his ex-girl. I've been tryin' to convince him I'm not, so please forgive me. I apologize for comin' off so hard on you."

"Oh, no problem," he said. He looked her up and down appreciatively. "I can see why the dude was on like that. You's a nice-lookin' jawn."

Tonya smiled. "What you say?"

"What do you mean?"

"That word 'jawn.' What you know about that?" Tonya asked.

Na'eema interrupted, "Where you from? Philly?"

"All day, every day," he stated. "I'm from the Bottom!"

They knew from the time the guy opened his mouth that he wasn't a hard-core thug from the streets of Philly. Rather, he was a good kid who, through his love of music, managed to succeed in this world despite his environment. Tonya was smitten by the DJ. He had a thuggish appearance, yet he retained a certain innocence about him. Tonya knew from the moment she laid eyes on him that this college kid was the type of dude she would definitely give some to.

"Damn, it's a small world," Tonya commented. "We're from Philly, too."

Instantly the wheels in Tonya's head began to turn. She wondered how she could parlay this chance meeting into something more.

"You drink?" she asked. "Can I get you somethin'?"

"Yeah, what we drinkin'?" he replied.

"Whatever you want to," Tonya replied seductively. "There's buckets of champagne just layin' around in the VIP. I say you follow us over there."

"Yeah, young boy," Na'eema said, catching on. "Come hang out wit' some real chicks from your hometown."

"Bet," he replied. "I'm wit whateva. Let's go."

He grabbed Tonya's hand and, not wanting to be separated, Tonya grabbed Na'eema's as they navigated their way through the crowd. Just as they made it to their destination, they were met at the VIP entrance by Q and his large entourage, which included several bodyguards, a few close friends, and gorgeous females.

The two sides each exchanged pleasantries before making their way through a tight security checkpoint into the VIP area. DJ Jus was still holding Tonya's hand, something that even Q had taken notice of. He couldn't help but pull Tonya to the side and make her aware of it.

"Hey, who you holdin' hands wit?" Q asked. "Ain't that DJ Jus from the Miss Jones mornin' show? What, he onna ya long-lost sisters from back home? He onna those down-low brothers or what?"

If Tonya hadn't heard the words come out of Q's mouth herself, she wouldn't have believed it. Was Q jealous? She almost didn't know how to take it.

Suddenly Tonya recalled an old saying her mother was fond of, "When people show you who they are, believe them."

"Trust me, he not gay," Tonya said, smiling. "Why you worried about him for?"

Tonya let her last statement hang in the air while Q stood there looking like he smelled something bad.

"And anyway, it looks like you got your hands full wit' ole girl," she said, testing him further.

"Oh, that ain't about nothing," Q told her. "She's just a friend."

"Yeah, right! Ya'll friends all right, friends wit' benefits," Tonya responded. "Q, you need to stop it. I know you. Anyway, you feelin' the party? It's poppin', right?"

"Don't try and change the subject," he said. "What you say you lose the dude and I send girlie on her way and we hook up tonight?" Q knew his approach was all wrong, but he couldn't seem to stop himself.

"Q, can we talk about this later?" Tonya playfully suggested. "I gotta check on something."

Q was fit to be tied. He had been watching guys trying to push up on Tonya all night. And to make matters worse, she had been flirting right back with them when she wouldn't even give him the time of day. What the hell was up with that?

Just then Q's "friend" came sashaying over. She slid her hand around his arm like she owned him and pressed her body against his.

"Q, baby," she said, giving Tonya an unfriendly look. "You coming?"

Still heated, Q slid his arm around the female and gave her a kiss on the lips. "Oh, yeah, I'm coming." Tonya would have had to be a fool to miss Q's double meaning. She rolled her eyes.

"I'ma catch you later, Tonya," Q said, then walked off with his dime piece.

Her blood boiling, Tonya turned and rejoined Na'eema and DJ Jus in their quiet little corner of the VIP area. They chitchatted over a few drinks, but it was clear Tonya wasn't the same happy-go-lucky person she was before her encounter with Q. As she watched Q with his current dime piece, she realized she was the one who had jealousy issues.

"Excuse me for a minute, y'all," she suddenly announced. "But I gotta go to the bathroom."

"You want me to come wit you?" Na'eema asked.

"No, I'll be right back," she insisted. She smiled seductively. "Anyway, I need you to keep an eye on our friend here. Make sure he don't holla at no other chicks while I'm gone."

"Don't worry about that. I got my eye on him," Na'eema joked. "Won't none of these broads come near him. He's all yours."

Tonya exited the VIP lounge with every intention of getting lost for a little while. At this point, anybody or anything would be a welcome diversion to get her mind off Q. She realized she hadn't seen Shakira in a minute. Tonya headed over to where she had last seen her. She didn't know if it was the liquor or what, but if Shakira was still around those guys, she was going to tell them to kick rocks.

Shakira sipped on yet another apple martini and continued to listen to the incessant talk of the would-be manager. She didn't notice that a short distance away, to her immediate right, there were a few groupies hating on her. They mean-mugged her and gave her the finger. They did anything and everything they could to disrespect her except approach her.

"Look, Ma, my man is hot!" the manager said. "His lyrics are sick. Ain't no rapper in the industry go anything for him. I'm tellin' you, if your boss hear 'em he gonna sign him on the spot! I guarantee it! All I need is for you to set up an audition for your label's A&R."

"I told you before, I don't work in that department," Shakira said with a sigh. "What do you want me to do?"

The man replied, "But you work for that label, right? You can't tell me that you can't get the A&R's number if you really wanted to. I understand that you usually don't do this, but do me this favor. Please? All I'm trying to do is get my foot in the door. I'm sayin', maybe we can exchange numbers or some-thin'?"

This guy was really working Shakira's last nerve, but she didn't let on. Shakira wasn't the type of person to tell someone to get lost even when they deserved it. Her one fault was being too friendly, and this guy was a pit bull who had latched onto her and wouldn't let go. At this point she would do anything to get rid of him.

"I usually don't give my private number out like that. I like to leave my work at work. They don't pay me enough to take it home," Shakira began. "But I'll tell you what I will do. Here, take my business card. Give me a call on Monday and I'll see what I can do for you. I'm not making you any promises, though."

"Good lookin', Ma!" he exclaimed. "You the realest person I ever met in the industry. All these niggers is fake. Thanks! I'ma call you on Monday. Whatever you can do for me I'll appreci-ate."

To show his appreciation, the man quickly hugged Shakira affectionately. She almost spilled her drink, he hugged her so tight. From a distance the women took in the whole scene. And it really got under their skin.

"All right, Ma, I'll catch you later. I'm about to go see who else I can politic wit'. A lotta very important people in here, you know," he said. "You be safe now, you hear?"

The man and his friend marched off, heading for another part of the club, leaving Shakira alone. She was glad that they had finally left. Shakira didn't know how much more bullshit she could possibly take. It had gotten to the point where she couldn't even enjoy herself. Soon as she downed the rest of her drink, she realized she needed to pee badly and made a beeline for the ladies room before anymore wannabe rappers and their managers could latch onto her.

She didn't notice when her three stalkers followed her.

When Tonya got to the spot near the bar where she had last seen Shakira, she was surprised not to find her there. Tonya's mind began to race. She hoped that Shakira hadn't left the club with that lowlife she had seen her talking to and that she had more sense than that. But if she didn't, Tonya would extend the benefit of the doubt to Shakira like she once had done to her.

Curiosity was killing Tonya. Finally she decided to ask someone if they had seen her.

"Excuse me, did you see a tall chick dressed in a business suit that was standing here talkin' to two dudes a lil' while ago?" Tonya inquired.

A guy replied, "Yeah, she just went that way."

"Was she wit' any dudes?" Tonya wondered.

"Naw, she left wit' a group of girls," the guy told her.

"Girls?" Tonya repeated. "Which way they went?"

"That way," the man said, pointing in the direction of the bathroom. "They left not too long ago. She was just here."

"Thanks," Tonya said, making her way through the crowd.

Shakira stepped out of the stall and came to a halt when she saw three women standing there looking like something was about to jump off.

"Lemme ask you a question," one woman began. "How the fuck do you know my man?"

Shakira unconsciously took a step back. "Your man?" Shakira repeated. "What are you talking about?"

"Oh, you can't remember who you was all up on? You got fucking amnesia all of a sudden?"

Shakira's mind raced. She didn't know what this chick was talking about. Then it hit her. "Are you talking about that guy just now?"

"Bitch, don't play stupid wit' me!" the woman said. "I'll beat ya muthafuckin' ass up in here! You fuckin' homewrecker. We gotta kid together. I know you my man's lil' jump-off. Now why don't you just admit it! Be a woman about it."

They had already surrounded her. Shakira didn't know what to do. These weren't the rational or professional type of women that she was used to dealing with, and the threat of violence was in the air. Things were about to get ugly at any second.

"Listen, I just told you, I don't know that guy," Shakira told them. "I was only being nice. He said he was a music producer or a manager. And I'm in the industry. I work for a record label. Any conversation that you seen us having was purely from a networking standpoint. To be honest with you, he's not my type."

"Not your type?" the woman yelled. "So you just go around givin' hugs to niggas you don't know and ain't attracted to?"

Another woman added, "Look, I'm tireda talkin'. This bitch keep playin' dumb. Every other word outta her mouth is a fuckin' lie."

Suddenly, without warning, Shakira's main antagonist began removing her jewelry as if she were preparing herself for a fight. Shakira just stood there, unsure of what to do next. She was so scared, she felt like she was going to cry. A tear slowly trickled down her cheek.

"Bitch, all that cryin' ain't gonna help your ass now. You 'bout to get ya ass beat," the woman stated.

At that moment, Tonya burst into the bathroom with her heels in hand, ready to do combat.

"What the fuck is goin' on in here?" she said to no one in particular. "Why you bitches surroundin' my people like that? Shakira, why is you cryin'? Oh, hell, no, it ain't even goin' down like that!"

Tonya's outburst had taken everyone by surprise. No one expected anyone to come to Shakira's aide. Previously, anyone who wasn't involved with the incident had scrambled to get out of the bathroom, sensing trouble. Now this chick had come out of nowhere, looking for trouble.

"You need to mind your goddamn business," one of the little flunkies advised.

"Bitch, this is my business," Tonya replied, shoving them out of the way.

Immediatedly they recognized that this new arrival was cut from the same cloth as they, the street. Even so, being from the same background made it hard for either party to back down. In their respective hoods, disagreements like these were usually settled one way: violently.

So from the moment Tonya had entered the bathroom, she set her sights on the leader of the pack, the chick who had so much to say. Her thinking was if there was going to be trouble, then it would come from this person. Quietly she waited for the right moment to strike.

"Look, ho, I suggest that you bounce right now," the woman warned, "before you get what's comin' to your friend here."

Suddenly the woman began walking toward Tonya, shouting insults and pointing her fingers in Tonya's face. As soon as she came within arm's reach, Tonya balled up her fist, and with all her might she delivered a crushing blow to the woman's throat region. The punch floored her instantly. The woman lay on the floor holding her neck, gasping for air, as the friends frantically attended to her.

"Now, bitch, look at you," Tonya said, glaring down at her. "You ain't so fuckin' tough now."

Quickly Tonya grabbed Shakira's arm and led her out of the bathroom. When they were free and clear, Tonya turned her attention to Shakira, who appeared to be shaken.

"You okay?" Tonya asked gently.

"Yeah, I'm cool," Shakira responded. "Thanks, Tonya. I don't know what I would have done if you hadn't walked in here when you did. I owe you."

"Don't say that, you don't owe me nothing," Tonya told her. "Just get yourself together and walk out there like nothing happened."

Shakira took a deep breath and said, "Actually, I think I'm going to head home now. I've had enough for one night."

"All right, whatever. You want me to wait with you?"

"No, I'll be all right," she told Tonya. "I'm just going to hop in a cab." She waved to Tonya. "I'll see you tomorrow."

Tonya watched until Shakira made her way out of the club to make sure none of those chicks tried to be slick and follow her outside. She had just turned to make her way back to the VIP section when she felt someone grab her arm. Tonya whipped around, ready to go off, thinking it was one of them hoes from the bathroom. She lowered her arm when she saw that it was Q.

"You all right?" he asked.

"Why you askin'?" she wanted to know, still heated from the fight and from her little run-in with him earlier.

"Looked like something jumped off with Shakira," he said, nodding in the direction of the bathrooms.

"Oh," Tonya said, waving a hand dismissively. "Some hoes just wanted to get it crackin'. I took care of them. Wasn't nothing."

"Is Shakira all right?" Q asked with a frown.

"Yeah, yeah. She just decided to call it a night." Tonya looked down to where Q still had his hand on her arm. "Um, Q?"

"What? Oh," he said, releasing her.

"Are you all right?" she asked this time. He looked a little funny.

"I'm always good."

"Okay," Tonya said, nodding slowly. "Well, then, I'm goin' to get back to the VIP."

"Back to ya friend?"

Tonya folded her arms over her chest. "Don't start that shit again, Q."

"Oh, now I'm startin' shit?" he asked.

Tonya held up a hand. "Q, we ain't seeing each other. We ain't even fuckin', so why do we keep having this conversation tonight? You know what? Never mind. You go do you, I'll do me, and we'll just leave it at that." She turned to go.

"Hold the fuck up, Tonya, stop talking crazy. Let me talk to you a minute," he said. He grabbed her hand and yanked her into a dark corner.

"What, Q? Damn!" she said, highly annoyed.

But Q didn't say one more word. He just pushed Tonya up against the wall, pinning her hands above her head, and before she could even open her mouth to say anything, he leaned in and laid a serious lip-lock on her.

Tonya was so stunned that she didn't even react at first. But that didn't last long. Q's lips felt so good that Tonya was soon moaning. Q quickly slipped his tongue inside her mouth. Tonya immediately responded, giving as good as she got. She didn't know how long they stayed there in that dark corner, kissing passionately, but before she knew it Q was unbuttoning her jeans and slipping his hand down her panties. It was a tight fit, but he knew what he was doing. She was glad they were hidden from view because she couldn't have stopped him if she wanted to. Slowly he slid one finger, then two inside her, finding her already wet. Tonya held on for dear life as he pumped his fingers in and out of her. She would have cried out when she came if he hadn't been kissing her at that moment. He continued to hold her until she stopped shaking.

Then Q stepped back, licked his fingers clean, and said, "Think about that while you're doing you."

Then he turned and walked away.

Tonya stayed there, slumped against the wall, trying to pull herself together, but after a while she saw, from her vantage point, Q leaving the club with his dime piece on his arm.

"That muthafucka," she said, straightening her clothes and heading back to the VIP lounge.

He had just blown all her resolutions where he was concerned straight to hell. There was no way she could stay away from him now.

Despite what she might have said, Karen was feeling real salty about the success of Tonya and Na'eema's party. She secretly hoped that an incident would happen to cast a shadow over their shining moment. Something like a club shooting wouldn't be bad. Karen seriously doubted that, not with all the security personnel in place.

"Here you go, baby," Young suddenly announced, handing Karen her drink.

He wasn't in a real social mood himself. He was currently in hater mode. Young couldn't believe that the label was doing it up this big for Shizzy Mack. He felt that he was better than Shizzy Mack all the way around the board, from looks to lyrics. He couldn't understand why he was in the position he was in and Shizzy Mack was a rap star.

"Thanks. I needed this," Karen said. "Certain people have been getting on my nerves all night long."

"Who?" Young wondered, hoping it ain't him.

"Them two new bitches that my brother brought in to work for the label. One bitch is named Tonya and the other Na'eema. I can't fucking stand either of them," Karen admitted.

Just then Tonya and Na'eema entered the room.

"Well, speak of the devil," Karen said. "Here come these two bitches right now." As they passed by, neither party spoke to each other. They merely exchanged fake pleasantries in the form of a weak smile. Being the dog that he was, Young took a good hard look at Tonya. To him there was something about her that looked vaguely familiar. At the moment he couldn't quite put his finger on it, though. But for some reason he couldn't seem to get Tonya out of his mind.

"Yo girlfriend looks real familiar," he stated. "I know her from somewhere."

"Nigger, you're just saying that because you probably want to fuck her," Karen spat, her jealousy rearing its head.

"Nah, it ain't even like that. I got who I want," he assured her. "But I never forget a face. I'm tellin' you, I know her from somewhere."

"Nigger, where?" she asked. "That bitch is from Philly."

"Well, damn, ain't that where I'm from?" he countered.

Young Fresh ta Def was right. He was from Philly. He had been in New York so long that he took on a lot of the slang and mannerisms of a New York rapper. It was a common misconception he faced. In the past Q had been accused of being slightly biased toward Philadelphia rappers, because he had signed so many. Currently there was only one Philly rapper on Prestige Records' roster of artists.

"Oh, shit!" he said, snapping his fingers. "I know where I know that broad from."

"Where?" Karen inquired in disbelief. "Where do you know her from? Please tell me."

"She's a stripper!" he proclaimed. "As much as I used to play them strip clubs, I know my strippers."

Karen could barely contain herself. She couldn't believe her ears. No, he didn't say what she thought she heard him say. Miss Goody Two-shoes, Tonya, was a stripper. She wondered if Q knew. She wouldn't be surprised if that Tonya had hidden it from him. She wouldn't put it past her to be a tricky bitch like that. She wondered if she should tell Q, but then quickly decided against that. She didn't want to seem like she was telling tales out of school. Q hated things like that. But she sure as hell was going to use the info to get that ho out of Prestige once and for all.

"You sure?" she asked Young. "Don't spread lies about people. That shit isn't cool."

"Yo, what the fuck I gotta lie about some shit like that for?" he snapped. "What I'm going to get out of that? If she's a stripper, then she a stripper. I'm just calling them like I see 'em. . . . Anyway, how's everything coming along with those funds? You took care of that yet? I gettin' tired of all this waiting shit. Maybe I should have did what I started to do."

"Look, don't start that shit again. I said I'm working on it.

Good things come to those who wait," Karen told him. "Just give me a little more time. I got you. Don't worry about it. And you're coming home with me tonight. This liquor is making me horny as hell."

"I don't know," he replied, smiling. "It depends on how you act . . ."

10

"Niecey, I know you're happy to finally be going home, huh?" the corrections officer said.

Niecey didn't bother to immediately comment. She was too busy shedding the drab prison garb with her inmate identification number stamped all over it. Still, she pondered the statement for a moment while donning her street clothes.

"What you think?" Niecey snapped. "You go home to ya family after every shift. Don't you think I wanna go home to mine? I'm not like the rest of these bitches who ain't got nuttin' to go home to. My family loves me. And my husband is rich!"

Only a few days ago, had Niecey pulled a stunt like this, it probably would have gotten her a one-way express ticket to solitary confinement. But since today was her release day, she knew that there wasn't anything the corrections officer could say or do to prevent it. This was payback for Niecey. Today she was finally a free woman.

Niecey had never adjusted to her incarceration. She fought constantly with other inmates and prison guards alike. There wasn't a day that passed by that she didn't think about escaping. In Niecey's mind she didn't belong there, despite the fact that she had pleaded guilty in a court of law. Despite the fact that she had taken someone's life.

The corrections officer regretted even trying to make nice with her now. Niecey had been labeled a troublemaker and a big mouth throughout her entire stint in prison by the prison staff. So she should have known better than to open a conversation with her.

"Hey, Howard, watch your mouth," the corrections officer demanded.

"Fuck you, bitch. I ain't gotta watch my mouth," Niecey cursed. "I can say whateva the fuck I wanna say. I'm goin' home. And ain't nuttin' y'all can do to stop me!"

The corrections officer glared at Niecey evilly, knowing full well that the inmate was one hundred percent correct. An image of Niecey's face was suddenly seared into the corrections officer's mind. She promised herself that she would take care of Niecey if and when she came back. She knew that eventually most inmates do return. The recidivism rate was high across the country.

"I'll see you when you come back, smartass," the corrections officer warned.

"Bitch, get a life," Niecey barked. "Don't hold ya breath waitin' to see me up in here again. The only place you're goin' to see me is on TV."

Knowing that she had the upper hand, Niecey strutted out of the prison intake area, where she walked through a series of mechanically opened steel grilles until she inhaled her first taste of freedom. She savored the moment. At times during her lengthy incarceration, she thought that this moment would never come.

Enjoying every moment of this, Niecey took her time walking to the chauffeur-driven limousine that Q had sent to pick her up. Once she reached the car, she turned around and gave the prison the finger as a parting shot.

"Fuck all y'all!" she stated loudly.

All of this was quite amusing to Niecey. She had waited for a long time to show her ass in this manner. For the first few miles, she couldn't stop laughing.

From a cozy seat in the back of the limousine, Niecey's thoughts suddenly began to shift to more serious matters. Her thoughts began to shift between Q and her son. She just assumed that they would all pick up where they had left off, that they would be a family again. In Niecey's mind there was no period of adjustment as far as her and Q's personal relationship was concerned. After all, she was his first love, the mother of his only child. That meant a whole lot to her. And it meant Q was hers for life, whether he liked it or not.

Niecey knew damn well that Q had been sleeping around while she was locked up. When Niecey used to see him in some of the tabloids with another woman on his arm, it used to drive her crazy. That was the reason why she was in prison in the first place. Even now the mere thought of it drove her mad. Niecey knew she would have to be very careful not to let her emotions get the best of her. It was a well-known fact that she was very jealous and crazy over Q.

Pushing Q out of her mind, Niecey decided to focus on the fact that she was now free. She smiled to herself. Today was a good day, and now it was time to enjoy life to the fullest.

11

Tonya and Na'eema were fast becoming the "it" girls in the company. The word of mouth on Shizzy Mack's album had been huge, and the first week's sales put him in the top five on the *Billboard* charts.

Q took all the top heads who had been involved in the album's success out to dinner. It was Tonya and Na'eema's first time at such an event, but they had a ball. They also got to know a few of the other Prestige employees better, since it was a social setting. The only odd moment of the night came just as they were finishing up dessert. Tonya noticed an odd exchange between Q and one of his bodyguards in the restaurant. Q swore under his breath. She was pretty sure no one else had heard him, but she couldn't help doing so since she was sitting right next to him.

Tonya looked up and saw him glaring at someone across the restaurant. Following his line of vision, she saw that he was looking at an older white gentleman. He appeared to be in his late forties, early fifties. He had dark hair tipped in gray at his temples, which made him look very distinguished. She couldn't tell his eye color from here, but his gaze was sharp and very intelligent and she doubted anything got past this guy. He was dressed in an obviously expensive dark blue suit, which made him look business sharp. This was not a guy anyone wanted to mess with. He looked like he was having dinner with a sophisticated-looking woman around his age, possibly his wife and a younger man who looked like him minus the suit, possibly his son. The man raised his cup of coffee in acknowledgment of Q as if he were toasting him. He smiled and then turned back to his dinner companions.

Tonya leaned over and asked Q, "Who's that?"

"Manhattan's district attorney, Robert Fera," Q said in distaste. "He's got dreams of becoming the city's next mayor. That's his wife and his son with him."

"He seems to know you."

Q smiled bitterly. "Yeah, he knows me. Nothing would make him look better than to have brought down a few prominent rappers in this town. We're all criminals anyway to him. His dick gets real hard when it comes to me and my empire. The hip-hop police have been watching me since the beginning, trying to get something on me, and I know he's behind the pressure they've been putting on me. That's why we can never be too careful with how we do things. All they need is one slip-up."

Tonya stared at Q, surprised he had even shared that much with her. Q had never really shared his business, but maybe it was because she was part of his camp now. Tonya looked back over at the Fera family. There was something familiar about Fera, but she just couldn't put her finger on it. Tonya pushed it out of her mind and went back to enjoying the dinner.

Over the course of a few months, Tonya and Na'eema began dealing directly with artists and their managers on various projects. But when the artists and their managers began bypassing Karen with their problems and going straight to Tonya and Na'eema, Karen became furious. One day, Karen came bursting into Tonya's office, furious.

"Who in the hell gave you permission to change Ron-O's album cover?" she fumed.

Tonya had been going over the budget for the newest album that was going to drop in two months. She looked up at Karen. "What?"

"You heard me!" Karen snapped. "Who in the hell gave you permission to change Ron-O's album cover?"

"Nobody," she admitted calmly. "It happened that day you were out of the office. I called you several times and left you messages on your answering machine. You never returned my calls. So I figured it was cool."

Truth be told, Tonya and Na'eema had a slight problem conforming to the corporate structure. They were so used to calling all the shots, making every last decision, that sometimes they forgot they now worked for someone else. Their decisions had turned out so well in the past, they saw no reason for them not to work now.

"You figured it was cool?" Karen repeated. "You keep taking liberties like that and I'll personally see to it that you figure out how to get a job somewhere else!"

With that said, Karen turned on her heel and left their office, leaving Tonya and Na'eema alone to digest the scolding.

"I hate that bitch!" Na'eema cursed. "Ohh, I wanna piece of her skinny narrow ass so bad."

"Me too!" Tonya admitted. "That bitch kills me how she be talkin' to me. I'm not no fuckin' kid!"

Na'eema added. "For real, this fuckin' job is startin' to get to me. It ain't all that I thought it would be."

At times the pressure-cooker environment got the best of both Tonya and Na'eema. There were some days when they dreaded even coming to work. The vast amounts of work and the pressure that came with it made Na'eema question herself on more than one occasion. There were a few times when they both wanted to curse Karen out. Yet they remained poised and professional, choosing to take the high road, hoping that what was done in darkness would one day come to light.

Na'eema may have been ready to abandon ship, but Tonya wasn't. She knew this was her last chance to make something of herself. It was either this or back to the street, back to stripping or the constant grind of a party promoter. She didn't see much room for advancement in either occupation. So she knew she had to pay her dues at the record label. Tonya knew she had to expect the worst and hope for the best. There was no way she was walking away from this. There was no way she was giving up her dream without a fight. She wasn't about to just let Karen run her away from there.

A few weeks later, while attending a meeting, Tonya and Na'eema were hit with another surprise by Karen.

"What happened to Ron-O's album? Who changed it?" Q wondered aloud, speaking to no one in particular. "It's a good look!"

Before anyone could say anything, Karen spoke up.

"That was my idea, Q," she claimed. "I wasn't really feeling the other concept. So I had the graphic artist change it right before the deadline. Since you were out of town, I couldn't run my idea past you, but I knew you'd like it."

Tonya and Na'eema sat in the meeting, stunned. They couldn't believe Karen had taken credit for Tonya's idea. And she did it right in front of their faces. Tonya just maintained a blank expression and managed not to leap across the table and snatch Karen by her hair. Na'eema just shook her head in disgust.

A wicked grin donned Karen's face as she accepted all the accolades.

It was stunts like these that made Tonya question the integrity of everyone in the corporate world. She began to question the

principles and morals of her co-workers, subordinates, and su-
pervisors. After being hit with example after example of office
politics, she began to wonder: what kind of people did she work
with?

"We had it better back in Philly when we were our own
bosses and didn't have to answer to nobody!" Na'eema would
often say.

Speak for yourself, Tonya said to herself.

With an attitude like that, Tonya didn't see Na'eema sticking
around too long. Figuratively speaking, Na'eema had talked
Tonya off of many ledges, saved her from doing a lot of stupid
things. Still, for some reason Na'eema wouldn't let her return
the favor.

"Na'eema, you can't let that shit get to you like that. I don't
like half the shit that go on either, but truth gonna come to light.
Shit comes out in the wash. Watch," Tonya said. "You can't feed
into that nonsense."

She fired back, "Easier said than done! One day you might
not be around to talk me out of beating that bitch down. One
day I'm not goin' ta be in the mood for her shit."

Tonya would listen to Na'eema's daily rants and complaints
about their new job. But she just chalked it up as crazy talk.
There was nothing Na'eema could say that could make Tonya
even entertain the thought of leaving. She had come to New
York to make something of herself and she'd be damned if she
left before she did.

With each passing day, Tonya was getting her act together as
she became more and more acclimated to the business. Although Na'eema was there with her, she began to feel that they
were going in different directions.

12

Having recently returned from a West Coast business trip, Q and his entourage took a limousine straight to his Manhattan headquarters. Once back in familiar surroundings, it was business as usual.

Q reclined in a cozy chair in his office, his feet kicked up on the desk, multitasking, talking on the office intercom while looking over publicity photos from his publicist. Also spread on his desk was an electronics magazine. Q liked to keep abreast of the latest technological advances, especially with computers and cellular phones. The items were like lifelines to him here in the twenty-first century. While he multitasked, his Blackberry vibrated repeatedly on his hip, like a pulse.

He laid the photos on his desk and removed his phone from its holder, glancing down at the screen. There were numerous fresh text messages from everyone from his attorneys to his mistresses. They all seemed to want one thing, a moment of Q's very valuable time. Quickly he scanned through each text message to determine the level of urgency. Seeing no emergencies, Q carefully replaced the Blackberry back in its holder, continuing on with his conversation.

"Hey, Annie, could you bring me a Red Bull, please? I'm feelin' a lil' tired," Q said into the intercom. "Is there anything out there to snack on? If there's any chocolate donuts, could you bring me one?"

"Coming right up," she said.

Q was drained. He had gone to an album release party last night, and immediately after he had boarded a red-eye flight to New York. Still, that didn't stop him from coming into the office to check on a few business matters. This was his company, and Q was determined to lead by example. If his workers saw the boss still coming into the office, and he was a millionaire many times over, then that would inspire them to give that extra effort and work harder.

After being served his coffee and donuts, Q went back to looking over spreadsheets and profits-and-loss statements. Q knew he had to be on top of things now more than ever. Getting on top was only part of the problem. Staying there would really cement his legacy in the entertainment world. Longevity would silence his critics, who said he was an overnight sensation or a flash in the pan. He wasn't making music, he was making history.

Slowly but surely, Prestige Records' employees began to trickle into the office. And one by one, they stopped at Q's office to pay homage to the boss. There they found a solemn Q, deep in thought, reading financial reports. At times he barely made eye contact or acknowledged whoever it was who was greeting him. Sometimes Q got like that while poring over mathematical figures in his mind. At times like these, what was in front of him had his undivided attention and required complete concentration.

But when he heard little feet running toward his office, Q looked up with a smile on his face.

"Daddy!" his son yelled as he burst through the door.

"Lil Q!" he said, rising up from behind his desk to greet his son. "What's good?"

Paperwork scattered everywhere, but Q didn't care. The only thing that was more important than his money and his company was his family, his son in particular. His life's struggle had been for his family. Family was what made success worthwhile.

Quinton Phelps and his son embraced warmly. One could feel the love these two shared for each other in the air. It was a habit for them to openly display affection for each other. At all times Q wanted his son to know he loved him; he never ever wanted him to question it. The roots of Q's displays of affection could be traced back to his childhood. He grew up without a father. He had had to compensate by loving his mother and sisters that much more. Father and son continued to hug as if they hadn't seen each other in months. But the truth of the matter was, they had only been separated for a few days. Q had sent his son back to Philly to be there to see his mom after her release from prison.

So that meant his baby's mother was somewhere around.

"Yo, where your mother?" Q asked.

In response to his question, Lil Q pointed toward the hallway.

Q braced himself for the worst. One thing about Niecey was that one never knew what to expect out of her. She was totally unpredictable, subject to mood swings. While Niecey was away he had become quite reckless with his relationships and it had all played out in the media. So Q was sure she had caught wind of that, even in prison. He was also sure that she would approach him about that, too. Niecey wasn't one to hold her tongue, and they had been together so long, Niecey thought she owned him. But the truth of the matter was, during her lengthy incarceration, they had grown apart. But Q would cross that bridge when he had to. In the meantime, he wanted to enjoy Lil Q.

The father and son's joyous reunion spilled out into the hallway, where Q and his son engaged in a childish act of playfighting. It ended up with his son tackling him to the floor and the two of them giggling their hearts out.

At that very moment, Tonya stared down the hallway at Q and his son, playing. She was mesmerized. Tonya had never seen this side of Q. She knew Q the player and Q the businessman, but not Q the father. Right now she was just getting a glimpse of that person and she loved every minute of it, as if she needed something else that was going to make her want Q even more.

Then Niecey came strolling around the corner. The sight of her shocked Tonya. She wracked her brain trying to figure out how in the hell Niecey had gotten out of jail so quickly. For a short period of time she had followed Niecey's murder case closely in the newspaper. She assumed Niecey was finished when she pleaded guilty to involuntary manslaughter and aggravated assault. Tonya didn't follow the case after that. If she had, she would have known that Niecey only received one and a half to three years in a state prison and she had served every day of the sentence. Now she was scot-free.

Niecey's sudden appearance brought a halt to Q and Lil Q's activities. They stopped playing long enough to pick themselves up off the floor.

For long seconds, Niecey and Q stared at each other. Q admired her beauty, as if suddenly remembering what it was that made him fall in love with her in the first place. The time she had spent in prison had agreed with her.

Although Niecey had always looked good, Q had never remembered her looking quite like this. Niecey looked like one of those gorgeous eye-candy models in *Don Diva* magazine. She was the complete package, honey-golden complexion, light brown eyes, and high cheekbones, with thick, juicy, pillow-soft lips. The prison food had done Niecey some good because prior to her incarceration she had always been a petite girl. Even childbirth hadn't put a significant amount of weight on her. Now her measurements had to be 34C–26–43. She was thick in all the right places.

The low-rise Frankie V jeans Niecey had on were so tight that they made his nature rise. He could only imagine how she got her big behind in those jeans. Q stared at her crotch region, realizing that she didn't have any underwear on. There were no thongs or panty lines to be seen.

Q was sure he would be the first to receive some of her pent-up sexual energy after her lengthy bid. *I can't wait to get all up in that,* he thought to himself.

To Q it was a given that he would get with Niecey, it was just a matter of when. After all, Q had paid for her legal defense, he had taken care of her financially throughout her entire incarceration, and he had raised their son while she was gone. Q had suffered through all kinds of negative publicity as a result of Niecey, so in his mind he felt she owed him some mind-blowing sex. And this was one debt he aimed to collect on.

Now, Q had to admit to himself that Niecey was better looking than a lot of those chicks he had on the side. She was a natural beauty straight from the hood who would give a lot of actresses, R&B singers, and runway models a run for their money. He thought about Tonya and how she was the only one who could give Niecey some competition. But he didn't want to think about Tonya right now. He had made it clear he wanted her. The ball was in her court now.

"What? You ain't got no love for me no more?" Q asked Niecey. "It's like that, huh?"

Niecey struck a defiant pose, hands on her hips, rolling her eyes and sucking her teeth.

"I shouldn't even talk to your ass. I saw a picture of you in *XXL* magazine hugged up with one of your jump-offs. You been doin' you while I was gone, huh?"

"C'mon, Niecey," he began. "Why you even go there wit' that?

It's not the time or place to talk about that. Damn, it's been a long time since we last seen each other. Why I just can't enjoy ya company for a few minutes witout you jumpin' all down a nigger's throat? You trippin' right now."

Niecey hadn't been around Q a hot five minutes and already she had pissed him off. Niecey's overpossessive ways had gotten the best of her once again. One would think that the passage of time had mellowed her somewhat, but it hadn't. She was still crazy as ever when it came to Q.

I see now this chick ain't changed a bit, he mused. *She ain't nothing but trouble, always was and always will be.*

Q glared at Niecey, his anger temporarily getting the best of him. Finally he broke down and took Niecey into his arms. They both broke out into a giant grin. As they embraced, Q let his hands run freely over Niecey's voluptuous body.

Niecey realized now wasn't the time to show that crazy side of herself, so like Q suggested, she just enjoyed the moment.

Down the hall Tonya soaked all this up. The sight of Q holding Niecey in his arms made her sick. She could only stand so much of this before she turned and walked away. It hurt her to see Q showing affection to Niecey. It was enough to ruin her whole day. Dejectedly, Tonya headed back to her office. At that moment the feelings she had for him seemed so far away.

From her vantage point she had just viewed the perfect couple. Whether that was true or not was debatable.

By the time Tonya got to her office, she was in a foul mood.

Soon as Na'eema reentered the office, she could tell that something was wrong with her friend. The evil look that was currently plastered across her face was a big sign.

"What's the matter wit you?" Na'eema asked. "You had a run-in with Karen or somethin'?"

"Yeah," Tonya stated flatly, not really caring to reveal the true source of her anger.

Tonya had never gone into depth about her and Q's prior relationship. Na'eema never asked and she never told. Ironically, her friend was probably the only person close to Tonya that she could confide in. Na'eema was the only person with enough compassion for Tonya to understand the emotional turmoil she was currently experiencing.

"Well, what did she do now?" she wondered.

Tonya replied, "Nothin'. I don't wanna talk about it."

Although she was dying to know what allegedly had happened, Na'eema left it alone. Her friend wasn't in a talkative mood. She respected that. She and Tonya had never had an argument or a major disagreement since they met. And Na'eema wanted to keep it that way. So as a friend she respected her space and backed off.

Once Q and his entourage left the office, Tonya began to cheer up almost instantly. She became less antisocial, and she and Na'eema began to tackle their daily workload together, in peace and harmony. Within a few hours things were back to normal. By now it was lunchtime. Tonya and Na'eema decide to head outside for lunch. Needless to say, they both weren't in the mood for anything fancy, so instead they opted for a street food vendor to buy a hot dog that the streets of midtown Manhattan are so famous for.

The two women were so hungry that they practically inhaled their two hot dogs. Then they washed the food down with a soda. During the course of their makeshift luncheon Na'eema could feel the good vibe that they always shared continuing to slowly return.

Being that it was such a nice day, Tonya and Na'eema took a walk around the block before returning to the office building. As they made their way closer to the building entrance, Tonya noticed Karen outside smoking a cigarette.

"I'm in love with a stripper," Karen sang as Tonya went through the door.

At first Tonya thought it was just a pure coincidence, until Karen passed by her office later that afternoon, singing the hit R&B tune again. Na'eema noticed it, too. At first Tonya didn't know what to make of it, but Karen kept repeating it as they walked by. This forced Tonya and Na'eema to really pay attention.

"Yo, Tonya, you heard that bitch?" Na'eema asked while they boarded the elevator.

"Think I didn't, when I did?" she replied.

"You think she just sayin' it to be sayin' it? Or she found out somethin' 'bout you?" Na'eema inquired. "This ain't a coincidence."

"I don't think so, either."

It seemed like every day Karen would come up with a different way to irk them. To Tonya and Na'eema it seemed like she stayed up nights conjuring up ways to get under their skin. But before this Karen had been a little more subtle with her games. Not anymore.

She definitely knows about me, Tonya thought. *Who she been talking to?* She knew just who to ask.

Tonya met Shakira for lunch at a small midtown delicatessen well within walking distance of the Empire State Building. The place was bustling with corporate and blue-collar types who stopped in to grab a quick bite to eat. Shakira thought it was strange that Tonya had insisted that she meet her there, rather than the two of them walking to the delicatessen together.

As soon as Tonya entered the deli, her eyes scoured the place for Shakira. She found her sitting alone at a corner table. Tonya couldn't ask for a more discreet spot than that. Tonya knew the chances of her uppity co-workers coming here were slim and none. This wasn't the type of dining they opted for. Immediately she rushed over to her.

"Hey, Shakira," Tonya said. "C'mon, let's get something to eat."

Together they went to the counter and stood on the rapidly moving line, waiting to place their individual orders.

"Miss, can I helps yous?" an older man asked in a thick Italian accent. "What yous havin' today?"

"Umm, lemme get a honey-roasted turkey with American cheese on wheat bread."

The man countered, "Mayo, mustard, lettuce, or tomatoes?"

"Nah, leave it plain," Tonya said.

"What about you?" he said, pointing his pencil at Shakira. "Whatyahavin'?"

If Tonya hadn't stopped talking, Shakira would have never known it was her turn to order. She couldn't understand a word the man had said. That was one thing she hated about New Yorkers, they talked so damn fast. With the man's heavy Italian accent thrown into the mix, she was utterly lost. One thing she liked about her small hometown, they all seemed to speak the same language. People were either black or white; that made life so simple.

As Shakira rattled off her order, the man quickly scribbled it down. Then he handed it over to his assistant on this makeshift production line. While they looked on, their sandwiches were made to order in a hurry. When they received their sandwiches, they both slid down the line and reached the cash register, where Tonya ordered two additional beverages to go with their respective sandwiches.

Sitting back down, Shakira didn't get to take a bite out of her sandwich before Tonya began questioning her.

"So, Shakira, what's the word?" she asked.

"What do you mean?"

"What's the deal with Karen?" Tonya inquired. "Has she been saying something about me?"

From the look on Shakira's face, Tonya knew she was on to something.

"All I know is that Karen is letting it drop that you're a strip-per," Shakira said. "She said some artist's manager or his friend, I don't know, recognized you from the strip club back in Philly. And ever since she found that out she has been telling anyone with two ears who'll listen. Personally, I don't think that's right. Even if you were a stripper, that's your business. She shouldn't be volunteering that kind of information about people. If God can forgive people, why can't man? Sometimes I just don't un-derstand how people can be so malicious."

Shakira's revelation about Tonya's past hadn't upset her in the least. Tonya stood fully accountable for her past. Still, she wasn't happy with the way Karen had played her. Other than that, she could live with everything that was being said about her because it was the truth. Besides, she and Q had been pre-pared for the time when someone would find out. She just didn't think it would be his sister. Tonya had to think about how to handle this. She had been careful not to trouble Q with any beef between her and Karen. And she wanted to keep it that way.

Tonya had not expected her past to collide so soon with her present. It seemed like no matter what Tonya did, her past had a way of catching up with her in some of the strangest places. But this time Tonya planned to own up to this accusation, hoping it might take some wind out of Karen's sails.

"Shakira, I'm goin' to be honest with you," Tonya began, "Yes, I was a stripper. Certain things happened in my life, wit' my family, that I really don't wanna go into at this time, that kinda forced my hand. I had to do what I had to do to survive. And maybe it wasn't right, but I had little to no other choices at that time."

Shakira admired her brutal honesty. "You don't owe me an ex-planation," she told Tonya. "I'm not sitting here passing judg-ment on you. I have a lot of respect for you. You made the best of a bad situation. Not many people could do that. That takes a lot of resiliency. God knows your intentions. Who am I? I wish this whole incident never happened. I mean, everybody has done something that they aren't so proud of." She got a funny look on her face. "Even Karen."

Tonya sensed that there was more to that comment. "Like what?" she asked.

Shakira looked a little uneasy. She leaned in and said, "I didn't know who I should tell this to. I mean, she's Q's sister, but I've been noticing that some of the money in the marketing budgets don't look right."

Tonya frowned. "In what way?"

"Well, she's been appropriating money to a company called Millennium. I've never heard of them before, but when I tried to call to find out who they were, I got a dry-cleaning place. And when I asked Karen about it, she just took the invoices out of my hand and told me that she would handle it. Tonya, thousands of dollars have been paid out to this so-called company, but there's no record of them."

Tonya was stunned. "You think she's stealing from Prestige? From Q?"

Shakira shrugged uneasily. "The only thing I'm saying right now is that something isn't right."

Tonya and Shakira reentered the office separately, each going back to their respective offices. Their new alliance would be their little secret.

"Well, what you find out?" Na'eema asked as soon as she saw her friend.

"Ole girl, Karen somehow found out about me stripping," Tonya admitted. "She's been runnin' her mouth to everybody, basically bad-mouthin' me."

"Yo, this bitch on some high school shit, talkin' 'bout people,"

Na'eema said. "Muthafuckas should be worried about gettin' they paycheck on Friday. That's it and that's all. Wait till I see that bitch. I'ma give her the bizness."

Now Tonya regretted even telling Na'eema. This was not how she wanted the situation handled. It wasn't the time or the place to be stepping to people. This was a place of business, Q's business. She felt as though she had to respect that at all costs. Q had given her a shot at a different life. There was no way she was going to take that for granted.

"I ain't feelin' that there, Na'eema," Tonya expressed. "Yo, we gettin' too old to be fightin' broads. That ain't the way to handle this. I'm gotta talk to her, see what she gotta say."

Na'eema just sucked her teeth, signaling her frustration. She wanted to handle Karen her way, but it was Tonya's call.

Tonya got up out of her seat and proceeded to walk down the hall toward Karen's office. Although her door was closed, under the circumstances Tonya saw fit to barge in completely unannounced.

Entering the office, Tonya found Karen on the phone. Before Karen could object to her unwanted presence, Tonya was upon her.

"We need to talk," Tonya said. "Like right now."

"Listen, Frank, can I call you back?" Karen spoke into the receiver. "A co-worker of mine just burst into my office unexpectedly."

Coolly, Karen placed the phone down on its cradle. An innocent expression was on her face, as if she didn't know what was going on.

"What's the meaning of this?" Karen asked with attitude.

"Look, don't play stupid wit' me. You and I both know the reason why I'm here. You been runnin' your mouth about me and that shit ain't cool. My past life don't have nothin' to do with my job performance. I do everything that y'all ask of me and more.

If you got a problem with me doin' my job, well, that's one thing. Talkin' about me behind my back to my fellow co-workers, well, that's something else. This is some real kiddie shit. You need to grow up and stop participating in that he say/she say shit. You suppose to be a grown-ass woman."

If Tonya was trying to appeal to Karen's human decency, her cries had fallen on deaf ears. Karen chose to play stupid, knowing if word of this incident got back to Q, then she would be in hot water. As it stood, it was just Tonya's word against hers, and that was the way she wanted to keep it.

"Look, I don't know what the hell you're talking about," Karen told her. "And I don't like the fact that you just came barging in here, unannounced, hurling accusations at me. What I suggest is, if you don't like what's going on around here, there's the door, leave, quit, resign. Good riddance. Do yourself a favor. We don't need your kind around here anyway."

The nasty tone of voice Karen had taken with Tonya really bothered her. She was tempted to take it to the street with her. She started to reach over the desk and snatch Karen up by her shirt collar and give her a Philly ass-whipping. She managed to restrain herself by reminding herself that this was Q's sister.

"Look, bitch," Tonya spat. "If you waitin' on me to quit, don't hold your fuckin' breath. You better get used to me 'cause I'ma be here for a good while. Just thought I'd share that with you. And another thing, you can't fool me. I know it was you who started the rumor about me bein' a stripper. Guess what? It's no rumor, it's real. I was a stripper. A fuckin' good one, too! I made more in one week than your dumb ass probably made in a whole month. Now, don't that make you mad? You went to school all those years, wastin' Q's money, and we almost got the same position. So if it's anyone's leavin' here it'll be you. One day, I'ma have your fuckin' job, so watch your back!"

She continued, "And don't even think you're going to drop

this bomb on Q because he already knows I was a stripper—emphasis on *was*." Tonya turned to leave. "One more thing. My name ain't dick, so keep it out of your mouth!"

Tonya stormed out of Karen's office, slamming the door behind her. She had made a bold proclamation and she had no idea just how she was going to carry out the threat or if she even wanted to. That bitch had just made her so mad. One thing was clear, however. Things weren't over between them. Not by a long shot.

After her verbal confrontation with Karen, Tonya kept an extra-low profile. She had no idea what Karen was going to do—if she was going to go running to Q or keep her mouth shut. But Tonya knew that now it was on and she had little room for error.

"Tonya, you have a call on line three," the receptionist said through the intercom.

Tonya picked up the phone, pressing the button for line three.

"This is Tonya," she said.

"Tonya Morris?" the caller asked.

"Yes, who is this?"

"It's me!" the caller said. "Ya cousin, Nay-Nay! Natasha."

"Nay-Nay?"

Instantly, Tonya was suspicious of the identity of the caller. Yes, Tonya did have a cousin named Nay-Nay, but she was much younger than Tonya. And her little cousin had been just a baby when the family turned their back on her.

Tonya continued, "I don't believe this is my cousin Nay-Nay. If you my cousin, tell me my grandmother's name."

"MaryAnn Morris," she instantly replied.

Hearing the correct answer was enough to make Tonya a believer that the person on the other end of the phone was indeed her family. Now Tonya's only other concern was, how did she find her? And why was she calling her?

Not that Tonya had anything against Nay-Nay. She didn't. She was too young to know what was going on or to help her. Everyone else in her family was subject to Tonya's wrath except her. Nay-Nay had a pass when it came to the hate Tonya felt in her heart for her family.

"Okay, you are who you say you are," Tonya said. "Now what's the deal? How the hell you find me? And why you callin' me?"

"Damn, cuz. It's like that?" Nay-Nay stated. "You ain't got no love for me? I ain't got shit to do wit whatever happened wit the rest of them tired motherfuckers that we call family."

Tonya interrupted, "Look, I don't got time for a long conversation. I'm at work. So matter of fact, I don't care how you found me, all I really need to know is what do you want?"

Tonya's strong statement caused Na'eema to come to her office door. She raised her eyebrows in puzzlement.

"Who that?" she whispered.

By placing one finger to her lips, Tonya gestured to her friend to be quiet. "Wait a minute," she mouthed.

"Look, I know you don't fuck with the family like that. But this is something I thought you should know. It about your mother. She's in the hospital and it don't look good. They say she on her deathbed. So irregardless of how you may feel about us, that is your mother. You need to go see her before she passes away," Nay-Nay explained.

"Nay-Nay, who put you up to this?" Tonya asked. "Which one of them sorry sonofabitches told you to call me, huh?"

"Tonya, does it matter? Real talk. Your mother is in Temple University Hospital and it don't look good," Nay-Nay said. "Fuck the dumb shit, you need to carry your ass back to Philly and see about her."

The years hadn't done anything to quell Tonya's anger toward her mother and her family. If anything, this phone call opened up old wounds. Tonya's hatred for her mother was blinding her to the reality of the situation.

"Nay-Nay, nuttin' against you, but it's personal between me, my mother, and the rest of her family. So fuck my so-called family. And the hell wit' my mother! I hope she does die! It shoulda happened a long time ago! Bye!"

Tonya slammed the phone down with such force and fury, she almost broke it. She was hurt by the audacity of her family, contacting her after all these years. How dare they? The last time she had seen anyone in her family, it was the time one of her male cousins had come to the strip club and tried to blackmail her. Tonya and company had assaulted him and then the bouncers joined in and finished what they started.

Only catching bits and pieces of a one-sided conversation, Na'eema could tell that it was someone from Tonya's family who had called.

"Tonya, who the hell was that?" Na'eema asked.

"My fuckin' family!" she raged. "Do you believe that shit? They got some fuckin' nerve callin' me. I told you what they did to me, right? Never fails soon as a bitch start doin' good. Muthafuckas come outta the woodwork. They talkin' 'bout my mother in the hospital and she might die. Like I care."

It took more than a few minutes for Tonya to calm down. But when she did, Na'eema gave her the business. She chastised her friend for her ignorance, telling Tonya of her own family problems.

"Tonya," she began. "I couldn't help but overhear ya conversation. You know I love you to death, but you're wrong. I don't think you should do your mom like that. You should go see her."

Tonya replied, "Look, I appreciate your concern, but frankly that was an A&B conversation. You see where I going with this. . . . My mother and my family did some shit to me that was totally uncalled for. No child should have to go through what I went through. That shit was inexcusable. That bitch turned her back on me and didn't think twice."

She replied, "I understand that, Tonya."

"No, you don't!" Tonya snapped. "You don't understand what it was like to be abandoned by your mother at a young age and forced to sell your body just to get the basic necessities in life."

"You think you the only one on the face of the earth that has family issues?" Na'eema asked her. "Because you're not. Lemme tell you something. My mother was on drugs real bad for most my life and my father was a good-for-nothing, deadbeat dad. He never gave a dime. Everything I ever had was hand-me-down clothes from my older cousins. I had to wait until they outgrew their clothes before I could get some new ones. I grew up despising my mother and hating my father. I blamed my father for everything that went wrong in my life. Because he promised he was going to come take me to live with him but he never came. . . . When I got older he suddenly fell ill with a life-threatening illness. And I didn't even bother to go see him. He died shortly after that. I regret not going up there to see him. I regret not making my peace with that man before he died. Please, I'm begging you, don't make the same mistake I did. Go see your mother. Irregardless what happened between y'all, she's still your mother and you at least owe her that much respect. You only get one mother. When she goes you won't get another."

Although Tonya had Q's private number, she had never before even thought about using it. She had no reason to, at least not until now.

"Hello?" she heard Q say.

"Um, hi, Q?" she said. "It's Tonya."

"Hey, Tonya, what's up?"

"Listen, I need some time off," she told him. "Seems like my mother is in the hospital."

"Yo, I'm sorry to hear that. Take as much time as you need. When are you leaving?"

"Tomorrow morning if I can."

"I'll send a car over, then, so you can ride down in comfort," he told her.

"Oh, no, that ain't necessary. I'm just going to hop on Amtrak."

"Ain't no point dealing with them crowds when you trying to go see your people in the hospital. Just take the car."

Tonya sighed. "All right. Thanks, Q."

He must have heard something in her voice because he said, "You sure you're all right?"

"Yeah, yeah, it's just . . . family, you know?"

Q laughed. "Yeah, I know, baby girl. But listen, don't let anyone get you too down. Just keep ya head up, all right?"

Tonya smiled. "Yeah, all right."

"Let me know if you need anything, okay?"

Tonya felt better just having Q make the offer. This dude always seemed to know the right things to say. But then the picture of him and Niecey, all hugged up on each other, popped into her mind and Tonya felt her heart grow heavy again.

13

A black chauffeur-driven Lincoln limousine awaited Tonya as she stepped out of her New Jersey residence. The car was befitting the executive that she now was. It wasn't a flashy vehicle, but a comfortable and reliable one. Q had offered to send Tonya a luxurious stretch limo so she could go back to Philly in style, but Tonya had declined. She claimed she didn't want Q to waste any money on her. She was thankful enough for the time off the job he had given her to attend to the matter.

As soon as the chauffeur saw Tonya approaching, he quickly exited from the driver's side and offered her some assistance.

"Let me help you with that, ma'am," he said, reaching for her bag.

"Oh, I'm okay. The suitcase isn't as heavy as it looks," she replied.

"Nonsense," he countered, taking the bag from her. "I insist."

He popped the car's trunk open and she watched as he carefully placed her Louis Vuitton suitcase in the spacious trunk. Swiftly the chauffeur moved toward the back passenger door and opened it. Immediately Tonya stepped inside. She found the interior much to her liking. It was roomy, with black butter-soft leather seats. Once Tonya got settled inside, she knew if the ride was as comfortable as the interior was cozy, then she would have a good trip back home.

After buckling his seatbelt, the chauffeur adjusted his seat and mirrors, preparing for the short drive to Philadelphia. Suddenly it occurred to him that his passenger might like to listen to the radio, a special station in particular.

"Ma'am, would you like to listen to the radio?"

At first Tonya was tempted to have the driver turn the radio on to New York's hottest radio station, Hot 97 FM, the *Miss Jones Morning Show.* Quickly she decided against it. She had some work to look over. The radio would only distract her.

"No, I'm good!" she explained. "If you don't mind, I'd rather not listen to anything."

The chauffeur replied, "As you wish, ma'am."

From that point on the two were in their own worlds. While the chauffeur concentrated on the road, Tonya busied herself with her work.

As the car maneuvered down the New Jersey Turnpike toward Philadelphia, Tonya found it harder and harder to devote her full attention to the task at hand. Her mind began to wander and her thoughts began to drift as she recalled the words of her cousin, Nay-Nay.

"Your mother's very sick. She's in the hospital. She might die!"

Tonya didn't know how to take the news. Why was Nay-Nay calling her now? She couldn't help but feel a little suspicious. Tonya felt like a lottery winner who had recently come into a large sum of money and everybody and their mother was trying to get a piece of it. It was funny to her how they had even found her after all these years. She always felt that if she never saw her family or her mother again in this life, then it would be too soon. Thoughts of her mother and her family evoked bad memories for Tonya. It had been a bad time in her life.

She hadn't seen or heard from her mother in close to five years. For a young girl making the transition from adolescence to adulthood in a sex-driven environment, it felt like a lifetime.

Things happen for a reason, Tonya thought. *Maybe my life was supposed to turn out like this to get me to this point.*

Tonya was desperately trying to put a positive spin on an ugly situation. But try as she might, she couldn't. There wasn't any right to what her mother had done. No matter how she looked at it, her mother had chosen to take a man's word over her own child's and she had abandoned her. The rape had pushed their already volatile relationship over the edge.

Still, Tonya knew of plenty of kids from her North Philly neighborhood who had difficult upbringings that included absentee fathers and drug-addicted mothers, but none of the remaining parents had ever done their children like this. Her mother just packed up and split, leaving Tonya to fend for herself, alone in the cold, cruel world. Coming home from school to an empty apartment was the moment that haunted her the most. The realization of her mother's betrayal had suddenly sunk in.

Every day that Tonya danced at the strip club, she prayed that her mother would appear and save her from that life. Whenever the doors of the club swung open, she hoped to see her mother's face leading the charge to rescue her. But it never happened. As the days went by, Tonya lost all hope and faith in her mother.

Once upon a time, Tonya had dreamed of finishing high school, going to college, and having a family of her own. Then reality had intervened, altering her plans, shattering her dreams, and damn near ruining her life. The grace of God and a never-say-die attitude was what kept her alive. It was what allowed her to succeed where many others had failed. She took the road less traveled and still managed to make something of herself.

Tonya had made many mistakes in her life. Matter of fact, her life had been one big trial and error. But right now things were so good that even she couldn't complain about the things that had come before it. Her sudden reversal of fortune had made life worthwhile. That was, until her family decided to resurface and contact her on her mother's behalf.

She had finally agreed to see her mother with the intent of putting that part of her past behind her. Na'eema was the one who made her realize that it wouldn't do her any good to dwell on the past. It was she who made Tonya see that human beings are fallible. So what if that irresponsible person is your parent, they still deserve the benefit of the doubt. Veronica Morris still deserved a second chance.

Tonya thought that that was easier said than done. But she would hear her mother's side of the story, if nothing else.

She also couldn't help having the sneaking suspicion that something else was up.

Tonya rode in total silence. All she could hear was the whistling of the wind. She swore that she could hear herself thinking. As Tonya sat silently in the back seat, quietly reflecting on her problems, she didn't even realize just how much distance the chauffeur had put between them and New York City. She looked out the window, hearing the whistling of the wind, and a light sprinkle began to fall, further dampening her spirits. Rain had always been her mood-swing drug.

The car crossed the Ben Franklin Bridge, which separated New Jersey from Pennsylvania, and she was home. Tonya was Philly through and through. The whole essence of the struggle that was her life embodied the city. She was born and raised here, so naturally she missed her city. Even though she had only been gone a few months, she missed it more than she could have imagined.

"Excuse me, driver," Tonya said suddenly. "Before you take me to the hospital, I wanna go somewhere else first."

The chauffeur made eye contact with Tonya through the rearview mirror and nodded. He carefully followed her instructions and shortly they were there. The chauffeur couldn't help but wonder if he had taken a wrong turn or something. The landscape of the City of Brotherly Love had changed from inviting to downright menacing. Tonya knew that her chauffeur was uneasy about being in the hood, but she didn't care. He was getting paid handsomely to perform a service, to take her wherever she wanted to go, and right now that just so happened to be her old North Philly neighborhood, the Badlands.

Now that Tonya had a taste of the high life, her old rundown block on 9th Avenue looked like a battle zone. The homes were even shabbier than she remembered. Stolen and stripped cars littered the street. Trash dotted the landscape. Tonya had wanted to look at her former residence for perspective. She had wanted to look at where she had come from. It made her appreciate everything that she had gone through thus far.

The significance of the moment may have been lost on her chauffeur, but to Tonya it was perfectly clear. She saw where she had been, the bottom; now she knew where she was going, to the top. Tonya had dealt with adversity all her life, and still managed to make something out of herself. She felt proud. At the same time, she felt sorry for those who weren't as fortunate as her, who didn't see the light at the end of the tunnel.

"Slow down," Tonya advised him. "I'm trying to see if I see somebody."

Intently Tonya searched the deserted street, taking mental notes of her childhood friends' homes. She hoped to spot someone she knew. But all she saw were signs of decay and despair. It was moments like these that made her realize that nothing was like it used to be. Things were getting worse not better.

How could Tonya come back to this? There was nothing left to even come back to. This wasn't Center City, a tourist magnet. This was the hood, the Badlands, the place that was forgotten by city officials.

Still, Tonya let these images of poverty burn into her mind so she would never forget where she came from, so that she would be forever grounded, humble, and hungry. Scenes like these made her appreciate her new life that much more.

After taking a brief diversion back down memory lane, Tonya instructed her chauffeur to go back to downtown Philadelphia to her hotel. Once she checked in and dropped off her luggage in her room, Tonya went to the hospital.

When the car pulled up outside Temple University Hospital, Tonya took a deep breath and stepped out of the limo, unsure of what to expect inside.

"Oh, my God, Tonya?" Veronica Morris weakly called out. "Is that you?"

The moment Tonya set foot inside her mother's room, she was recognized immediately. Although it had been some time since they had last seen each other, Veronica knew her child's walk anywhere.

Staring in disbelief at her child, looking so beautiful and fashionable, Veronica couldn't help but think, *I used to be young and beautiful.* Her mind raced backward to yesteryear. There she was a young girl, a sophomore at Simon Gratz High School, falling in love for the first time. By her junior year, she was pregnant and a high school dropout. A few months later she was a single mother, raising Tonya on her own. Fast forward several years, she was abusing then abandoning her daughter. Now the young girl she had left stood before her as a grown woman.

Tonya was shocked by her mother's poor physical appearance. Her complexion had darkened and she had lost a lot of weight. Tonya almost didn't recognize her. She had no idea that her mother was doing this bad.

"Tonya?" Veronica asked again. "Is that you?"

"Yeah, Veronica," she said dryly. "It's me."

Under normal conditions, Tonya would have rushed over to her mother's bedside and embraced her, maybe even shed a tear or two, after not seeing her mother for so long. But she kept her distance, as if her mother had an infectious disease that she didn't want to catch. Tonya stood at the foot of the bed with a stoic look on her face.

Though heavily sedated, Veronica could feel the air of negativity in the room. She could feel the hurt in her heart. She still heard those demons in her head that told her to leave her daughter. Now she regretted bowing out of her daughter's life when she needed her the most.

"Where is he?" Tonya asked. Long ago she had promised herself that if she ever saw her mother's boyfriend Pete again, she would try her best to kill him. Another reason she needed to know was that if her mother was still with him, then there was no reason for her to even be here.

Her mother knew who she was talking about. She took a deep breath. It pained her to talk about Pete, the man who had raped her daughter and whom she had run off with. The thought of his violation and deceit caused her great heartache.

"Pete gone!" she said. "He's dead! That no-good nigger passed away the year before last. He died from a heart attack."

"Good!" Tonya exclaimed, her voice boiling with anger. "I hope he suffered, too!"

Tonya had always heard it was bad to speak ill of the dead. Normally she would have respected that, but not in this case. Whenever she thought of the bastard who had stolen her virginity, the man who basically turned her life completely upside down, naturally it evoked some ill will in her. With those words she unleashed all the bitterness, frustration, and anger in her heart. There was a sick feeling inside her that led her to celebrate the demise of another human being.

Unable to do anything to comfort her daughter, Veronica did

the only thing she could do and cried. She felt totally helpless. She kicked herself for being ignorant of the fact of what really happened between Tonya and Pete.

Veronica was overcome by emotion, but Tonya showed none. Nothing could make her change her stone-faced expression. To her this admission was too much, too little and too late. Her mother had done her wrong. Now it was time that she dealt with it like a woman. She had run from the truth and Tonya for all these years.

It was too bad that Tonya had so little empathy for the woman who birthed her. The streets had made her that way. There was a divide that now existed between the two women, and it had to be conquered before they could resume their roles as mother and daughter.

Tonya wasn't the same person her mother had walked out on some years ago. No, this wasn't the lost little black girl looking for her mommy.

Just then Veronica's physician walked in. This brief interruption in their conversation saved Veronica from further embarrassment. Immediately he asked to see Tonya in the hallway.

In a heavy Indian accent he asked, "Excuse me, ma'am, are you related to the patient?"

"Yeah, I'm her daughter," she reluctantly admitted. "If that's what you want to call me."

"I see," he said. "Please, try not to upset your mother. She is a very sick woman. She needs all the rest she can get."

"What's wrong with her, Doc?" Tonya wondered.

The doctor fell silent for a moment as he searched his mind for the layman's terms to describe Veronica Morris's ailment. He was so used to medical jargon that the task proved more difficult than it really was.

"Your mother is inflicted with a disease called focal glomerulosclerosis. The disease attacks the tiny filters in the kidneys that remove waste from the blood. That makes the kidneys spill protein from the blood into the urine, resulting in kidney damage that could lead to kidney failure, which requires dialysis or a transplant. In your mother's case it is the latter, because she wasn't properly diagnosed earlier."

Suddenly Tonya knew the reason why she was called. She suspected that her family members believed that she could be a possible kidney donor, that she could save her mother's life. If that was the case, they better think again. Tonya wasn't about to donate an organ to a woman who had left her for dead. Why should she? In her book her mother was a rotten bitch who deserved everything that happened to her. It was unfathomable to her that anyone in her family would fix their face to even ask her that question. She guessed that was why those cowards had put the doctor up to it. Still, it didn't matter who it came from, the answer was no.

Tonya could remember when, as a child, her mother was the center of her universe. Everything she did was an effort to please her. Her mother was a strict disciplinarian whom she obeyed. At times she waited on her mother hand and foot.

It was probably fitting that the mother now needed the daughter after all those years that Tonya had needed Veronica and she wasn't there. Tonya was all but certain she was going to let her mother die. She wasn't about to risk her life for the likes of her mother.

The next day when Tonya arrived at the hospital she had convinced herself that she had done all she was going to do. But she wanted to look Veronica in her eyes, like a woman, and tell her there was nothing she could do for her. Now that their roles were reversed she wanted her mother to know what it was like to feel unloved.

Veronica Morris was propped up in her bed, watching a game show, *The Price Is Right*. She hadn't noticed Tonya as she silently entered the room, so Tonya took the opportunity to lean against the wall and study her mother. Tonya was disgusted by the person she saw. The longer she stared at the woman, the more she remembered how Pete had violated her and the look of hate in her mother's eyes when she tried to tell her. The one person who was supposed to protect her had thrown her to the wolves. The rage, pain, and loneliness built and built up inside Tonya until she felt like she wanted to hit, pull, tear, and hurt her mother the way she had been hurt.

"Bitch, I hate you!" she spat all of a sudden. "What you did to me was unforgivable!"

Veronica jerked her attention from the TV in shock. She stared in surprise as her daughter slowly walked toward her. Tonya's harsh words cut her down. She was hurt that Tonya would fix her mouth to talk to her like that. She raised her remote and turned off the TV with a click. But Veronica was all cried out. Yesterday after Tonya had left, she had cried and cried and cried.

"You musta lost your goddamn mind," Veronica said, becoming heated. "How dare you talk to me like that? I know you hurting, but I'm hurting, too."

"Yeah, I did lose my mind. Right around the same time I lost my mother," Tonya replied. "Do you have any idea of what my life was like after you left? Do you know what I had to do just to survive?"

Veronica stared at her daughter, then closed her eyes and took a deep breath. She opened them again and looked at Tonya. "No," she replied, "I don't know what life was like for you. Sometimes I wondered, though."

"Well, you ain't got to wonder anymore!" Tonya informed her. "Veronica Morris, your daughter used to strip for a living. This is what I had to resort to just to get by. Night in and night out, I was shaking my ass up onstage in front of men old enough to be my father. Do you know how that made me feel? Bad! But I got over it."

Veronica put her hands over her eyes as if she could keep herself from seeing Tonya's pain. Her selfish acts had caused a devastating domino effect, the aftereffects of which Tonya was still struggling to overcome to this day. Although the news tore her apart inside, Veronica knew that there was nothing she could do about it. She couldn't undo what she had already done. She desperately wanted to say something in her own defense, but she thought better of it. What could she possibly say to ease her daughter's pain?

Tonya felt so much better now that she had confessed her sins to her mother. It was as if a burden had suddenly been lifted off her chest. *Let Veronica take that to her grave with her,* she thought.

"Look, I gotta go," Tonya said, shaking her head. "I've already expended too much energy dealing with this situation. I'm done with you. There's nothing I can do for you. That's all I came to say."

Veronica Morris watched her daughter turn around and march out of her hospital room for what she thought was the last time. She knew that she would never see her daughter ever again. Just as Tonya was about to exit the room, Veronica called out. Tonya froze with her hand on the door handle

"Tonya! Tonya, I'm sorry for what I've done to you! I can't take it back. All I want you to know is, if I never see you again, I love you."

I love you. Those words echoed in Tonya's ears. It seemed as if her entire life, Tonya had waited to hear those words. Throughout her entire adolescence Veronica had been so hard on her. She had constantly chastised her for the tiniest mistake she had made. Not even once could Tonya remember her mother uttering those words to her like she just had. It seemed like she had waited a lifetime to hear them. All she ever wanted was to love and be loved by her mother.

"You love me, huh?" Tonya repeated. "It's funny how it took something like this for you to say that to me. You don't love me. What you really meant to say is you need me. If you ever loved me there's no way in the world you ever would have done what you did to me. How could you leave something you love as easily as that? Your child. And never come back to get me?"

Tonya stared angrily at her mother, demanding an answer to a lifelong question that had dogged her to this day.

"Tonya," her mother began painfully. It seemed as if the words were being ripped from her. "Believe it or not, when I was much younger than you, I was . . . raped, too."

Tonya stared at Veronica in shock. She had expected her to say anything but that.

"I never told nobody," she said, staring down at her hands, which were clenched in her lap. "I was gonna carry that secret to my grave. It was my daddy's best friend who raped me. He told me if I ever told anyone he'd kill my whole family. . . . So I know what it's like to be violated. I know what it's like to have a grown man thrust his manhood inside the womb of a child."

Never in her wildest dreams would Tonya have ever guessed that her mother was also a victim of rape, that she, too, was robbed of her innocence.

"When that happened to you," she continued, "honestly, I didn't know what to do, how to react or how to believe. To tell you the truth, I didn't want to deal with the situation again. It brought back a lot of bad memories. So I left you, in part to protect you from that ever happening again at the hands of Pete. I was going to come back for you as soon as I got my mind straight. As soon as I got rid of Pete. But I was too finanically dependent on that man to ever leave him. Tonya, I'm sorry. But baby, I just lost it. That's all I can say."

Tears filled Veronica's eyes as she was forced to come to terms with her dastardly deed. Years and years of built-up frustration were released on a moment's notice as a floodgate of tears suddenly ran down her cheeks as her body was wracked by crying.

Her mother's heartfelt explanation had a profound effect on Tonya. Slowly tears began to trickle down her face. Tonya's tears were clear indications that she was not alone. Never mind that her mother's explanation of her disappearance was years late. Tonya turned and quietly left her mother's hospital room, her mind and heart heavy.

Tonya had stayed up way into the night thinking, and finally decided that there was just no way she could walk away from her mother now. After putting their differences aside, Tonya underwent the battery of tests to see if she could become an organ donor for her mother. Once she was identified as a positive match, emergency surgery was scheduled a few days later.

Although Tonya was afraid to go under the knife, she put her fear aside for the greater good. All she would remember about the procedure was being wheeled into the operating room and receiving anesthesia. Tonya and her mother would endure a three-hour operation to replace her mother's ailing kidney.

The operation was deemed a success. Still, there was a chance that Veronica Morris's body might reject her daughter's kidney. At Temple University Hospital the survival rate was ninety-five percent or better after one year and eighty-eight percent after three years. No medical procedure was one hundred percent perfect, though the chances were slim that something would go wrong. Yet still they were there. For the doctors and Tonya it would be a wait-and-see process.

Once Veronica and Tonya Morris's medical condition had stabilized, they were transported out of the ICU to the acute care unit of the hospital. Their stay there would be closely monitored under the watchful eye of a trained kidney specialist.

When the anesthesia finally wore off, Tonya awoke in a hospital bed with a physician monitoring her condition, naked as the day she was born, underneath the cheap hospital gown.

Tonya moaned in pain.

"Is everything okay, Ms. Morris?" the physician suddenly asked.

Tonya merely nodded her head as she waited for the pain to subside.

The physician continued, "Don't worry. The pain you are experiencing is normal after undergoing a kidney procedure."

"Doc, could I get something for the pain?" she asked. "It hurts."

"Of course. I'll notify the nurse of your request immediately."

With her eyes Tonya followed the doctor as he left the room. It was then that she took notice of her surroundings. Suddenly she realized there was an IV hooked up to her arm. To her immediate right she noticed her mother resting comfortably. Tonya lay there silently for a few minutes of quiet reflection while staring at her mother. Suddenly she became sentimental as tears glistened down both her cheeks. She said a silent prayer for her mother's speedy recovery. She had done her part; now hopefully God would do his, and spare her mother's life.

Veronica Morris looked so peaceful lying in her heavily medicated state that Tonya hated to bother her. This was the loving mother she had remembered as a child, the woman who had nursed her back to health when she was sick. This wasn't the monster who had administered a savage beating to her and later abandoned her for a man.

Talking to her mother had done a lot to help ease the pain. But it hadn't totally erased all the misfortune and mistakes of the past. But love conquers all. Though Tonya's wounds were slow to heal, they healed.

Now Tonya was in forgive-and-forget mode. Life had a strange way of administering doses of humility when one least expected it. If she learned one thing from this entire ordeal, it was that life was too short to harbor hatred in her heart for her mother. She vowed to get past that. It was a struggle, but somehow, some way, she vowed to get past it.

The healing process was slow. It came in small doses for Tonya and Veronica, both physically and emotionally. The two women talked for hours and hours while they recovered. Other times they lay side by side in their individual beds without uttering a word. Together they experienced more than their fair share of ups and downs. Some days were just better than others. Despite the pain, they got through it together.

After recuperating in the hospital for five days, both women were given a clean bill of health. Upon leaving the hospital, Tonya and her mother received a comprehensive schedule of follow-up doctors' visits for lab tests and checkups, which was common for all kidney transplant patients. The reason for this was to track the patient's progress and detect any potentially hazardous complications.

At home Tonya and Veronica continued to bond. Tonya told her mother all about her job, her friend Na'eema, and Q. She poured out her heart to her mother, revealing her innermost feelings. Veronica could hear the first hints of sadness in her voice as Tonya talked about her and Q's brief past relationship.

Recognizing young love when she saw it, Veronica encouraged her daughter to go after the man she wanted. As the days went by and she began to get better, Veronica urged her daughter to leave, to go find her true happiness.

Q sent a limousine to bring Tonya back to her Edgewater, New Jersey, apartment. The driver couldn't get her out of her old North Philadelphia neighborhood fast enough. Tonya wasn't feeling the hood anymore. The element of danger that she had learned to live with now made her uneasy. The Badlands was a place where crime was so prevalent and inescapable that she feared for the safety of her mother as well. Tonya promised herself that the next time she spoke to her mother she was going to talk to her about moving into a better place.

Tonya's sudden appearance in the hood may not have caused much of a stir, but her lavish exodus did. Certain people in the hood began inquiring about her.

14

After a full recovery, Tonya felt like a brand-new woman in more ways than one. Physically she was back on her feet and could focus on obtaining the ultimate: Q. She didn't care where she had to travel or how far she had to go to get him, but he was hers. So when Q offered her the opportunity to go out of the country, to the Bahamas, with some other staff members and recording artists to put the finishing touches on an album, she jumped at the chance. At this point she would do anything just to get close to him.

If this was Q's way of telling her to take a break after going through that lengthy ordeal with her mother, then she would gladly take it. To be honest, Tonya really did need a break. The last month or so had been nothing but drama. She needed to get away for a minute to recharge her batteries, and this was a welcome diversion. It would also be nice to get away from the winter weather and soak up some sunshine, take long walks on the beach, maybe just be a kid again.

Teterboro Airport in Bergen County in northern New Jersey was the rendezvous place. At the crack of dawn, two private Lear jets sat on the runway, waiting to whisk the two dozen or so employees of Prestige Records away to the tropical destination. Although this trip was strictly business and not pleasure, Tonya planned on turning it into a working vacation. She was going to take a sightseeing tour of the island the first chance she got. This would be only her second time on an airplane and her first time out of the country.

Unfortunately, Tonya had the misfortune to be on the jet that Q wasn't aboard. She just couldn't catch a break when it came to Q. He was never alone—there was always someone or something he had to deal with. Most of the time it was business. If this persisted, Tonya would have to rethink her plan of attack.

But even now she had moments when she wondered, *What would stop him from hurting her again?*

A million thoughts raced through Tonya's mind as she fastened her seatbelt and the plane prepared to take off. She also couldn't seem to stop worrying about her mother back in Philly. She had pretty much made up her mind that there would be no discussion. She was moving her mother out of the Badlands. Tonya wished Na'eema had chosen to come. Instead she had gone back to Philly to visit her boyfriend and check on her own ailing mother. Who was Tonya to suggest she do otherwise? When it came to that, Tonya totally understood. She couldn't wait to get back and tell Na'eema everything that happened down in the Bahamas. No matter how minute or insignificant the situation was, Tonya planned to tell all. That being the case, still, there was no replacing Na'eema. Her company was invaluable to Tonya. There was nothing like being with her girl, no matter where they were.

There was one person who was noticeably absent from the trip, and that person was Karen. Tonya didn't know where she was or why she wasn't there, but she was glad she wasn't. At least Tonya wouldn't have to deal with her bullshit. Karen kept something stirred up whenever she came around.

Bursting through fluffy white pillows of clouds, the Lear jet began to make its descent. Suddenly the jet hit pockets of turbulence that violently shook the plane, awakening Tonya from her sound sleep. She opened her eyes just in time to see the beautiful tropical paradise below.

Tonya was drenched by warm tropical rays of sunshine as she departed the plane. Already Q and his small entourage had gathered their bags and made the short trip across the runway to the awaiting limousines.

Tonya was still feeling sluggish from her long nap on the plane. Still, she wasn't in such a foul mood that she couldn't enjoy the sudden shift in temperature. The weather in the Bahamas was extremely different from that of New York City at this time of year. Although it was late March, the northeast was still dealing with Old Man Winter.

Tonya laughed to herself, already starting to leave her worries behind. She couldn't wait to call Shakira and rub it in her face. To actually think she had passed on the trip because it was her boyfriend's birthday this week.

She doesn't know what she's missing, Tonya thought.

The word *rest* wasn't in Q's vocabulary. He gave orders to all employees to go straight to their rooms, shower, and do whatever it was they had to do, but to be ready for work in an hour. Q had booked studio time for all his recording artists, and in the music business, time was money. Q didn't have any of either to waste.

Q's reasons for leaving the States became clear even to Tonya. This was done to limit distractions. He had intentionally taken them out of their environment to concentrate on making good music.

While down in the Bahamas, Tonya saw Q up close and personal and started to understand what made him tick. Tonya began to see that Q was a tireless worker, a relentless taskmaster who had a vision for his record label. He pushed every one of his artists to write the perfect hook or hit that high note. Whatever their forte was, he pushed to get the most out of them.

And now that they were working closely together, Q was starting to recognize Tonya's strong work ethic. Finally she was being appreciated by the man himself, and he realized that Tonya's value extended far beyond profits.

Over the course of the next few days, Tonya and Q spent endless hours at late-night recording sessions.

In Tonya's observation of Q, she quickly realized why he was in the position he was in as label owner. He was driven. Q worked long hours and slept only when necessary. Some days his work often left him wishing for more hours in a day. More often than not, it also left Tonya longing for sleep. This wasn't the way she had dreamed of being with him, but she'd take it.

Q found that Tonya had good instincts for what was going to help sell an artist when it came to the complete package. She made some suggestions along the way that he found himself taking into consideration.

They would often take small breaks together and she would ask him about his son, his family, his interests. And Tonya seemed like she genuinely wanted to know. She was different from any other female he had ever been with. Other women had only been interested in his money, his sex skills, and/or his fame, even Niecey. But Tonya was proving to be different.

Even more surprising was that he was honestly interested in her. He asked her about her mother and listened as she shared her concerns about where her mom was living. Q made a note to himself to see if there wasn't something he could do about that when he got back to New York. But the more he talked to Tonya, the more he realized how much she had been through and how much she had grown up since the last time they had been together. And it made him want her more—not just her body, but the complete package. And he planned to make her his before they left the island.

The torrential rains were the first sign of what was to come. A combination of high winds and intense rains battered the Bahamas and anything else foolish enough to stand in its path. It was as if Mother Nature had a point to prove. Forecasters had predicted that when the storm was over, the damage to the island would run well into the tens of millions of dollars. Everyone braced for the worst.

From the comforts of their five-star hotel, Tonya, Q, and the rest of the employees of Prestige Records weathered the storm. It was surreal to them how a bustling tourist attraction had been reduced to a ghost town in a matter of hours. It was like a scene out of a monster movie. The locals abandoned the streets like Godzilla was coming to town. They knew what the vacationers did not—that the forces of nature weren't to be taken lightly.

"I don't believe this fuckin' shit!" Tonya said.

From time to time she walked over to the window and looked out to witness the beating that Mother Nature was putting on the island.

Tonya was impressed by what she saw. After all, she was from the East Coast, so she had been in her fair share of inclement weather, but this was the worst she'd ever seen.

If the storm didn't kill her, Tonya thought the loneliness would. She had been holed up in her suite for almost a whole day now. Daylight had come and gone, and she was still doing the same thing—nothing. Nothing but sleeping, eating, and taking long showers. Although she had to admit that her suite was cozy, with all the comforts of home, it was too bad half of the electronic appliances didn't work, like the television or radio. The storm had knocked out power across the island.

Tonya began using room service as a strange form of entertainment. She would put in various orders for meals and snacks, and wait to see who the hotel would send to her room with the food. Each time she did it she hoped that she would get some handsome black Bahamian gentlemen to serve her. Then maybe that would entice her to have a one-night stand. She had even gone so far as to put on a bright pink satin and black chiffon nightie with matching thong along with some sexy high-heeled shoes. After a few failed attempts, Tonya quickly dismissed the notion. She left the role-playing fantasies to the Terry McMillan novels. Her luck just didn't run like that.

Growing tired of staring out the window, Tonya wandered over to the bed before deciding to take another long, hot shower. Exiting the shower Tonya began to apply lotion to every part of her body. She slipped on a white wifebeater and some gray coochie shorts that left little to the imagination.

Just as Tonya prepared to get into the bed and slip under the covers, there came a knock at the door.

Now y'all mothafuckas come? Tonya said to herself. *I forgot I even ordered anything.*

Picking up her game again, Tonya tiptoed to the door and looked out the peephole. What she saw on the other side of the door wasn't appealing at all. A short old black man, with a potbelly and receding hairline, stood on the other side of the door.

Oh well! she thought. *So much for that. Ain't no way in hell I'm givin' him some ass. I ain't that desperate.*

"Yes?" Tonya asked.

"Room service," the man stated dryly.

"Who sent you?" Tonya joked.

He repeated, "Room service."

"I said, who sent you?" she laughed.

"Look, ma'am, you want it or not?" he asked. "I don't have time to play games. I have other guests to attend to."

Seeing the man was clearly frustrated, Tonya quickly opened the door. She was greeted by a pleasant surprise.

Before she could even object, the waiter proceeded to wheel in two bottles of Dom Perignon champagne and a large fruit salad. Instantly his eyes became glued to Tonya's tank top and her nipples, which pressed against the thin cotton material of her top. The waiter almost pushed the cart into a wall, he was staring so hard.

"There must be some mistake. I didn't order this," Tonya said.

There was no way she was going to pay for those expensive bottles of champagne. It cost at least a quarter of her weekly salary.

"Excuse me, ma'am, is your name Tonya?" the waiter asked, reading off a card.

"Yeah, but . . ."

"This was sent to you by a gentleman by the name of Q," he told her. "Don't worry, he's already taken care of the bill. Enjoy."

"Oh, okay!" Tonya boasted while closing the door. "This nigger Q gotta lil' class about him."

Tonya's first thought was, *What's the occasion?* But she quickly put the thought out of her mind. She wasn't one to turn anything down, especially anything free.

Tonya normally didn't drink, but this wasn't a normal circumstance. She was bored out of her mind, frustrated about Q, lonely, and scared about the weather. She needed something to take her mind off these things. She could also use something that would help her go to sleep. And if this bottle of Dom could help her, then so be it.

Just as Tonya was about to bust open a bottle of champagne, she realized that she didn't have any champagne glasses to drink out of. She raced to the door and poked her head out, hoping to catch a glimpse of the waiter. Unfortunately, he was nowhere to be seen. Tonya closed the door and headed for the phone to call room service.

"Hello?" she said into the receiver. "Could I get some champagne glasses up in Room 894?"

"Yes, ma'am. As soon as possible," the operator stated.

"How long is that?" Tonya fired back.

"As soon as I get an available staff person," the operator explained before hanging up.

Tonya didn't like the way that sounded. She wasn't about to wait on them to start getting drunk. Taking matters in her own hands, she walked into the bathroom and retrieved one of the glasses in there. After peeling away the thin aluminum wrapping from the cork of the champagne, Tonya managed to pop the cork with her hand. She laughed as the cork flew across the room and hit the wall. Tilting her glass, Tonya poured herself a glass of some of the finest champagne in the world.

Bringing the glass to eye level, Tonya inspected it closely as if it were liquid gold.

"Here's to wives and mistresses. May they never meet," she toasted.

Tonya had always wanted to say that, ever since she had heard it in a movie. She thought the line was so fly, some real player shit. But by no stretch of the imagination did she consider herself a player. She merely said it out of lack of knowing a better toast.

With one quick motion she threw her head back and gulped down the champagne. The first glass was followed by another and another. Soon Tonya had a good buzz going on.

She looked up when there was a light knock on the door.

Tonya got up and went rushing across the room to answer it. When she stumbled and almost fell, she stopped momentarily to gather herself before she continued across the room.

Thinking it was the waiter bringing the champagne glasses she had requested, she didn't even bother to look through the peephole. So she was surprised when she opened the door and saw Q standing there holding two champagne glasses. He had intercepted the waiter just before he got to Tonya's door. Tonya had to admit that even in the midst of a storm, Q was fresh head to toe. He had on a baby blue Armani Exchange button-up shirt, a dark blue New York Yankees baseball cap, a pair of Red Monkey designer blue jeans, and blue Adidas flip-flops on his well-manicured feet.

"Well, whatcha gonna do? Just stand there or invite me in?" Q asked with a smile when she just stood there staring at him with a puzzled look on her face.

Q could tell by the glassy look in Tonya's eyes that she was slightly intoxicated.

"Oh, oh, my bad!" Tonya said, giggling. "I'm trippin'! I wasn't expectin' you."

Q replied, "So is that a good or a bad thing?"

"I dunno," she said with a devilish grin. "We'll see."

"Okay, that's what's up then," he stated, stepping inside.

"What brings you this way?" she asked. "You got lost or somethin'?"

Q countered, "Nah, I was just checkin' on my peoples, makin' sure everybody was all right. I'm tryin' to get outta here with all Prestige Records' personnel."

"Okay. I'm alive," she announced. "See ya!"

"Tonya, why you trippin'?" he asked. "Why you gotta be so difficult?"

With those few words Q had succeeded in blowing Tonya's high. She didn't know where the alcoholic buzz went, but she quickly regained her senses. She knew she had to say something in her own defense, tell her side of the story, or else it would never get told.

"Look, Q, you got some nerve, nigger," she began. "It's not like you feelin' me anyway. You busy doin' you! And I respect that."

Q looked thoughtful. "You know I always dug you since day one, Tonya," he finally said. "But a nigger stepped up his game and as a result, I got more on my plate. I'm tryin' to milk this music game for every penny that it's worth. I'm rich, but I'm tryin' to get richer. I'm tryin' to get every member of my family out the hood, even if they're just distant relatives. I don't want my wealth to begin and end with me. I want it to span from generation to generation. That's real wealth. So with that in mind, a nigger gotta work hard! Sometimes I get so focused I may not seem to notice you. But trust and believe I do. I really appreciate everything that you've done for me so far."

Q's statement made her feel better, but Tonya still didn't see where she could play a part in his life, other than being a valued worker for his company. For a while, that had been cool with Tonya, but now she wanted more. She needed more. And in her mind, she deserved more.

"Let me pour you a drink," he said.

"Yeah, you do that," Tonya said. "It's the least you can do."

As Q poured the champagne, Tonya studied his handsome features. Her body began to yearn for him as she once again recalled their last sexual encounter. Valiantly, Tonya fought the feeling.

"You wanna make a toast?" Q asked.

"Don't mind if I do." She raised her glass. "Here's to old times."

"And to new ones," Q added.

In unison they downed their glasses of champagne. These were followed by more glasses of champagne. Before long the good times began to roll. Tonya and Q went back down memory lane, chitchatting about everything and nothing at all. They laughed, joked, and continued to drink. Without even realizing it, they had downed two bottles of champagne. They both thoroughly enjoyed each other's company. It was a welcome diversion from the tropical storm that was currently battering the island.

"Yo, excuse me if I'm outta line, Tonya, but I could just eat you up, girl," he said. "Father Time been good to you. Fa sho!"

"Thanks," she answered, while trying hard not to blush.

Tonya desperately tried not to let the statement go to her head. She thought it was game anyway. It came off to her as a guy saying whatever he had to say just to get some. To Tonya those were the words of a true player.

"Look, I'm gonna lay it out, Tonya," he said, his tone dead serious. "I care for you. That threesome between you, me, and Kat all them years ago wasn't 'bout nothin'. I was just satisfying my male ego. Fulfilling every man's fantasy. Just bein' selfish. By no means was that ever a reflection on you. I ain't never looked down at you for that. I appreciated you getting down for ya man like that."

Tonya retorted, "So that's why you spent half the night freakin' off wit' Kat? Was that your way of showin' me you cared?"

She couldn't resist throwing that up in his face.

Q looked thoughtful. "I know this goin' to sound crazy but . . . I was just fuckin' Kat. That's all it's ever been for me—just fuckin'. Even with Niecey. But if you'll let me," he put his glass down and looked her dead in the eye, "I'd like to make love to you tonight."

Tonya stared at Q. Was this his way of telling her that he cared for her? Or was this some slick-ass line he was laying on her just to get in her pants? He had certainly been trying hard enough to do just that. Tonya decided right then and there that it didn't matter. She was going to take a chance. She was going to lay her cards on the table.

"Q, I love you," she told him.

For a long moment Q said nothing. He just stared back at

her. Tonya was about to lose all hope when he smiled and said, "Good." Then he leaned in and kissed her.

They kissed for so long and so strong, it was hard for either of them to catch their breath.

Oh, damn! Tonya thought as she hungrily tasted his tongue.

Q played Tonya's body like a musician making beautiful music. Her body responded to his slightest touch. He began to kiss, lick, and suck her neck as if his life depended on it. Tonya squirmed and moaned with each bite and suck. Q's dick throbbed against the denim of his jeans. He lowered Tonya to the floor.

"I want you so fuckin' bad," he growled.

"You can show me better than you can tell me," Tonya boldly stated.

Hurriedly, Tonya slipped her wifebeater over her head and wiggled out of her shorts. She lay butt naked waiting for Q to join her.

"Q, hurry the fuck up. I want you, nigger!" Tonya said as she watched him undress.

"Sssshhhh," Q replied. "I don't wanna hear nothin' but you moanin'. That's all I wanna hear when I stick this dick up in you."

Suddenly Q was on top of her and they were embracing, kissing, biting, and sucking as if they couldn't get enough of each other. Q ran his tongue along the dangerous curves of Tonya's body as his hands roamed freely. He started on her neck, then slowly worked his way down to Tonya's shoulders to her erect nipples down to her belly button, where he stopped to thrust his tongue inside.

Tonya moaned and clutched him to her. Pleasure clouded her mind as every part of her being throbbed in anticipation.

Watching Q lick on her was a turn-on in itself. Tonya made cute sex faces as the anticipation and pleasure intensified. But instead of fulfilling Tonya's burning desire to feel Q's face buried between her thighs, he took an unexpected detour to Tonya's well-manicured toes.

Placing Tonya's tiny right foot in his mouth, Q sucked her toes like he was possessed. Tonya's back arched as a strong euphoric sensation shot straight through her body. She began to rub her clitoris and was soon overcome by orgasm after orgasm. Never in her young life had Tonya experienced something so intense. These were the best orgasms she had ever had in her life.

Q didn't have to be told he had done good. Tonya's body told him as much. Q loved satisfying his partners, getting them off first. It was a turn-on for him to see them having an orgasm as a result of something he was doing.

Pushing her legs apart, Q had a good view of Tonya's neatly trimmed vagina. Tonya was still recovering from her last orgasm when Q buried his head between her legs and began to eat her out.

Tonya's body began to quiver as Q nibbled and sucked on her clitoris. Tonya's moans and screams excited him. She begged him to stop, but he wouldn't. He knew as well as she did that she didn't want him to stop. When she tried to pull away from his hungry mouth, he only chased her, locking his arms around her thighs till she couldn't escape.

Tonya thrust her hips wildly as she climaxed over and over again. She was unable to take much more of this. And although she was a willing recipient, Tonya was beginning to feel selfish. It was time for her to return the favor.

"Now it's your turn," Tonya said seductively, finally pulling from him. She pushed him onto his back.

Tonya went straight for Q's dick. She took as much of him as she possibly could into her mouth, testing her gag reflexes.

Tonya then began to go up and down, bobbing her head in a smooth rhythm. Saliva began to ooze from her mouth, saturating him. A few well-timed sighs and moans were her reward for a job well done.

Tonya sucked Q's dick for so long and so lovingly, her mouth began to dry. She raised up for a moment and crawled a short distance to the food cart. She removed a bottle of champagne, along with a bucket of ice.

After popping a few pieces of ice in her mouth, Tonya was right back at it. She commenced to sucking Q off with renewed vigor.

This shit is bananas! Q thought to himself.

The cold of the ice and the warmth of Tonya's mouth drove Q wild. He wanted to tell Tonya to stop, it was so ridiculously addictive, but somehow the words got lost in his throat. Q couldn't talk; he was too busy moaning. Over and over again, Tonya would repeat the process of popping ice in her mouth, whenever what she had in her mouth melted.

Q felt the head of his penis swell up. He was unable to contain himself any longer. Nor did he want to. He felt like he was going to explode.

"Cum in my mouth," Tonya whispered, well aware of what was going on.

Just before Q was about to climax, Tonya pulled one more stunt. She gave Q one last long, heavy suck, then stopped. Softly Tonya began to blow cold air on his penis as she stroked him firmly with her hand.

Q erupted like a volcano, sending a strong surge of sperm shooting through the air. Tonya managed to catch the second wave, taking him in her mouth again until she drank him dry.

"Oh my God!" Q managed to say.

But Tonya wasn't finished. Usually Q needed a few minutes to become erect again. He also liked to take that time to savor the moment. However, he wouldn't have the luxury to do that. She began to gently suck him until he was fully erect again.

Carefully Tonya spread her legs apart and lowered herself onto Q's fully erect penis. Her love juices were still flowing, so she was easily able to guide it right in. Tonya began to ride Q's penis like a true cowgirl. She loved this position because she was in total control. She could dictate the tempo of the sex. Up and down she went. Tonya was getting it how she liked it, hard and fast.

The two were too far gone to even think about the consequences of unprotected sex, like pregnancy or disease. The thought would undoubtedly cross each of their minds later, but for now they were adhering to the pleasure principle.

Sweat dripped off their bodies as Tonya went from reverse cowgirl to the missionary position and then finally to Q's favorite, doggy style. His strokes were long and steady as he penetrated her from different angles until he found her G-spot.

"Yyyyyeeeeeessssss!" she cried with pleasure. "Harder! Harder!"

Tonya felt like she was having an out-of-body sexual experience. If she died right now then she would die happy. Her clitoris was on fire, she began to frantically rub it with her fingers, stimulating herself even more. Sensing the urgency in her moans, Q began to pump harder and stronger, penetrating her even deeper.

They both seemed to climax in unison. Tonya's body jerked with the force of her tenth orgasm of the night. Moments later, a physically drained Q slumped down on her. They lay on the floor savoring the feeling.

Eventually, they shifted around until she found a comfortable spot in Q's arms and fell asleep. A while later Q fell asleep listening to the soft sound of Tonya's heartbeat. Together they slept through the worst part of the storm without even waking.

In the middle of the night Tonya awoke and lay there for a few moments. She had never felt safer in her life than at that moment. She couldn't help but think how wonderful that night had been. In the back of her mind she wondered how this passionate lovemaking session might change tomorrow. She hoped and prayed that this was the beginning of something special for them. For that answer she would just have to wait and see.

Secretly she feared that Q would do her dirty once again, that he would write her off as some passing fancy, thinking she was only in love with the dick and not Q the person.

The next morning when Tonya awoke, she was alone. It was like her worst fear had been confirmed. Like a fool, she had played with fire for a second time and gotten burned. She got up off the floor, knowing she would have to pull herself together. This wasn't the first time that life had shat on her and probably not the last. Tonya looked at her current predicament like this: she took a chance and gave herself to Q, gambled and lost, in the game of love.

Tonya got in the shower with a million thoughts running through her mind. She wondered how she was going to maintain a business relationship after they had been so intimate last night. How in the hell was she going to keep her job after they had crossed that imaginary line, mixing business with pleasure?

After taking a long shower, Tonya realized she was no closer to finding the answer to Q's abandonment of her than when she first stepped into the shower. She was just going to have to be a woman about it, admit to herself that she made a mistake by having sex with Q, and move on. She could only hope that Q would do the same thing. Still, he was in control, he was the boss. So it was Q's call to make, how he was going to handle the situation.

Worrying herself sick, Tonya never even noticed that the storm had subsided. The sun had come out and was poking its way through her room's closed curtains. Meanwhile, Tonya had begun to get dressed, unsure of what she was doing or where she was going.

A loud knock at the door had momentarily shattered the peace and quiet in the room. Tonya raced to the door, hoping it was Q on the other side. Not bothering to look, she opened the door and was disappointed. A waiter pushing a food cart stood in the hallway with a blank look on his face.

"Breakfast," he said.

"I didn't order any damn breakfast!" Tonya snapped, attempting to shut the door.

"Ma'am, this was sent to you by someone named Q," the waiter said. "And if I don't deliver it, I won't receive my tip."

Oh, how nice of you, Q. Fuck 'em and feed 'em, Tonya mused.

The waiter stood there, looking anxious.

She sighed. "Okay, you can bring it in."

She wasn't going to turn into a hater all of a sudden just because Q didn't want to be with her. Things were what they were, not what she wanted them to be.

When the waiter left, Tonya sat in the room, on the edge of the bed, staring at the tray. She refused to touch the food, thinking in some way that that might hurt Q. But soon hunger pangs from last night began to hit. The nice aroma from the breakfast filled her nostrils.

Tonya realized she wasn't hurting anyone but herself if she didn't eat. She walked over to the cart and uncovered a plate. French toast, lightly dusted with powdered sugar, a side of bacon and maple syrup. There was orange juice and coffee as well. There was another plate as well. *Just how hungry does this nigger think I am?*

Taking the first plate off the cart, she began to dig in. After Tonya ate the meal, she washed it down with the glass of orange juice. That marathon of a sex session had left her famished and she was actually still hungry after she finished, so Tonya decided to help herself to the other plate of food.

However, when Tonya lifted the cover she received the surprise of her life. A diamond-link chain with an attached diamond-encrusted capital letter P, for Prestige, lay on the plate, along with a note. Tonya picked it up and began jumping up and down like a little girl, unable to contain her excitement. She placed the long, expensive chain around her neck, then headed straight to the bathroom mirror to see how it looked on her.

Just as she was getting accustomed to the look and the feel of the chain, Tonya suddenly remembered something. She dashed out of the bathroom to read the note.

"Last night was bananas!!!!" the note read. "I don't know what happened to the last chain I gave you, but whatever happened, let's not let it happen again. Sorry I couldn't stay. I found out that the state of emergency was lifted off the island and I went to the studio to work on a few tracks. Call me when you get up, Q." And then scrawled at the bottom of the note was "P.S.—I love you, too."

Tonya reread the note over and over again, as if the words were suddenly going to change. Or someone was suddenly going to pop out of the bathroom and yell "Psych!" Q loved her. He really loved her. She almost couldn't believe it. It seemed so unreal after all this time.

Tonya could feel tears of happiness well up in her eyes. She had never in her life cried because she was happy, so this was a new experience for her.

Tonya held the chain to her heart. All her dreams were coming true.

For the remainder of their stay in the Bahamas, Tonya and Q were inseparable. They worked long days together and spent hot nights in Tonya's hotel room, making love. It was as if they were trying to make up for lost time. Either Q didn't adhere to his own policy of not dating within the company or he didn't care. Throwing caution to the wind, he decided that he had waited long enough for Tonya and he wasn't about to let her go.

All the things that usually ate into Q's time, he managed to find a way around them. The quiet time they shared together, having a romantic dinner in a secluded place, was all about them. Q turned off his cell phones and told no one where he was going. They discovered that not only did they enjoy each other's company, but they had a lot of things in common. Q felt like he had finally met his match in Tonya.

Neither of them brought up Nicccy and what she was likely to do when she found out about them. For now, they just wanted to enjoy each other.

Tonya couldn't ask for anything more. It felt unreal, but she hoped this was the start of a romance that would last forever.

Word of Tonya and Q's affair had arrived in the States before them. The island was only so big, and Q and Tonya had been spotted numerous times eating dinner, riding motorbikes, or just walking on the beach. On several occasions they were spotted in compromising positions. Someone even secretly took a picture of the couple with a camera phone and sent it to a newspaper. Fueled by the power of cell phones and gossip, the news spread like wildfire among the employees.

Karen sat in her office with the latest gossip sheet on her desk. She had just finished reading *The Star*. She glared at the picture of Q and Tonya kissing on the beach. She truly hated that bitch. Putting the paper down, she stared at the opposite wall for a while, her thoughts racing. She knew what she had to do. She picked up the phone and dialed a number.

When the phone rang, Niecey immediately looked down at her caller ID. She noticed that the number of the caller was blocked. Her first instinct was to ignore the call. But curiosity got the best of her. She answered the phone.

"Hello, Niecey?" Karen said.

"Yeah, this is she," she stated. "Who's this?"

"It's Karen," she explained.

"Karen?" she asked. *Why the hell is she calling me?* Niecey wondered. She knew Karen couldn't stand her and that if it weren't for Lil Q, the ho wouldn't even speak to her at holiday gatherings.

"Yeah, I'm sorry to have to call you, but I think there's something you should know."

Instantly, Niecey was all ears because she knew it had to be about Q. "What is it?"

Karen hesistated. She didn't want to officially be the one on record who called Niecey up and told her point blank that Q was fucking his new marketing consultant. So she said, "I think you should check out *The Star.*"

Niecey looked at the phone as if it had said something crazy. "*The Star?* What the fuck do I care about *The Star?*"

"It's who's in it and with whom. I think you'll be very, very interested, Niecey." She spoke slowly, emphasizing her words, so Niecey would catch on.

Niecey was quiet on her end. She was beginning to understand. Q was in the rags again with some other chick. She was heated, but she didn't understand why Karen felt compelled to call her this time, especially since it wasn't the first time her brother had been in the papers with a new sidepiece he had acquired.

"Okay, so why are you tellin' me?" she asked. "He's got another fuckin' sidepiece. What's new?"

"Listen, you can do whatever you want to do with the information," Karen said. "I just thought you'd want to know. Good-bye." The line went dead.

Niecey sat there for a while, thinking about her conversation with Karen. Any girlfriend or wife of someone in the music industry had to know about the endless supply of groupies. Niecey always figured that what she didn't know wouldn't hurt her. But what she did find out could possibly hurt Q. She didn't need this sort of thing to be thrown up in her face. Q knew how jealous she was and that she wouldn't take this sort of thing lying down.

Finally Niecey went out to the newsstand and got a copy of *The Star*. Sure enough, there Q was, kissing and hugged up on some ho. Niecey didn't recognize her.

She wasn't the least bit surprised, but still that didn't lessen the pain any. She couldn't wait until Q and his new flavor of the month got back.

15

Q and the entire Prestige Records staff boarded two red-eye flights back to New York City. When they landed in New Jersey, it seemed like everyone on board, except Q, was suffering from jet lag. The bags under Tonya's eyes were evidence of the frequent late-night romps with Q. Still, she returned from her business trip feeling physically drained but emotionally reinvigorated. She was glad it was Sunday because she could use the day to get some rest.

They were all pretty thankful to be back in New York. The tropical storm had shaken up just about everyone. Now they were glad to be back in familiar surroundings, back to the rat race, where at least the weather was a little bit more predictable.

It was mid-March in New York City and there was a chill in the morning air. It was cold enough to give Tonya the sniffles.

Everyone grinned and bore it as they made their way to a fleet of warm, waiting limousines.

"I'll see you Monday morning," Q told her before she got into her limo. He didn't kiss her since they were standing in full view of all the other employees. They were no longer on the island, where they had managed to be discreet. At least, that's what they thought.

"Not tonight?" Tonya asked, looking up into his eyes.

Q smiled. "What? You ain't get enough down on the island?"

Tonya actually felt herself blush. What was this man doing to her?

Q laughed. He didn't think he had ever made a woman blush before. It was nice. "I have to go see Lil Q and handle some business," he told her. He leaned into her a little. "But dream about me, okay?"

"Oh, that won't be a problem, Daddy," she said.

Q gave her a slick smile, then turned and headed for his own limo.

He suddenly turned and shouted, just as he was about to enter the car, "Ya'll go home and get some rest. In the next couple of days we are about to launch a national media campaign. We accomplished a lot down in the Bahamas, but we still got a lot more work to do. Can't stop, won't stop!"

"Yo, Na'eema. Where you at?" Tonya called out as she entered their apartment. "Na'eema?"

At any moment Tonya fully expected Na'eema to emerge from either the bathroom or her bedroom, greeting her with a big smile on her face. Tonya was dying to tell her the news about her and Q.

"Na'eema?" Tonya yelled for the third time. "Yo!"

After not getting any response, Tonya was now curious about her friend's whereabouts. She gently set her bags down in the hallway and proceeded to take a look around the apartment. She ventured down the hall, past the kitchen and living room, and nothing seemed out of place. Their apartment was as neat and clean as on the day she left.

As Tonya made her way to the back, she glanced into her bedroom. Nothing out of the ordinary there. When she reached Na'eema's door, she immediately noticed the door was closed.

Tonya knew something was up then. Na'eema never shut her door, not when she slept and not even to dress after taking a shower. So now Tonya knew something was wrong.

"Na'eema, you in there?" she said before walking in.

When Tonya entered the room she saw Na'eema's dresser drawers pulled open and emptied out. All her clothes were gone. Tonya continued her inspection of the room, opening her closet and finding it empty, too. Tonya did an about-face, turned, and left the room. She went into the kitchen and dialed Na'eema's cell phone number. On the third ring Na'eema answered.

"Na'eema?" Tonya said. "Where the hell are you? Why all ya clothes gone? You packed up and left without tellin' me?"

"Tonya, slow down, girl. Would you gimme a chance to say sumthin'! Damn!" Na'eema replied.

Tonya did as she was told, closing her mouth long enough to hear Na'eema out.

"Look, it went down while you were gone," Na'eema said, sighing. "Me and ole girl Karen got into it. While ya'll was down in the Bahamas, I went back to Philly to check on Moms. When I got there Moms was doin' a lil' worse than I expected, so I decided to stay a few more days. I call ole girl and explain the situation, tellin' her I wouldn't be to work that week. She tells me if I don't get back there tomorrow I'm fired. I said, what about my mother? What I'm suppose to do about her? She said she don't give a damn about my mother. So you know me, that's all I needed to hear. I came back to work the next day and beat the bitch's ass! They had to call security to get me off her ass."

Tonya let out a soft laugh, but the fact of the matter was that it wasn't funny at all. Now Tonya regretted even leaving to go on the trip to the Bahamas, at least without Na'eema. She couldn't believe Na'eema had fed into Karen's nonsense. After all, they weren't kids anymore; they had to find a better way of dealing with people they didn't like besides fighting.

After all, wasn't it Na'eema who had told her numerous times, "Don't worry about what was being said about you. You know who you are. You know what you did and why you did it. These people ain't no better than you, just because they educated."

Na'eema had held her down so many times, stopping Tonya from doing foolish things. And when it was her turn to be the voice of reason, she was nowhere to be found.

"Damn!" Tonya sighed. "I wish I was there to talk you outta that shit. Man, it wouldn't have even gone down like that. I swear, Na'eema."

Now Na'eema felt bad. It was almost as if she had let Tonya down. Initially, she had felt like she had done something slick by kicking Karen's ass. Only after this conversation with Tonya did she realize the stupidity of her actions.

"Look, Tee, my bad!" Na'eema said. "I ain't mean for it to go down like that, but it did. When Karen made that statement about my mother I completely lost it. You know how I feel 'bout my mother. Don't nobody talk bad 'bout her. I don't care who you is. Anyway, don't worry about me, I'ma be all right. I wasn't feeling that music shit anyway. I'll get my job back at the shop and start throwing parties again. At least that way I'll be closer to Moms. I couldn't really keep an eye on her way up in New York."

Tonya sat on the other end of the phone, completely numb. Her best friend was leaving her. And after hearing that, there was no way she could share the good news with Na'eema about her and Q. So Tonya decided to keep it to herself. She found it hard to believe that Na'eema could be happy for her at a time like this.

"Well, Na'eema, let me go. I just got back from the Bahamas and I'm tired as shit," Tonya said. "I'll call you later and tell you all about it."

"Oh, you mean about how you and Q decided to pick up where you left off?" Na'eema said.

Tonya's jaw dropped in shock. "How the fuck you know about that?"

"Bitch, pick up a paper," Na'eema said. "Your ass is all over the rags. Guess things weren't over between you two, huh?"

"Well, things just kind of happened while we were down there," Tonya said, sounding grumpy. "Damn!" she cursed. "I can't believe we in the papers!"

"Didn't look like you were tryin' too hard to hide it. Or maybe he just turned your ass out so good you forgot who you was with. What'd you expect fuckin' with a cat like Q?" Na'eema asked her. "He constantly under the microscope and now, so will you."

"I got to call Q," she told Na'eema.

"All right, play girl, you handle your business, but next time, don't let me find out this kind of shit in the paper, you hear me?"

Tonya felt bad. "I know, I'm sorry. It just happened so fast!"

"Whatever, girl. You just do you and make sure you wear his fine ass out for the both of us." Na'eema laughed and Tonya reluctantly smiled. "And be sure to call me on the regular. I want to know all about how nice you about to be living."

"Yeah, well, we'll see," Tonya said, studying her nails. "I ain't tryin' to rush into anything with this nigga."

"Stop tryin to play it cool, Tee. That nigga got you open and you probably got him open too from the way you two been eyein' each other for months."

"Well . . ." Tonya said, suddenly smiling. "He did say he loved me." She giggled.

"Oh, god, spare me before I start hearing about how y'all gonna move in together and get a dog and some horses and shit." But Tonya could hear the laughter in her voice. "But seriously, I'm happy for you, Tee. If there's anybody who deserves to be happy, it's you."

Tonya fell silent. Did she really deserve to be happy?

"What's wrong?" Na'eema said, noting how quiet she had gotten.

"Just wondering if you're right," Tonya told her.

"Tonya, what the fuck are you talking about?"

Tonya closed her eyes and took a deep breath. "I don't know if I really deserve this. There's . . . something I never told anyone about before."

"What? Like you killed somebody?" Na'eema said jokingly.

Tonya was silent once again. Na'eema's laughter slowly faded as she realized Tonya wasn't laughing with her.

"Tonya, you killed somebody?" Na'eema screamed.

Tonya pulled the phone away from her ear and glared at it. "Damn, Na'eema, you gonna make a bitch go deaf."

"Fuck that, Tonya! You better start speakin on it right now before I come up there—"

"All right, all right!"

"Did you kill somebody?"

Tonya sighed. "It's complicated. So just shut up and let me tell it," she said when she heard Na'eema take a breath in order to let loose another impatient comment.

"This was back in my stripping days when I was hooked up with Kat. Me and Goldie knew she was full of shit, but she looked out for us more than anyone else had at that time. And I was young and dumb enough to believe what came out of that bitch's mouth simply because I didn't know any better. But I learned the hard way. Anyway, Kat had beef with this stripper named Cookie. Thought she was stealing and shit, so she had us lay in wait for her and we beat the shit out of Cookie so bad that she was laid up in the hospital for a minute. It was pretty bad. I still see that girl's face sometimes in my sleep. But her pimp, Jules came after us. We had just takin' money out of his pocket. So he rolled up on us one night after we had left the club and was about to blow Kat's brains out. If I had known then, what I know now, I would have stopped Goldie from pulling the trigger. But Goldie shot him and Kat told us that we had to get out of town. So we headed down to Miami for a little while. That's where I met Q. When we got back, it looked like everything was going to be fine, but Goldie had talked me into getting out of the stripping business." Tonya stared down at the floor, remembering the look on Goldie's face as she pleaded with her to leave it all behind. "I admit that I was scared as hell, but I was going to do it because Goldie asked me to. But then everything turned to shit. Kat got brought in by the police, the cops knew it was Goldie who had killed Jules and all of sudden Goldie had to get the hell out of Dodge. She headed up here to New York to avoid being arrested. Kat said we would get her a lawyer, so we both started hustling in order to raise money for Goldie's lawyer or so I thought."

Tonya laid back on her bed and stared at the ceiling. "I had also hooked back up with Q, who was in Philly at the time. It wasn't nothin' serious. I was taking care of him and he was taking care of me. But then one day, he told me that he wanted to have a threesome. Him, me, and another chick. I didn't trust some stranger so I invited Kat. That was a mistake. Next thing I know, Kat's got her claws sunk into him, so I just decided to back off. I was still trying to raise money for Goldie's lawyer, but I had also decided to get out of the business even if I had to do it by myself. So I was all about stacking paper so I could make my move." Tonya felt a lump swell in her throat and she put her arm over her eyes to keep the tears from flowing. "Then one day I get a package in the mail. It's from the owner of the rooming house where Goldie was living. It was Goldie's diary. She had killed herself and had asked for someone to send it to me. I couldn't believe it. My girl, Goldie, was just gone. I didn't want to read it, but I made myself sit down and read her diary cover to cover. One of her last dying wishes was for me to have the thing, so the least I could do was honor her memory and read it like she wanted me to. And let me tell you, it was an eye opener."

"Why, what'd it say?" Na'eema asked. It was the first time she had spoken, which was unusual for her since she was always interrupting with questions and commentary.

"All kinds of shit," Tonya said. "But the worst was how Kat had been telling Goldie that I had turned her back on her and didn't want to have anything to do with her. I didn't even know Goldie had been calling or I would have set that shit straight. I also found out that she wasn't getting any money from Kat. So the bitch was just pocketing all the money and telling Goldie that I had left her alone in the world. I wanted to kill Kat. But instead, I just laid in wait for her when she got home and then beat the hell out of her. I told her she'd better have my money the next night or I was coming after that ass again." Tonya shook her head. "I was so stupid. I should have been ready for her, but she ambushed me that next night and she and some rough neck girls kicked my ass so bad that I ended up in the hospital. I lay in there, in pain, for a week, plotting that bitch's downfall. As far as I was concerned, Kat had killed Goldie. To me it was as if she had gone up to New York and poured those pills down Goldie's throat. All she knew how to do was destroy lives and she kept getting away with it."

"So what'd you do?"

"I knew that she was having problems with Q's baby mama, who was just crazy and jealous. So I called her up, pretending to be Kat, and cursed her out. Told her that Q and I were getting married and that I was pregnant with his baby. And I told her that if she had a problem with it, she could come to my house, but that I would have something waiting for her." Tonya rested her hand on her stomach while she stared up at the ceiling. "Niecey showed up at Kat's house and shot her. I found out in the paper the next day that Kat was dead."

Na'eema was quiet for a long time.

"Aren't you going to say something?" Tonya asked.

Na'eema was quiet for a little while longer. "That's some story," she finally said. "Did you know that Niecey was going to kill Kat?"

"No," Tonya said. "I thought she was going to fuck her up. But when I found out that she had killed Kat, I was . . . glad. I was glad, Na'eema. And I'm still glad." Tonya burst into tears. "I hated that bitch for what she did to me and to Goldie! I still hate her!" She began to sob. It took her a couple of minutes to pull herself together.

"All right, all right, listen to me, Tonya," Na'eema said. "I'm guessing you brought all of this up because now you're happy with Q and you're thinking you don't deserve it because of what went down between Kat and Niecey, his baby's mama. But that shit would have gone down between those two anyway. I know the type of bitch you're talking about when you talk about Kat. It was only a matter of time before somebody put a cap in her ass. The clock was ticking and she didn't even know it. And don't get it twisted. You ain't like Kat. You don't run around lying, stealing, cheating, and fucking people over. You've only done what you had to do to survive. Now you've got a chance to be happy. So grab that bitch with both hands and hold on."

Tonya wiped her eyes. "So you don't think I should tell Q?"

"What for?" Na'eema asked. "You played some little petty bullshit by calling the baby mama. Bitches do that all the time. But Niecey decided to kill a woman and you don't have anything to do with the actions she decided to take. Leave that shit in the past. You got other things to worry about."

Tonya sniffed. "Like what?"

"Like crazy baby mama now. Q's in love with you. What's she going to do once she finds out about that?"

"I don't know. But I do know that I'm not letting her keep me from Q."

Na'eema sighed. "Well, this is too much damn drama for me for one day. Listen, you watch your back and call me every once in a while. I meant what I said about not wanting to find out no more shit from the papers. All right?"

Tonya smiled. "All right."

Tonya hung up the phone and lay on her bed thinking about what Na'eema had said. When her head just started to hurt, she shook it off and tried to call Q instead, but his phone kept going to voice mail. She wondered if he had seen the papers already and was avoiding all phone calls, including hers. Tonya hoped this hadn't messed things up between them before they had even had a chance to get it off the ground. The thought depressed her. So she climbed into bed and pulled the covers over her head.

Not only had this situation with her and Q taken a down turn, but her girl Na'eema had lost her job because of this bitch, Karen.

Tonya was tempted to play her trump card and go over Karen's head and try to get her friend's job back, but it was obvious Na'eema didn't really want to be there. And besides that, Tonya didn't want to snitch on Karen to win favor with Q. She had managed to keep Q out of the office politics thus far and if she had her way, he would continue to stay in the blind. Besides, Q had enough to deal with now. This was between her and Karen.

The first thing on Q's mind was seeing his son. They had grown so close after Niecey got incarcerated and he became the sole caregiver for the child. Father and son had forged a bond now that was greater than the love the boy had for his mother. Even Niecey noticed and became envious of all the attention Q showered upon his son.

Although Q loved being in the music business, one of the things he detested the most was being away from his son for long periods of time. But when one is chasing a dream, pursuing goals, trying to secure his family's financial future, sacrifices have to be made. A harsh reality of the world was that time is money. The only thing that temporarily pacified Q was the fact that he was heavily compensated. However, he was slowly beginning to see that money wasn't everything. Money wouldn't get him into heaven and it certainly wouldn't make him a good father. Thoughts like these weighed heavily on Q's mind; they seemed to be a daily dilemma.

Two hours later, two stretch limos pulled into Q's southern New Jersey estate. Q leaped out of the vehicle and rushed inside his house. Normally when Q arrived he was greeted by a chorus of "Hey, Dad!" Today it wasn't to be. It made no sense for Q to look around the house; he knew his son wasn't home. His son wasn't where he was supposed to be.

As his bodyguards began to file into the house, Q walked to his main-level home office to get some privacy. Sitting down in a chair, he propped his feet up on the desk and frantically punched a few numbers into the house phone. He was calling Niecey to find out his son's whereabouts.

The telephone number that he dialed rang for what seemed like forever before it was answered by what Q thought to be Niecey but actually turned out to be her answering machine.

"Hold on for a minute, I can't hear you."

"Yo! Yo!" Q screamed into the phone. "Yo!"

The recording continued, "Psych! This is Niecey and unfortunately I'm unable to take your call right now, but if you would please leave your name, number, and a brief message I will return your call at my earliest convenience. Have a nice day and God bless. Bye! Bye!"

After repeated attempts to reach Niecey, Q gave up. He hung

up the phone, deciding against leaving a message, because what he had to say at this point wouldn't be nice. Q was angry. He didn't like to be ignored. He saw no reason for his son not to be here. It was a custom for them to be with each other after coming off a long trip.

Q couldn't help but take it personally. He had already called ahead and they had established the fact that he was returning from the Bahamas and he wanted Lil Q home when he got there.

Q and Niecey hadn't been seeing eye to eye on many issues pertaining to his son. Niecey didn't like the private school Q had placed him in, and so on and so forth. Q thought she was nitpicking. He felt Niecey's arguments had no basis. She hadn't even readapted to society yet, and here she was trying to change things, routines, that had worked for years, while she was incarcerated.

When Niecey had given Q temporary custody of their son, Q was free to raise him as he saw fit and he had. There was no way she could ever say Lil Q wasn't well taken care of. Q's wealth had afforded his son the best of everything. He was exposed to things that his parents had never been exposed to themselves. And that's exactly how Q wanted it. He was raising a well-rounded man, not some little street thug.

It seemed like Niecey wanted their son to be thuggish, though, as if she thought that private school, getting a real education, would make Lil Q soft. Over the years Q evolved into a big businessman and a better person, more civilized, while Niecey remained ghetto. She hadn't adjusted to the upper echelon of society at all. It seemed like Q couldn't take her anywhere without her getting into a verbal altercation with someone. She even beefed with his bodyguards. Niecey complained about them being around all the time.

Since she had been home, Q had overlooked a lot of incidents, trying to keep it real and keep Niecey an active part of Lil

Q's life. Now he was beginning to wonder if that was going to remain possible.

Q loved Niecey for a number of reasons. The main one, of course, was bearing his only child, Lil Q. But he wasn't in love with her, and that was a big difference. Their differences would have to be ironed out sooner or later.

Suddenly the phone rang. Q reached over and picked it up before it rang again.

"Yeah, it's me, Niecey. What's up?" she said nonchalantly.

"What's up?" Q echoed angrily. "What you mean, what's up? Ain't you supposed to have my son over here? I thought we agreed on that! Where the fuck are you?"

At that moment, if Q could have seen the smirk that appeared on Niecey's face, he would have smacked her. Niecey knew Q well and she knew exactly how to hurt him: keep him away from his son. This was payback for not taking her to the Bahamas and taking one of his side chicks instead. If they were going to play games, then they were going to play hers.

"Oh, my bad! I forgot you were flyin' in today," she lied. "We got caught up at a birthday party for one of Lil Q's cousins at Chuck E. Cheese."

"How long for ya'll get here, man?" Q snapped.

"We on the highway now," she replied. "We should be there in less than an hour. So hold ya horses!"

"Later!" Q said, cutting her off. "I see you when you get here."

After hearing Q's comment, Niecey knew what lay in wait for her once she got to his house—an argument. And she couldn't wait. In a strange way, Niecey wanted and needed attention from Q. If this was the only way she could get it, then so be it.

"Daddy!" Lil Q yelled as soon as he entered the house.

Q had dozed off, waiting on his son's return, but he woke up immediately when he heard Lil Q. It was like music to his ears.

He wished he could enter and reenter the house all day, just to hear the excitement and love in his son's voice.

As soon as Lil Q came running into the room, Q jumped out of his chair and scooped his son up in his arms. A big grin spread across Q's lips as he whirled the child around in a circle.

"Daddy!" his son exclaimed. "Did you miss me while you were gone, huh?"

"Is water wet? Is an elephant heavy? Do a rabbit do-do in the woods? Of course I miss you, what kinda question that?" Q asked, laughing.

From the corner of his eye he saw Niecey enter the room. All the humor fell away from him like a dropped cloak.

"Q, me and Mommy gotta talk, so go to your room and play a video game," he told his son. "Put on Madden. I'll be up there in a sec to whip ya butt."

"Okay, Daddy!" he joyfully replied. "What team you wanna play with?"

"The Eagles," Q replied as he glared at Niecey. "Don't play dumb, you know that's my squad."

Doing as he was told, Lil Q ran upstairs to his bedroom.

"Yo, what the fuck kinda games you playin'?" Q asked as soon as his son was out of earshot. "I thought I told you to have him here at a certain time! I wanted to spend some time with him. You know he got school tomorrow."

"Nigga, that's my son, too! He got more family besides you and your side of the family," Niecey fired back.

"Them muthafuckas ain't been wanting to see him. Ain't none of them call to see how he was doin' while you was away," Q insisted. "Now all of a sudden they wanna see him. Where all this love come from?"

He strolled over to her almost casually. "And lemme ask you somethin'. What you been doin' to my son? Except for today, every time he comes back home from a weekend with you, he's not himself. He really ain't got much to say. He just wanna stay in his room and be by himself."

"Why don't you ask him what's wrong with him?" she spat. "How the hell am I supposed to know?"

Q countered, "Oh, you know somethin'. You ain't as innocent as you seem. And don't think I believe that shit for one minute."

Coming over here, Niecey figured that they would argue, cuss, fight, and then fuck. They had had some of the best sex ever after they had fought. But now she sensed a new tone of hostility.

"Look, nigga!" she said. "Lil Q needs to know my people just as well as yours. And I don't give a fuck if they didn't call or come see him while I was away. They do it now!"

Niecey was shifting into her ghetto mode. She stepped all up in Q's face, making all kinds of gestures with her hands.

Q ignored her antics. He knew Niecey was only doing it to piss him off. If he fed into her negative behavior, it might lead him to smack her.

"Look, Niecey, let's not start nothin' new," he told her, disgusted. "Things were runnin' smooth while you were away. I ain't have no problems. Not one!"

"Maybe if you stop fuckin' all these hos and pay attention to ya family, we wouldn't have problems now!" she spat. "You down in the Bahamas with all kinds of bitches!"

Damn! Q mused to himself. *How the fuck she find out about that already?*

It never ceased to amaze him how fast rumors about him seemed to travel. Q loved his celebrity status, whether it was getting his picture taken by paparazzi, parlaying at parties with professional athletes and famous actors, or getting the VIP treatment at five-star restaurants or exclusive nightclubs. But there was one aspect of celebrity he could do without. Like most people, he didn't like other people up in his business.

Q didn't know how Niecey found out about what he did in the Bahamas, nor did he care. He felt disrespected, knowing that she had taken the conversation into an area it didn't have to go to.

"Look, I'm a grown-ass man. I don't answer to nobody, feel me! What I do and who I do it with is none of your fuckin' bizness. Let's just concentrate on raisin' our son! Sumthin' I been doin' fine while you were away."

"You weren't thinkin' about your son while you were down in the Bahamas fuckin' your new bitch! That's the problem right there, Q," Niecey said. "But you know I'm real good at makin' our problems go away. I always have, and I can do it again. Don't play wit' me."

Q got real still as he stared at Niecey. He knew that she was threatening to do something to Tonya, and rage like he had never felt before rose up inside him. In that moment, he felt like he could kill her. If somebody hurt Tonya, bodies would be dropping in the streets.

"Look, bitch," he said, his voice like ice. "You ain't been nothin' but a headache since day one. You ain't done nothin' right since you had my son. Now you startin' to bite the hands that feeds you. Who was it that paid your lawyer bill? Me. Who was it that got you out on bail till your sentencing? Me. Who the fuck took you outta the fuckin' projects, where half your family still lives? Me. If it wasn't for me your ass would still be there. Fucked up and doin' bad just like the rest of your family. Bitch, you must have lost your fuckin' mind, but don't you ever forget that!" He looked her dead in her eye. "I wish you would violate me like that again. Last time you got a pass; if there is a next time you will not be so lucky. If I were you I wouldn't press my luck."

Tears welled up in Niecey's eyes. Q had never disrespected her like this in the past. She couldn't help but think, *This is the man I love?*

Without warning, Niecey pulled her head back and let loose a mouthful of saliva, spitting directly in Q's face. Instantly he responded by viciously smacking Niecey repeatedly across the face. Niecey and Q began to scuffle inside his office, which quickly turned into a one-sided affair. Niecey's uncontrolled violence proved to be no match for Q's brute strength. Q's bodyguards were alerted to the situation by the loud sound of a struggle. They rushed to the office and pulled Q off of Niecey before he could do any serious damage.

"Man, get this bitch up outta my house," he ordered them.

The bodyguards complied, as nicely as they could, to remove Niecey from the premises. But not before Niecey let loose a few insults of her own.

"Nigger, you ain't all that! I knew ya ass when you was broke, player! Remember? You think 'cause you gotta couple of dollars now you better than everybody else. Fuck you, nigger! You ain't shit! And ya momma ain't shit! I got somethin' for ya ass! Watch! You gonna get yours!"

"Whatever, bitch!" he said. "You and what army gonna do somethin' to me? These ain't the old days, Niecey. You can't pay a nigger enough to go against me. Niggers don't want them type of problems, especially not over some bum-ass bitch like you!"

But Niecey wasn't nearly done with his ass.

As it turned out, Q wasn't the only one having issues. Tonya was dealing with the backlash of gossip about their affair. She was fully aware of the hit her reputation had now taken. It embarrassed her to know that her co-workers knew that she slept with the boss. Now it would appear as if she had been given her current position only because she was sleeping with Q, and she had wanted to get by on her own merit. But now all of the underlings were being a little extra nice to her, as if she had the power to fire them herself. Karen was the only person who didn't change. She was still her usual nasty self, only a little more smug, as if she knew something Tonya didn't.

16

T onya, you busy?" Shakira spoke softly into the phone. "No, why?" Tonya replied.

"Could you stop by my office? I have something you might be interested in seeing."

Shakira stared down at the papers on her desk in amazement. She couldn't believe what she had discovered.

A knock came at the door.

"Come in," Shakira commanded. "It's open."

"What's good?" Tonya asked curiously, stepping inside and closing the door behind her. "Why did you want me to see so bad?"

"Come take a look at this," she said, pushing the papers across the desk.

Tonya flipped through the papers, then looked up at Shakira, confused. "What the hell am I looking at?"

"I've been checking the marketing accounts to see if any more checks were being written to Millennium," Shakira explained. "There have been, and they've been in larger amounts than before, so I decided to find out just who owns Millennium. I started with the tax filings for the company with the Securities and Exchange Commission and went from there." She took a deep breath. "Tonya, it's owned by Young Fresh ta Def."

"Young Fresh ta Def?" Tonya asked, surprised. "He has his own company? Doing what? And why is she writing him checks?"

"He doesn't have his own company. It exists on the books only. But Karen has given him close to two hundred thousand dollars so far."

Tonya sat back, stunned and not sure what to think. Why would Karen steal from her own brother? Well, it wasn't like she hadn't seen family do worse to each other. Hell, her family was a prime example of that. But what were they involved with? And why this particular rapper? Then it hit her. A woman only gave a man money when she loved him, owed him, or was fucking him. Karen might love him, but she was probably definitely fucking him.

"What arc you going to do?" Tonya asked Shakira.

"I've got to tell Q," she said.

Tonya nodded, feeling horrible. She couldn't stand Karen, but it was going to break Q's heart when he found out that his sister was stealing from him and his company.

This was the beginning of the end for Karen. Her blunder had set off a chain of events that were going to have some pretty devastating effects upon her and were sure to shake things up around the record company.

Lil Q was visiting with his mother another weekend. This time Q hadn't brought him down, telling her that he had some urgent business to attend to. She hoped that wasn't code for "I'm gonna be fuckin' my girl." Never mind that he had never done that before, but Q wasn't acting the same, either. He had been polite ever since their fight and he continued to support her financially. And in the meantime, she had managed to keep her mouth shut—in front of him at least—since she didn't want to hurt her cash flow. But in the past, they had fought and Q would end up right back in her bed. But not this time. She began to suspect that this new girl of his was the reason.

"So, Quinton," Niecey asked. "Does ya daddy have a girl-friend?"

"Ummm, yeah," he replied.

"Oh, yeah?" Niecey casually said. "What's her name?"

"Her name's Tonya," he told her. "And guess what, Mom? She's from Philly, just like you."

Once Lil Q got started talking, it was hard for him to stop. He told his mother everything she wanted to know and then some.

"When do you see her?" Niecey asked. "Does she come over the house?"

"Most of the time, I see her like going toward the weekend, right before I leave to come here. She works for my dad."

"Is that a fact? What does she do?"

"She works in the marketing department," he said. "I forgot what she said she does."

Niecey asked, "Well, how does she look? I bet she's ugly, right?"

"Umm, no, she's not, Mom," he replied honestly. "She's cute."

"Well, would you date her if you was old enough?"

"Yeah, I would," Lil Q quickly answered. "But I'm not old enough yet. Maybe later, if she still looks good."

Never ask a question you really don't want to know the answer to.

She snapped, "Oh, shut up! You wouldn't know cute if it walked up to you and slapped you in the face. Ya father probably filled ya head up wit' that nonsense, just so you could come back and tell me."

"No, he didn't," the boy answered. "Dad doesn't talk about you. He said small minds talk about people. Great minds talk about ideas."

"To hell wit ya dad. Don't be quote that nigger to me," she cursed.

The truth hurt, and Niecey boiled with anger. Suddenly she burst into tears.

Lil Q was immediately alarmed and tried to comfort her by patting her on the back the way his father did with him whenever he was sad or got hurt.

"Ma, what's wrong?" he asked. "Why you cryin'?"

"Your father doesn't love us anymore," Niecey cried. "He's tryin' to break up our family. But I'm not gonna let him. He can't take you away from me. You don't wanna go, do you, Quinton? You wanna live wit' me, right?"

Lil Q was utterly confused. How could he tell his mother he didn't want to live there and not run the risk of upsetting her? But all his friends were in New York. And his father. He didn't want to leave them. And his mother had a nice house, but his father's was nicer. He wanted to live there, not here.

"Don't worry, Mom," he explained. "I won't leave you."

"I'm glad to hear you say that," Niecey said. "'Cause you know you're all I got. We all we got. Now, don't forget to tell the law guardian that the next time you go and see her, all right?"

"Okay, Mom," he replied.

"Thank you, baby!" she sang his praise. "We gonna have so much more fun when you come here to live for good. Ya father won't even miss you. He don't love you! He don't love nuttin' but his money and what's her face!"

And just as quickly as they had come, her tears were gone as something else occurred to her. "Quinton, does your father have any woman sleeping over his house?"

"Yeah, sometimes," Lil Q admitted. "But it's only Tonya. She the only girl he ever let stay there."

Niecey countered, "Oh, there's others?"

"No, just Tonya," he replied.

Now Niecey knew things were serious between Q and Tonya. Q didn't let anybody come to his house, let alone spend the night there. This revelation was like a slap in the face to Niecey. The thin thread of hope, of reconciliation, had just gone out the window. She flew off the handle into a jealous rage.

"Fuckin' bitch!" she cursed. "Quinton, listen to me. The next time you see ya dad's girlfriend, don't you say a fuckin' word to her. You hear me?"

"Yes," he answered meekly.

"That bitch ain't shit to you," she told him. "You don't gotta talk to her or listen to her. She's nobody!"

Niecey threatened, bribed, and coached her son. She did anything to sway his allegiance to her, making promises she couldn't keep and showering him with gifts. To her, all was fair in love and war.

There comes a time in every person's life when they're forced to face some harsh realities and to make some difficult decisions. Q had reached that point. When Shakira first explained to him the situation involving his sister and his artist, Q didn't believe her. He gave Shakira the third degree, questioning the messenger and almost disregarding the message. It wasn't until she placed the paperwork to substantiate her claims in front of him that he believed her. There it was in black and white, money wire transfer slips from the bank, signed by his sister, Karen Phelps, to Millennium Entertainment.

Shakira explained the whole scenario to Q, and what she suspected was going on with his sister and the rapper. With the evidence in hand, Q was easily able to connect the dots. The picture it painted forever shattered the innocent image he had of his sister. It wasn't the money that she had stolen that hurt him so much. He had tens of millions. It was the trust that he bestowed upon her that made the situation so difficult. This was his kid sister. He had sacrificed a lot so she could have. Q began to blame himself. Maybe he shouldn't have brought her into the music industry. Maybe he shouldn't have hired her. Maybe he shouldn't have kept his word to her. After struggling with these thoughts, Q erased these doubts from his mind. He had done nothing wrong.

So this is what they mean when they say don't go into business with family, huh? he mused. He had fought that notion. He had thought, *Why can't I go into business with my family? Why can't I surround myself with people I know and trust?* His sister's actions disappointed him, but he had to deal with them and with her.

But he grew angrier by the moment when he thought about all the times Young Fresh ta Def had tried to wiggle out of his recording contract, and all the time he had been using his sister to take from his plate. Q had personally discovered him, signed him, and brought him to New York, where he enjoyed a comfortable life and made an honest living. Had it not been for Q, Young Fresh ta Def probably would have been a statistic, either dead or in jail. Q had literally saved his life, and this was the thanks he got for his efforts.

Later that night, Karen was surprised when her doorbell rang. She wasn't expecting anyone. Young said that he had to take care of some business. She just hoped it was nothing illegal and that he was keeping out of trouble.

She was surprised when she looked through the peephole and saw Q standing there. Karen quickly unlocked the door.

"Q!" she exclaimed when she opened the door and saw him standing there. He was the last person she expected to see. She hugged him. "Come on in. What you doing here? I thought you were going to be in the studio all night putting the finishing touches on Ron-O's album."

"Yeah, I was at the studio all day today and all night last night," he said, walking into her living room.

"So what brings you by my spot?" she asked.

"What? I can't come by and see how my little sis is doing?" he said, turning to face her. "Do I need a reason to be concerned about you? Is loving you and being your family not enough?"

"Oh," Karen blushed, "that's so sweet. Thanks for thinking about me. I know you got a million things on your mind."

"Never too busy to forget about my family," he told her. "Now come in here and sit down. Let's chop it up for a minute."

Karen sat on her leather couch and Q sat on the love seat across from her. They made small talk, discussing the new homes that Q had just bought for his mother and his other sister, Roshaunna, in the Pocano Mountains region of Pennsylvania. They exchanged stories about distant relatives and who was doing dirt. When she was nice and relaxed, Q cut to the chase.

"Listen, Karen," he began. "I need to ask you something and I need you to be totally honest with me."

"Okay," she responded, wondering what he wanted to know.

"Why are you transferring large sums of money out of the record label's bank account? And what are you and Young Fresh ta Def planning to do with the money you stole?"

Karen stared at Q in shock. All she could think was, *How did he find out?*

The color drained from Karen's face and she sat there pale and at a loss for words. She had never anticipated Q finding out about what she had done, let alone confronting her. Caught, Karen did the only thing she could—cry. Tears streamed down her face as she dropped her head into her hands. But if she was looking for sympathy from Q, she would find none.

"Look, it's too late for all of that," he told her calmly. "Didn't you know the consequences of your actions? Karen, I can't believe you would cross me like this. Not you, anybody but you." He took a deep breath. "Now, tell me why you did it."

"I was going to put the money back," she sobbed. "I didn't think anyone would miss it. It was only a loan. He said he would pay it back."

"Calm down. You're not making sense, Karen. Pick your head up and look me in the eye and tell me why you did it."

Karen lifted her head, but she couldn't look her brother in the eye.

"Me and Young have been seeing each other. I wanted to keep our relationship on the down-low because I didn't want you to feel funny about me messing with the help. He began telling me about all the problems he was having with the label. So I began acting as an emissary for him. You remember a couple of times I called you on his behalf, but that went nowhere. So he had his lawyers try to get him released from the label, but you made it clear to them that the only way he could get out of his recording contract was to buy himself out. Whether you knew it or not, he was broke. Realistically, Young thought he was never going to get off the label. He thought his rap career would be stuck in limbo forever. He was about to get some kilos of cocaine from somebody and go down South to sell them. That's what he told me. I was in falling in love with him at the time. I couldn't let him make a sucidal move like that. My initial reaction was, 'What about your career?' I felt he had too much talent to revert back to the street life. So . . . so I intervened. I did what I did. And now I feel terrible about it."

Q couldn't believe his ears. Young Fresh ta Def had basically conned his sister into stealing from him. Deep down inside he had himself to thank for that. Q had helped shelter Karen all her young life. He made sure her focus was on school and nothing else. He routinely chased away any little boy who came around trying to holler at her. As a result, Karen grew up with tons of intellect but no street smarts. She couldn't recognize game when she heard it.

Q was deeply disappointed after listening to Karen recount

the events that led to her betrayal. Still, he had to do what he had to do, for the sake of his family and his company.

He stood up. "Karen, get your shit. I'm sending you up to Mommy's house until I can figure out what to do with you. Don't try to call or contact me. I'll call you when I'm good and ready. And another thing, whatever you do, do not involve Mommy in this. She doesn't need to know. It'll only stress her out. You know how she is," Q told her before he turned to leave. "Oh, yeah, one more thing. You call that motherfucka Young Fresh ta Def and have him meet you in front of your building around twelve o'clock tonight. If he asks you why so late, tell 'em you have a late meeting with me. If he acts funny, like he ain't going to come, tell 'em you got something for him and you don't want to talk about it over the phone. If he wants it, he'll have to come get it."

Young Fresh ta Def took the bait and arrived at Karen's Upper West Side condo right on time. He had taken a cab straight from a recording session at a Times Square recording studio. In his mind this was going to be fast. He was going to get whatever Karen had for him and be gone. He didn't plan on spending the night or having sex with her, although he wouldn't turn down some head from Karen, as long as it was a quickie. Tonight time was money. He had left some artists from his newly formed label in the studio to finish laying down their vocals. Studio time wasn't cheap, so he had to get back as soon as possible.

He didn't see Karen anywhere out front, so he buzzed her, thinking she might have gone upstairs, but got no answer. There was no way he was leaving there empty-handed, so he took a seat on a nearby car and waited.

After ten minutes he was looking up and down the block, and inside every passing cab, for any sign of Karen. He called her cell phone repeatedly but it kept going straight to voice mail. He was getting more and more frustrated by the minute. Then he spotted a shapely female form a short distance away, her provocative walk capturing his attention. Every step she took, her hips swayed, to some beat that only she could hear. Distracted from thoughts of Karen, Young Fresh ta Def stared, mesmerized. He couldn't wait until this female got close enough for him to engage her in some conversation. He might be able to bag this chick or at the very least walk away with her number.

The *click-clack* of her high-heeled shoes was like music to his ears. As she came closer, Young Fresh ta Def realized that she had a pretty face to match that banging body. Now everything was a go.

"Excuse me, miss, what you doing outside this time of night?" he said, smiling. "Don't you know there's all kinds of dangerous criminals running around the streets of New York?"

"Oh, really?" she said flirtatiously. "You wouldn't happen to be one of them, would you?"

He joked, "Me? I'm just a concerned law-abiding citizen, ma'am."

"Okay, I believe you. You didn't look like the killer type. You're too handsome for that. Unless you're a lady-killer? Now that I might believe," she said. "By the way, what's your name?"

"My bad. We doin' all this rapping and we don't even know each other's name. My name's Anthony," he replied. "And yours?"

"I'm Monica," she told him. "You live around here?"

"Nah, I'm supposed to meet my friend here. This is his building," he lied. "If you don't mind me asking, where you live at?"

"Oh, right on the next block," she told him. "My car is parked in the garage around the corner. You know you can't leave your car on the streets of New York. When you wake up tomorrow it might not be there."

"You ain't lying about that," he said. "This city is money hungry, they'll tow ya car in a minute."

She pulled a cigarette out of her purse. "Would you happen to have a light?"

Although Young Fresh ta Def was happy to be receiving all this rap from a beautiful young lady at this hour of the morning, he had to find a way to get her number and get her away from him before Karen made an unexpected appearance. He didn't want to blow whatever Karen had for him by her getting jealous about him talking to some other chick.

"Yeah, I got one," he said as he patted himself down. "Here you go." Monica smiled, revealing two rows of ultrawhite teeth.

Damn, this bitch got some white-ass teeth to be a smoker, he mused.

Had the aspiring MC bothered to do a quick surveillance of his immediate area, he would have noticed the dark late-model cargo van that was rapidly approaching with the headlights off.

"You smoke?" she asked, blowing a cloud of smoke into the air.

"Nah, Ma, I'm good," he stated. "Do you!"

"Can I keep this lighter?" she asked.

"Sure, no doubt."

He watched as she dropped the lighter and the pack of cigarettes in her bag. Then, in one swift motion, Monica produced a .25 automatic, stepped back, and pointed it straight at his head. His only response was to throw his hands up in the air in submission. He thought this was a robbery.

"Yell and I'll shoot!" Monica barked.

The van came to a quiet stop, the side door flew open, and out hopped two rugged, muscular thugs. They snatched up Young Fresh ta Def and threw him inside the van. The incident happened so fast that no one saw a thing.

"Yo, what the fuck is going on?" he yelled.

In response the goons began to savagely pistol-whip him. They rained blow after blow down on his face and head until Young Fresh to Def was beaten to a bloody pulp.

"Yo, you like taking things that don't belong to you, huh?" one goon asked. "Look, my man want his money back. All of it. Don't call no names, you know who we talking about and you know what you did. Tomorrow, you go to the bank and reroute that money back where you got it from. Don't call the police or try anything funny. Niggers don't want to have to swing past your mom's crib and snatch her up. Keep ya mouth shut, and everything will be all right. Nobody else will get hurt."

After that speech they rode in complete silence until they kicked Young Fresh ta Def out of the van on the West Side Highway. His head was still spinning as he picked himself up off the ground. Still, he had the presence of mind to know who was behind all this: Q. This was clearly a setup. He had heard stories about Q back in the days in Philly. Only now did he really begin to respect his gangsta. He had played a dangerous game with a very dangerous man, and lost.

Surrounded by five eyewitnesses at home, Q got the word about the accident Young Fresh ta Def had had. Since he was a boss, he made sure not to involve himself or his bodyguards, in the incident. He had other people on the payroll for that. Although he would have loved to have personally done his artist some bodily harm, Q knew he had to be smart. He had too much to lose. Besides, bosses didn't personally handle dirty work like that. They gave the orders and things got done.

Overcome by a sense of satisfaction, Q made love to Tonya all night long.

17

The next morning, Q went into Prestige early. He wanted to get in the studio, hoping it would clear his head. As he entered the building lobby, Q and company were approached by two white men in plain clothing. Q's bodyguards immediately surrounded him. The men flashed their badges.

"Quinton Phelps," one cop said. "We need to have a word with you."

"About what?" Q replied calmly. "Speak on it."

"It's about an upcoming rapper on your label," he told him. "The kid goes by the name of Young Fresh ta Def. It appears that the kid had a little accident last night. Somebody busted him up pretty good and we were wondering if you knew anything about this incident?"

"Wow!" Q exclaimed. "Is he hurt bad? I feel awful for the kid. But why are y'all wasting time even questioning me? I was at home last night with my bodyguards and my lady."

"I wish things were that simple, but sorry, it's not. There's a little bit more to the story than that. For instance, somehow your sister is mixed up in all this. Now, you can voluntarily come down to the station with us or we can pick you up later with a warrant. The choice is yours."

Immediately, Q knew he had no choice. If Karen was involved, then he needed to know what the cops had on her. He was furious. *She better not have lied to me,* he thought.

"Yo, Blue," he said to one of his bodyguards. "Y'all follow me downtown and call my lawyer and have him meet us there."

Down at the police station, every passing police officer seemed to stare at Q when he entered the building. Although they had had high-profile criminals here before, they had been investigating him for some time now. It wasn't until Q reached the interrogation room that he saw the culprit behind this. District Attorney Fera was inside the room, leaning against the wall, with a hot cup of coffee in his hand.

"If it isn't the infamous DA Fera, live and in the flesh," Q said coolly in greeting, "What's up? What's the meaning of this?"

"Mr. Phelps, how nice of you to join us on this beautiful morning."

Q smirked. "Y'all muthafuckas need to get off my dick, seriously. What's your problem with me? You mad at me 'cause my car cost more than your house? Black man can't make an honest living anymore? He gotta be doing something illegal?"

Fera sipped his coffee, unruffled. "Let's just see how smart your mouth is after your little chat with the detective." He smiled at Q. "The next time you see me I'll have an indictment with your name on it, smartass. I promise you." Then he turned and exited the room.

Q's stoic facial expression didn't let it show, but he was worried. Something about Fera was making him uneasy. The DA was just too sure of himself. It was as if he had an open-and-shut case. Without betraying himself, Q took a seat. His criminal lawyer, Matthew Schabb, walked in.

"Counsel, I'd like to inform you that no charges have been filed against your client, and at any time he is free to leave. However, it's in his best interests that he fully cooperate with us on this matter."

"We'll be the judge of that," Matt Schabb said.

"Okay, suit yourselves," the detective said. "Here's what we have so far. Your boy, aka rapper Young Fresh ta Def, has been using money funneled to him through his dummy company, Millennium, to buy large amounts of drugs and stockpile an arsenal of guns, which have been sold and distributed in the New York metropolitan area. Apparently he has taken the words 'keepin' it real' to a whole 'nother level, having decided to live what he raps about. Talk about art emulating life, huh? Christ! This guy's ridiculous."

"This is all you got?" Q snapped. "You bring me down here for something Young Fresh ta Def is doing?"

Matt Schabb cautioned, "Q, please let the detective finish speaking."

The dectective continued, "Anyway, before I was so rudely interrupted by Prince Charming here, as we speak the DA is building a very strong case for money laundering, interstate gunrunning, drug distribution, you name it. We have confidential informants willing to testify to those facts. Via a paper trail of bank transactions, we can directly connect the rapper and your darling sister Karen to a trail of death and destruction, drugs and guns, all financed by your bulging record sales. My colleagues assure me that they can almost guarantee that once they get ahold of the rapper, and we have several units combing the streets looking for him at this very moment, he'll roll over on you, Q. And with your prior criminal record, you'll serve a minimum of twenty years, with the possibility of a life sentence if you're convicted. And I promise you this, the DA will move to seize your assets if you're convicted or cop out in court, so it's back to the projects of Philly for you and your immediate family. All those fancy mansions, condos, platinum jewelry, and expensive luxury cars gone! Everything that you worked so hard to achieve will be taken from you. Listen to me: if you want to continue to support your dear old mom and live the glamorous life, cooperate with our ongoing investigation."

Bad Girlz 4 Life

Upon hearing the detective's story, Q was furious. Now he wished he had given the order to kill Young Fresh ta Def. That would have eliminated his problem. He couldn't believe that he had used his money for some shit like this.

"Here, gentlemen, take a look at these," the dectective said, sliding three thick manila envelopes across the table.

Q dumped the contents of the envelopes on the table. Numerous pictures fell out. Q filed through them. He immediately recognized them as some of his contemporaries in the music industry. One was the CEO of a rival rap label, and like him, he also had a questionable background. Slowly Q filed through the pictures of bodyguards, entourage members, managers, rappers, and promoters. Q knew almost every one of these people, but he also knew that he had no dealings with them besides the usual industry stuff.

The detective continued, "Q, I know you can easily recognize the people in those pictures. They are all involved in the music industry in one way or another. But what you may not know is that the New York City Police Department suspects them of being involved in a large-scale drug operation that stretches from here to across the country."

"Oh, yeah?" Q said. "That's news to me."

"Oh, yeah, this is big," the detective said. "And that's where you come in. We haven't been able to fully infiltrate this organization, but with your help . . ."

"My help?" Q interrupted him. "Look, Detective, don't insult me like that. I ain't nobody's rat. I'm a man. I don't play those type of games. You got the wrong man. Matt, let's go!"

The detective watched as his case walked out the door. Q might have turned down his offer to become a confidential informant, but he still knew that Q had problems of his own. He could only hold out the hope that Q would change his mind.

"That's what they all say, Q. If you change your mind, give us a call," the detective said. "But know that when you go down, your sister and your empire are going down with you. You've got twenty-four hours to give us a formal answer."

Suddenly it was clear to Q that the district attorney wanted him badly but was willing to sacrifice Q in order to get the others. Still, Q knew he wouldn't let the authorities flip him. He was prepared to stand by his word. *I ain't no snitch!*

Because the cops had approached Q quietly, the media hadn't gotten wind of the ongoing investigation. If they had, the police station would have been a madhouse, surrounded by photographers and reporters.

Q arrived home, where he found Tonya waiting for him. He filled her in on everything that had happened. By now she had become his closest confidante. They sat in his living room on the couch. Q had his eyes closed and his head in Tonya's lap while she stroked his head.

"Q, what are you going to do?" Tonya asked.

"What do you mean?" he replied. "I'll tell you what I'm not doing and that's telling."

"No, I didn't mean it like that. I know you a stand-up nigger. You ain't gotta tell me that," she replied.

"To tell you the truth, I don't know," he said.

Tonya stared down at him as she continued to stroke him. "You know," she said, "sometimes I do my best thinking when I take my mind off the thing I'm thinking about. So how about we just watch a movie or a basketball game on cable?"

Q just nodded.

While channel-surfing, Q asked where Lil Q was.

"Up in his room," Tonya told him. "I asked what he wanted for dinner, but he didn't seem interested. Looks like he's not in a good mood."

Q rubbed his eyes tiredly. "Yeah, he's been acting funny for a while now. I think Niecey's behind it."

Tonya frowned. "In what way?"

"I don't know, but I been thinking I should put a stop to Niecey's visits, at least until she straightens up and acts right. I hate to do that, but that's what her hand is calling for."

Q looked genuinely disturbed by the thought of separating Lil Q from his mother. Tonya felt helpless in the face of all the troubles that seemed to be piling up on Q. She wished she could make it all go away for her baby. Feeling a bit depressed, Tonya continued to flip through the channels, hoping to find something that would distract them both.

She stopped when she saw Manhattan District Attorney Robert Fera's face on the screen. He was holding a press conference to announce some secret indictments that were being handed down by the grand jury in a high-profile case he was involved in. At his side was his son, basking in his father's fifteen minutes of fame. It was clear he was being groomed to follow in his father's footsteps.

Tonya stared at the screen, struck once again by the feeling that she knew him from somewhere, another place and another time in her life. Her eyes widened when it hit her. Tonya jumped off the couch, knocking Q to the floor, and pointed at the screen while jumping up and down.

"Q! I seen this nigger before!" she said. "The DA's son. I know him!"

"What?" Q said, sitting up, disgruntled over being knocked down to the floor. "Is that a good or a bad thing?"

"Bad!" she told him with a smile. "Very. He used to come to some private locked-door stripper parties. The nigger was a regular. A freaky lil' mothafucka, too. A lot of girls didn't want to fuck with him. He was into golden showers and shit." Her smile widened. "And guess what? I recorded a lot of those parties. I was thinking of possibly turning the footage into DVDs to make some more money. But Na'eema talked me out of it. She said I might get somebody in trouble."

Q stared at her in disbelief. "Well, where's that film at now?" he asked.

"I got it in storage in Edgewater."

"Get your shit. We taking a little trip," he told her as he picked up the phone, called Lil Q's nanny, and told her to come over there to watch Lil Q for a couple of hours.

Q couldn't believe his good fortune. He hoped like hell that Tonya was right. This was the only chance he had to keep his sister out of a serious jam and clear the company's name. So with the clock ticking, Q and Tonya sped off in one of Q's European sports cars up the New Jersey Turnpike, their destination a twenty-four-hour storage facility.

After retrieving the tapes, they brought them back to Q's and stayed awake all night until they hit the jackpot. There on tape was Robert Fera Jr. engaging in illicit sex. Q's hopes began to soar. Maybe, just maybe, there was a light at the end of the tunnel.

Q's next step was to contact his lawyer. He informed him about what he had and instructed him to personally contact the district attorney's office. Robert Fera consented to the meeting, thinking Q was going to agree to being an informant.

In a quiet little coffee shop in midtown Manhattan, Robert Fera arrived twenty minutes late. He was wearing a big arrogant smile on his face, like a cheap suit. He strolled through the coffee shop like he owned the place. Matt Schabb, Q's attorney, offered him a handshake. Fera looked at it as if it were a poisonous snake and sat down.

"Good morning, Rob," Matt Schabb said, sitting down also.

"Morning," he replied. "Has your client come to his senses?"

"Umm, not exactly," Schabb said. "That's not the purpose of this meeting."

"Well, just what is the purpose of this meeting, then?" Fera inquired. "If your client isn't ready to play ball, I'll nail his ass to the cross myself when I'm done with him."

"Calm down, Rob," Schabb said, raising a hand. "I have something here that may interest you. Take a look at this."

Q's attorney pushed the PLAY button on his laptop computer and the video began to play. At first nothing made sense to the district attorney. He saw nothing terribly interesting, let alone incriminating. Clearly this meeting was a big waste of time.

"What am I supposed to be looking for?" he wondered. "This DVD is totally irrelevant."

"Hold your horses," Schabb insisted. "The show is about to begin."

As if on cue, Robert Fera Jr. suddenly entered the picture. He was led by a scantily clad female into what appeared to be an office. The tape showed the district attorney's son clearly handing the woman some money. Soon it was evident what the money was for. The two took turns performing oral sex on each other before the camera faded to black. Q's attorney fast-forwarded the video to numerous instances where the district attorney's son was caught in more compromising positions, each one worse than the one before. By the time the show stopped, Robert Fera was pale and barely breathing.

"In exchange for disposing of this damaging footage," Schabb said, "my client would like you to make this case just go away."

"That's impossible," Fera stated, shaken. "I can't do that."

"Nothing is impossible," Schabb stated. "Aren't you your party's leading candidate for the upcoming mayoral election? If this tape gets out you might as well kiss that good-bye. This could cause a lot of unnecessary problems. We wouldn't want that, now, would we?"

Fera recognized when he had been checkmated. He was caught between his political ambitions and the parental responsibilities of protecting his child. Reluctantly, he agreed to let Q off the hook. He left the coffee shop with a gentleman's agreement in place that this tape would make its way to the six o'clock news if Q so much as felt Fera breathing down his neck again. The district attorney knew that if it did, he would be ruined.

Q's attorney phoned him with the good news. Q let out a long sigh, knowing that he had dodged another bullet. Now to tie up one more loose end.

The *New York Daily News* and the *New York Post* ran front-page stories about the death of rapper Young Fresh ta Def, who died in a fatal car crash while eluding the police. The media was having a field day. Each paper had sensationalized headlines in their effort to outdo each other.

Q read the paper and merely shook his head. Fortunately for him, his company was able to retrieve most of the funds that had been stolen from their accounts before Young's untimely demise. When Q got the news, he turned off his phone. He was unable to be reached for comment.

18

One nightmare ended and another began.

"You can't be serious!" Q said into the phone. "This is a joke, right?"

"I wish it were, Mr. Phelps, but unfortunately it's not. This is very real, something I suggest you not take lightly. I have the paperwork in my hand to prove it," his lawyer told him. "Are you near a fax? I can fax these documents over to you right now for your review."

For a few seconds Q stayed on the phone, speechless. He was too upset to comment. Niecey had filed paperwork in family court, petitioning for full custody of their son.

Even after their fight, Q had maintained a cordial relationship with Niecey. He still provided for her financially. He continued to let Lil Q interact with his mother, even dropping him off for visits. He didn't do anything out of the normal to Niecey except stop sleeping with her. Q felt she wouldn't take him seriously if he continued to be intimate with her.

But Niecey's motives for taking Q to court were simple: revenge and financial gain. Q was her meal ticket, always was, and, if she had it her way, always would be. Since he wanted to be a whore and sleep around, then he would have to pay for his unfaithfulness. The court proceeding wasn't about who would best provide for the child, but rather who the father was and wasn't sleeping with.

"Mr. Phelps. Mr. Phelps, are you still there?"

"Oh, oh, yeah. I'm still here," Q replied. "You can send the paperwork over to my office. The fax number over there is 212-555-4815. Could you please put "Attention Mr. Phelps" on the paperwork?"

"All right," his attorney said. "But one more thing before I go. Will you be needing legal representation on this matter, or do you plan to handle this thing on your own? If you do need an attorney, I have a brother-in-law, Jameson Friedman, who works for the law firm of Walker, Lezman, & Brown. When it comes to family law they're the best in the business."

It didn't take much convincing on Q's part. He absolutely wanted the best. As a matter of fact, he had warned Niecey a long time ago that he would fight her to the ends of the earth should she ever try anything like this.

"If you ever involve the white man in our business, bitch, I swear I'll spend every last dime I got on the best lawyer money can buy to make sure you don't get custody," he had vowed. Now it was time to make good on that promise.

"Okay, that sounds good. I want him working on my case," Q said.

"That's wonderful. I'm glad to hear that," his attorney responded. "So what I'll do is, after my secretary sends the fax, I'll have her forward him your contact information, and he'll be contacting you immediately."

As soon as he hung up the phone, Q was almost overcome by a strong impulse to call Niecey and give her an earful. It took all the willpower he had not to. He wasn't about to stoop down to her level. But from now on there would be no direct contact with him, physical or verbal. If Niecey had a message for him, she'd better send it to him through her lawyer.

Fuckin' bitch! he cursed to himself. *Niggers told me not to*

*fuck wit you. See what the fuck I get for not listenin'? Fuckin'
problem child.*

In a foul mood, Q canceled the rest of his appointments for
the day. He and his bodyguards convened in Manhattan at his
Chelsea residence in Manhattan.

Niecey's betrayal left him feeling very bitter. He needed
someone to talk to, someone to hear his side of the story. He
called Tonya. He was relying on her not only for his physical
needs but his emotional ones as well.

"Yo, Tee, you ain't gonna believe this shit!" he said into the receiver.

"What happened?" she asked, never having heard Q this upset before.

"Pardon my language, but this bitch Niecey done took me
downtown," he told her.

"She did what? Downtown? What's that?"

"Niecey filed a petition with the courts for custody of Lil Q,"
he explained. "Now ain't that some shit? Do you believe that
broad? After all I did for her! Guess this what I get for bein' a
good nigger. I coulda did that chick dirty and left her ass when
she went to prison, but I didn't. I stayed there and held her
down, like I was suppose to."

Tonya could hear the pain in Q's voice. And although she
didn't like Niecey herself, she was careful how she chose her
words. Q and Niecey would always have some sort of relationship because of their son. Out of respect for that, Tonya never
bad-mouthed Niecey or tried to turn Q against her. As long as
what they did didn't interfere with her and Q's relationship,
Tonya had no beef with anyone. She would remain neutral and
play her position.

"Damn, that's messed up!" she replied. "Don't let her bullshit
get you, though. She just tryin' to fuck wit' you, that's all. All she
tryin' to do is inconvenience you."

"You think?" he asked.

"C'mon, man, she just wants some attention. Once the court takes a look at her record, there ain't no way they'll grant her custody," Tonya explained.

"You right, you right," Q said, calming down. This was exactly what he needed, someone to put things in perspective for him. There was nothing worse that someone could do to him than mess with his son. "I didn't even look at it like that," he cheerfully said. "I forgot all about that. That ain't a good look for her."

But Tonya radiated optimism. That was one of many things Q liked about her. Another was that she seemed to always have his back. Being from the street, he placed a high premium on those kinds of things.

After restoring Q's fragile confidence in the legal system, Tonya hung up the phone and went back to work. She was grateful that Q had even picked up the phone to consult with her on the matter. Little things like that meant so much to her.

With his day in court rapidly approaching, Q's anxiety was building. Although his lawyer had virtually assured him of a favorable outcome, he still had his doubts. Q had no faith in the judicial system whatsoever. During his tenure in the streets, he had seen some strange things, innocent men found guilty and guilty men found innocent. To him it was still a crapshoot, and no one could convince him otherwise.

Just before his court date, to add insult to injury, Q was served with a temporary order of protection by the sheriff's department, courtesy of Niecey. She claimed Q had physically abused her and verbally threatened her. Allegedly she was in fear for her life. If this was any indication of how their court proceedings were going to go, then things were about to get real ugly.

The family court line was long. It snaked around the corner.

It was filled with deadbeat dads and disgruntled mommas. Q arrived bright and early to no fanfare, accompanied by only two bodyguards. Like everyone else, he was made to wait his turn to enter the building. When he reached the entrance, his personal belongings were inspected and he had to pass through a metal detector for security reasons. Once that was done, he was directed upstairs to wait some more.

Once upstairs, Q met with his attorney, and he basically outlined today's events to Q. There was nothing noteworthy to mention; basically he was here to make an appearance. His attorney would handle everything.

For his appearance in court, Q opted to wear a suit and tie, something appropriate for the occasion. When Niecey finally made it upstairs, she sauntered through the courthouse corridor provocatively dressed in a tight black miniskirt with a matching black sweater. Her outfit showed off everything a man coveted in a woman: shapely legs, nice firm breasts, and junk in the trunk. Q took one look at her and shook his head. She smiled slyly back at him. He felt Niecey was inappropriately dressed. What she was wearing was better suited for the club, not court. She just wanted Q to see what he was missing and what the next man was now getting.

"Parties of Phelps and Howard," a court officer announced.

Q sighed. "'Bout time."

Their scheduled morning session had dragged on well into early afternoon. For approximately three hours Q and company had sat on the hard, cold wooden bench, waiting to hear his case called. He watched countless other people who came after him go into the courtroom before him.

Q entered the courtroom, followed closely by his attorney. He couldn't help but think that this place didn't look anything like the courtrooms that he had seen on one of those television dramas. It was small inside, and there was an absence of courtroom spectators and seats. There were two tables, one for the petitioner, which was Niecey, and her attorney. And the other table was for the respondent, Q, and his attorney. The only other people inside the room were the stenographer, the court officers, and the law guardian, all of whom seemed stoic and unapproachable.

Suddenly the presiding judge appeared from his chambers. He was an elderly, clean-shaven, bald white man, fragile in appearance. Though he was a diminutive figure, he seemed to have a commanding presence about him. Q didn't know whether this could be attributed to his job title or what.

After the judge took his seat on the bench and briefly reviewed the petition, court was in session. Like clockwork, a court officer positioned himself in front of the petitioner/respondent tables.

"Will both parties please rise?" he said. "Would you please raise your right hands and repeat after me. Do you swear to tell the truth, the whole truth, so help you God?"

Stone-faced, the court officer trained his laser-beam, no-nonsense stare first on Niecey before focusing on Q. The man definitely took his job seriously. It was as if his look was some form of truth serum that could detect a liar.

"I do," they both seemed to say in unison.

"Good afternoon, ladies and gentlemen," the judge began, as if he were carrying on a casual conversation. "Ms. Howard, I see that you don't have legal representation. Will you be representing yourself?"

"Oh, my lawyer had a trial scheduled for today," Niecey explained, "but he told me that he would be available for the next court date."

The judge didn't bother to address Q. He could see that he was well prepared and accompanied by his attorney.

If Q was expecting more from his first day in court, then he was sadly disappointed. The judge never spoke to him directly.

He spent just a few minutes chatting with his attorney before each party was assigned another court date.

When Q exited the courthouse, he was in for a surprise. He was besieged by half a dozen or so reporters and photographers, most of whom were paparazzi. He didn't know how they found out about his day in court or who told them, but this was a personal matter, and he was not open to discussion. Still, he tried his best to ignore this midday media blitz. He tried to deflect attention by proceeding straight to his limousine. But the media just wouldn't leave him alone.

"Excuse me, Mr. Phelps, can we get a word with you?" one reporter shouted while shoving a microphone up in his face.

"No comment," Q dryly stated.

Another reporter interrupted, "There are allegations swirling around this case about possible child neglect and/or child abuse. Would you like to comment on that?"

"What?" Q replied, caught off guard, then said, "No comment."

Using roughhouse tactics, Q and his bodyguards made their way through the mini-sea of leeches and parasites otherwise known as gossip columnists to a waiting limousine. All the while, pictures were being taken. Once inside, they were whisked away.

This was the flip side of fame that Q was now experiencing. His every little move, missteps included, was blown out of proportion. For no good reason at all, the press was willing to invade his privacy.

Once the main attraction was gone, the reporters turned their attention to Niecey, who gladly stopped and answered every question. The message was clear: Niecey was willing to try her case in the court of public opinion as well. She painted a false picture of herself as an innocent victim, a single mother, fighting for the right to be with her child, hoping the public outcry would shame Q into giving up custody of their son.

To Q, the show Niecey put on with the reporters wasn't a cause for concern. He wouldn't lose any sleep over her antics. What he did was have his attorney petition the court for a gag order for their case.

If Niecey decided to run her mouth to the press now, there would be a heavy price to pay. It would be one less distraction in what was quickly becoming a circuslike atmosphere.

In the days, weeks, and months between the next court date, Q busied himself with his music empire. It was business as usual. Niecey was the furthest thing from his mind. Too bad the same couldn't be said for Niecey. Q was constantly in her face. In the media, magazines, music videos, and television, she was constantly being bombarded with Q's image. Even though it was just entertainment, to see Q with another girl would drive her crazy. In her mind, he was her man. Sure, they were going through something right now, but they would get over it and reunite.

During this downtime, Niecey never felt lonelier in her life. She began to really look forward to her son's weekly visitation. Lil Q became the highlight of her week. Though Niecey might have put up a brave front, she feared losing the very thing she held dearest in this life, her son. She continued to try and brainwash her child against his own father and his new girlfriend.

Tonya was the first person Lil Q turned on. He completely shut down when it came to dealing with her. He went from interacting with her to avoiding her whenever possible. In his young mind Lil Q saw Tonya as the enemy. She was the reason for his parents' breakup.

To her credit, Tonya picked up on Lil Q's negative vibe and tried to defuse it. One day while running an errand to the grocery store, she broached the subject.

"Lil Q," she began. "I noticed over the past few weeks that you've been actin' funny toward me. Why?"

Lil Q totally ignored her. He didn't even bother to glance up from the PSP video game he was currently playing. It was like Tonya didn't exist to him. She had no authority over him. The only reason he was even in her presence was because he had to be.

"You hear me?" she asked. "It's not nice to ignore people."

Once again, Lil Q didn't respond or even look in her direction. Fed up, Tonya reached over and snatched his game away from him.

"Gimme that!" he shouted.

Tonya replied, "So you are alive, huh? Look, I know you think that I'm this and that. But what your mother and father are goin' through ain't got nothing to do with you or me. So you need to stop actin' funny toward me, okay? Whatever the problem is, I ain't got nuttin' to do with it. So can we go back to the way we were?"

With a defiant look on his face, Lil Q just stared at Tonya. It was like what she was saying wasn't even registering.

"What's good? We cool again or what?" Tonya asked.

"Can you gimme my game back?" Lil Q dryly stated.

At her wits' end, Tonya reluctantly shoved the game back into his hands and continued to drive. Still, she wasn't about to let their conversation end on that note.

"Listen, Lil Q, I know ya mother be bad-mouthin' me and talking about me. You ain't even gotta tell me that, I already know," she explained. "But what you need to do is ask her why I never talk about her."

After making that statement, Tonya decided to just let it go. She figured Lil Q would understand when he got older what was really going on.

Q saw how his son continued to change. He felt helpless as Lil Q became more and more distant and moody, to the point where he didn't want to interact with his dad anymore. Lil Q's grades began to suffer as he began to act out in school. The tight bond that they had forged while Niecey was in prison was slowly deteriorating. And there was nothing Q could do to stop it. Niecey's underhandedness was driving them apart.

Though the court procedure was still in the infancy stages, Q attended faithfully. He suffered through long hours of downtime in the waiting area, waiting to get his case heard before the judge, only to receive a postponement. There were so many false starts that Q was starting to believe the whole process was designed to discourage him from attending. He would endure months of this before the real fireworks began.

Niecey's original lawyer had tried to convince her not to have a custody trial. He did everything in his power to talk her out of it. He warned her of the hefty legal bill she might incur. And he told her of the unnecessary stress that might be placed on the child. In turn, Niecey rewarded her attorney for his efforts and honesty by firing him and hiring new legal representation. Her new attorney was a man named Lee Smith. He would become an extension and a reflection of his client, a complete asshole. Lee Smith would do whatever Niecey said to do, just as long as his client paid him.

On the day the trial was scheduled to begin, Q arrived at the courthouse in his usual attire, an expensive Italian business suit. Niecey showed up shortly thereafter, looking tacky as ever, in a tight pair of low-rider designer jeans, the kind that called too much attention to her butt. Quickly their names were read from the court docket and they were led into the courtroom, where their custody case was about to be heard.

As soon as the judge entered the courtroom from his chambers to preside over the custody case, he asked one last question.

"Before we begin this trial, let me ask, has there been any resolution in this matter, Counselor?" he asked, directing his question to the petitioner's attorney.

Due to an overworked legal system, the judge had no way of knowing what had transpired during the months since the case was first brought before him. He had seen countless others in the interim. They were all faceless and nameless, just numbers on the court's overcrowded docket. "No, Your Honor, there hasn't been any resolution in the matter," Lee Smith replied.

Niecey refused to even try to come to a civil agreement on the custody issue. Any invitations made by the defense to settle this thing amicably and out of court were rebuffed. Niecey remained steadfast in her hope to gain full custody of her son. She continued to push toward that dream, no matter how unlikely it might seem.

"All right, then," the judge said. "How many witnesses will be testifying?"

"We will call two witnesses," Lee Smith replied.

"How about you, Counselor?" the judge asked, redirecting his attention.

"We will call one witness, Your Honor," Jameson Friedman told the judge.

Both parties submitted their witness lists to the court. And immediately following that, court was adjourned to the following week. It didn't seem right to Q to be wasting all this time in court and to be no closer to the ending than when they started. But he couldn't do anything about the court's proceedings. So he just had to bear with it.

The seemingly endless wait for their court date was now over. From the start of the trial, both sides knew that this would be a hotly contested custody case. The main goal of any custody battle was to win, not to be considerate of the other parent's feelings. More often than not, child custody disputes warranted nasty tactics. Lee Smith was under direct orders from Niecey to assassinate Q's character, any chance he got.

"Mr. Smith, will you please call your first witness?" the judge asked.

"I call Bernice Howard to the stand," the attorney said.

Since the courtroom was so small, the court officer had to go out into the corridor to retrieve each witness as they were needed. When he returned, the court officer was followed by a medium-height, average-looking woman who bore a striking resemble to Niecey, because she was her mother. After being sworn in, the witness took the stand.

"Ma'am, would you state your name and your relationship to the petitioner to the court?" the attorney said.

"My name is Bernice Howard. And I'm Niecey Howard's mother," she replied.

The attorney began, "Mrs. Howard, how long have you known the defendant?"

"For a long long time," she answered. "I knew him when he was broke. We usta live in the same project."

"Mrs. Howard, would you please be more specific?" the attorney asked. "How long have you known the defendant? Five, ten, fifteen years?"

"More like ten or twelve years," she said. "We go way back."

"Is it safe to say you know the defendant Mr. Quinton Phelps very well? Correct?" the attorney asked.

"Yep," was the answer she came back with.

"Would you please tell the court about Mr. Phelps's former occupation," the attorney said.

"Q was a well-known drug dealer in the projects," she stated.

Q's attorney, Jameson Friedman, leaped out of his chair,

showing his immediate displeasure with the witness's statement.

"Objection!" he said. "That's purely speculation. My client doesn't even have a criminal record to substantiate that claim."

"Objection sustained," the judge interjected. "Counselor, would you not mislead the witness. Stick to the facts."

"Yes, Your Honor," the attorney continued.

When Bernice Howard left the stand, she was careful not to look in Q's direction. She was ashamed of herself, of the things she had said about Q under oath. She felt it wasn't necessary to say those things. Q had been very good to her in the past, showering her with expensive material things, like a car. It was her daughter, Niecey, who had gotten her involved with this madness. Now she was using Bernice like a pawn. Niecey was spoiled. Everything had to go her way. Bernice knew that she was partially to blame for Niecey's childlike attitude. She had given in to her demands all of Niecey's life. Still, Bernice had a hard time comprehending her daughter at times. She couldn't understand how something so right, Q and Niecey's relationship, could go so wrong.

Niecey Howard had been a problem child/drama queen all her life. She had been raised in a one-parent household in the Richard Allen projects in North Philadelphia. Her mother showered her with material possessions and attention, thinking that would help ease the pain of the absence of the child's father. Her plan backfired miserably. By solving one problem, she created an even bigger one. Niecey began her journey through life with a "me" attitude. In her mind, it was all about her. She never liked to share, and for that matter, she was never a good sport when she played with other children.

Without a father figure in her life to discipline her properly,

Niecey grew up fast. The streets became her outlet, her way of dealing with the absence of her dad. They gave her verification that she wasn't able to find anywhere else. Out there she was somebody.

Life in the Richard Allen projects was never a cakewalk for anybody, but Niecey had a bad habit of making things harder than they had to be. She went from a rebellious child to a wild adolescent in no time. As she got older, it became next to impossible for her mother to chastise her. Routinely she would publicly embarrass her mother, wherever they were, whenever she didn't get her way.

Bernice was a gentle person who didn't believe in hitting her child. Her theory stemmed from her own childhood experiences when her parents would routinely whip her and her brothers and sisters for the smallest violation of their strict rules. To her credit, she tried to treat Niecey like she wanted to be treated as a child. Unfortunately, that approach didn't work on Niecey. She took advantage of her mother at every opportunity.

Soon Niecey began running with an older crowd, moving fast. She dabbled in everything from being sexually promiscuous to involving herself in the project drug trade. While her mother was hard at work, Niecey would use their apartment as a stash house for young up-and-coming drug dealers. Her house became the cool hangout spot for all the kids in her building.

Around the same time Niecey started showing out, Q began his ascent up the slippery ladder in the drug game. His street notoriety soon caught Niecey's attention. She made it a point to get his attention. Every day she would pass by the building he sold drugs in front of. She was attracted to his power as much as he was attracted to her beauty.

Up until she met Q, Niecey had run over her mother, her ex-boyfriends, and everyone else. Q put an immediate halt to that. He became the first person strong enough to stand up to her. He didn't let her boss him around just because she was cute. And Niecey liked that. It made her want to be with him even more.

Initially, Bernice Howard wasn't too happy with the idea of her teenage daughter having a boyfriend. But once she met Q and got a chance to know him, she recognized that he was a good person. Q seemed to have a calming effect on her daughter. She especially liked that fact. He had a way of keeping her in line. When Q was around, Niecey seemed like a different person. She never disobeyed her mother.

One thing led to another, and soon Bernice allowed Q to move into her home. She turned a blind eye to his drug-dealing activities just as long as he respected her house. She could live with it, just as long as she didn't see it. Q had brought law and order to her home that hadn't been seen since Niecey was a child.

Over the years, Q and Niecey's relationship deepened, finally culminating in the birth of their only child, Quinton Phelps Jr. Although their relationship wasn't always peaches and cream, they had somehow managed to survive. If there was a turning point in their relationship, Bernice Howard would have to point to her daughter being charged with murder. Even though Q was a regular visitor at the prison, she felt that this marked the beginning of the end.

To Jameson Friedman, Smith's trial strategy was primitive. Lee Smith attempted to lead the witness with a calculated line of questions. It was a weak strategy he would employ over and over again in an attempt to damage Q's reputation. His tactics would backfire on him as he used them on each witness. He soon lost credibility in the court's eye.

Witness testimony that probably could have taken less than a week to be heard by the courts was stretched out over a few months, due to time constraints. Niecey and Q's custody case was given an allotted time of an hour or two every month. If they were lucky, some months they were scheduled for two court sessions a month. To Q it just didn't seem right. They had been in court for a little over a year and he still hadn't gotten anywhere.

Q's lawyer didn't bother to cross-examine Niecey's witnesses due to the fact that he thought the petitioner's attorney was doing a great job of digging a hole for himself. It wasn't until Niecey took the stand that Jameson Friedman exercised his option to cross-examine the witness.

"Good day, Ms. Howard," Friedman began.

"Hey!" she replied flatly.

"Ms. Howard, or is it Niecey? Which do you prefer to be called?"

"Niecey's fine!" she stated.

Friedman cut straight to the chase.

"Niecey, isn't it true that you're a convicted murderer?" he asked.

"No, I plea-bargained to a lesser charge," she snapped, attempting to clarify the matter.

After pointing out that fact, Q's attorney proceeded to make a case for his client receiving full custody of his child. Jameson Friedman began to address more relevant matters, like why and how his client's home was the best place for a child. He stated his case for who should get primary custody: the pickup and dropoff schedules and locations, who would pay for the child's education, how the child's time would be split between the two parents on weekends, summer vacations, and holidays.

Jameson Friedman's case was shaping up nicely, and he hadn't even begun to call his own witness. Q was pleased with his legal representation. He felt that his high-priced legal defense was worth every penny.

Niecey must have sensed that her case was falling apart, so during a lunch break, she did the unthinkable: she fired her lawyer. This added to the already lengthy delay in the trial.

Niecey's stupidity had its telltale signs from the beginning, but it culminated with her firing her attorney and representing herself. There was an old saying that came to mind whenever anyone in the courtroom looked at Niecey: "He who represents himself has a fool for a client."

If nothing else, Niecey brought entertainment value to the proceedings. She did and said one outrageous thing after another. She quickly became the talk of the entire courthouse. Everyone from judges to court officers talked about her custody case.

With every court proceeding Q felt like he was losing a piece of himself, a piece of his dignity. He found it hard to keep his hands clean when Niecey was slinging so much mud. Soon even he got caught up in Niecey's nonsense. When Niecey brought a male friend whom she was currently seeing to court, Q responded by doing the same one week later. He had Tonya come with him to family court for emotional support. Niecey definitely didn't take too kindly to this. As soon as she got a chance, she picked a fight with Tonya.

"Excuse me, Mr. Phelps, can we discuss something in private for a moment?" his attorney asked.

"Yeah, what's goin' on?" Q fired back.

Tonya stepped away to give Q some freedom to discuss his case with his attorney. Not to give the impression of being nosy,

Tonya wandered off, away from Q's security team. Tonya strolled off near the elevators. There she was met by Niecey, who immediately approached her.

"Look, bitch, why don't you make yourself useful and tell ya man, Q, to take my son outta that fuckin' private school he got him in. He ain't learnin' nothin' and he don't like it there!"

Niecey needed a reason to come at Tonya. If not, she would come across as trying to be a bully. So she used her son as an excuse to have a confrontation with Tonya.

"What?" Tonya spat. "What are you talkin' about?"

Tonya didn't know what to make of Niecey's statement. She didn't have anything to do with what Niecey and Q were going through, so she didn't know why Niecey was even involving her in the situation. Besides that, Tonya didn't like the way Niecey had approached her. She didn't know who Niecey thought she was talking to her like that anyway.

Tonya continued, "I ain't tell him nothin'! You tell 'em, bitch! He right over there!"

At that point Tonya was vexed. All kinds of thoughts ran through her mind. She was from the hood just like Niecey. There, people tended to settle their disputes violently. If someone offended someone else, then better be prepared to fight. Tonya always had the attitude of fighting where she got mad at.

I should just sucker-punch this bitch! She ain't crazy! I'll show her crazy! Tonya thought.

Niecey must have been reading Tonya's mind. It seemed like the moment she conjured up the thought, Niecey acted on it. As soon as Tonya turned her head, Niecey struck her with a wild blow on the side of the head. The punch didn't have anything behind it, so Tonya was able to recover quickly. Once she did, it was on from there. Tonya and Niecey went toe to toe exchanging punches, much to the surprise of stunned onlookers and court officials.

By the time Q and his entourage had turned to see what all the commotion was about, dozens of court officers had begun to converge on the scene. Within seconds they had successfully separated the two combatants. Q couldn't believe his eyes. He stopped to talk to his attorney for a minute, and all hell had broken loose. Though he didn't see what had happened, Q still placed the blame for the fight on Niecey. If anything, he figured that Tonya was just defending herself, which was something he had expected her to do.

Amazingly, Tonya and Niecey got away with fighting in family court without getting arrested. But that didn't mean the fight went unnoticed. Tonya was forbidden to ever attend another court date. And the presiding judge was told of Niecey's involvement. Unfortunately for everyone, Niecey was just getting warmed up.

As it turned out, Q felt really bad for Tonya. He felt it was as much his fault as anyone's that she had an altercation with Niecey. From that day forth he promised never to ask Tonya to accompany him to court again. So a few days later, on the spur of the moment, he went to a Mercedes-Benz dealer and leased a Mercedes Benz S500 luxury sedan in the company's name for Tonya. Initially she balked at accepting it, but after lots of encouragement from Q, Tonya gratefully accepted it.

A few weeks later, it was Q's attorney's turn to present his case. Q was the only witness he planned to put up on the stand. But Q would be giving lengthy testimony—his attorney would make sure of it.

As Q gave a glowing testimony, Niecey sat at the table taking notes. At times she scribbled furiously on a yellow legal pad.

She would stare at the notes and shake her head, as if she had something on Q. Niecey acted as if she were going to poke holes in his defense during cross-examination. The few times that Niecey and Q did manage to make eye contact, Niecey smirked at him. But it was a weak attempt to hide her misery. Niecey was growing increasingly frustrated listening to the rosy picture the opposing attorney was painting of Q. In her mind, this wasn't the Q she knew.

Throughout the entire trial, the judge had appeared to not be giving the court proceedings his full attention. Suddenly he appeared very alert and vibrant during Q's testimony. Everyone in the courtroom saw it as a good sign for the defense.

Jameson Friedman made it look easy. He did a brilliant job of portraying Q as a loving father, a philanthropist, and a pillar of the community. When he was done there was no doubt in his mind that the case was over. However, in Niecey's mind the fight was far from over; on the contrary, it was only beginning. Now it was her turn to cross-examine the witness.

She began, "Mr. Phelps, is it true that you are a record producer and owner of a record company?"

"Yes," Q admitted.

"Isn't it also true that the majority of the music industry is on drugs?" she asked.

"Objection, Your Honor," Q's attorney interrupted.

"Sustained!" the judge said. "Ms. Howard, please get to the point you're trying to make."

"If you will allow me to, Your Honor," she said.

"You may proceed," the judge commented.

"Mr. Phelps, isn't it true that you take a drug called Ecstasy?" she asked him.

"What?" he replied, clearly upset. "You know me, you know I don't do drugs!"

"I don't know, Mr. Phelps," she replied. "I only thought I did."

Once again, Q's attorney leaped from his seat to make an objection. The judge ultimately agreed with him and reprimanded her for her line of questioning.

"Tell me somethin', Mr. Phelps," she said. "How can you be such a wonderful father when you work such long hours?"

"I get the majority of my work done while my son is in school," he declared. "My hours are flexible. I own the company, I can come and go as I please."

"Oh, really?" she remarked. "Ain't you lucky!"

Q shot her a look that seemed to say, "You can't be serious." Just when he thought she couldn't sink any lower, Niecey took it to an all-time low.

She continued, "Mr. Phelps, what if I were to inform you that the child you think is your son really isn't your child at all?"

Now Q, his attorney, and the court had seen and heard it all from Niecey. She had gone from assassinating Q's character to leveling false accusations in a desperate attempt to gain the upper hand in these custody proceedings.

"Objection!" Jameson Friedman shouted.

"Sustained!" the judge agreed. "Ms. Howard, the question of paternity is not an issue for the court to decide at this point in time. This is a custody trial. Please refrain from making comments or questions pertaining to paternity."

"Okay, Your Honor," Niecey replied. "I have no further questions for Mr. Phelps."

Now that each side had rested its case, the fate of Quinton Phelps Jr. was in the hands of the presiding judge. It would be his decision and his alone where and whom the child would end up with. He had the final say after taking into account the reports and recommendations of the law guardians and Child Protective Services. He was the judge, the jury, and the executioner.

After the presiding judge mulled over his decision for close to a month, the courts and everyone involved in the case were made aware of the final outcome of the case.

"Hello, Mr. Phelps?" Jameson Friedman spoke into the phone.

"Yeah," he replied.

At that moment there were butterflies in Q's stomach the size of bats. He was nervous for a reason. A phone call from his attorney could only mean one thing: the court had come to a decision on his custody case. Although this was the moment he had been waiting for for close to two years now, now that it was here he wasn't so sure if he wanted to hear it.

"The court has made a ruling in your custody case," his attorney explained. "Congratulations! You won. The courts awarded you full custody of your son. You and Ms. Howard are to alternate holidays, and she gets to keep her weekend visitations along with six weeks in the summer, which you are responsible for providing transportation to and from."

Q took a deep breath and exhaled. Instantly a smile creased his face. He was elated that the court had ruled in his favor. Right now he would give anything to see Niecey's facial expression when she heard the ruling. To see the look on her face would be priceless. Tonight Q planned on taking Tonya out to dinner to celebrate. He knew she would get a kick out of it after what had happened between them. Surely they would have a laugh at her expense.

Meanwhile, in Philadelphia, Niecey was informed of the court's decision by mail. She was irate. Niecey couldn't believe that the courts would award Q full custody. The decision completely ruined her plans to file for child support. Her cash cow was now gone. Now Niecey had to live with the fact that her son had been removed from her everyday life by the court system, at least until he was old enough to decide for himself. She felt everything that she held near and dear in this world, her child, ripped away from her. Angrily she balled the decision up and threw it in the trash. To her it wasn't worth the paper it was printed on. Niecey had every right to be mad at someone for the court's ruling, and that person was herself. Whether she knew it or not, Niecey had supplied the judge with all the evidence he needed to make his decision. Her erratic behavior and her malicious line of questioning had doomed her. The judge's decision was almost unprecedented. The mother almost always retained custody of her child, unless there was evidence of drug or sexual abuse.

In Niecey's twisted mind, she wasn't to blame for her troubles, Q was. Niecey vowed to get back at him, no matter what it took.

19

The results," the doctor said, "have come back positive."
Tonya couldn't believe her ears. Immediately she trained
her eyes on a spot on the ceiling. This was just unbelievable. She
inhaled deeply as she digested the news and pondered her next
move.

Though Tonya hadn't had a checkup in years, here she was in
the doctor's office. After having a battery of tests performed on
her to check her health, she was totally stunned. The only reason she was here today was because she had been feeling funny
as of late. And she had this beautiful thing called health insurance. She felt it was time that she used it, since she was paying
for it anyway.

"Are you sure?" she asked.

The doctor stared back at her blankly. She was trying to remain professional, but clearly her patience was wearing thin. She
had been in the medical field for over twenty years and counting.
Yet there was always some patient who doubted their diagnosis.

"Ms. Morris, no test is one hundred percent accurate. But
this one is close to it. You are indeed pregnant," the doctor said.
"Now, if you would please excuse me, I have another patient to
attend to."

"Thank you," Tonya solemnly said.

Tonya still couldn't believe it. At that moment she realized she had never expected to hear those words. There was no way in the world she could have foreseen this. Admittedly, she wasn't ready for parenthood.

What the hell I'm supposed to do now? she wondered. *What the hell is Q going to say? Damn!*

Thoughts of her pregnancy tormented and teased Tonya. On the one hand, she didn't want to be pregnant; on the other hand, she was thrilled that it was Q's. Yet she didn't want to be anyone's baby's momma. She wanted to be some man's wife. And with all the current drama that Niecey was giving him, she couldn't see Q rushing into another potentially similar situation.

On a dark, rainy day in New York City, Tonya exited the doctor's office and aimlessly walked the streets of midtown Manhattan. In her mind she was coming to terms with some of the most disturbing news in her young life. Tonya took turns fighting the urge to cry and then making a joke out of the situation. She had to laugh to keep from crying. Tonya's thoughts shifted to Q. She wondered how he would take the news. She knew Q's reaction to it, one way or the other, would play a role in how she would ultimately handle the situation. How would this affect their relationship?

After Tonya was nearly hit by a yellow taxicab while crossing a busy intersection, she was convinced that she was dwelling on the subject too hard. She was pregnant, not dying. This wasn't the end of the world. If nothing else, she would go into work today to get those thoughts off her mind.

When Tonya arrived at the office, she barely spoke two words to anyone. She made a beeline straight to her office and closed the door. She wasn't in the mood for anyone's mess. Once she settled in, she reached inside her drawer for some headache medication. After gulping down the aspirin dry, Tonya mentally prepared herself for work.

Tonya started her workday the way she normally would, by looking at her calendar for any scheduled meetings, appointments, or conference calls. When she looked down at the calendar, suddenly she was reminded of something very important. Today was her birthday. In the midst of all the drama, she had almost forgotten. But there it was, circled and highlighted, with the words "B-day" written inside the box.

Well, I guess I already got my birthday present this morning. Wow, some fuckin' present that was, she mused.

In Tonya's book this was a day for celebration. Although she didn't have anything special planned, this was still a joyous achievement. She had lived to see another year. A few people she knew hadn't. For that fact alone she was grateful. To her, any day aboveground was a good day.

Suddenly her grouchiness was replaced by happiness, as if she were struck by a ray of sunshine on a dark, cloudy day. Instantly Tonya had peace of mind. Just as she was getting herself together, there came a knock at the door.

"Come in," she said.

In walked Shakira and Annie, wearing silly little birthday hats and holding a chocolate cupcake with one lit candle. After entering her office, they quickly closed the door behind them, so as not to call attention to their mini-celebration.

"Happy birthday to you! Happy birthday to you!" Annie sang softly.

Shakira countered soulfully with a different chorus. "Go, go, go, Tonya, it's ya birthday. Go, Tonya, it's ya birthday!"

As they crooned their individual renditions of birthday songs, Tonya was touched by the gesture. It lifted her spirits. She thought this was so sweet of them. She couldn't believe that they had even remembered her day. Tonya was thankful that at least someone had. Thus far the same couldn't be said for Q.

"Ya'll too much!" She shook her head.

"Make a wish and blow out the candles!" Shakira said. "Hurry up before the wax begins to melt on ya birthday cupcake."

Tonya lowered her face until it was at eye level with the cupcake, and like a child she closed her eyes tight, made a wish, and blew out the candles.

"Yay!" Annie added. "Well, hate to spoil the fun, but I gotta go. I'm the first line of defense around her. Catch ya later, ladies!"

"Bye, Annie, and thanks!" Tonya said. "I appreciate this."

"It's time for me to get a move on, too," Shakira said. "I gotta pile of work sittin' on my desk waitin' for me."

"Don't I know it," Tonya replied. "Shakira, you the hardest-workin' exec in the music biz. I don't believe in role models, but you mine!"

Shakira shot back, "Girl, what you talkin' 'bout? Flattery will get you everywhere."

"Thanks for stoppin' by. See you later."

All jokes aside, Tonya really admired Shakira's strong work ethic. She felt that in a couple of years Shakira could quite possibly be running Prestige Records.

With her makeshift birthday party over, Tonya settled in to begin a hard day's work. Just as she began to check her e-mail, there was a knock at the door.

"Come in," Tonya announced, wondering who this could possibly be.

Annie walked in with a long, rectangular-shaped box in hand. From the moment Tonya saw the box, she knew what it was flowers.

"These just came for you. A local florist delivered them," Annie explained.

As she laid the box across Tonya's desk, the sweet aroma of the roses escaped the box. Quickly Tonya removed the envelope that was attached to it. Within a fraction of a second she tore into it. The opening of the envelope revealed a card stuffed with hundred-dollar bills and a gift certificate to a luxurious day spa.

Tonya waited until Annie left before she read the card. Yes, everyone knew that she and Q were dating, but that didn't mean she had it out there more than it already was.

She knew females have a tendency to run their mouths. This was why she didn't have too many as friends. This was where she drew the line with Annie and Shakira. Tonya summed up their relationship as work related, although she was becoming quite fond of Shakira. She felt like she got closer to her every day.

Now that Annie was gone, Tonya was free to read her birthday card from Q.

Hey birthday girl. I know you thought I forgot about you but as you can see I didn't. What kinda man would I be if I overlooked the most important day of the year, huh? Anyway, I didn't know what your pockets looked like so I sent u some cash. And a gift certificate to a day spa. You work hard, take the rest of the day off to pamper yourself. I booked you for a two-hour time slot this afternoon. Enjoy. I appreciate everything that you do for me. We'll get up together later. I'll take you out to dinner tonight to celebrate.

Love is Love.

Q

That's what's up! Tonya mused to herself. *Q, you didn't forget about me after all.*

Sitting at her desk, Tonya must have reread the letter half a dozen more times, as if the words on the card would somehow change. Q had scored major cool points for even remembering her birthday. Never mind the gifts, it was the little things that meant so much to Tonya. And this was one of them.

After gathering up her things and shutting down her computer, Tonya was off to the day spa. She could have floated there, that was how good she was feeling.

The spa at Mandarin Oriental Hotel was a short trip by taxi, even in the hectic midtown afternoon traffic. Tonya arrived at the spa unsure of what to really expect. The only time she even had a massage performed on her, it was done by an amateur, some guy who was trying to get into her pants, someone who didn't have the patience or expertise to properly soothe her aching body.

After entering the hotel, Tonya was directed to the thirty-fifth floor, where the spa facilities were located. She took the elevator upstairs and got off on the prescribed floor. From the moment she exited the elevator Tonya could tell that the spa catered to a distinguished clientele. The spa exuded elegance with its Oriental-influenced décor. She was greeted by the spa concierge as soon as she entered.

"Hello, may I help you?" he said.

"Yes," she replied. "My name is Tonya Morris. I believe I have an appointment scheduled for this afternoon."

Quickly, the spa concierge punched her name up in the computer to confirm the appointment. The computer validated what Tonya told him. Once Tonya handed over her gift certificate, they each prepared themselves to conduct business.

"What kind of treatment would you like?" he asked. "Will it be a facial massage or a body massage? Or would you like both?"

Tonya replied, "I don't know. What do you suggest?"

"Well, ma'am, is this your first time here?"

"It's my first time in a spa period."

"Oh, okay, I see," he said. "Then what I suggest to you is our Swedish massage. It's the most popular among first-timers and very relaxing."

The spa concierge went on to explain the differences in the various types of massages that the spa offered, including therapeutic and deep-tissue massage. He expounded on the health benefits of each. Ultimately, Tonya opted for his first suggestion, though they all sounded good to her. After all, this was her first time, so who was she to disagree? At this point anything that was suggested, she basically went along with.

Tonya was escorted to a private changing room. There she was given a robe and a pair of slippers. Tonya slipped out of her clothes and into the garments she was given. Underneath the robe she was naked as the day she was born. Tonya had no problem getting naked. After all, she was once a stripper. One couldn't be in that profession for as long as she was with hang-ups about getting naked.

Shortly afterward a female massage therapist came by the changing room to retrieve Tonya. She escorted her to another place called the treatment room.

Once inside the room the massage therapist instructed Tonya on how to properly get on the massage table and which position to lay in. Then she left the room.

When she was gone, Tonya took off her robe, hung it on the hook and got underneath the crisp white sheets. Suddenly there was a knock on the door. It was the therapist, signaling her reentry into the room.

"Excuse me, miss. No disrespect, but I would really feel very uncomfortable if you're the person giving me the massage. I'm not into women," Tonya explained.

"No problem," the woman replied in a thick foreign accent. "I will send someone else."

If anyone was going to get their kicks off on her, Tonya preferred it to be a man. She always thought that if a woman touched her in a sensual way, then she might like it and that might make her gay. Tonya's head was full with all sorts of ho-

mophobic nonsense. As dumb as it was, she adhered to it reli-
giously.

When the treatment room door swung back open, Tonya was
glad to see that the person entering the room was a man, although she had her suspicions about his sexual orientation. He
looked a little feminine to her. Tonya decided not to make a big
fuss about it. She was anxious to get going.

"You ready to get started?" the massage therapist asked.

"Yup!" Tonya said. "Ready as I'll ever be."

"Good. Get ready to relax your mind and let your body be
free," he said. "This is the closest thing to heaven on earth."

"If you say so," Tonya said.

"You'll see. Some say it's better than sex."

"Oh, really?" Tonya said, laughing.

"Really!" he added.

The massage therapist began to rub Tonya with special oil.
For the next fifty to sixty minutes, the massage therapist worked
his magic. He stroked and kneaded Tonya's muscles, working
them over tirelessly. Tonya would spend a good part of the day
being poked and prodded on the massage table.

"Ummmm," Tonya moaned.

"See, I told you."

With her eyes already closed, Tonya merely smiled in response. She didn't want to engage in too much conversation.
She was enjoying this too much. Sensing as much, the massage
therapist concentrated on his job.

The invigorating feeling Tonya was currently experiencing
was unlike any feeling she had ever felt before. It felt so good
that Tonya dozed off a few times, drifting in and out of con-
sciousness. The feeling was addictive. Tonya planned to come
back sometime soon.

Before Tonya knew it, it was time for her to get a facial. Reluctantly, she did so. She didn't find this massage as enjoyable

SHANNON HOLMES

as the last, but it felt good just the same. By the time Tonya's session was done, she swore by its mysterious healing powers. It seemed like the spa de-stressed her mind and rejuvenated her body. Tonya's satisfaction was reflected in her tip. She gave her personal massage therapist a hefty tip of two hundred dollars.

As she dressed, Tonya couldn't help but think to herself that this was shaping up to be the best birthday she ever had.

Right before Tonya exited the day spa, she received a phone call from Q. She explained to him that she was finished with her massage and she didn't know what she was doing or where she was going next. He then dispatched a limousine to pick her up and bring her to him. The limousine took Tonya to a music studio called Baseline, which had recorded every prominent rap figure at one time or another in their career. Q was there, helping one of his artists put the finishing touches on a remix of one of his hit records.

As soon as Q saw Tonya, he immediately stopped what he was doing and went over to embrace her. He gave her a big affectionate hug, the kind that lovers share when they long for each other.

"What's up, birthday girl?" he hollered. "How you like your massage? That shit was bananas, right?"

"All I'm going to say is, I'll be back," she said with a smile. "You do know you done started somethin'."

What Tonya didn't know was that Q got just as much enjoyment out of turning her on to new things as she did. He wanted to show her another slice of life. But she already saw for herself that this was a whole different ballgame. She had stopped being in awe of Q and the things his money could buy a long time ago. Tonya carried herself with amazing dignity for someone from the ghetto, someone lacking the proper home training. She seemed to make adjustments on the fly, and act accordingly. Unlike Niecey—Q couldn't take her anywhere.

"Look, this shit gonna take a lil' longer than I expected," he explained. "But since it's still early, I'ma give you my American Express Black Card and let you do a lil' shoppin'. Okay?"

Okay? Tonya thought. *Was that a question? Of course it was okay.*

"Go to the Gucci store on Fifth Avenue or SoHo and buy yourself somethin' nice," he ordered. "By the time you come back I should be ready. We go out to eat then."

"All right, I'll be back," she told him.

"Don't take all day, either," he warned playfully.

Tonya happily exited the studio, Black Card in hand, off to do what she was told. She hit all the trendy boutiques and well-established department stores like Tiffany's and Century 21. When her shopping spree was over, Tonya had rung up over ten thousand dollars on Q's Black Card. It was a struggle for her to fit all her bags into the limousine's trunk. Somehow Tonya and the chauffeur managed.

Amid the dimly lit, calm atmosphere of the restaurant, Tonya finally had a chance to relax, slow down and enjoy her meal. The day had been full of surprises, one after another. Aside from the material gifts she had received, it was the quality time that she spent with Q that she valued the most. This meant the world to her. She would give back all the gifts just for moments like this. For her they came few and far between, because of Q's hectic work schedule.

Tonya had been on both sides of the coin. She had dealt with guys who were broke, and now she had a man with money. One thing she realized: broke guys' girlfriends wanted time and rich guys' girlfriends wanted time. From either person there was no way you were going to get both; it was one or the other.

"I don't know how many times I'm gonna say this," Tonya began, "but thank you again. I appreciate everything you've done for me."

Aside from Tonya receiving the shock of the hour from the doctor, her birthday had been everything she could have ever hoped for and more.

"C'mon, now," Q said smiling. "Once was enough. I get the point."

After exchanging a few more words, Tonya and Q went back to eating their individual salads while waiting on their meals to arrive. Hungry, Q was a bit more attentive to his salad, focusing solely on his food. Meanwhile, as they ate, Tonya couldn't help gazing at the handsome man sitting across from her. She really did love him. Suddenly she could see herself giving birth to Q's baby. She could see herself with him for the rest of her life.

"What you over there thinking about?" he asked when he noticed she wasn't eating.

"Oh, nothing!" she quickly replied, going back to her food.

"You sure?" he asked, concerned. "You ain't gotta lie to me. C'mon, tell me whatcha was thinkin' about. I wanna know your innermost thoughts."

She thought to herself, *Do you really wanna know what I'm thinkin' about, mister?*

"You really want to know?" Tonya asked aloud, giving Q a way out.

"Yeah," Q said. "I wanna know. Whatever it is, I can handle it. I'ma big boy!"

The moment of truth had come and Tonya could feel it.

"Okay, big boy," she said, putting her fork down. She took a deep breath and looked him in the eye. "I'm pregnant!"

Q's jaw damn near dropped in disbelief.

"Wow!" Q finally managed to say.

He struggled to find something meaningful to say, but he couldn't find the right words at the moment.

Q couldn't believe this was happening again. They had always used condoms. After Niecey, Q had always been careful, but here was Tonya telling him that she was carrying his seed. No, Tonya and Niecey were nothing alike, and yes, he loved this girl more than he had ever loved anyone, but . . . he couldn't help wondering if Tonya hadn't done this on purpose, as a way to guarantee that she would always be a part of his life. Maybe telling her that he loved her wasn't enough. Maybe giving her everything her heart desired wasn't enough. He had definitely learned from the past that for some females there was never enough. He didn't want to believe that Tonya was like that, and part of him was telling himself that he was being a damn fool to even think this. But another part of him was saying that this was some fucked-up history repeating itself. And after everything he had just gone through with the trial and Niecey . . . Lil Q still wasn't back to his old self. *Damn!* Q thought. *Why is this happening?*

Tonya felt as if she had been punched in the chest. Q didn't want this baby. It was written all over his face, in the way he now held his body. If he really loved her, then why would he be sitting there looking like he had just swallowed something bad? Tonya swallowed a lump in her throat and tried not to cry.

"That's all you have to say?" she asked. "Wow?"

Q heard the pain in her voice and it immediately made him feel bad, which then made him angry. What did she expect him to say after dropping a bomb like that on him? He found himself going on the defensive. "What do you want me to say? It is what it is. The ball is in your court."

Tonya stared at him, so hurt she couldn't even speak. She hadn't expected Q to do her like this. Well, she guessed it really was all fun and games for him. It had never been about love. She felt like a fool. Once again she had opened herself up to this man and he had crushed her like a bug.

Right now, all she wanted to do was get away. Maybe she would go to Philadelphia, visit her mom for the weekend. Just for a little while, so she could get her mind right and figure out what she was going to do. She didn't want to make any drastic decisions based purely on emotion.

"Before I leave, I just want you to know that if I had known it was going to go down like this, I never would have gotten with you again. But I didn't get pregnant by myself and I didn't do it on purpose."

"Well, since you brought it up, did you?"

Tonya wanted to punch him right in his face.

She had been accused of being a lot of things in her lifetime, most of which came from disgruntled clients in her former profession, but she had never been accused of trying to trap a man with an unwanted child. Tonya knew a baby didn't keep a man.

"You know what, Q? Fuck you! And your money!" she cursed. "If I decide to have this baby, I can do this shit by myself!"

Tonya shoved her chair back, grabbed her purse, and stormed out of the restaurant, ignoring the shocked and curious stares of the other diners.

Tonya commandeered one of his two waiting limousines, ordering the driver to take her home. Tonya sat in the back of the limo fighting back tears. Q's accusation had rocked her to her soul.

Right now she was very uncertain of what the future held for them, or even if there still was a future with Q. All she knew was that she wanted to go home to her mother, now.

20

Ma, lemme get ready to go," Tonya said. "It's gettin' late and I still gotta long drive up the turnpike."

"Okay, Tonya," her mother said. "I wish you could stay a little longer, though. I love having you around, you know that. Sit ya tail down and rest ya bones a little longer."

That was all Tonya needed to hear. In many ways, her mother was still the dictator she had always been, but Tonya didn't mind this time. She wasn't eager to head back to New York. She still hadn't decided what she was going to do about the baby.

"Ma, what kinda baby was I?" Tonya asked suddenly. "Was I one of those fussy babies?"

"You was a good baby. You slept all night. You didn't wake up in the middle of the night like most babies. I could leave you with anybody and you would never cry. Shoot, you was a good baby."

Their conversation dragged on for hours. Every time Tonya glanced out the window, she could see it was getting later and later. But still she stayed.

The quick passage of time could be credited to the enjoyment each one received from the other's company. Visiting her mother had become a ritual for Tonya, although she had been motivated by a spat with Q to drop by this time. Tonya and her mother were getting to know each other all over again. They learned each other's likes and dislikes. Time had changed Tonya, not so much her mother. Veronica was pretty much stuck in her bossy ways. Tonya, on the other hand, was still evolving as a woman and a person.

It was utterly amazing how success seemed to make everything right. Tonya and her mother had never really seen eye to eye. They had been having verbal and physical altercations since she could remember. They always ended up with her beating Tonya or berating her, saying things that no mother should say to her child. If there was anyone in her life presently unworthy of reaping the benefits of her success, it was Veronica. She had played no role in nurturing her talents. Though she had long since forgiven her, Tonya would never forget.

For the sake of peace, harmony, and family, she let bygones be bygones. Her success was her mother's success. And her financial gain was hers, too. To a stranger on the outside looking in, she was the perfect mother. Tonya let her play that role of loving, supportive parent. The truth would be their little secret. To her it was family business, and that ugly aspect of her home life she wanted to keep hidden from the public.

"Woooo!" Tonya sighed. "Ma, I really need to be gettin' a move on. I gotta work tomorrow. Look, it's dark outside now."

Tonya was very much aware of where she was at—the Badlands. This section of Philadelphia was home to the have-nots. This was where extreme pockets of poverty existed and drugs and crime were commonplace. Here the residents were known to go hard. Wandering these streets, especially after dark, one could be asking for trouble. Most law-abiding citizens got off the street when the streetlights came on.

Tonya knew it, too. That was why she was in such a rush to get out of there. Although she grew up in the Badlands, on 9th, so much had changed. Things had gotten worse and not better. She was now a stranger on these streets. Besides that, her mother lived on 5th and Cambria. In the Badlands it didn't get much worse than this. After dark the streets belonged to those who lived outside the law.

A few months ago Tonya had begged her mother to move now that Tonya had a couple dollars in the bank. But Veronica wouldn't hear of it. Her excuse was, "I was born here and I'll die here." No matter how bad things got, to Veronica this was home. The only home she had ever known.

"All right, Ma, I'm gone!" she announced.

Then Tonya did something unprecedented and totally unexpected. She walked over to her mother and gave her a kiss on the cheek. The sudden show of affection had taken them both by surprise. But neither one of them said anything about it. They accepted it and quickly moved on.

"I'll see you later," her mother said. "Call me as soon as you get home."

Something wasn't right with her daughter. Veronica Morris could feel it. Ever since she had arrived at her home, she had sensed that something was bothering Tonya. Whenever she asked, the answer would be the same: nothing. As her daughter prepared to depart for home, Veronica wished she could work up the nerve to ask her one more time.

"I will," Tonya promised.

Tonya went to the door and gathered up her things. Before she stepped outside Tonya tucked her platinum and diamond chain with a diamond capital P in her shirt. She had rarely taken it off, and it was something that could get her into a lot of trouble in this neighborhood.

The confines of the streets that had once seemed so friendly, that had once housed her and been her safe haven, now seemed inhospitable to Tonya. Once she got outside, she picked up her pace as she headed for her car. It was better to be safe than sorry.

"Yo, she's comin' out now!" a shadowy figure said into a Nextel cell phone/walkie-talkie.

"Okay, we see her!" his phone chirped in response. "We got it from here."

After hearing that, the lookout left his post and proceeded to the predetermined spot. There he would wait for his co-conspirators' arrival. He hoped everything went well. It looked like this broad had money and he, like everybody else in this neighborhood, could use some.

Up the block, after placing her bag in the trunk and getting in the car, Tonya started her black Mercedes-Benz S500. As she waited for her vehicle to warm up, Tonya's thoughts went back to her mother.

Next time. I'll tell her about it next time.

But fate had other plans.

PART III

The Beginning
of the End . . .

21

Quinton Phelps rarely sat still. He was always doing some work-related task, even at home. His life had become the music business and the music business had become his life. On the rare occasion when he did manage to come home, it was commonplace to find him alone in his den, in front of the computer, burning the midnight oil. Q was a tireless worker who believed in outworking the next man. To him it was a mantra he used to get ahead and stay ahead. But for the past couple of days, he had been using work as a distraction.

Q was torn up about how things had gone down between him and Tonya. He hadn't been able to sleep that night, and first thing in the morning he had gone over to her apartment, only to discover that she wasn't home. He had tried to reach her on her cell but she wouldn't accept his calls. He figured that she was either at her mother's house or with Na'eema. He was about to track down her mother's address from the chauffeur who had brought her home after her surgery when he made himself pause for a minute. He had really hurt her, and she probably needed a second or two to regroup. Just because he was now ready to talk about the baby didn't mean that she was ready to talk to him. She would be back on Monday and they would talk then. At least, that was his hope.

It hadn't taken him long to realize that he was being foolish and letting this situation that had gone down with Niecey affect how he had responded to Tonya. He didn't believe any of that stuff he had said to her and he couldn't wait to look her in the eye and tell her just how stupid he had been.

Just then his cell phone vibrated.

Q snatched it off his hip and was relieved to see Tonya's name on his caller ID. *Finally!* he thought, hitting the TALK button.

"Baby," he said quickly, not giving her a chance to talk, "I'm so sorry! Please believe me when I say that I didn't mean the things I said to you. When are you coming home so we can talk face to face?"

"Shut the fuck up and listen!" a deep voice snapped into the phone.

Completely caught off guard, Q did a double take. He looked at his phone to make sure this was indeed Tonya's number. Satisfied, he resumed the call.

"Yo, I don't know who the fuck this is playin' on Tonya's phone, but dig, I ain't got time for no games!" Q said furiously.

"Nigga, this ain't no muthafucka game," came the response. "At least we not playin'. Dig, we got ya peoples. And if you wanna back you better come up off a mill."

"What?" Q stated in disbelief.

"Oh, you think this a joke, huh?" the man barked. "I'ma 'bout to put ya ho on the phone right now!"

Faintly, Q could overhear the kidnappers giving Tonya orders in the background. Now he knew this wasn't a game. Tonya was got.

"Q, they got me. They said they gonna kill me and the baby if you don't come up off the money," Tonya said.

"All right, that enough info, bitch!" the man said, coming back on to the phone. "Now look, you got three days to get the cash. Not some of it, part of it, but all of it!"

Q sat there, stunned, listening while the kidnappers did most of the talking. He took note of their instructions about how they wanted the money, where they wanted the money, and when they wanted the money. More important, they warned him not to call the cops. If the police should happen to get wind of this, then they promised to kill Tonya. Their exact words were, "The cops would find her when they smelled her."

As suddenly as the phone call began, it ended. Q was left with his jaw agape, at a loss for words. It didn't take him long to spring into action, though, and he started to make some phone calls. The first call was the most crucial.

"*As salaam alaikum*, sister," he spoke in hushed tones. "May I please speak to Jihad?"

"*Wa laikum as salaam*. May I ask who's callin'?" the woman replied.

Q started to say his name, but on second thought he thought better of it. He was so paranoid he didn't know who was listening. All he knew was that he didn't want to implicate himself in anything.

"A friend," Q merely replied. "A very good friend."

"He'll be home in about two hours if you would like to call back."

Q was relieved that she accepted his response and hadn't pressed further for a name. "Thank you, sister. I'll do that."

After he was done with that, he made the call he least wanted to make.

"Hello?" a groggy female's voice answered.

"Ms. Morris," Q said, "is that you?"

The unfamiliar voice on the other end of the phone could have been anybody. Q didn't know what Tonya's mother's voice sounded like, since he'd never even talked to her before. The only reason he had her number was because Tonya had called him on Ms. Morris's house phone on several occasions, to let him know she had reached Philadelphia safely. To his credit, Q had saved the number just in case he ever needed to reach Tonya and couldn't get through to her on her cell phone. He never imagined he'd be using her mother's number for something like this.

"Yes, this is me," she countered angrily. "Now, who in the hell is this? And why are you calling my home so late?"

Veronica Morris was wary of receiving phone calls so late at night. She knew they almost never brought the receiver any good news. Now that she was on the phone with a stranger, that only heightened her suspicions.

"Ms. Morris . . ." Q stated, his voice quivering. "I have something to tell you. Ya daughter . . ."

"What? What's wrong with Tonya?" she shouted. "What the hell have you done to her?"

Q interrupted. "Calm down, Ms. Morris. Would you listen for a minute? I ain't did nuttin' to ya daughter. I'm a friend of hers named Q."

How can I tell her something like this? he wondered.

Q searched his mind looking for the right words, the right way to phrase this. It seemed like the right words just wouldn't come. Nothing could prepare him for something like this. How does one tell a parent that her child has been kidnapped?

He continued, "Ya daughter . . . ya daughter's been kidnapped."

"What? By who?" Ms. Morris fired back. "Why? You had somethin' to do with this!"

"No! No! No, I didn't, Ms. Morris. I promise you it wasn't me. Why would I be calling you then? I care for ya daughter. I wouldn't want somethin' like this to happen to her. Besides, what does she possibly have that I can't get? She works for me," Q explained.

Q went on to vigorously deny any and all accusations. It took some time for him to convince Ms. Morris otherwise, but finally he did. She saw the logic in what he was saying.

"I'm callin' the police!" Ms. Morris stated. "They'll get to the bottom of this. The police will find Tonya."

This was exactly what Q feared. Now he wished he hadn't called her. Q realized that if she did act on this threat, then ultimately she would give her daughter a death sentence.

It took a lengthy conversation and a whole lot of promising on Q's part to finally convince Ms. Morris not to call the authorities. Q vowed that he would get Tonya back safely. He put that on everything he loved. Niggas had forgotten who he was and where he had come from. But he was about to remind them.

22

Q stood in his driveway, alone, pacing back and forth among his numerous and expensive SUVs and European luxury sedans, waiting for Jihad to return his call. There was a candy-apple-red Ferrari 599 GTB, a midnight-blue Aston Martin V12 Vanquish, a platinum Bentley GT, and a raven-black Cadillac Escalade, just to name a few. Q had more automobiles than there were days in the week. Although he walked among his toys, as he liked to refer to them, the finer things in life weren't on his mind at this time. His lone thought was of Tonya and getting her back from her abductors safely. He prayed that no harm would come to her. If it did, he would know no limit in seeking out his revenge. He would even go after the kidnappers' loved ones if he couldn't get them.

Q knew he should have moved her when they got back from the Bahamas. In hindsight he guessed that that was a way of him keeping his bachelor pad and denying the strong feelings that he had for Tonya. Q knew he should have protected her like he did everyone else he loved, his mother, his sisters, his son, even Niecey. He should have even moved Tonya's mother to a safer neighborhood, because if someone could get at them, then they could get at him.

He should have at least warned her about certain elements of the streets. Q's lack of oversight had set the stage for this. His overlooking a potentially dangerous situation had put her in harm's way.

He had all this money, surveillance cameras and security around him and his home, yet he had failed to adequately protect the love of his life and the mother of his unborn child. Q was overwhelmed by guilt and yet he felt empty inside. The center of his universe was gone.

The reason Q contacted Jihad was he needed someone on the outside to handle this job. There were lots of shooters and killers from his old neighborhood who would jump at the chance to handle this type of thing for Q. But he knew that to get in bed with these hungry young killers was almost like writing his own obituary. No amount of money would satisfy their insatiable appetite for power. He would be forever in their debt until death did him or them. Q was a public figure; he had to be smarter than that.

He also needed someone who wasn't closely or remotely associated with him, just in case things went wrong. He needed someone the hip-hop police couldn't link to him. He didn't need some young, bloodthirsty, gung-ho, trigger-happy murderer who might snitch on him if he got caught. He needed someone who was a stone-cold killer and battle-tested. He needed someone who would ride or die, whatever the situation called for.

Noting the time, Q reached on his hip for his cell and quickly punched in an area code and phone number.

"*As salaam alaikum*, brother," Jihad said.

"*Wa laikum as salaam*," Q said. "Yo, sumthin' came up. I need you. You know if it wasn't important I wouldn't even have called."

Jihad didn't even have to ask the caller his identity. He knew Q's voice from anywhere, after all the collect calls he had made to him from prison. It didn't matter that Q's voice was slightly altered due to all the stress he was currently under, he still picked up on it immediately.

"Is the person a believer?" Jihad asked. "Are they Muslim?"

Although Jihad was down to ride or die for Q, there was one thing he wouldn't do and that was shed blood of another believer in the Islamic faith. That was where his loyalty began and ended with Q. He couldn't bring himself to harm another Muslim unless it was a holy war being waged. He knew that to do so would be like punching a one-way ticket straight to hell, according to his religious beliefs.

"No," he flatly replied. "I don't think so."

"Come over. You remember where I live?" Big Jihad asked.

"Yeah, I'll be right there." Q replied.

"*Inshallah,* I'll see you when you get here," Big Jihad promised. "I'll be waitin' for you."

With that the phone line went dead.

Q didn't even bother to tell his bodyguards where he was going; he just hopped into his Ferrari, the fastest car he owned, and sped off. Before anyone could stop him, he was gone. Q knew time wasn't on his side. Time was slowly ticking for him to comply with the kidnappers' demands or they would kill Tonya. Q was in a race against time. It was a race he planned to win.

Like a madman, Q frantically drove toward the City of Brotherly Love, with evil thoughts racing through his mind. He began to conjure up horrific ways of death and torture. Retaliation had to be swift. He began to focus on just what needed to be done. There had to be an unprecedented public display of violence against these kidnappers. The streets were watching and waiting to see just how Q would handle the situation. If Q didn't take action, and quickly, then it would surely harm his street credibility.

Seventeen miles northwest of Philadelphia was a small sub-urban community called Norristown. Q had come to this quiet town in search of Big Jihad. With the navigational system inside his vehicle, Q had no problem finding his house. At top speed, he arrived at Big Jihad's house in less than an hour.

Exiting his vehicle, Q proceeded to walk up to the door of the nondescript ranch-style brick house. Before he could knock, the door slowly opened and he stepped inside. After closing the door, Q and Big Jihad embraced. It had been quite some time since they had last seen each other. To each man, it was evident that the love was still there. Still, it was unfortunate that they had to meet under these strenuous circumstances.

Big Jihad was a huge guy, hence the name. He was a moun-tain of a man standing six foot six and weighing close to three hundred pounds. His barrel chest was attached to two thick arms like tree stumps. Even in his glory days, Q never remem-bered Big Jihad looking quite this menacing. It seemed like he was bigger each time Q saw him.

Q followed Big Jihad into the kitchen, and they both took a seat at the kitchen table. From opposite sides of the kitchen table, they began to talk. Sitting down at the kitchen table, Q could hardly believe that the gentle giant sitting across from him was once a drug addict. Father Time had been good to Big Jihad. He was in tip-top shape. It seemed like his physical appearance hadn't suffered in the least.

"Jihad, they got my girl," Q began. "They snatched her up comin' outta her mother's house."

Big Jihad replied, "Who's they? You know who snatched her up?"

"I don't know," Q countered. "So 'they' could be anybody."

"Okay, tell me the whole story. Start from the beginning," Big Jihad suddenly announced.

Quickly Q ran down the entire story to him, recalled all the trips Tonya had made to see her estranged mother back in Philly, in a valiant effort to make up for lost time. He told him about the phone call he received from the kidnappers. He told him about the latest, including their ransom demands. He spilled his guts to Big Jihad, telling him of their relationship, Tonya's pregnancy, even how he thought the whole thing might have happened, giving him many different scenarios.

Big Jihad sat quietly, spellbound by a combination of what Q was saying and how he was saying it. A few times Big Jihad thought he heard Q's voice crack and his eyes water. His heart went out to him. Big Jihad not only saw this as an opportunity to help his friend but as a chance to prove his worth.

Although Q painted the perfect picture for Big Jihad, there was just one problem. This picture had just one flaw, but it was a huge one. The identity of the kidnappers was still unknown. It was one thing that both these men knew, being street people, that most extortionists and kidnappers worked under the premise of keeping their identity secret. That way they faced no form of retaliation. And they could possibly seek out the same victim again, if they chose to.

Since they both subscribed to the same school of thought, Q had already used this same form of reasoning when the kidnapping first happened. Immediately everyone fell under some form of suspicion, from his former employees to all his ex-bodyguards and ex-lovers. Conspiracy theories were abundant in that room. If there was a motive, Q explored, researched the person, and had their whereabouts checked out. He financed a thorough investigation that left no stone unturned.

"Q, we gotta problem," Big Jihad told him. "If we don't know who got her, then how can we get her back? You don't have no choice but to go along wit' the program and give 'em what they want. I can't hit what I can't see."

Big Jihad was careful how he chose his words normally, so in this case he knew he had to be extra-careful. This was a tense situation, and feelings tended to run high. But Big Jihad had another reason for holding his tongue. Q's money had bought this home for his wife and children. It was Q's money that had helped him live such a pious life. So Big Jihad was especially careful not to appear ungrateful for everything Q had done for him and his family.

It was then that a defeated feeling began to wash over Q. He had never felt more helpless in his life. In an instant he started to search the inner recesses of his mind, looking for that one clue that would swing things in their favor.

Big Jihad felt his pain, but there was nothing more he could do for Q until Q had concrete evidence of the identities of the kidnappers. Big Jihad wasn't about to take innocent lives just to settle a score. For Big Jihad to move out for Q's cause, he would need a whole lot more than that. As it stood, his hands were tied.

Murder had become Big Jihad's calling card while he ran the streets of Philly. But those who knew the man behind the gun knew he brought more to the table than just that. Big Jihad was fiercely loyal and protective of his friends. There was a method to his madness. He killed for a reason, not for the season. It was as if he was God's personal instrument of destruction to punish all bad men.

Suddenly the solution to the problem came to Q. The kidnappers had used Tonya's phone to contact him. And soon they would do so again. Being a gadget kind of guy, Q knew that most of the latest cell phones had tracking devices called GPS systems. The system worked two ways. It helped cell phone owners find their destination, but what the general public didn't know was that it could also be used to find them.

"I got it, Jihad," he said. "This is how we'll find her . . ."

With the aid of a laptop computer, Q was able to successfully pinpoint the location of the phone. He was willing to bet his life that Tonya was somewhere close by. If he was right, then Big Ji-had might be able to rescue Tonya and extract a measure of re-venge all at the same time. But if he was wrong, then Tonya was dead for sure. This was a helluva dilemma Q had to face.

At the end of their lengthy conversation Big Jihad extended his large hand in Q's direction, offering him a handshake. It was a handshake Q accepted graciously. To both men it meant the sealing of a deal. It was as if they had just sworn each other to se-crecy without saying a word. They each knew that one way or an-other there would be bloodshed. The only question was, whose?

As Q drove away, he realized that every move he had made throughout his life and in his career had been the correct one. It seemed like they had all been methodical steps that brought him to the pinnacle of success. He hoped like hell the decision he had just made was the right one, or his musical empire, his world, was about to come crashing down.

On 9th and Butler in the Badlands of Philadelphia, the early-morning sun shone brightly. Innocent children and working-class people walked down the block like they normally did, completely unaware of what was transpiring. Inside a narrow, nondescript brick house, there was a low level of physical activ-ity, but mentally everyone was excited. The kidnappers were in a celebratory mood. The strong scent of marijuana permeated the house. They all assumed that their ransom demands would be met. They had no reason to believe otherwise. They figured they held the trump card: Tonya, Q's emotional attachment and sig-nificant other. After all, a million dollars was a small price to pay for the safe return of your future baby's momma.

"Yo, what you gonna do wit' ya share of the loot?" Hector asked, in between taking pulls on the marijuana blunt.

"I'm up outta this bitch, my nigger," Mally announced. "I'm gonna go to ATL, chill wit' my peoples down there, just lay low. I probably cop some coke or weed just to keep that money turnin'. If ya money ain't makin' you money, it's only a matter of time before you go broke."

Hector added, "Yo, you right. That's a good idea."

"Yo, you know how many niggers I done seen blow loot in the hood? A lot! Remember that bitch Trina, we usta call chicken wing 'cause her right arm was fucked up?"

"Yeah," Hector replied. "We usta make fun of her when we was young."

Mally continued, "Well, what we didn't know was the bitch had some kinda lawsuit against the fuckin' hospital and the doctor for causin' that birth defect. When she turned like twenty-one they gave her all that money. A couple hundred grand. First they moved out the hood, to Nice Town, she copped a house somewhere up there. She usta come back through the hood pushin' BMWs, Porsches, and Mercedes-Benzes. Nigger, you name it, she had it. Man, before you knew it, that bitch was dead broke. She ran through all that money, spendin' it like there was no tomorrow. Then tomorrow came. By the time she hit twenty-five she was broke, livin' back in the hood with three kids by three different niggers and she was smokin' crack."

"What?" Hector exclaimed. "She fucked up like that?"

Mally fired back, "Is she? I wouldn't even putta bad bone on her like that if it wasn't true. That bitch is smokin' like a broke chimney!"

"Fuck that bitch! Anyway, I know what I'ma do wit my loot. I'ma buy some land in Puerto Rico, you know, houses and land is dirt-cheap down there. Plus I always heard you can never go wrong wit' real estate. I mean, you can't lose no dough in it anyway. You know?"

"Now you talkin', nigger! That's what's up," Mally said. "As soon as you get ya spot down in Puerto Rico, I'm comin' down to holla atcha! We gone be down there blowin' on some Kush and fuckin' some bad mamis."

"No doubt!" Hector chimed in.

The longer these three talked, the higher they became. Their train of thought blurred the lines that separated a lie from the truth. Soon their conversation turned into a contest of who could tell the best lies. Deep down inside, none of them was even considering leaving Philly. They didn't know anyplace else. They were born in Philly and most likely would die there. Besides that, they really couldn't enjoy their riches elsewhere. They needed people they knew to see them balling. Visions of fast cars, money, and loose women danced in their heads. What good would their come-up be if they couldn't show it off?

Nightfall couldn't come quick enough for them. It was then that Brian, the fourth man involved in this, would go pick up the loot from the designated dropoff point. Although Mally and Hector were childhood friends, when it came to money, neither of them trusted the other.

Subconsciously they both feared that if one went to pick up the money, that person might make off with it. For the sake of argument, they both agreed that Brian should go, since he was the least ruthless of the quartet.

Meanwhile, inside the bedroom, a baby-faced Boo kept a close watch on his captive, Tonya. It was his job to thwart any and all escape attempts, to feed her and take her to the bathroom. In other words, he was in charge of keeping Tonya alive, at least until after they collected the money. Then it was safe to say that they didn't care what happened to her.

As a matter of fact, Mally and Hector didn't plan on letting her leave there alive. They figured that they had to kill Tonya to cover their tracks. Tonya was the only witness to their crime. She saw their faces and on occasion, when someone slipped up, she heard their names. So what would stop her from going to the police? Or even worse, Tonya telling everything that she knew about them to Q, and then he put a contract out on their lives? Mally and Hector didn't feel good about the possibility of that happening. It was a hell of a probability that they would have to look over their shoulders for a good while, out of fear of retaliation.

One thing about Boo that both Mally and Hector loved, other than him being trustworthy, was that he didn't ask any questions. The only thing he wanted to know was how much was he getting paid? End of story. The who and what didn't matter to him. As long as there was some sort of compensation involved, then one could count him in. This was their caper, their car. He was just enjoying the ride.

Neither Mally nor Hector was aware that Boo was a sexual deviant. So in essence they had just let a fox in the henhouse. Boo was careful to conceal his intentions, but occasionally he complained to them.

"Ay! Ay!" Boo whispered. "Bitch, I know you hear me!"

Convinced that she was indeed asleep, Boo resumed playing his video game. This was how he passed his time, playing PlayStation for hours on end, with little or no contact from Mally or Hector. Lately, evil thoughts had been creeping into Boo's mind. He wanted Tonya sexually in the worst way. Secretly he had been sneaking feels on Tonya whenever he could. He even went so far as to masturbate while watching her. Before the day was out, he planned to "take the pussy," as he put it.

Tonya lay there motionless, hog-tied on the bed, bound and gagged, pretending to be asleep. But the truth of the matter was, she hadn't slept a wink since she had first been abducted. She couldn't sleep worrying about the baby and whether Q would fork over the money for her release. She nearly worried herself to death over the latter. At times she refused to eat or drink any water. Between that and Boo constantly groping her, Tonya couldn't sleep. She prayed for a moment to catch Boo off guard. She prayed for any lapse in judgment that would lead her abductor to untie her. Though she hadn't been raped, Tonya knew from the way this guy was acting, like he was "pressed for some pussy," it just might happen.

All night long Big Jihad had held a vigil-like watch on the house. Inconspicuously, he sat in a freshly stolen, tinted-window Honda minivan, observing the comings and goings at the location. Overnight, until now, he had noticed little to no movement, other than an occasional light turned on or off in various rooms. He saw no one enter or leave the house from the time he got there. According to Q, there were definitely two people, maybe more, in the house besides Tonya. From Big Jihad's vantage point, there wasn't anyone else there. If so, surely they would have gone to the store at night, or to work or school in the morning. The only thing Big Jihad really worried about was shooting or killing innocent bystanders in the house. He never liked spilling innocent blood. He prided himself on making the right person bleed or suffer.

Big Jihad had contemplated his murderous plans in his head all night. By now he was very familiar with his plan of attack. Now it was time to execute his plan with deadly precision.

The belief that what he was about to do was right spurred Big Jihad on. On the strength of that, he was about to put his life on the line. Thoughts of Q and their last conversation came to mind.

Q's mandate to him was simple: "Bring Tonya back alive. But I want them all dead! Anybody who had something to do with it!"

When the coast was clear, Big Jihad exited the car and lumbered a few feet across the street and up the block to the house. Had anyone seen him approaching the house, Big Jihad would have looked pretty suspicious, wearing a brown UPS deliveryman uniform with package in hand, but with no delivery truck. As luck would have it, no one noticed or no one cared.

When Big Jihad reached the house in question, he looked around cautiously, surveying his surroundings for witnesses or the police. Satisfied with his observations, Big Jihad pressed the bell. He patiently waited for someone to answer the door.

Mally was high as hell. The weed that he had been smoking had taken effect. He felt so good, as if he could do or say no wrong. He was currently preoccupied with eating a cold slice of pizza while listening to a boom box located on the kitchen counter. At first Mally didn't hear the initial ringing of the bell. He thought it was some kind of sound effect coming from the music track currently playing on the radio. Mally reached over and lowered the volume to be sure he wasn't just tripping. When he did that, the bell suddenly rang again.

"Yo, Mal!" Hector called out from the upstairs bathroom. "See who the fuck that is on the door."

"I am, nigger!" he shouted. "Calm ya fuckin' nerves. I headed to the door right now. Finish takin' ya shit!"

One thing Mally hated about Hector was that he was overly cautious. It was to the point that if you didn't know him, one would have thought he was scared. But that wasn't the case at all. Hector was a killer; he could kill at will. He was good with a knife or a gun, it didn't matter to him.

Stepping out of the kitchen, Mally passed the slightly cracked bathroom door. As he did, he caught a glimpse of a red-faced Hector, straining while he defecated.

"Damn, nigger!" he shouted. "Flush the muthafuckin' toilet! Ya azz smell like you wanna be alone. You fuckin' stink! Goddamn!"

Mally scrunched up his nose and proceeded to walk toward the front door, braving the foul odor as he did so. He advanced to the door quicker than he normally would have, due to the stench.

"Who!" he barked.

"UPS," came the gentle response. "I have a package for . . ."

Either the stench or just plain stupidity led Mally to open the door. Whatever the case might have been, it wouldn't be a decision he would live to regret.

Meanwhile, upstairs, Boo had just finished playing a lengthy game of Grand Theft Auto. He had played the game so long that his hands began to cramp. One glance over at Tonya's round ass, as she lay on her stomach, and Boo's penis became erect. Suddenly he yearned for a different kind of excitement, that of the sexual nature.

Undoing his zipper, Boo freed his penis and began stroking it. He was about to help himself to a piece of Tonya. After he got his, he didn't care who knew. In his sick, twisted mind, he had earned the right to have Tonya.

"Damn, that fat ass muthafucka!" Boo said. "It's time we got to know each other better."

Boo proceeded to unfasten the handcuffs that had not only restricted Tonya's arms but threatened to cut off her circulation. Tonya played possum, faking sleep, while her abductor began to remove first her shirt and then her bra. Just before Boo was going to pull down her pants, Tonya suddenly came to life and scrambled across the bed, making her way toward the window.

"Bitch, where do you think ya goin'?" Boo growled. "Get ya ass over here."

Boo reached out and grabbed Tonya by her belt loops and dragged her back to the bed. He was intent on succeeding in this violation of her. As Boo pulled Tonya toward him, Tonya pulled the sock that served as a gag out of her mouth and yelled her head off.

Downstairs, Hector flushed the toilet simultaneously as Tonya screamed. Still, he heard her cry of distress loud and clear. Hurriedly, he performed a rush job wiping himself. Leaping up off the toilet, Hector merely pulled up his baggy jeans. He had no time to fasten his belt. His high was now officially blown. He exited the bathroom prepared to address the problem upstairs.

"Can I help you?" Mally said bravely.

"I have a package for Maria Santiago." Big Jihad's baritone voice boomed into the house.

Big Jihad stood there with an empty box and a clipboard in hand, giving the man at the door his best deliveryman impersonation. Immediately his eyes were drawn to the man's neck region. There he spotted the sign he was looking for, an admission of guilt. The man blatantly wore a diamond-link chain with a letter "P" pendant, which was clearly a logo belonging to Q's company. This confirmed to Big Jihad that he was in the right place, so heaven knew that what he was about to do wasn't wrong.

At that very moment, a scream came from upstairs, temporarily diverting Mally's attention from the gigantic UPS deliveryman. Mally looked over his shoulder. Back inside the house, he saw Hector rapidly approaching, heading for the stairs. Instinctively, Mally tried to slam the door. But a funny thing happened: for some reason it didn't close. Mally turned to see just what was preventing the door from closing, and he received the surprise of his life.

"Yo, git ridda that nigger!" Hector snapped as he raced down the hall. "Shut the fuckin' door!"

Big Jihad had already cocked back his huge arm and launched his big fist into the man's face, breaking his nose in three places, sending blood spewing everywhere. Reeling from the blow, Mally fell backward into the house, flat on his back, holding his nose. Rolling on his back with his knees in the air, the kidnapper held his face in his hands in a desperate attempt to keep blood from leaking out.

In one swift motion, Big Jihad kicked the door closed and retrieved his twin black nine-millimeter fully automatic handguns from his waistband. From that point on, he went on a murderous rampage.

Big Jihad didn't have time to figure out who was the ringleader and who were the followers. Whoever was inside the house was being held accountable and would be dealt with accordingly.

Standing over a dazed and bloodied Mally, he proceeded to pump slugs into his face. The bullets did exactly what they were intended to do, killing Mally instantly.

Murder wasn't for the faint of heart. To Big Jihad it was just a job that needed to be done. He showed indifference to death. Most of the time when he executed people it was to preserve life, to protect the innocent and punish the guilty.

The sound of gunfire froze Hector in his tracks. At that moment he knew something had gone horribly wrong. A few feet from the door he paused, momentarily in a state of confusion. Suddenly Hector decided to turn his immediate attention toward the sound of the shots. He reversed his tracks and headed downstairs. He wanted to know who or what had caused Mally to discharge his gun.

When Hector hit the bottom of the stairs, he saw an ominous figure headed directly toward him, guns drawn. Realizing his mistake, Hector frantically attempted to remove his gun from his pocket. But he couldn't draw it quickly enough. Two more gunshots echoed though the house and slammed into his body. Desperately Hector tried to draw his gun, but it was too late; death was already upon him. Big Jihad fired his gun again, placing a slug into the back of Hector's head. That ended any delusions he had of getting up out of the hood.

Big Jihad climbed the stairs, stepping on the body, making his way toward the sound of the screams. With one strong kick, he broke the lock, flinging the door wide open. He entered the room like the one-man wrecking crew he was, with his mind bent on death and destruction. He burst in leading with his weapons, quickly scanning the room for any signs of danger. He saw none. What he saw was a shirtless woman crouched low in the corner.

"Anybody else in here, sis?" he quickly asked as his gaze darted back and forth.

Tonya didn't know who this big man was, but she knew he wasn't with her abductors. At least, he wasn't with the ones who had initially abducted her. With her head, Tonya signaled toward the closet. Big Jihad immediately caught the hint and proceeded slowly toward the closet, gun drawn.

Not wanting to endanger himself any more than he already had, Big Jihad let off a single shot near the closet door in hopes of frightening whoever was inside to come out. He needed to take someone alive. Big Jihad needed information on who was behind this.

"Don't shoot! Don't shoot!" a muffled voice said. "I'm comin' out!"

The fear in the man's voice could be heard loud and clear. It was evident that he was in way over his head.

Instinctively, Big Jihad backed up and kept his two guns trained on the door, just in case this was some sort of trick. If it was, he was going to let loose a deadly barrage of gunfire.

"Git on ya knees, nigger!" Big Jihad ordered. "Crawl out! Slowly!"

Doing just as he was told, the man crawled out with his head bowed, defeated. He surrendered himself to a killer. Boo hoped that Jihad would take mercy on him and spare his life.

"Yo, I ain't have nuttin' to do wit' this shit!" He began copping a plea. "It was Hector and Mally. They responsible for everything. They just asked me to watch her, they told she was some big drug dealer's girl who had owed them some money. That's all I know."

Upon hearing that, Big Jihad knew that getting information out of him was going to be easy. He would just have to coerce him into telling the truth.

In one swift motion he raised one of his pistols and viciously brought it down on top of Boo's head. The wound almost knocked him senseless and opened up a nasty gash.

"Nigger, stop lyin'. Tell me the truth and I'll let you live," he growled.

The man balled up into a fetal position at his feet. He writhed in pain on the floor from the force of the blow. Blood leaked through his fingers as he held his head in pain.

Tonya had a front-row seat to the beating that Big Jihad was administering to her captor. She got a sense of what might happen next and turned her head. Tonya had seen this before and knew how it ended.

"Wait a minute. I'll tell you! Just don't hit me no more," the man cried. "It was Niecey! Niecey put them up to it."

The revelation stunned both Big Jihad and Tonya. Not once did they ever think that someone they knew was behind the kidnapping. Big Jihad's job suddenly got a whole lot tougher.

Without warning, Big Jihad raised his gun and fired one shot into the man's head, silencing him forever. He crashed face-first into the floor and his body lay in a lifeless lump. Even though the kid was young, Big Jihad didn't care; he eliminated him. Death didn't discriminate.

"C'mon, sis, hurry up and put that on. We gotta get up outta here now!" Big Jihad said.

He grabbed Tonya's shirt from off the bed and threw it to her. As she donned her shirt, Big Jihad worked on freeing her feet. In seconds he successfully removed the extension cord that bound her feet together. Once that was done, they fled the house, leaving out the back door. Down the alley they dashed, to another stolen car that had been strategically placed there by Big Jihad.

Taking the back blocks, they fled the scene of the crime. The more distance they put between themselves and the house, the easier Big Jihad breathed. Now the chances of him getting apprehended for these murders were very small. One could get away with some heinous crimes in the hood, as Big Jihad well knew. So much stuff happened in the Badlands that in a few days people would forget all about the three lives lost in that house.

Within minutes of their departure, several squad cars descended on the scene, responding to an emergency call of shots fired. The first group of policemen on the scene would find a trail of blood and dead bodies scattered all about the house. Each victim had died as a result of multiple gunshot wounds to the head.

"Don't worry, sis, everything is gonna be okay now," Big Jihad gently assured her. "You're in good hands. A friend sent me to get you. So relax, I'm takin' you where you need to go."

Silently, Tonya sat in the passenger seat and blew a sigh of relief. She was glad to be out of that house. Inside, the stench of death was everywhere. Although she had escaped the house, still she would probably relive that hideous sight for the rest of her life. But at least she was alive. Tonya closed her eyes tightly and thanked God.

23

After her successful rescue, Tonya was taken immediately to a five-star hotel in downtown Philadelphia, where there was a room reserved in her name. Tonya proceeded to follow instructions. But before she did, she turned and thanked the stranger for putting his life on the line.

"I don't know your name and I don't want to know, either," she began. "But thanks. You saved my life."

Tonya now had time to digest everything that had happened. This would be the last time she would see her big protector or even make mention of him. Tonya understood that what had taken place in that house in North Philly had been done for her sake, to save her life.

"Sis, thanks isn't necessary. I did what I had to do to get you up outta there in one piece," Big Jihad explained. "Just remember, forget what happened. See no evil, speak no evil. Let's go to our grave with what took place. Peace be unto you."

Big Jihad was a pretty good judge of character. If he even thought that Tonya was the type to snitch, then there would have been four dead bodies instead of three. As things stood, he was comfortable with the fact that his deadly secret was safe.

Once Big Jihad dropped her off, it was the last time they would ever see each other. He still had more business to tend to.

He wouldn't stop until everyone involved in the kidnapping was dead and stinking.

Alone in the hotel room, Tonya took a shower and changed into the clothes Q had had delivered before falling asleep on the bed. It was the first peaceful slumber since the kidnapping. It wasn't long before Tonya's sleep was broken. Shortly after she nodded off, the phone rang. Tonya answered it on the first ring. She was anxious to see who it was.

"Hello?" she gently said.

"Excuse me, ma'am, there is a car service here waiting for you," the hotel concierge told her.

"I'll be right down," Tonya replied.

Getting downstairs as fast as the elevator could carry her, Tonya fully expected to see Q's smiling face when she entered the limo. She was somewhat disappointed when she did not. But she soon would.

Q was careful to keep his hands clean. He had far too much to lose. This would be the extent of his involvement in the crime, other than issuing the hit—sending a limo to pick up his girlfriend. It was as simple as that.

"Hey, where are you takin' me?" Tonya asked.

"Look, ma'am, I'm not paid to answer questions," the driver replied. "They pay me to drive. Sorry. You'll see when you get there."

Feeling completely safe, Tonya settled down for what she thought would be a long ride. But they reached their destination sooner than expected.

When the limo arrived in southern New Jersey at a beautiful house in a gated community, Tonya knew where she was, at Q's house. He stood a few feet away from the limo, leaning on one of his exotic automobiles, just waiting for the limo's doors to open.

The driver exited the limo, walked around to the back

passenger-side door, and opened it. Tonya hopped out and ran over to Q, leaping into his arms. She had two words running through her mind.

"Thank you! Thank you! Thank you!" she said repeatedly.

The moment Q laid eyes on Tonya, he was overcome by joy. Finally Q had something to celebrate, something to be happy about. The good feeling he was currently experiencing went far beyond getting Tonya back from her abductors. What Q was feeling was something called love.

Q's eyes welled with tears. He wanted to run up to Tonya and throw his arms around her. But she beat him to it. Quickly he abandoned the thought. He had to play it cool, because after all, he was Q. Still, the whole scene was unbelievable to him. Though he had faith in Big Jihad and what he could do, even so, he knew no plan was foolproof. He had reason to wonder if this day would ever come again, if and when he would see Tonya's beautiful face again.

Throughout his lifetime, Q had grown used to dealing with uncertainties. But the idea of a future without Tonya was something Q did not ever want to think about. Q never expected to feel like this, complete, so soon after his life had taken such a terrible twist.

Their reunion seemed to make everything worthwhile. It brought a fitting end to a long ordeal. Now Tonya knew Q loved her, she could see it and feel it. Love was in the air, it was everywhere.

"I'm happy as hell!" Tonya blurted out. "I feel so lucky just to be alive."

"Let's not talk about that," Q told her. "We don't know who's listenin'."

Q refused to even engage Tonya in any conversation pertaining to the kidnapping. In his book some things were best left unsaid. Silence was good for all parties involved.

Q continued, "For what it's worth, I missed you, too. How's my baby doin'?"

If this was Q's way of telling Tonya that he cared for her, then she would accept that.

Happily, Tonya embraced Q again, squeezing him tightly. Suddenly a thought crossed her mind. It was one that had escaped her during this joyous celebration. She hated to dampen the mood, but Tonya felt like she had to do what she had to do.

"Q, I hate to bring this back up, but . . ." she whispered. "Ya baby mother, Niecey, was behind this whole thing. She set everything up."

"What?" Q replied, shocked.

Tonya moved her lips even closer to his ear, speaking in hushed tones reminiscent of Mafioso soldiers. Quickly she explained how she knew what she knew. As soon as Tonya was done telling Q the story, he immediately excused himself and ran into his house.

News of the triple homicide was splattered across the news. The grisly discovery made not only the local news, it captured headlines across the country. Everywhere Niecey turned, there were live reports. She didn't know how, but somewhere along the line the kidnapping had taken a deadly turn. Niecey sat through countless news reports waiting for an account of the dead. When the reporter finally did read off the names of the dead, Niecey was shocked not to hear a woman's name mentioned among them. Niecey was angry. Not only had her plan failed miserably, but her rival was still alive. After her anger subsided, it dawned on Niecey that there would be an extensive investigation. She began to worry, thinking up the worst possible scenario, being implicated in another murder. Niecey fretted over the possibility of being returned to prison, possibly for life. She did what any other criminal in her shoes would do. Niecey packed her bags and prepared to flee the city until things died down, until she knew for sure what was happening.

Finding Niecey's whereabouts was easy for Big Jihad. She stayed in Philly. And he knew Philly like the back of his hand. He had another factor in his favor. Q had once occupied the condo that Niecey currently stayed in before turning it over to her once she was released from prison. Big Jihad knew the precise location of the condo for security reasons.

Jihad already knew what she looked like. He had seen her on dozens of occasions, being that they were from the same hood. Their paths had crossed a time or two. And like most people, Big Jihad never did like Niecey. But murder wasn't a popularity contest. It was business.

As much as Big Jihad was an expert in the art of killing, he was equally as patient when stalking his prey. He sat in the underground parking lot of Niecey's Center City condominium, parked a short distance from her luxury SUV, waiting for her to show up. He knew that sooner or later she would. It was human nature.

Suddenly Niecey entered the parking lot, struggling with two large duffel bags. Periodically she stopped every so often to catch her breath. It was a chore carrying her stuff to the car. Still, she managed to make it to her car all by herself.

Ever alert, Big Jihad leaned back in his car seat, hidden behind a dark-tinted window. Patiently he waited for her to come closer. That way he wouldn't have to give chase should he miss with his first shot. The cleaner the kill was, the better. He wanted to end this as quickly as possible.

Unexpectedly, another car entered the garage, putting Niecey on alert. She was so paranoid that she mistakenly thought the white man driving the vehicle was coming to arrest her for her role in the botched kidnapping. She froze in her tracks, momentarily paralyzed by fear.

"Hey. How are ya?" the man said, exiting his car. "Need some help with those bags? They look pretty heavy."

"No, I'm okay," Niecey replied. "My car's just right there. Thanks anyway."

The man responded, "Okay, travel safe, ma'am."

Once the man passed Niecey exhaled deeply in relief, then continued toward her car. Now she was ever so close to her vehicle. Beads of sweat began to form on her forehead as she began to physically overexert herself. Niecey was so close to her car now that she could throw her keys at it and hit it if she chose to.

Just a lil' closer, Big Jihad mused.

Niecey arrived at her red Cadillac SRX SUV, winded. She dropped her bags at the back lift gate. With the push of a button, her trunk door slowly began to rise. Niecey bent down and picked up her duffel bags, slinging them into the car one at a time. When that was done she pushed the button again, closing the trunk. Walking around to the passenger side, she opened the door and entered the car. After placing the key in the ignition, the car's engine came to life.

Instantly, the car's interior was filled with loud rap music. While the car warmed up, Niecey busied herself setting the car's navigational system. She was completely oblivious to her surroundings. Her mind was on fleeing the city.

Meanwhile, a few feet away, Big Jihad was ready to make his move. The time was right to strike. As he mentally prepared himself for the hideous sight of death and destruction, his cell phone vibrated in his pocket. Big Jihad cursed himself for forgetting to turn off his phone. It was small mistakes like this that could cost him his freedom or his intended target.

Reaching inside his pocket, Big Jihad touched a button, sending the caller to his voice mail. He figured whoever it was, it wasn't important right now. When his cell phone vibrated again, needless to say, Big Jihad was pissed. He saw his opportunity to kill Niecey slipping away. Repeatedly, he ignored his calls, but they kept on coming in one after another, to the point that it might jeopardize Big Jihad's mission. Finally he relented and answered the phone. He wanted to know: what was the emergency? What was so important that they had to call him back to back to back?

As Big Jihad retrieved the phone from his pocket, he looked at the number that came up on the screen. The phone number looked very familiar. Suddenly he knew who the caller was—Q.

"Yeah?" he answered. "What's up?"

"If it ain't too late, leave it alone!" Q commanded. "That's dead."

When Q had issued the order to kill everyone involved, never in his wildest dreams did he think that Niecey would somehow be tied up in this. Although Q could be cold and calculating when it came to matters involving the street life, he didn't think he could look his son in the eye, knowing he had a hand in his mother's death. And Niecey might have deserved to die for her role in the kidnapping, but still, Q couldn't see himself issuing the order. After all, this was his child's mother, someone he once loved. They had a history together that not even murder could erase.

"Okay, whatever you say," Big Jihad replied. "I will leave it alone. Peace."

Big Jihad respected Q's wishes; it was his call to make. Since Q said there would be no further bloodshed, then that's what it was. Slowly, Big Jihad replaced his murder weapon in the glove compartment. He watched as Niecey put her car in gear, backed out of the parking space, and exited the garage. She was on her way to God knew where. Niecey would never know how close she had been to becoming a murder statistic, how close she had been to death.

Epilogue

Tonya and Q sat side by side at a lavish baby shower thrown in her honor in a posh midtown Manhattan hotel ballroom. Mentally the couple counted as many gifts as they did their blessings. At times they both seemed to marvel at how far and fast their relationship had come. Neither believed that their relationship was a coincidence. They tended to romanticize the situation by calling it fate or destiny, but they both believed that they had found a partner and a relationship that would last a lifetime.

Despite Na'eema's advice, Tonya had decided to share everything about her past with Q, including that fateful phone call she had made to Niecey that resulted in Niecey killing a woman, going to prison, and being separated from their son.

Q had been disturbed to learn this to say the least.

"I didn't mean for it to go down like that," Tonya told him, calmly. "I was so focused on Kat getting what she deserved that I didn't think about anyone else. And while I'm not sad that Kat is dead, I'm sorry that Lil Q has suffered." Tears welled up in her eyes. "And I didn't want to keep a secret like this from you. If we're going to be together then I want you to know everything, so you can never say I lied or kept secrets from you."

Q had sat there not saying anything and not looking at her for the longest time. Tonya remembered thinking, *That's it. It's a wrap.* Finally Q shook his head.

"It doesn't matter," he told her. "Niecey is a grown woman, Tonya, and she always knows exactly what she's doing. She just likes to blame it on other people." He turned to her. "And as far as Kat was concerned, if I had known the full story, I would have taken her out my damn self." He pulled her into his arms. "I don't want to keep focusing on the past. I'm all about the future now and as long as you're in it, then I'm cool."

And that was apparently all Q wanted to say on the subject.

Looking out on the crowd of people who had come together to celebrate this momentous occasion, Tonya broke out into a wide grin. She gave a courteous smile to the unfamiliar faces, people who had shown up just to support Q, like his entire staff at the record label, his mother and sisters, and a few of his peers in the music industry. But her real reason for smiling was the familiar faces like her mother, Shakira, and Annie from work, and of course Na'eema. To her it was extra special to see Na'eema's face in the crowd. She was a friend indeed. She felt like she was her long-lost sister from another mother. To Tonya it didn't matter how or where they had met. Their friendship was just as special as two kids who had grown up knowing each other all their lives. It didn't matter to her how long she had known Na'eema, only that she had been there for Tonya every time she needed her. For that Tonya was eternally grateful to Na'eema, so much so that she planned on bestowing the honor of godmother on her.

As Tonya smiled, posed for pictures, and opened up more presents, her mind began to flash back to her years of running the streets, when the strip club was the center of her universe. It was then that Tonya realized that she wouldn't have traded what she had gone through for anything in the world, from her chaotic adolescence to her current position as soon-to-be baby momma to one of the most powerful men in the music business. All her trials and tribulations had helped shape her into the woman she was today. Now she knew that tough times didn't last, tough people did.

After bearing witness to her own personal amazing journey, Tonya could truly say her life had changed for the better. She believed that if a person made a concerted effort to change their life, then God would grant them a second chance. She was living proof of that. Here she was having a baby by the man she loved, living in the lap of luxury without a care in the world. Two years ago, who would have thought this was possible? Certainly not her. For once in her life, the future was indeed very bright.

Turn the page for a sneak peek at the explosive sequel

B-More Careful II

SHANNON HOLMES

When the dust settled, Netta barely escaped B-More with her life. Her man, Tone, was dead and she was pregnant with his child. Now when her child faces a life-threatening disease, Netta is forced to come back to B-More to seek treatment. But when the money that she needs to save her son's life becomes tight, Netta steps back into the game, determined to rule B-More once again. But gone does not mean forgotten and it's not long before sex, murder, and mayhem rule the streets once more with Netta right in the middle of it all.

COMING IN 2009
FROM ST. MARTIN'S GRIFFIN

I'm still that bitch! Them young hoes ain't got nothin' on me! Netta thought to herself, as she prepared for a night of clubbing.

After admiring herself in the mirror, she returned to her bedroom and sprayed herself lightly with Issey Miyake. Netta wanted to smell as good as she looked. Just as she was about to call Hope to see how far she was from her house, she heard the sound of a car horn blowing in front of her house. Peeping through her curtains she spotted Hope's black Honda Accord.

Quickly, Netta looked in on her son, to make sure he was fast asleep. The television was tuned to the Cartoon Network while Little Tone rested peacefully. Suddenly, Netta was overcome by guilt. She felt bad about going out on the town at a time like this. Especially with the medical condition her son was in, but she had no choice. It was for Little Tone's sake that she needed to make some moves tonight.

The sound of the doorbell interrupted her thoughts and she reluctantly went down to open the door.

"Hi, Netta!" Tara greeted her cheerfully. "That outfit is da bomb!"

"Thanks! Listen, look in on my son every so often. Make sure he's okay and if something go wrong or he should wake up and not feel good, call me on my cell phone. I left the number on the refrigerator, okay?" Netta said.

"Okay! Don't worry—everything gonna be all right," Tara told her.

There was something about the young girl that put Netta at ease—besides the fact that she was Hope's sister. She just felt like her son was in good hands. Armed with that knowledge she left the house.

"Y'all have a good time!" Tara shouted.

Almost as soon as Netta entered the club, it started again. The eye-rolling, finger pointing, and whispering. Just by the salty expressions painted on their faces, Netta knew that these chicks felt threatened by her presence. She wasn't in here to take anybody's man, at least not tonight. Netta was just trying to scope out the scene, see who's who and what's what for future reference. And maybe have a good time.

"Maybe it's me and maybe I'm trippin', but is these bitches mean muggin' a lil extra hard tonight or what, yo?" Hope asked. "I feel a little tension up in here tonight. Bitches are starin' like we got bull's eyes on our backs."

Netta smiled. "You know how that go. They got haters everywhere. Especially up in here."

Without even trying Netta always shined when she went out. She was just always a little flossier, more extravagant than the other chicks. Armed with good looks, a devastating body, and sexy attitude, Netta had the ability to make a bullshit bargain store outfit look good. By any measure, Netta was sexy.

Netta continued, "Don't even pay these bitches no fuckin' mind. They don't want no trouble. All these hoes gonna do is stare, roll they eyes, or suck they teeth. All that catty coward shit. It ain't bout nothin'."

"I feel you on that, yo," Hope replied. "Guess it's just in a bitch's nature to hate . . . Anyway, fuck 'em and feed 'em pork! I could care less whut a bitch say or think 'bout me. That shit don't pay my rent. Ya heard?"

After awhile, Netta and Hope began to order rounds of drinks. As they did so Netta began to scan the area, paying close attention to faces, and kept her ears perked for name recognition. To Netta, a select few in the sea of faces were recognizable. But she didn't know these people well enough to go up to them and strike up a conversation. No, she only knew them in passing. More often than not street people traveled in the same circles.

Besides that, Netta's attention was focused mainly on the champagne-popping, jewelry-wearing, and skirt-chasing drug dealers. She wouldn't settle for meeting anyone less than a baller.

"Hope, who are these bitches right here?" Netta asked, turning her attention toward the club's entrance.

Like lasers, Hope focused her eyes on the group of loud young ladies who had just entered the club. Immediately, she recognized them. Their reputation had preceded them.

"Them hoes right there call themselves the 'Knock 'em Down Girls,'" Hope told her. "See the little one in the middle? That's Keisha. She's their leader, head of the clique or whateva you want to call the hoe. But she get that money, yo! She straight rapin' these so-called hustlin' ass niggas. Knock 'em Down clique the shit in Baltimore now."

"Oh, yeah?" Netta laughed. "It's like that?"

"You better know it!" Hope assured her. "Ever since them bitches called the Pussy Pound disappeared. These bitches been what's up to every money-makin' nigga in the city. But I wonder whatever happened to the Pound?"

"Me, too," Netta replied sarcastically.

Though Netta and Hope were real cool, she had never told Hope about her affiliation with the Pussy Pound. Her motto was "Everything wasn't for everybody." If and when the time was right she would tell her. Until then, Netta kept her little secret to herself.

"That red bitch right there, that's Lisa. Next to her is Shawnie and that other chick's name is Tosha," Hope said, identifying them all.

As the clique passed by, Netta got a close-up look at Keisha. They seemed to lock eyes briefly. Keisha frowned. It was as if she recognized Netta from somewhere, but couldn't quite place her.

Until this very day, Netta's name still rang in the streets of Baltimore. Not only did her peers know her name and game, but the younger generation did too. Every young tramp, ride, or die chick or gangstress looked up to Netta, as if it were a law or something. Many females may not have liked Netta, personally, but quietly they admired her from afar.

But Keisha was different. She didn't bow down to anyone. She never liked hearing about the legendary Netta or the Pussy Pound. As far as she was concerned they were has-beens, a thing of the past. The Knock 'em Down posse was what was happening now. Even though they were no longer officially in existence, the Pussy Pound, Netta in particular, had something Keisha so desperately wanted: fame, for herself and her clique, and street notoriety. Netta's status was cemented and unparalleled in that aspect.

"Lemme tell you 'bout Keisha, yo," Hope began. "She fucks with one of the biggest hustlers in Baltimore. This nigga named Littles. Peep this though, the nigga know she do her thing and he still wifed her. Ain't dat some shit? What nigga in his right mind gonna make a hoe a housewife?"

"You be surprised," Netta said. "That's the power of the P-U-S-S-Y. Men can't get enough of that shit."

From past experience, Netta knew that the irresistible power of sex could take a broke female from the projects to the penthouse, in no time. It never ceased to amaze her, how men would lay up and catch feeling over any pretty-face chick.

When she passed by, Netta was surprised at how short Keisha actually was. Keisha stood five feet two inches. But even her small stature didn't take away from her beauty. She was honey golden complexioned with large seductive eyes. And even though her hair was styled in a short hairdo, she looked good in it. Her shapely body was impeccable, more than enough for any man. What she lacked in height Keisha more than made up for in attitude. And everyone knew not to get it twisted. Keisha was a feisty little thing, equipped with a take-no-shit attitude. She was as wild as they came.

To Netta, the rest of her clique were just average broads at best. She was definitely not impressed by their looks. The money that they made allowed them to buy the finest clothes, which in turn made them look better than they actually did. But Netta saw through all that smoke and mirrors. To her they were merely dressed up chicken-heads.

So the game appeared to be wide open. Netta thought to herself, if she could wrestle control of the sex-for-pay trade away from Keisha and the Knock 'em Down girls then the money was hers for the taking.

Netta had a key element in her favor: experience was the best teacher. She had practically invented this part of the game, so she felt no one would do like she did. She did it before and she felt she could do it again. Her son's well-being literally depended on it.

"I can't believe these bitches got the city on lockdown," Netta stated, in disbelief. "The game must really be fucked up. Business must be really bad."

"Believe it or not, it is what it is!" Hope smirked. "The game ain't the same no more."

"Shit, I see!" Netta replied.

Clearly, a lot had changed in her absence. Now, she caught the tail end of the golden era of the drug trade. Gone were the good old days when there was literally a drug kingpin in every neighborhood.

Now there were only a handful of drug lords scattered about

the city. This huge drop-off could be attributed directly to snitches. The streets and the drug game in particular had been infiltrated by them. Everybody who committed the crime didn't necessarily want to do the time.

From an illegal standpoint, Baltimore was nowhere near ready to return to its money-making heydays of the late eighties and mid-nineties.

The night quickly progressed. Netta and Hope managed to actually enjoy the rest of their night. From Netta's point of view, she had achieved two things. One, a night out that had taken her mind off her problems temporarily. And two, she had seen the heart of Baltimore's underworld, friends and foes, hustlers and hoes. She now knew what route she had to take and she had to do what she had to do.

The path Netta was about to embark on to make money was cold, calculating, and deliberate. But drastic times called for drastic measures. When she was done there would plenty of dead bodies left in her wake.

The passage of time had made Netta forget exactly how dangerous it was for her to show her face in Baltimore, but there were those who were going to be quick to remind her.